The Private War of Sidney Reilly

Second Edition

By Allan Torrey

A.T. Chesterton Publisher
New York, NY

Copyright Information

Torrey, Allan
A.T. Chesterton Publisher
37 West 72nd Street, Suite 16A
New York, NY 10023

First Edition entitled:
The Private War of Sidney Reilly

Second Edition and Publication
A.T. Chesterton Publisher, trade paperback
November, 2015, New York, NY.

For information on special discounts for Library, Academic, Professional and bulk purchases, contact A.T. Chesterton at 1-212-799-3002
or email ST1@sidney-reilly.com
ISBN-13: 978-0-615-79162-3
ISBN: - 10: 061579162X

Web: www.sidney-reilly.com

In memory of

Robin Bruce Lockhart

F. Reese Brown

With gratitude

CONTENTS

Introduction: Masterspy / Spy Masters

The Sidney Reilly of *Private War* is not the spy of MI6 legend or of the popular Reilly TV series. He is not the mythical Reilly, promoted as the real-life prototype of Ian Fleming's fictional James Bond, the spy who never made a mistake.

Private War reveals an authentic Reilly whose Achilles' heel enables two brilliant spy masters to gain unheard-of behind-the-scenes political power. *Private War* exposes how they kept this amazing feat hidden for nearly ninety years.

In 1917 the British Prime Minister sends masterspy Reilly to Moscow to stop the Bolshevik Lenin from seizing power over Russia. Reilly fails, but after returning to London gradually discovers that his failure resulted from betrayal.

Reilly's investigation leads to a shocking conclusion that sends him back to Moscow on one final, ultra-high-stakes mission. He never returns, thus entombing the spy masters' secret forever.

Immediately thereafter the British Government issues its own cover story: Reilly was a double agent who betrayed Britain. The Soviets, too, announce their version of the Reilly legend: he was a murderous British adventurer and provacateur bent on seizing the Revolution for himself.

Private War is the first account of what really happened.

Read what two experts have said about *Private War:*

Dr. Lev Bezymensky, Soviet journalist and chief KGB propagandist who promulgated the Soviet version of Reilly's story, said: "Torrey's novel is unconditionally a remarkable piece. There are versions of Reilly's story by "court historians," but Torrey's version is far closer to the truth ... I am inclined to recommend publishing this book in Russian."

Robin Bruce Lockhart, author of ***Reilly: Ace of Spies***, said, "I am excited that Allan Torrey's fascinating, well-researched historical novel is to be published ... it may well be true ... it merits the attention of film-makers."

Readers' comments about the First Edition

The book that all enthusiasts of the Russian Revolution should read. - Marina Osipova, Author, August 27, 2015

"The Private War of Sidney Reilly is part detective story and part brilliantly clear explanation of a very intricate and horrifying period in the history of Russia.

The story of the spy who wanted to stop the unstoppable makes for a gripping read and I devoured the book in a couple of sessions.

Scrupulously researched, peopled with real characters, it is a thrilling historical novel, which I would recommend to anyone, especially those interested in the Russian Revolution and its soiled aftermath."

An Epic Novel that Reveals the Secrets Behind the Russian Revolution - Dr. John B. Gingrich, January 16, 2015

"If you've ever been curious about the Russian Revolution, and its historical aftermath, this novel by Allan Torrey will strike a very significant chord. This was a very confusing period in Russian history, with multiple socialist factions competing to bring down the czarist regime and gain power. Concurrently, the western European powers were very heavily involved in trying prevent Russia from falling into the most radical of these socialist groups, the Bolsheviks.

The Bolsheviks were intent not just on revolutionizing Russia, but also on spreading communism throughout the western world, which was in a precarious state following the end of WWI. Enter private citizen and master spy Sidney Reilly, who the British spy services employed to further British interests in keeping Russia in its sphere of influence.

(Gingrich, continued)

Loaded with secret dealings and hutzpah, masterspy Reilly struggled mightily to overcome the competing socialist forces, playing one off against the other, and at times looked that he might succeed. However, of course, the ultimate outcome is well-known.

Allan Torrey draws upon excellent factual sources – such as Richard Pipes and N.N. Sukhanov – in taking the novelist's license in filling in gaps of the known facts about the Revolution and drawing very plausible conclusions about what happened to bring down the forces of the western European opposition and propel the Bolsheviks into power. Great characters, including romance and deception among the spies, brings all of this intrigue to a very personal level. All in all, this is a powerful novel full of twists and turns, intricate plots, and an amazing ending. Any reader interested in revolutionary Russian history will be delighted with this insightful work."

Fabulous Read - Which Side? - NYC on January 9, 2015

"Stunning read. Based upon a review, I read this book. The story was riveting as the saga of a British agent thrust into the Stalinist era unfolds. Extremely well written, the thread is one you keep reminding yourself it's true and not a novel. Great backdrop to the new Steven Kotkin's Stalin book. Would make a wonderful screenplay. Highly recommended"

Great read! - ByAnnonymous on December 5, 2014

"Amazingly well written. Thoroughly well researched."

More than a spy book - Gerald Waterfield, 12/ 19/2014

"*The Private War* is more than a spy book. It is not flat description of facts or feats told by a historian. It is a well-researched novel that provides the unique experience of seeing Reilly in context and feeling what it must have been like to live through the Russian Revolution-- how frightening and horrifying it must have been. I think it did this just as well as the 1980s TV series, but with a much more striking and satisfying conclusion. The fictional family device helps to establish intimacy and a sympathetic connection to the characters, some of whom were actually close to Reilly in real life. (Disclosure: I line-edited the manuscript [unpaid] prior to publication.)"

The real subject of this book... Dr. Irina Degtyarovaon, November 13, 2014.

"I think the real subject of this book is the Russian spy services. It discovers a direct link between the institution of terror invented by Djerzhinsky called Cheka-KGB-FSB, to the present Russian Government. It ruled by deception and murder in order to control the minds of the masses.

This direct link from the past to the present is the highest value of "Private War of Sidney Reilly." For even Russian people."

(translated from Dr. Degtyarovaon's Russian language comment, as follows:)

"думаю объект кинги- русская служба шпионажа .. Автром открыта прямая связь между изобретением ДЗЕРЖИНСКИМ установок террора, названными ЧЕКА-КГБ-ФСБ-МВД, и сегоднешним ПРАВИТЕЛЬСТВОМ РОССИИ!

это kak управение- метод обмана и убиист в порядке контроля умов масс. Это связь прошлого с настоящим, для каждого РУССКОГО и есть высочайшей ценностью книги" Частная воина СИДНЕИ РЕЙЛИ"!"

- докт. И.В. днепропетровск, УКРАИНА

Private War is a great read... The climax took me....

- Rhona Danzeisenon November 11, 2014

"Private War is a great read, exciting and suspenseful with a climax that took me completely by surprise. Just on those terms I would say it's a highly successful first book. It is a work of fiction that poses realistic explanations for the mysteries surrounding Reilly's life and tells an original spy story set inside British-Soviet espionage tensions of the 1920s. The author sets very high standards for the novel and delivers nicely. Private War deserves recognition for doing extremely well what good fiction should do, that is, to teach us a truth that we have not already discovered on our own."

If a rogue elephant . . . charges at me out of the thickets of my past and gives me a second shot at it, I intend to shoot it dead. But with a minimum of force.

George Smiley, in *Smiley's People*
by John le Carré

Book One:
Revolution!

Characters & Organizations Introduced In Book One

Reilly and His Allies

Sidney Reilly – A British spy and adventurer
Katya - Reilly's friend
Anna - Katya's daughter
Natasha - Anna's friend
Laurent – A French agent
Ilya - Katya's son
Volodia, Sasha, Arkady – Friends
Savinkov - Reilly's close friend, an SR
Suvorin – An important newspaper publisher
Semyenov and Filonenko – SRs

The Provisional Government of Russia

Alexander Kerensky- High official, then Prime Minister
Duma –The legislature, mostly liberal
Soviet - Left Opposition, socialist
Sergei Mikhailov- Intelligence Dept, ex-Okhranist

White Officers, ex-Russian Army:

General Yudenich
General Kornilov
General Deniken
General Krymov

Ex-members of the Tsar's secret "Okhrana" police

Sergei Mikhailovich – Ex-Okhrana Intelligence officer
Yusepov – Ex-Militia officer
Malibaev –Ex-Militia officer
Krepov-- Ex-Militia officer
Aladin –Ex-Militia officer

British Intelligence Agents, Spies

Reilly - Spy and adventurer
Bruce Lockhart – Diplomatic agent
Weber – Phantom agent, Moscow
George Hill– British spy in Russia
C – The Director of British Intelligence, at London Centre
Boyce – Moscow Station Chief, British Intelligence
Somerville – Somerset Maugham, writer and secret agent.

Bolshevik Party, Communists

Lenin - Bolshevik leader
Feliks Derzhinsky – "Cheka" Founder and President
Peters – Second in command of the Cheka
Trotsky –In line to replace Lenin
Stalin - Lenin's eventual successor

Various Groups, Political Parties, Cabals

Bolshevik Party - Communist Party of Lenin
Menshevik Party - Left wing socialist party
SR, SRs - Socialist Revolutionary Party oppositionists
Okhrana – Tsar's secret police, defunct and dispersed
Right wing - Conservative to fascist philosophy
Left wing - Liberal to Communist philosophy
Monarchy - Government under the Tsar
Phantom Group –Secret British spy group in Moscow
London Centre –London Spy Service headquarters
NY Station - British spy station in NYC

Prelude: Moscow, 1926

Reilly stood at the edge of his grave, his shovel thrust upright into the ground and the cold barrel of a pistol at his neck. He had done everything possible to bring his scheme to fruition. He had sacrificed his fortune, friendships and reputation. In moments he would surrender his life.

He had set his master plan in motion knowing that he would probably not live to see the outcome. The plan would succeed or fail without him.

Reilly put a cigarette between his yellowing teeth. He had been captive in a Soviet prison for months, during which time he had received American cigarettes as a reward for his cooperation. The Inquisitor had promised him tooth powder too, but later confessed that there was not a gram of tooth-powder left in Moscow. It was the only information Reilly got from his Soviet captors that he believed.

The Senior Inquisitor took a match from the front pocket of his black tunic and lit Reilly's cigarette. As Reilly took the smoke into his lungs, he mused on one remaining question. The Senior Inquisitor read his mind. "Well, was it worth it?"

Reilly offered a slight smile.

Ibrahim, the second Inquisitor, raised his pistol to Reilly's skull. The Senior Inquisitor, far less excitable, said, "What's funny about that? Did you think we would *not* execute you?"

"I couldn't ignore what Lenin and Derzhinsky were doing to Russia," Reilly said. "People were starving in Petrograd. They killed millions with the Red Terror. I had to act."

"It's over now. Perhaps you want some archaic ritual, like Last Rites or incense?" the ex-Catholic Senior Inquisitor said.

"Get on with it." Reilly took a drag on his papirosi and flipped it into the freshly-dug grave as the Inquisitor backed up behind him and said, "Goodbye, comrade."

Two pistol shots followed. A lifeless body collapsed into the grave. The gunfire echoed for a moment. Then the hills overlooking the city of Moscow fell silent.

Part I: Doomsday

January-February, 1917

1. Jelly Roll Blues: New York City, January, 1917

I'll be down to get you in a taxi, honey
You'd better be ready 'round half past eight
I want to be there when the band starts playing,
So baby, don't be late...

Nick LaRocca tucked his cornet under his arm and smiled at the applause. He bowed with the others in the Dixieland Band and wiped sweat from his brow with a kerchief.

W. Curtis Robinson stood in a tuxedo at the entrance next to an upright piano. Seated at the upright, a young man crunched a cigar between his rear teeth and pencilled a change on some sheet music. He struck a chord and sang, "When you want 'em, you can't get 'em." A maître d' took Robinson's overcoat and led him to a table where a polished gentleman greeted the approaching cornet player.

"Swell, Nick," Sidney Reilly said.

Nick LaRocca beamed and shook Reilly's hand.

W. Curtis Robinson stood by, his hands on his hips, just part of the scenery at Reisenweber's Columbus Circle Café.

"Well, bye, Mister Reilly," Nick said, took his kerchief to his forehead again and wove around the tables to the exit.

Reilly lit a cigarette and said to Robinson, "Well?"

"He'll test you," Robinson said. "It's a big investment."

"It's not an investment, Robinson. It's insurance."

"Let him see your eyes when you tell him the cost."

A young man joined the pianist with sheet music, said, "Faster, like this" and read two lines from Darktown Strutter's Ball in metered prose: "Remember when we get there honey, two steps gonna handle them all. *Two* steps. Two *steps*?"

"Who's in?" Robinson said.

"Morgan, the Nobel brothers, Carnegie, Rockefeller, the billionaires. But I have some competition. The socialists are raising money for Lenin. The Germans, too."

Robinson said, "Everybody's got a plan for Russia. Socialists, Capitalists, Bolsheviks, Germans. Makes the war in Europe look small-time by comparison."

The maître d' escorted a man to Reilly's table.

Robinson said to the newcomer, "Sidney Reilly, sir."

"Good show," Reilly said, shaking Henry Ford's hand.

"Jazz?" Ford said. "Coloured music."

"Ragtime," Reilly said. "Great investment."

"Coloured music." *Bah.*

Gonna dance off both my shoes, when they play those Jelly Roll Blues.

Ford knew Reilly hadn't come to talk about jazz, but about what the barons of American industry stood to lose unless they could stop the Bolshevik called Lenin from seizing power over a failed Russia state. They had to keep Russia in the war or the German Army might win. Men like Ford had billions invested and billions to lose in Europe and Russia. Ford thought Reilly's plan might work but questioned how strongly Reilly believed in it himself.

"I'd be better off with the Bolsheviks in power," Ford said. "They know nothing about economics. Lenin would wreck the Russian economy for a century. The Germans agree."

Robinson shook his head slowly. Reilly went poker faced.

The pianists did another song. The three leaned in to hear one another. When the song finished, Reilly said, "If you're in, have Robinson deliver a letter of credit to Morgan Bank."

Ford shook Reilly's hand and left the room.

Robinson said, "He's buying. See you at the Plaza in the morning. Say, Reilly, Russia really that bad?"

"Worse," Reilly said. "Soldiers are eating shoe leather. They can't get food or fuel to the cities. Food lines go a cross-town city block, longer every day. And it's turning out to be a bloody cold winter. It's no good at all, Robinson. The socialists come out for demonstrations and police beat anyone who looks at 'em crooked. Everybody's depressed."

The Dixieland Band filed back and took their instruments.

"See you tomorrow," Reilly said and went to the door. He stopped near the piano and dropped a five on a silver plate.

"Gee, that's swell of ya', Mister Reilly."

"G'night, George."

The maître d' gave Reilly his overcoat. Nick LaRocca's cornet started out. A voice in the band sang: "I want to be there when the band starts playing..."

Anna, too, wanted to be there when the band started playing. But Reilly kept her away from Reisenweber's, in a flat on St. Mark's Place. The young lady was restless: tradecraft meant waiting, watching and boredom, which could disrupt concentration. It was a new agent's first test. Anna had watched the house across the street for days.

Reilly meanwhile paged through the morning's Times. They had moved the dining table to the window, parted the curtains slightly and took turns watching. Anna leaned forward with a spy-glass close against her eye.

"Anything?" Reilly said absently.

"Yes. Man with a beard. A light on the fourth-floor."

Reilly lifted his binoculars. "Trotsky," he said. "Can't go in while he's there." He put the binoculars on the table.

"Somebody else with Trotsky," Anna said after a moment.

Reilly looked again and seemed disappointed. A man he called "White" sat opposite Trotsky. An American employed by Reilly's superior officer at London Centre. He worked in New York, but outside of channels. A phantom.

Reilly took the phone and said, "Five hundred Madison." Then, "Wiseman, Reilly here. Is London running anything with Lenin's agents in New York? No? Thank you."

Wiseman was a truth-teller, sworn not to lie to a brother.

Reilly wondered whether the mainstream Wiseman would know a phantom like White, an off-the-books agent.

"Who is he?" Anna said.

"Just an American," Reilly said. He had to manage Anna's exposure carefully. Explaining White would give too much away too soon. But he could explain Trotsky.

Several nights running Reilly had gone to Reisenweber's Café on Columbus Circle and had seen Trotsky work his charm on society women, performing financial seduction with stories and solicitations made "in the cause of justice." People said he was visiting the jewellers, offering gems at low-fashion prices.

"Probably the pawn shops too."

Trotsky was raising cash, hustling for revolution in Russia.

"Might buy him a seat near Lenin."

Maybe London Centre wants to buy a seat near Trotsky. That might explain White's visit.

The subject changed. A third man sat at Trotsky's table. Anna saw Reilly's apprehension.

"Someone you know?" she said.

"I thought it was one of Lenin's hatchet men. Derzhinsky. A dangerous revolutionary. But no."

Had Reilly not come to New York, Anna would have stayed uptown, far from Lenin's men. She had arrived in 1914, when her mother prevailed upon Reilly to get her out of Russia. In New York, Reilly arranged a position minding two young children. But her independent spirit and speedy mastery of the English language took her to an East Side grade school that needed a French teacher. When Reilly returned a year later he found a beautiful woman with a craving for "more life." Reilly trained her to observe, put her to work at the British Consulate and then at New York Station. Her mother wanted her to stay in New York. Anna wanted to return to Russia.

Trotsky was in the way. The Bolsheviks *had* to believe Reilly was a German agent. But Trotsky would recognize him and that meant a delay in delivering the small package. He hoped Trotsky would go to Russia soon.

Then boredom overtook Anna. "Give me the package," she said. "I'll tell them I work for your German identity, Colonel Schaefer, that he has something contagious so he sent me in his place. Call the German Consulate and tell them I'm taking Schaefer's place, in case Trotsky calls to confirm."

Reilly agreed with Anna's logic and thought he had trained her well enough to carry off a small delivery. That evening, he watched through binoculars as Anna appeared on the third floor of the Bolsheviks' safe flat. Trotsky greeted her, offered her a seat and opened a bottle of wine. They toasted and drank seconds. But Trotsky was moving too close. Reilly thought Anna might be getting too excited and feared she might lose sight of her mission.

When she returned, Reilly took her to task. "Never drink or socialize when you make a run. A slip means danger. Our personal relationship could force me to make a bad choice. Don't put me in that situation again."

Anna said, "It's done," and gave him an envelope with a receipt. "What's so important?"

Reilly sat Anna down at the dining table. "My job comes with very high stakes. It's not an adventure and it's not just about money. It's about the fate of Russia."

"I love Russia too," she said.

"It's more than that," Reilly said. "The monarchy will collapse. There are good people who can save Russia, but dangerous ones too, men like Lenin or Trotsky. They rob banks and candy stores and kill without a thought. They want power over Russia just to squeeze the wealth out of her. They'll kill anyone who gets in the way. They wrap their scheme in a philosophy like a religion. What they do stinks. If they take power over Russia, it will be a disaster."

"Then why are you here," Anna said, "and not in Russia?"

"Because we may need something that hurts the Bolsheviks and discredits Lenin. The package you delivered from the German Consulate could help."

"What was in the package?"

"Money. From the Germans to Lenin. What's important is the signed receipt you brought back. It's evidence that Lenin and Trotsky are traitors to Russia, that Lenin's in bed with the Kaiser. It could discredit Lenin with the Russians when he tries to take power. And he does intend to take power."

2. Petrograd, Russia, February, 1917

Petrograd was hungry. Anna's mother, Katya, had posted a food queue schedule in the kitchen. Katya herself normally took the longest walk, down the Nevsky, almost to the monastery, through the poorer section. Volodia, a family friend and boarder, went to the lines on Vasilievsky Island.

Anna took Kamenovstrosky, a wide street with lamps that still worked, which let Katya imagine that her daughter would be safe. But Anna had kept Reilly's pistol and did not think she needed any greater protection. On the far side of the River Neva, a palace-like mansion was home to a ballet dancer named Matilde Ksheshinskaya. Anna's brother, Ilya, worked that area and beyond, where Anna and a friend studied ballet.

Anna discovered that the hospital on the north end of Kamenovstrosky Boulevard received early food supplies at a nearby carriage house. She stayed close. One night, hospital shifts changed and many people came and went and the food queue was at its longest. A military vehicle rolled slowly in from the north, long, covered with armour and filled with armed men who shot at everything while guzzling vodka. Anna stood behind a tree as people fell around her. The vehicle stopped though the shooting continued. She took out her pistol, but the vehicle rolled away before she had time to do anything foolish. She helped others carry wounded men and women into the hospital, aided the few nurses too young to serve at the front and tended to the wounded.

Inside, she said, "Bolsheviks" to no one in particular.

"Anarchists," one said. "They occupied a house up the street, come out when they're drunk and shoot for sport."

"I'd have shot them, but I couldn't get my gloves off."

"Good thing, young lady, if you don't mind my saying so."

When she could do no more she went back to the line but kept her hand in her pocket and her pistol loaded. Her prize was black bread, which she carried away in between layers of her clothing, a sweater and a shirt, rolled up to prevent the loaf from slipping. Her hands pushed her pockets to the centre of her overcoat but the cold in her belly made her feel naked. It was a colder-than-usual Russian February.

That night Anna got home first and put wood in the fireplace. The back door opened and Volodia carried Ilya inside. It was Ilya, wasn't it? His face was cut from eye to chin, and filthy. His hat was gone and his hair thick with snow and mud. He limped, with Volodia's support.

"Take him to the sofa while I heat some water," Anna said. Volodia helped the boy with his overcoat, put a few pillows on the sofa and guided him down on his back. Ilya cried out and winced as his leg fell straight.

Anna wiped his face with a cold wet cloth and apologized.

"Never mind," he said. "It's good. My face is on fire."

Ilya told his story before Katya returned, in order to avoid a fuss. He had gone to the far side of the Neva River at the Troitsky Bridge. He'd had no luck with several lines but finally found one that was not too long. A pensioner standing just ahead passed out from hunger and his wife shrieked in panic. Ilya ran to the front and pleaded with the shopkeeper for food, anything the man might eat. He took out his money and offered it to the owner, when militia men pushed him down, accused him of attempting bribery and beat him.

While the elderly citizens cursed the police, they could do little else. The militia took Ilya to the Admiralty Prison, where the convicts further abused him. But after a while a little man, a Chechen Bolshevik called Ibrahim, bribed a guard and got him released. Volodia, on his way back from the queue on Vasilievsky Island, met him by chance and took him home.

Anna looked more than she listened as she tended to Ilya's cuts and bruises. "Who was it? The secret police?"

"Yes," Ilya said, "But a Bolshevik helped me out."

"One Bolshevik," Volodia said. "I found him outside the Admiralty Prison. His name is Ibrahim. He bribed a guard to open the door. An investment. A handsome recruit is always a star on a red soldier's cap."

"Wait 'til your mother sees you," Anna said.

"I'll do the talking," Volodia said. "We won't use the word 'prison.' I'll tell her you were attacked by ruffians who stole the food you got after standing in line."

Katya came in and said, "What have you done to yourself?"

Volodia said, "Hooligans beat him up for a sausage."

"I told him it was a bad neighbourhood."

It was a more peaceful exchange than might have been.

Ilya's incident faded but Anna and Volodia worried that it might have swayed the boy's sentiments toward the Bolsheviks. Reilly had schooled Anna on the dangers they represented. Volodia, a judge in the Russian judiciary, knew their crimes first hand, had sent many to prison but had tried to treat socialists with objectivity and sympathy.

Volodia said, "If the Bolsheviks come to power, they'll try to destroy the bourgeoisie as a class. Starting with judges like me." His best friend, he said, was the cold weather, which kept the riff-raff off the streets.

"When it warms up, they'll come out with a bang."

On Wednesday afternoon Volodia donned a black judicial robe and walked from his office through a freezing corridor to the courtroom. A man in a greatcoat sprang up, removed his hat, bowed and gave Volodia his card.

"Kerensky," he announced with pride and another bow, "Alexander Fyodor'ich. At your disposal, Your Honour." He patted his own closely cut hair with a kerchief.

"They say, Kerensky, that you are a socialist, and that if we have a new government you may be its leader."

"I am honoured and prepared," he said and bowed again.

Volodia said to the bailiff, "Where's the prosecutor?" He looked at his watch and saw that the hearing was scheduled to begin. He called the prosecutor, who had a sickly wife.

"You know the socialists, Your Honour. Keep 'em in jail."

Volodia returned as Kerensky paced the room, rehearsing his case with gestures, his greatcoat flowing over his boots.

"Be seated, Kerensky," Volodia said and sat at the judge's bench He glanced at a document and said, "No prosecuting attorney today. But you can't win by default, so proceed."

Kerensky arose, took off his greatcoat and draped it over a chair. He cleared his throat and then, taking short, measured steps near the judge's chair, began in a deep voice, "Six weeks ago an injustice was committed: two men were jailed for no crime other than holding incorrect political beliefs."

Kerensky summed up: "Can we fight for Russia's honour at the front and dishonour other citizens at home?"

"No," Volodia said and closed the file. "I order the defendants released. This case is closed."

Kerensky bowed once again, smiled and swept up his overcoat and fur hat. "Would Your Honour arrange a meeting with Sidney Reilly? Sooner would be better."

Volodia nodded and Kerensky sped off.

Restaurants were closing in Petrograd, for cold, caution and waiters' disaffection. The Metropol on Sadovaya was still open and had private booths. Kerensky sat in one with his arms folded. Reilly slid in across from him.

"Judge Orlov said you wanted to speak with me," Reilly said.

Kerensky said, "I hear you were in America taking bets on our revolution. Why are you here now?"

"I want Russia to survive, honour intact."

"You want to keep Russia in the war against Germany? They say you've talked to all the bankers and industrialists in New York and Russia. What's your plan?"

"A coalition that will stand up to Lenin," Reilly said.

"Let me be blunt. You can't rule Russia with a dictator."

"A coalition," Reilly said. "People with varied political interests and views, the old world and the new. We need a Constituent Assembly and an agreement to abide by elections. Only Lenin is out. Does that satisfy you?"

"No military dictator?"

"The generals are fighting a war and hate politics. What do

the socialists want?"

"A central government. The Duma legislature. As you say, a Constituent Assembly. We should resurrect the Soviets."

"The old workers' committees?"

Kerensky said, "Exclusion leads to violence. The Soviet will give the socialists a place to stand so the new government can keep their loyalty."

"I'll back you. I have a lot of money to spend, and good connections. But no Lenin and no Bolsheviks."

Kerensky slid the curtain aside. "Democracy means we include everyone. Otherwise we have nothing to talk about."

3. Russian Spring

Anna awoke on Thursday morning in a feverish sweat. Embers glowed in the fireplace near her bed. Moisture trickled down the outside of the windows. At first she thought she was ill. But when she heard laughter in the street she tore the blankets away from her body. Outside, people walked with unusual lightness, overcoats open, some without hats. She dressed and went out.

On the way, she paid little attention to the crowds gathering on the nearby Nevsky Prospect or to the long queues that had already formed. But on the next street a stranger in a fur hat and greatcoat sped around a corner with a briefcase. His strides were long and swift and his eyes fixed on a tram about to depart from the nearest stop. He did not look away until he crashed into Anna and sent her flying into the snow. As quickly as he had arrived he spun around, lifted her to her feet, swept off his hat and bowed.

"Forgive me, my dear," he said as he presented his card: "Kerensky. Member of the Duma. Servant of the people."

"You're in quite a hurry, Citizen Kerensky," Anna replied, unhurt, brushing snow from her overcoat.

"I don't know what came over me," Kerensky said.

"I thought the revolution had started," Anna said.

"If it were revolution, my dear, I shouldn't be running from it." He looked nervously past Anna, backed away to resume his flight and said in an anxious voice, "But for now, I must be going." At the last instant Kerensky leaped from the walkway to the step of the departing tram. He turned to Anna and shouted, "Au revoir, mademoiselle!"

Anna mimicked Kerensky. "If it were revolution I wouldn't run away from it. My dear. Reva-loo-tion, my dear."

Thursday might have marked the start of the revolution.

Friday was International Women's Day. Police and protestors filled the streets, some separated by barricades. Chants and songs came from every direction. Militiamen on rooftops shot machine guns into the crowds. Anna ran home.

At home, a breathless, frightened but exhilarated Anna told Reilly a slightly enhanced version of her story, clinging to him as tears trickled from her eyes.

Reilly said revolution had no room for romantic illusion.

"Do you understand? No going out on your own without orders or a plan. Not if you want to work with me."

Anna opened her eyes and pulled slightly back. "Of course I promise," she said. "But if it's revolution, my dear, you shouldn't find me running away from it."

Friday, too, might have been the first day of revolution.

Reilly asked Sasha, his confidant and Anna's uncle, to leverage his friendships inside the legislative Duma. He asked family friend and judge Volodia Orlov, to cultivate his contacts among the socialists. Covering both Left and Right.

"I'm the Tsar's Judge," Volodia said. "The Reds will want to hang me and you want me to infiltrate them?"

"For a while it's open season on government men. But you might find you have your own constituency, people you were easy on in the docket. Might include Derzhinsky."

On Saturday the revolution seemed closer. Violence escalated. Sunday was worse. Reilly, Anna and Natasha converged off Suvorovsky as clusters of people mushroomed into a mob. The pop of a pistol shot returned echoes of long rifles from the militia at the edge of Znamensky Square. Then staccato blasts of machine gun fire answered a political speech, dropped men into red-spotted snow and sent carriages, sledges and motorcars careening around corners into thick crowds, trampling dozens of children.

"You have two choices," Reilly shouted. "Either go home or help get these children to the hospital. What will it be?"

They hurried after him, carrying children to the hospital. Reilly pulled a doctor from his conversation to treat them. He thanked Anna and sent her home.

On the way, Anna saw more shooting from the rooftops, more blood in the street and local regiments who were drunk, singing patriotic songs and shooting randomly. She could not distinguish provocateurs, police and rebels from one another. At the sight of a local regiment, policemen tore away their own uniforms and put on civilian clothes. At a small cluster of shops, vandals smashed windows and beat guards.

"Death to the police traitors!"

"Hurrah, Litovsky! Hurrah Pavlovskii!"

The army reserves have come to save us!

More machine-gun fire, followed by a roar from behind the shopping centre, sent Anna running home.

Reilly took her aside and said, "I cancelled a meeting at the British Embassy because of you. I asked you not to do this again." Anna had no regrets. She loved that she was experiencing life intensely. Reilly quietly admired that.

That evening, when Reilly tapped on Ilya's door, the youngster said, "What?" more in exclamation than invitation. Reilly opened the door. Ilya stood at the window, his injured leg wrapped but his cheek unbandaged. Smoke filled the room. A mound of cigarette butts and ashes spilled out of an ashtray on a small table next to a copy of Bunin's *Village.*

"What's all this?" Reilly said, nodding to the ash tray.

"What's all that?" Ilya said, nodding toward Volodia's room. "The secret police? Your allies? Men who beat me?"

Reilly came close, examined Ilya's wounds and promised to find his attackers. "They'll get what they deserve."

On Monday, the revolution came.

Before sunrise, Volodia and Reilly reviewed a list of contacts. Volodia went to the courthouse to assess the damage. He took back streets in order to avoid trouble with the rebels. Reilly went to the Admiralty and then along the river to observe activities among the local regiments.

The city seemed cast in a colourless veneer, deserted and bleak, grey above and underfoot with rows of dreary stucco houses on rows of desolate, ugly lanes. Guards at every corner looked at Reilly suspiciously and asked for papers.

Reilly showed his British Passport. If the soldier could read, he would nod approvingly. If not Reilly would say, "I'm British, here to help get food to the Russian troops at the front." True, though few knew. Young soldiers replied, "Good luck. God save the king!" The English king.

A train arrived at the Moscow Station. Passengers detrained and stood outside to wait in vain for taxis. Cars arrived for foreign diplomats or family members. A woman put a dozen young ladies on a southbound train, the flowers of the Smolney School, and waved goodbye as the train rolled toward Kiev and the war, much safer than Petrograd.

On the near-barren Nevsky, a woman scurried along, her head wrapped in a black scarf, walking with a gait of wounded arrogance in steps quick and uncertain. On any other day she was a patron of the Nevsky's finest stores. But today she heard Reilly's boots crunch into the icy walkway, glanced back at him and hurried around a corner.

Boards covered the glass-fronts of empty shops. A car slid around a corner, careened against the walkway and then crawled away. An older man just searching for a way out.

The Trinity Bridge, normally heavy with traffic at this hour on a Monday morning, was empty. On the far side, Ksheshinskaya's palace was as dark and empty, as forsaken as the nearby mansions. The Winter Palace seemed like a coffin. Across the river, the imperial flag hung limply under a low, grey sky that almost hid the Litany Bridge in its mist.

On Mars Field, three different battalion flags waved over silent men who smoked cigarettes, drank or stood guard in fear. They were soldiers, probably also rebels.

The British Embassy had lights. On the top floor, two or three consular employees studied the city with binoculars. Next door, at the French Embassy, men peered out with spy glasses, keen to witness history from a safe distance.

A block away, three officers lay dead in blood-speckled snow. The three battalions on Mars Field had joined together against the police and government, for the revolution.

Four rifle shots echoed from across the river, where more officers, factory owners, policemen or judges lay dead in the snow. Workers set out across the frozen River Neva when shots came from Mars Field, where another officer fell. Then a cheer, "Hurrah Pavlovskii!" for the men crossing the river, the fourth regiment to join the revolution.

A mob approached the main administrative area. Reilly ran along the river and passed the embassies to the Artillery Building. Before he could ring the bell, the door opened and two army officers ran out, tore the epaulets from their military overcoats and ran away. Reilly rushed up the stairs to an officer's room, where a general stood at a window looking at the mass of soldiers and workers outside.

"What do your reports say?" Reilly said.

"They've taken all but three government buildings."

An adjutant shouted from the floor below: "General!"

The general went to the stairway and said, "No shooting!" Then, to Reilly: "They'll kill us bourgeoisie, you know."

Volodia arrived safely at the courthouse, where his colleagues cleaned out files and burned documents. The front door crashed open and half a dozen men rushed in with weapons drawn. They took six judges downstairs and into the street and shot them dead in the bloodied snow.

Volodia heard screams and hurried to the second floor in the hope of jumping to the roof of the adjoining building. But someone jumped in front of him aiming a pistol. "Stop," he said as he lit clusters of documents in the fireplace and scattered them through the room. He held his gun at Volodia's head and shoved him into the next room where he set fires. He said, "Don't worry, pal, I'm not going to set you on fire. I'm going to execute you." He took Volodia outside and aimed his pistol. But a shot from elsewhere dropped the rebel to the snow.

"Go home, Your Honour," someone said.

"Who was it?" Reilly said breathlessly as he arrived.

"Derzhinsky, I think," Volodia said.

The crowd was thick and large. Fire took the courthouse, rebels took the Artillery Building and some frightened young soldiers ducked inside.

"It's over," Reilly said. "The only question is how much damage they'll do. The Duma's at the Tauride Palace. Let's go. We don't want to be caught by this bunch."

An explosion ripped through the courthouse upper floors. Flames shot through the windows. Broken glass and debris rained onto the crowd below as fire devoured the building.

"Let Nicholas' judges burn in hell!" the crowds shouted.

Reilly and Volodia headed toward Tauride Palace.

Anna went past the Admiralty Building to Saint Isaacs Square, where the cathedral dome dominated the close end and balanced the Mariinskii Palace at the far end. Rifle fire came from all over, echoing against the buildings. Machine gun blasts from the rooftops thumped into the ground.

Two men in fedoras, whose opened raccoon overcoats revealed plaid vests and neckties, led two frightened courtesans around the corner of a street that came from the Nevsky. They stopped short when shooting echoed against the buildings and shattered windows in the fashionable homes across the square. The echoes died away. The four rushed into the Astoria Hotel. Residents' faces appeared in windows that had not been shattered. Small dark clouds dotted the crystal blue sky. Anna hurried to the cathedral.

Rebels will respect the cathedral. I'll be safe.

A limousine careened around a corner at Mariinskii Palace and drove onto the square with rifles protruding through its open windows. Anna ducked as they fired at apartment windows across the square and then turned on the hotel. Glass fragments flew all over and faces disappeared from the windows. Pedestrians fell. The limousine screeched away.

Who and what was that? Hooligans or policemen?

Anna climbed the cathedral steps. A machine-gun blasted from high above her, its charges shattering hotel windows.

The ones on top of the cathedral are militia, shooting at pedestrians to terrorize, to clear the streets, to stop the revolution. Killing people!

Then, from the far side of the square rifle shots echoed against adjacent buildings. In front of the Mariinskii Palace, clouds of smoke rose from behind an abandoned tram, turned on its side with its windows broken, lying alone in the street like a dead elephant. From atop the cathedral came screams. A dozen men sprinted through the square toward the cathedral, shooting as they ran. Anna pressed against a column as they jumped up the steps and ran through the doorway. Bodies thumped as they hit the cathedral floor.

The commotion inside stopped and the square became silent. Above someone shrieked desperately. Blood shot through Anna's body as the sound grew to a crescendo and abruptly ended with a horrifying thump. She drew back and covered her face with her hands. A policeman's body lay bloodied just steps away. Rebels appeared in the doorway.

"You can't stay here!" one said.

"Where should I go?" she cried.

"Go home!"

One pinned a red ribbon to her overcoat. Then they raced across the square beyond the tram, past the canal.

Another volley of gunfire came and went. Anna ran toward the hotel and then toward the Nevsky, where smoke filled the sky. Inside her overcoat, she felt Reilly's pistol. She slipped into alcoves or archways, looked up at rooftops, vigilant and prepared to defend herself. She felt the city pulsating around her. She had outrun the spectator inside her and become a part of the chaotic rhythm of the city.

The crowds thinned out on the far end of Fontanka, where the Mikhailovsky Palace peered across the canal at a wide three story building with tall windows on each side of thick doors. A truck filled with armed men stopped. They jumped out, stood close and awaited orders. Troops from the local regiments came and stood at ease in rows of six with an official at the entrance.

Men brought out the contents of the building, built a pile of desks, bookcases and chairs and set it afire. Flames reached high. File boxes went to a truck, which sped off.

"Residential," a man said. "No burning buildings here."

From inside came shouting, screaming, pleading. Dozens of Okhrana secret police officers streamed out of the building at gunpoint, terrified, their arms raised. These were the most feared and hated men in Russia. Rebel workers formed a semi-circle, held their pistols straight out and fired for fifteen seconds. Their secret police victims jerked left and right and dropped to the red speckled snow.

Volodia and Reilly arrived at Tauride Palace, where a rebel crowd tried to persuade the Duma ministers to accept power. But most of the Duma ministers locked the main entrance and ran off in fear, unable to understand the rebels' pleading .

"They're here to support you," Reilly said.

The Duma ministers resisted. "When Tsar Nicholas hears about this we'll be executed. We don't want power!"

The soldiers screamed, "Cowards! Take power!"

Reilly said, "They'll hang you and follow the socialists."

The men of the Duma looked outside to see the crowd of soldiers open up and a contingent of determined-looking men stride through with one man at their head.

"It's Kerensky," Volodia said quietly. "And I'm a dead man."

The delegation came in. Most of the ministers rushed off.

When Kerensky stepped up, Reilly took him to the side and

said, "I've thought about your proposal to include the Bolsheviks in the Soviet. You're right. I'll support you." Then he spun Kerensky around and looked at him as though he had not just spoken. "Lovely day, Alexander Fyodor'ich."

"I'll say." Kerensky beamed at the few Duma ministers, his warm smile stretched under a red nose. He took off his gloves and hat and bowed. Then, with the enthusiasm of a brush salesman he said, "Say, fellows! We're here to organize the socialist revolution. Can you give us a room?"

Reilly and Volodia slipped away from the Tauride Palace. They avoided the barracks and went along Suvorovsky, where the street was quiet.

At the station they waded through crowds of people hoping to buy tickets out of Petrograd, through a sea of soldiers and civilians arriving on an inbound train and others just standing around, happy to be off the street. They got to the platform, where someone appeared at the top of the train steps and said, "Hello, gents" with a crooked smile.

Volodia said, "What are you doing on a southbound train?"

The train whistle blew. Steam hissed under the wheels.

Reilly helped Sasha down. They walked to Katya's house.

That night an eerie calm descended upon Petrograd. Rebel groups guarded intersections. Above the city a glow of red flames, and thick clouds of smoke, cast a surreal pall over everything. By midnight everyone was relaxed, relieved simply to have survived the day and willing to accept an exhausted peacefulness. That is, until Anna started up to bed, looked out the window and said, "Oh, no!"

Outside, motorcars stopped, soldiers shouted and rushed to the house with drawn weapons.

Sasha took Katya upstairs. Anna pulled out her pistol. Ilya limped across the room and stood in front of Anna.

Volodia started to the side of the house and then stopped. "They've come for me," he said with resignation. "I won't resist. It'll be easier for everyone that way."

Anna set the safety and hid the pistol under her sweater. Ilya held up his cane. Something pounded on the door.

Volodia walked through the foyer and opened it. A tall man with a full beard and a pistol stood there, red ribbons on his greatcoat. Behind him troops stood with bayonets ready.

"Judge Orlov of the District Court?"

"Yes," Volodia said.

"Soviet Chairman Kerensky sent this message," the man said, holding up a document. "We value your sympathy to the revolution. Will will meet tomorrow at the Tauride Palace."

Volodia stood quietly as the officer continued, "Comrade Kerensky ordered us to ensure your safety. Blood-thirsty police gangs are looking for revenge. We have reports of murders, pogroms, police terrorist attacks. Our troops will guard your house tonight, until we take the terrorists into custody. Should I tell Comrade Kerensky to expect you?"

Volodia replied shakily but quickly, "Yes, thank you."

Part II: Kerensky Rising

February – July, 1917

4. Superman at The Soviet

"Where have you been for so long?" Katya said.

Both Anna and Volodia believed drinking had led to Sasha's temporary resettlement in Moscow in late 1916. Ilya guessed it was secret business of Reilly's. Katya thought the departure had dual causes: drink, and her insistence that Sasha go to avoid setting a bad example. Reilly was not surprised to hear their answers.

Ilya was right: Reilly had devised a scheme to create the impression in the household that drink was the reason for Sasha's longer-than-expected visit to Moscow. He even had Sasha play-act an episode of drunkenness while the children were absent, so the fear of God would touch Katya, stifle the protective affection she held for her brother and lead her to banish him for a while. Sasha's performance secured a rationale for his extended absence.

"Moscow," Sasha said. "As you insisted." Since October.

Reilly, before going to New York, was at General Army Staff Headquarters in Mogilev. His meetings with Russian Intelligence convinced him that the Russian Monarchy would fall. The rail lines, in disrepair, had frozen. Delivery of food and military supplies failed, both to the cities and the Front. Shortages led to demonstrations and ultimately waves of police violence. Talk of schemes to overthrow the Tsar filled the salons. The government was clearly doomed.

"Five months?" Katya said. "I expected you long before this. We had to suffer the revolution alone. What kept you?"

"It was your idea," Sasha said.

Reilly judged that a broad coalition of liberal Duma legislators and socialists could prevent the worst outcomes of the Russian monarchy's failure, such as defeat by the German Army or a bloody Russian Civil War. He found support for building an organization to guide a coalition government, not to stage a putsch but to pressure the successors of the monarchy, to keep Russia functioning as a state and a military ally of Britain and France.

Within days of his first pitch, he raised more than enough money from Russian industrialists to get the project off the ground, to buy supplies and loyalty. Soon cables came in from everywhere promising financial support. A fortune arrived in cash and letters directing various American, British, French and Canadian banks to transfer funds to Reilly's accounts. Sasha took over the Moscow operation. Reilly went to New York.

But Katya smelled a rat. "One month was my idea. But this is Sidney's work."

Sasha's presence in Moscow had bought time for Reilly to work the American industrialists such as Ford, who had investments in Europe or Russia, and to transfer funds once they agreed to his scheme. It had also allowed him to devise a plan to discredit the Bolsheviks.

"I love him," Katya said, "but he's got the devil in him."

"Nonsense," Sasha said and kissed her on the temple.

On the day following Red Monday, Sasha and Volodia went to Tauride palace, home of the bourgeois Duma and now also of the left socialists. The palace had survived its first night in rebel hands without its royal aura. Troops stood lazily in the corridors and hallways, smoked cigarettes and looked absently at the rich trimmings and paintings of the European and Russian masters. They cleaned rifles or slept alongside workers who, as they, had nowhere to go, or had been too exhausted to go anywhere the previous night, when the first meeting of the Soviet finally broke up. Litter was everywhere: crumpled papers, cigarette butts, empty bottles, overcoats thrown on the floor or over antique chairs.

Word spread that the Duma would form a government and call for a Constituent Assembly that would give way to an elected government. A bloodless coup.

The socialists reinvented an organization called the "Soviet," a workers' brain-trust for opposing everything the new liberal bourgeois government would propose.

For the moment both socialist Soviet and liberal Provisional Government called Tauride Palace their home. Volodia and Sasha passed through the wide corridor. Sasha went toward the rear of the palace, to the Duma. Volodia went to the 'Soviet Cafeteria' where troops from the local garrisons prepared millet in a large black pot and spooned it out to men who stood in a long queue with porcelain dishes that had the imperial seal. Soviet members ate breakfast and tentatively congratulated one another on their victory.

Volodia carried a bowl of millet to a table and sat among some men he did not know, discovering quickly that his good reputation among the Socialists was intact. He immediately accepted their offer to join the Soviet and took his oath at the breakfast table over a bowl of millet.

Suddenly Kerensky materialized in the cafeteria. "Fellow democrats!" he said. "The Soviet will convene in the Catherine Hall! It's the first day of democracy in Russia!"

On the way out Kerensky ran into one of the Soviet delegates. "Comrade," he said, encircling the man and following him, "How would Soviet members respond if the government offered me a ministry? Say, Justice?"

"We are the Opposition, Kerensky, not the government. You'd have to resign from the Soviet first."

Soviet members surrounded Kerensky, who shouted, "I've got them in my pocket, you know! A coup for the Soviet."

Kerensky approached his Soviet colleagues one by one, trying to persuade them to allow him to become the new government's Minister for Justice and to retain Soviet chairmanship. They rejected his plea

"Unless the rank and file demand it."

The rejections weighed on Kerensky's cheeks. He ambled through the corridor, his pointed jaw low and his lips curled down. He stopped at an Oriental vase with flowers from the Winter Garden. His eyes suddenly twinkled.

"Rank and file," he thought. "Of course."

Kerensky approached a vase of flowers and inhaled their scent. Then he sneezed. He took out a handkerchief, blew his nose and straightened his necktie. He smiled confidently, walked to Catherine Hall and stopped at a hanging mirror. He studied his swollen eyes, took a deep breath and went into the large room. "May I have the floor?" he said.

A few people turned around. No one responded.

"I'm Kerensky," he shouted and jumped onto a table.

The speaker fell silent as everyone turned to Kerensky.

"Comrades!" he said. "Do you trust me?"

"We do!" they shouted.

"I speak," he said emotionally, "with all my soul, and if necessary – if you do not trust me – then I'm ready to die!" Tears welled in Kerensky's eyes and ran down his cheeks.

"Comrades! The Duma formed a new government and I had

to give an immediate reply when they asked me to be Minister of Justice. I have the men of the old government in my hand and have made up my mind not to let them go!"

Over the applause came shouts: "Hear! Hear!"

"I've freed the political prisoners from exile in Siberia!"

Applause thundered through the hall.

"Must I resign as Soviet Chairman in order to do this?"

"No! No!"

"I am ready to accept that title from you again if you..."

"Oh, yes! We want you!" they shouted.

Kerensky spoke on, begged his audience for approval at each step and at each got a ringing endorsement. He buried his face in his hands. "O-oh," he said, "you've filled my heart with faith and restored my spirit." He waited for more applause, got it and then blew his nose, jumped from the table and disappeared.

That afternoon the Bolshevik Military Committee, Lenin's army, appropriated the palace of Matilde Ksheshinskaya, Russia's prima ballerina, and evicted everyone but the servants.

At the same time, Lenin arrived in Petrograd from Europe.

5. Terrorist, Patriot, Novelist, Poet

Early one unseasonably warm morning in March of 1917, a cyclist crossed the northern city limits of Paris and pedalled along a narrow dirt road through the French countryside. He had a policeman's whistle in his mouth and a cigar between his fingers. A thick black moustache spread over his lip, and on his nose coloured spectacles protected his intense dark eyes from the dust and debris in the air.

He wore an official round hat and the jacket of a French officer's uniform, but his pants were dark khaki, with legs rolled at the bottom. He carried a rifle in a sling across his back, two pistols inside his jacket and a gun the size of a derringer in his boot. A canteen and fishing knife drooped from his belt. A thirteen-inch Arabian Scimitar lay in a scabbard beneath his jacket, its handle protruding just enough to satisfy his reach and its blade very close to his skin. A pouch attached to his belt carried three live hand grenades.

His black boots covered legs that had pedalled distances, outrun pursuers, and were determined to drive him to his destination on the northern coast of France by nightfall.

A man of many names, he carried numerous passports. In London he was Thistlewaite, in Paris, Jean Claude, in New York, Mister Chase. To a casual observer he could have been an athlete or a gendarme, a general or poet. But police knew him as 'Boris Savinkov, Russian terrorist and revolutionary.'

Savinkov disdained safety but had long sought sanctuary. He had lived for thirteen years in exile from Russia and now wanted to return. His journey through the French countryside could have been easier. He might have cycled to Abbeville and along the coast to Calais. It would have taken several hours longer but would have been safer. Instead he went north, through nervous French forces near Complegne and dangerously close to the German Army at Roye.

Perhaps Savinkov's decision to ride through the line of fire was brave, dictated by the importance of his mission and conscience. He feared the German Army but, even more, the thick grey mist that rolled across the coast every evening at seven o'clock. He preferred the possibility of death by cannon fire to the anxiety of standing blindly in one place for a few hours to wait for the fog to lift.

At noon he stopped at a farmhouse outside the town of Albert, where he put oil on his bicycle chain. He sat under a tree and ate bread and cheese. He poured wine from his canteen into a crystal claret and savoured the bouquet. He washed his hands, brushed his teeth and rode away without incident. Late in the afternoon he arrived outside Calais.

Knowing that what would follow would probably be the most difficult part of the journey, he stopped to study a map. He found the road that led to the ocean and identified the jetty to which he would have to walk in order to keep his appointment. The mist was thicker near the ocean. His blood surged: he needed half an hour or the British trawler waiting offshore would return to England without him.

For a mile the road was straight and easy. But closer to the shore it turned into a narrow dirt path surrounded by tall weeds. At the end of this path, he heard the ocean pound and hiss and left the bicycle to continue on foot. The fog drifted inland; he stepped carefully on stones he hoped would lead the right way. But the soil was wet and the stepping stones submerged. He held out his arms to keep balance. As the fog got thicker his heart beat harder and faster.

The water receded; the stones ended in sand. He went a few steps further until his boot hit wood. He brushed away a thin layer of sand, touched the dock and strode out over the water.

A shadowy figure appeared in the fog at the end of the dock, wearing a sea captain's hat and long dark cape. He held a fishing rod and leaned on a cane. A rowboat, tied to the pier, rocked with the waves.

"Stop there," the stranger said. "I've got one on the line."

When Savinkov stopped, his boot thumped on the dock.

"Blast!" said the stranger. "Lost him. Well, Savinkov."

Savinkov nodded, stepped near and offered his hand. But the old fisherman turned around and cast out his line.

"Hello, C," Savinkov said.

C carefully rested his pole. "So, you want to go back? But not like Lenin, with Germans."

"Right."

"Do you promise to keep Russia in the war?"

"Yes. Russia's honour is at stake."

"Very well. There is one further condition. One of my spies in Petrograd has been shot dead. I want you to occupy two of his agents until further notice."

"Assassins?"

"Marksmen." He gave Savinkov their names.

"Filonenko and Semyenov. I don't know them."

"They're expecting you to contact them."

C reeled in his line and dropped the rod into the boat. He

raised his stiff right leg, perched like a pelican and lowered himself to the dock. He sat on the edge with one leg dangling over the water while he removed a wooden leg. He climbed into the rowboat and put the prosthesis beside him.

"Well?" he said, looking up sternly. "Are you *coming*?"

"Yes," Savinkov replied, his answer more like a question. "How far do we have to go in that...dinghy?"

"The question, dear Savinkov, is not how far *we* have to go, but how far *you* have to go. Get aboard."

Savinkov nervously looked out at the fog and climbed into the back of the boat. The rear sank several inches, rocking the small craft as he clumsily seated himself. He locked his hands onto the sides as a ghastly expression covered his face.

C held out the oars and then drew them toward his chest. The rowboat rode up and veered slightly port-side as C's arms thrust the oars forward, drew them back and drove the dinghy against the waves. "Sing with me, Savinkov!"

Savinkov stuck his head overboard, moaned and vomited.

"Poor Savinkov!" C said. As the boat rose abruptly over a high wave, C sang, "Rule, Britannia! Britannia rule the waves! Bri-tons ne-ver ev-er shall be slaves!"

6. Kerensky and Savinkov

Kerensky waited at the train station for Savinkov with a brass band. Upon his arrival, Savinkov quickly conceded, "I was a terrorist but have renounced unnecessary violence. I am a socialist but a peaceful politician. I am a thinker, a Political Philosopher but I don't mind getting my hands dirty. The Soviet is my natural home."

He was sceptical that an idealist like Kerensky could run a political organization. They would need the help of Reilly's syndicate, socialists, monarchists, the military, secret police and people who knew how to run a government. With Reilly in the game, Kerensky and Savinkov might succeed.

Kerensky said, "I knew you'd take the right side. Come tomorrow. The socialists will accept you immediately. Then we'll meet with some of the generals."

"All right," Savinkov said.

"Now," Kerensky said, "there's something else."

"I knew it," Savinkov said.

"The Soviet will elect representatives to the army. But they want to exclude the Bolsheviks from the vote."

"Idiots. Lenin will say he's the real Opposition."

"How can we make the Soviet include them in the vote?"

Savinkov asked to be taken to see Judge Volodia Orlov.

"I'll talk to him."

Kerensky said, "By God, we'll be unbeatable."

"You sound crazy, Kerensky," Savinkov said gently.

"I am crazy with the passion of a single idea, Boris: democracy in Russia."

The carriage pulled left. The force of the turn sent Kerensky leaning into Savinkov as the carriage swung across the street and headed back in the opposite direction. The ashes from Savinkov's cigar fell onto his blue trousers. He leaned forward, blew the ashes away but then left a wide smudge as he tried to sweep his trousers clean. Farther along the street the carriage turned again and rolled along the Fontanka Canal past the Nevsky, where it came to rest in front of a red stone house.

"I'll see you tomorrow at the Soviet?" Kerensky said.

"Yes," Savinkov said, pulled out his duffel and strode across the street through the red brick arch.

The following day Kerensky and Savinkov took Volodia to the Soviet meeting, where His Honour argued that the Soviet should let the Bolsheviks participate. The argument failed, as Savinkov knew it would. But it got the Bolsheviks' attention.

7. Derzhinsky

Volodia stood at an intersection not far from the Tauride Palace. He glanced at a note that one of the Bolshevik deputies had given to him and imagined they had heard his seemingly sympathetic plea in the Soviet. Perhaps, he hoped, they had summoned him for the purpose of extending an invitation to join. He took back streets and came out on Suvorovsky, away from the affluent section. He looked for a house number, ambled slowly along the sidewalk and found a small block of flats behind an archway leading to a decrepit courtyard. He found the door and tapped on it.

"Come in, Your Honour," a voice said.

Volodia went in. Close by stood a slender man with blond hair, a slight beard and cold blue eyes. Volodia was nervous.

"Thank you for coming," the soft voice continued, carrying with it the mysterious power of deep eyes that suddenly held Volodia motionless and dried his mouth.

"Feliks Edmundovich," Volodia tried to say, though the words hung somewhere inside as he swallowed.

Get hold of yourself, man. This is your opportunity.

"Are you well, Your Honour?"

"I didn't know the invitation was from you." But was it an invitation or an order? In an earlier encounter he had sentenced Derzhinsky to prison. Did Derzhinsky want revenge?

Derzhinsky took Volodia's hands, squeezed them gently and grasped Volodia's forearms. His sleeves were rolled, exposing his wrists and wide manacle scars that seemed to say, "I earned the right to call myself a Bolshevik in *your* prison."

Volodia took an involuntary deep breath as a vision appeared: Derzhinsky as a quiet defendant standing before him, wrists manacled, Volodia himself draped in the magical protection of a judicial robe. Now Volodia felt naked.

"What is it, Your Honour?" Derzhinsky said. When Volodia answered only by involuntarily tensing his forearm, Derzhinsky continued gently, "Tell me the opinion of a virtuous man, about what best serves Russia? This aimless tugging between the Soviet and an impotent liberal government? Or a strong Soviet determined to set Russia on course to repair the damage of war, neglect and profiteering?"

"A strong Soviet, of course."

"But the Soviet has no strength, Your Honour. Its leaders mean well, but you know, the road to hell..."

Volodia took the bait. "The road to hell is paved with indecisive leadership." He felt Derzhinsky's gentle grasp tighten around his forearm and knew he had struck the right chord: the Bolsheviks will win because only they are decisive. Still, Volodia could not allow Derzhinsky to believe he would be easy. "But who will care what I think?"

"Your Honour, I admire your courage. You fought the Tsarist system as a judge. You fought the Soviet on our behalf the other day, in defence of fairness and democratic values. Your character and conviction could help lead Russia to a better future. Will you to join us?"

Volodia had prepared himself to engage in the kind of dialogue he thought Derzhinsky wanted.

"Who would take me seriously? I sentenced Bolsheviks to prison. I tried to be fair. But comrade, prison is prison."

Derzhinsky looked expressionlessly into Volodia's eyes, as though reading his thoughts and intentions. "Are you concerned that your experience with the monarchy will lead our people to ignore you, that this would make you ineffective?

"I'm concerned that they'd have me shot."

Derzhinsky studied Volodia intensely. Volodia had given Derzhinsky something to rebut, something to make him work harder to persuade him.

"Should the Soviet take a harder stand?" Derzhinsky said.

"I work in the Soviet, Feliks. It lacks will."

"What about you, Your Honour? Have you served democracy in your life as a judge, a man on the sidelines even in judicial robes, a spectator, a witness? Or do you say that a man must do more? Is it better to take action in this lifetime even though it may be perilous, or should one preserve safe passage from birth to death through passivity?"

Volodia knew that Derzhinsky wanted no less than real, critical self-examination. He would have to exude agony over the essence of his life, over whether he believed his career had served justice, over whether it was better to be satisfied with an honest judge's life of near-spectatorship, or to risk action that might lead to great danger. Before he could say yes to Derzhinsky he had to exhibit and perhaps endure the agony of self-examination.

Volodia thought: "Why have I been lenient with the socialists? Sympathy for Socialism, for the socialists, for the victims of the awful system in which I worked? Or was that a device I invented to limit my responsibility?

"How else could I exist?" he thought. "Have I lived a life of impossible contradiction inside an evil system, taking quiet, invisible action against it? Or was leniency a tool to define limits, to protect myself and not to serve humanity?"

"Are you a religious man?" Derzhinsky said.

Volodia was in the docket and Derzhinsky was his judge.

"I left the church," Volodia began.

"Did the Church fail you?"

"Perhaps, phrasing it like that..."

Derzhinsky tightened his grasp of Volodia's forearm. "Yes!" he said in a strained whisper. "Christ thought man could tame himself through faith and discipline. He failed for want of fear and force, the only true tools in subduing man."

Now I see why he inspires such terror. He believes himself Christ's heir.

Volodia said, "Those very tools."

"Can you embrace the danger?"

"I can..."

"Let's take it up together, Your Honour."

Volodia sensed success.

"Your Honour, however you assess your contribution to a just world, whether you have succeeded or failed, what I am offering you is the chance to begin your quest for justice again, in this lifetime but in a completely different life."

Volodia thought that Derzhinsky must have observed his agonized expression. "Of course," Derzhinsky said, "if you think we'll fail just as ignominiously as Christ failed, you should go save yourself as we would save ourselves."

"Have we really a chance?" Volodia said.

"Our time is coming soon, Your Honour."

"Soon?" said Volodia, forcing a grim smile.

"We will soon be the majority in the Soviet. When the workers and soldiers demand the Soviet take power, they will in fact be demanding that the Bolsheviks take power."

Volodia's head spun. "What about the local regiments?"

"Come tomorrow," Derzhinsky replied. "You'll see the regiments flock to us and clamour for Soviet accession."

They have troops? "What do you mean?"

"Neither government nor Soviet knows how to use power. The Soviets don't want power. We Bolsheviks do want it and one day we *will* control the Soviet."

"How?" said Volodia. "And when?"

"Events are closing in on the Soviets. England and France demanded reassurance from the government that Russia will not quit the European war. The government's sabre-rattling response terrorized the reserve troops stationed in this city. They called on the Soviets to intervene. But the Soviets hesitated, which cost them the troops' confidence."

Volodia said, "Well, if the Soviets intervened for the troops, people would say they want their own private army. The White generals would ride on the city, arrest the Soviets and declare martial law. We'd be crushed."

"Almost," Derzhinsky said. "There *would* be an attack, but we'd be in *Finland*. Soviet hesitation will convince the troops that the Soviets are no different from the government."

"So now we should act, and speak up for the troops."

Derzhinsky shook his head subtly and said, "No, no. If we spoke up it would look like *we* wanted the private army. As in the Soviet case, the generals would attack."

"What will the Soviets do? What will we do?"

"We'll wait as the Soviets dither, allow themselves to be seen as allies of the government and enemies of the revolution. Then they cannot claim they are the Opposition."

"By default," Volodia said, "*Lenin* will be the Opposition."

"Precisely, Your Honour. When the government falters we will speak as the Soviet and replace the current deputies one by one until we rule. The troops will know the difference between the old Soviets and us, and will demand a transfer of power to the Soviets, which we will lead."

Derzhinsky embraced him and kissed his cheeks. Volodia opened the door and stepped into the dull grey hallway where a window under the ceiling let in a ray of dusty light. He climbed down the stairs to the filthy courtyard.

"Bang, bang!" came a child's voice from behind a pile of rubble. From behind another pile of decayed wood and rusted metal fragments came more laughter. Volodia walked through the archway with a shiver and hurried along Suvorovsky Boulevard. His mind swirled as he passed the rows of low houses that sat in disrepair along the boulevard: now, and not before, he questioned the wisdom of his decision and considered how his success in seducing Derzhinsky had changed his life, probably forever and not for the better.

Volodia asked Anna to find him a safe flat. He could no longer live with the family without putting them in danger.

The first Bolshevik attack came in April with a determined-looking facade, pushed twice and then faded in the face of crowds organized to support the government.

General Kornilov, Military Governor of Petrograd, positioned twenty thousand troops just outside the city to keep the peace. But the Soviets successfully twisted the government's arm and kept Kornilov's army out. Though some violence occurred, the Soviets prevented the bloodshed of an attack, either by Kornilov's troops or by the Bolsheviks.

Kornilov was befuddled, a military man unable to understand why the government had not ordered him to act. Anger and humiliation hit. He resigned his post and retreated to Army Headquarters to fight a war with greater clarity. This, some believed, was the first great casualty of revolution. Russia needed a government, which needed an army, which needed a general. It needed General Kornilov.

Reilly awoke at midnight to a pounding on his hotel door. He got up, opened the door and saw Savinkov smiling with a bottle of champagne. Sasha stood quietly by.

Savinkov strutted in, got three glasses and opened the bottle. "I have good news and bad, you know," he said gingerly.

"Start with the downside, Boris."

"The Prime Minister and Defence Minister resigned. The government has fallen." He dropped a typewritten statement on the dining table. "Here," he said. "We can no longer administer the country. Therefore we wish to enlist creative forces in this country that have not taken a direct role."

"Who's that?" Reilly said.

"The Soviet," Sasha said.

Savinkov said, "They said they were The Opposition and couldn't join the government. But when the whole government threatened to resign, the Soviets let six deputies join. Now it's a coalition government."

"Kerensky is the new Minister for War," Sasha said.

"Oh, Lord," Reilly said.

"Yes," Savinkov said, "Guess who will represent the Soviet to Army Headquarters in Mogilev!"

"Who?" said Reilly.

"I will!"

Sasha leaned back, balancing his chair on its rear legs.

"Imagine, me, a former terrorist," he raved. "I'll go to Mogilev with Kerensky! They'll call me 'Colonel Savinkov'! Colonel!"

When the glasses were empty Reilly got up and marched to a credenza that sat against the adjacent wall. He took out a bottle of vodka and a glass, filled it and gulped the vodka down.

They sat quietly, as the events and changes of the day gelled into a coherent moving image of a present and a future. When the image reached its final frame, they glanced at one another and uttered a single word: "Volodia."

For Volodia was now on the inside of a burgeoning cabal that they knew would become Lenin's personal secret police.

Reilly and Volodia met the following evening at the safe flat. Reilly attributed Volodia's nervousness to his deep cover spy mission. He smoked cigarettes continuously and spoke with an uncharachteristic abruptness:

"Why didn't Kornilov bring fresh troops to the city?"

Reilly said, "Kerensky and the Soviet got in the way."

"That may cost us," Volodia said. "Lenin ordered a test of the government's will, not an attack. He made secret plans for an escape to Finland if opposition came. But the government's failure to use force changed everything."

"When they told Lenin that Kerensky was the new Minister for War," Volodia said, "he laughed until tears came to his eyes. He laughed even harder when Kornilov resigned as Military Governor and ran off to headquarters."

The Bolsheviks weren't ready. They were a month, five or six weeks away from a real attack. But they had seen the government's reticence and now were psychologically prepared.

Volodia said, "The government needs to use the army. You need to get Kornilov back into the picture."

"I've got the book on Lenin," Reilly said. "That might help."

"What book?"

"His deal with the Germans. They bought Lenin. Cash in exchange for a separate peace. I can prove he made a deal with them to pull Russia out of the war. He's a traitor."

"If that could bring Kornilov back, go to the newspapers."

"Both Germany and Britain will suspect that I set it up, and either one would have me killed. Not to mention the Bolsheviks. Timing is important because I'll only get one chance." He explained that he had copies of documents.

Reilly said. "I know a French agent. Reliable. I'll have him take the documents to Russian Intelligence."

"Twist it around so no one recognizes your hand."

Reilly said, "Right. It was a French operation. First they only wanted to sell decrypted cables. But patriotism got hold of them when the Germans brought Lenin back to Russia."

The story would appear to show that rogue French agents

had deciphered cables to sell. But when they saw that Lenin had come to Russia on a German train, they knew he had betrayed France and Russia and was really a German agent. A separate peace could destroy France, Britain and Russia. No self-respecting French agent, rogue or not, would allow that. And neither would most Russians. And If it brought Kornilov back into the picture, an angry Russian Army would chase Lenin into the Crimean Sea.

8. Laurent

A man in a tan suit stood in the doorway with a shy smile, small and hefty, his thinning hair brushed back over beads of liquid that could have been cheap hair tonic or profuse sweat. His big eyes gave the impression that he was both curious and modest, but not at the same time.

"Well, Laurent," Reilly said with a half-smile.

The man said, "Good evening, Mister Reilly."

Reilly smiled. "Laurent, did you get my message?"

"I certainly did," he replied. "What scheme does the famous Sidney Reilly have for me?"

Reilly led Laurent to a small bar. "Brandy?"

"Napoleon?"

"Of course."

"I don't mind if I do."

Reilly took a large snifter from the bar and poured an inch of brandy. He gave it to Laurent, took a glass himself and rested his elbow on the bar not far from the glass. His posture was casual and his expression light and amused as he watched Laurent study the rich fixtures in his room. Then he lectured, "Gold-painted moulding between the ceiling and walls, an ivory mirror frame hand-carved in Mesopotamia, sterling candlestick holders on a wall papered blue and grey. It hasn't peeled or frayed but doesn't look new."

"Yes, very prosperous," Laurent said, impressed.

"You want to help France?" Reilly said with a soft smile.

"That depends," Laurent said.

Reilly clicked his fingernails on his glass.

"How much is it worth?"

"Are you French, Laurent, or Russian?" Reilly said.

"I am French, Mister Reilly," he said.

"You love your country, I'm sure."

"I do, especially Paris. When I can get there."

"When the police aren't looking for you."

"Why do you ask?"

"If Lenin took power here, what would happen there?"

"Lenin is a very nasty man," Laurent said.

"Would he honour Russia's alliance with France?"

Laurent's eyes opened wide, like little globes, as though amazed at the prospect. "No, I don't think so," he said.

"How many German troops are in Russia and Ukraine?"

"I think a lot of them, very many. How many?"

"Millions. If Lenin made peace, where would they go?"

"France?" he said, as though stunned.

"Then where would you go?"

The prospect of not returning to Paris weighed on Laurent's face. "I don't know, Mister Reilly. Where? Not to France. Not if the Germans were in control."

"You see, Laurent, your country needs you. Russia too."

"What can I do?" Laurent said and shrugged.

Reilly gave Laurent a document, which said: "Lenin's entry into Russia successful." It was signed, "Schaefer." He looked at Reilly. "Where did you get it?"

"Never mind that."

"Is it a forgery?"

"A reproduction," Reilly said. "Just like the original."

"Are you selling it?"

"No," said Reilly. "I want to put Lenin out of business."

"You'll need more than that."

"I'll have more," Reilly said.

"You don't need me."

"I need a delivery channel."

"Where to?"

"Russian Intelligence."

"They'd pay dearly," Laurent said, wide-eyed.

"We're not selling. The idea is to discredit Lenin."

"With one letter?"

"This is just the first."

"Just deliver it?" Laurent said.

"Sell the idea. We'll give them material if they agree to make it public at the right time."

"When is that?"

"When the Bolsheviks make their next move."

"When is that?"

"A month," Reilly said. "Two months. I don't know."

"You want a regular delivery boy? Just a mail man?"

"I need someone who can sell the idea that the documents came through the normal military decryption process, that they were held back until verified at the highest levels."

"You work for the French, too, Mister Reilly?"

Reilly frowned. "Not for what *they* pay. Can you do it?"

"It might work."

Reilly said, "You'll have two dozen more, and some information about how money went from Berlin to Lenin. It depends on what the government does with it. You can't go to the trouble of getting it from the field if they're not going to use it and use it properly to get rid of the Bolsheviks."

"Just like that."

"Just like that," Reilly said. "What do you think?"

Laurent replied, "I don't know if I want to work for you again. I remember Arabia, when I delivered something for you that got me arrested. And Port Arthur, when you sent me to the Russian commander while you went out and made a fortune on sulphur. I never saw a ruble. I don't know."

"You're a professional, Laurent. We'd be good partners, you and I working together to put Lenin out of business. Of course, I wouldn't ask you to do it for free."

Laurent's eyebrows went up across his wide brow and slipped back down, bringing out crow's feet around his eyes as he smiled. "We'll have to review the details."

Reilly took an envelope from his pocket and offered it. "I thought you'd prefer dollars," he said.

"Dollars are very good." Laurent stuffed the envelope into his pocket and wiped a bead of sweat from his forehead.

"There's something else," said Reilly.

"What is it, Mister Reilly?"

"It is important not to connect me to this in any way."

"I understand," Laurent said.

"Because if you do, great harm will come to both of us."

"Great harm?"

Reilly drew his forefinger across his throat.

"Both of us?" Laurent said.

"That's danger pay," Reilly said, pointing to the envelope.

"It *is* a thick envelope."

"Take this letter to Sergei at Justice. He can read it but not keep it. Tell him if he wants it he'll have to keep it secret for now. You'll deliver more, maybe dozens. You'll tell him when to release them because the French insist it be used in the most effective way to discredit Lenin."

"Two dozen more deliveries, two dozen more envelopes?"

Reilly said, "Don't forget about Paris, Paris."

"I like that, when you call me Paris. I'll go in the morning. I'll come back at night with my report. You'll see how reliable I am." Laurent took a few steps toward the door.

"Laurent," Reilly said.

The Frenchman stopped and turned around.

"Your country needs you, you know."

"Trust me, Mister Reilly."

Reilly rested his elbow on the bar and took a sip of brandy as Laurent scooted through the doorway and disappeared. His expression of amusement vanished.

Reilly turned onto Mikhailovsky Street. He waited between a pair of tracks as a tram glided slowly along the other and rolled to a stop at Nevsky. A whip cracked. In front of the hotel a horse jumped forward, jerked the carriage behind and trotted toward the park at the far end of the street. A car followed it to the corner, sped around and disappeared from view. A truck veered onto the street and squeaked to a stop in front of him. A man jumped out.

"Commander Reilly?"

A delivery from the embassy. Three crates stacked inside his door. He took them to a desk and opened each with a screwdriver. First he saw green metal and a white label that said, "Underwood." In the next box he found a Remington and in the third an Adler. English, Russian and German.

Laurent showed up in the same suit he'd worn the night before. Reilly asked how he'd done at Intelligence Headquarters, and Laurent's looked confident. He put his hands on his hips and studied the accoutrements. "Mister Reilly," he said, "I like this hotel room. I might take one for myself. How much?"

"Plenty," said Reilly. "More than you could afford."

"Oh, I don't know. Prospects are good. Revolution is a time of opportunity for a smart man."

"What did Sergei have to say?"

"Brandy?"

Reilly went to the bar to pour two stingy shots. "Well?"

"You were right, Mister Reilly. He liked the letter."

"What did he say?"

"He wants to see more and will work with French Intelligence to help get them out." Then with a grin, "He loves France as much as I do."

Reilly relaxed. A smile crossed his face.

"Good work, Paris."

Laurent held up a small brandy snifter.

Reilly leaned on the bar with his left elbow, his right forefinger scratching gently against the stubble on his cheek as his thumb stroked his chin. "Just what I wanted."

"I said to trust me, Mister Reilly. I'm a good partner."

The Frenchman waved Reilly's cigarette smoke away. "I told him I'd bring more soon. Tomorrow or the next day."

"I may have something tomorrow night."

Laurent glanced at the typewriter on the desk and then at the stack of three wooden boxes. He looked delighted. "Will it take you so long? Even on a precision German machine?"

"What?"

"To write the letters on those typewriters."

"Don't second-guess me," Reilly said, shaking his finger.

"It's a chance to serve my country. I don't want to wait."

"I won't make you wait," Reilly said. "But I have some things to take care of first. You come back at noon on the day after tomorrow and I'll have something for you."

"Very well, Mister Reilly, I'll see you on Friday then." Laurent looked around. "You never told me what you pay?"

"I told you, plenty."

"I think I'll see if they have another one I can rent, maybe not so big. Maybe something down the hall, to help us."

"Sure, Paris, do that," Reilly said. "Tell me on Friday."

"I'll find out," Laurent said, "and tell you on Friday."

Reilly nodded, the smile still on his face.

Laurent walked through the corridor to the lift. Reilly closed the door and went to the desk He put a piece of paper in the Adler typewriter, rolled it in and started to type.

Two small lamps cast a dim light at one end of the room. The window beneath the basement ceiling at ground level faced the rear of the palace and let in tiny amounts of daylight for a few moments each morning. Volodia carried a stack of files to a box and took a new stack to his work table.

"How is it?" Derzhinsky said, his deep blue eyes penetrating Volodia's. "The files you sent were interesting."

Volodia rose, went to the stack of boxes against the far wall, brought back a file and gave it to Derzhinsky.

Derzhinsky's expression was unchanged as he read it. But the pupils of his eyes widened. "You didn't send this to me with the others. Did you just find it?"

"I waited to give it directly to you. You've been busy."

"Very good, Your Honour," Derzhinsky replied, tucking the

file under his arm, an infinitesimal squint in his eye.

"In similar situations, you'd prefer similar treatment?"

"Yes." Derzhinsky said he planned to give Volodia a position reporting directly to him, even before the Bolsheviks brought up the issue of taking power. Some Party members still wanted a delay, and Stalin's support would be important. As Volodia had imagined, Derzhinsky would use the information, which showed that Stalin had been an informant of the Tsar's secret Police, to secure Stalin's support.

Emboldened, Volodia pressed, "I wouldn't mind a day or two away from this basement. When the Congress convenes, send me there and I'll bring you an independent report."

"Independent?" Derzhinsky said.

"Yes," Volodia said, his mouth dry. "For perspective."

Derzhinsky said, "I see," and went away.

That night, in a nervous state, Volodia reproduced a document and judged it identical to the original.

Sergei Mikhailovich had worked in the Tsar's government. When revolution came he sided with the Provisional Government. Now, as an Intelligence Department official he invited Reilly to his office.

Reilly dropped a document on Sergei's desk.

Sergei changed his expression and said, "Lord. Where did you get this?"

Reilly shrugged deliberately. "Does it matter?"

"It's a forgery, to be sure, but a damned good one."

"It's a true forgery," Reilly said. "From the Okhrana files."

"What?"

"Stalin worked for the Okhrana," Reilly said.

Sergei stood up, walked around his desk and slid a small chair close to Reilly. "Something is finally happening but I can't discuss it yet. At least not with anyone here."

"Why not?"

"Rules of engagement," said Sergei.

"Who have you engaged?" said Reilly.

"Some renegade French agents. They have the book on Lenin. Intercepted codes, names, much more. Evidence."

Laurent followed instructions.

Sergei said, "Lenin's on Kaiser Wilhelm's payroll. We knew it all along but the French beat us to it."

"The French, eh? Well, good for them. Good for you."

"That's why I'm interested in your letter. With that and with what's in the works, I'll discredit Lenin as a German agent, a traitor both to Russia and to the revolution."

"When?" said Reilly.

"Not until Lenin makes his next move," said Sergei. "That's a condition set by the French. But they're right. By that time I'll have dozens of documents to prove Lenin's ties to Germany: money the Bolsheviks have been paid, secret account numbers, agents' names, contacts, everything."

"I'll do what I can to help. But Lenin's got thousands of men in his 'factory militias' and next time he'll use them."

Sergei shook his head. "General Kornilov went back to Mogilev. He slammed the door behind him. Doesn't want anything more to do with politics. He won't be much use."

"He needs something the Soviet can't stop."

"Can you talk to him?" said Sergei.

"I could go to Mogilev," Reilly said.

"I'll get you a private berth. When can you leave?"

"Day after tomorrow."

"Why not right away?" said Sergei.

"I'll need more evidence to convince him," Reilly said.

"I'm not sure what I can do in two days, Reilly."

"The French must have something."

"Laurent promised more but he's got to clear it with his superiors before he delivers anything."

"Who is he?" said Reilly. "I'll go have a talk with him."

"It's an off-the-books operation," Sergei said. "They're rogue agents who could pull out if I talk to anyone."

"Who is Laurent?" Reilly persisted.

"For now, just a name," said Sergei.

"What do you know about him?" said Reilly.

"He's a French intelligence agent."

"Are you sure the documents are real?"

"The documents are real. But I'll insult the French if I push for too much too soon. I can't do anything until I've got them in my hand. But it won't be long."

"Well I can," said Reilly. "Where is he?"

"He gave me no address."

"The embassy must know him. I'll make some inquiries."

"You wouldn't mind?" said Sergei.

"Nah," Reilly said, "I'll be back tomorrow."

"Then you'll have it."

"By the way, Sergei, what's the Frenchman charging?"

Sergei looked back with a questioning expression.

Reilly said, "One more thing. I need a list of the Okhrana officers who worked the Vyborg area before the revolution."

"I'll have it for you tomorrow."

Reilly stood in the doorway. "You'd have thought the British might pull this off. But the French? Never would have guessed."

The configuration of the hotel suite had changed. Reilly had moved the desk to the bedroom and put the Underwood and Adler typewriters on it, the first with Cyrillic keys and the other with the classic German. Stacks of paper sat on the floor nearby, each different in texture, colour and origin. A crystal ashtray sat between the two typewriters, filled to the top with butts and ashes. On the desk were recently-typed documents in German and Russian. Air was sparse.

Reilly looked at his watch, coughed and got up to open a window. He stood there for a minute and filled his lungs with the sour taste of Petrograd, mildly preferable to the thick substance that he had finally begun to notice after smoking furiously for eight or nine hours in the bedroom with the door closed. He coughed again, looked at the door and heard a sound in the other room. He got his pistol, went to the main room of the suite and opened the door.

"Good evening, Mister Reilly," Laurent said.

Reilly tucked his pistol away and opened the door.

Laurent came in. He waved his hand in front of his face. "You must have worked all night," he said, squinting. "I see you moved your desk into the other room and typed and smoked all night. It was very kind of you to try to spare me from the miserable smoke that you produce with your cigarettes, but it wasn't successful."

"Brandy, Laurent?"

"A double, if you don't mind."

"Can you go to Intelligence headquarters tomorrow?"

"I'm at your disposal," said Laurent. But when he leaned forward, he seemed secretive. He squinted, shifted left and right and then looked up at Reilly. "I can go in the morning. But Sergei may not be ready to accept the documents."

"What do you mean?" said Reilly.

"He could be in a meeting. Something might come up."

"What do you mean?" said Reilly.

"You said Friday. I'd look suspicious if I went too soon."

Reilly grinned. "Oh, I wouldn't worry about that, Paris. You've set the whole thing up just right. You've got him eating out of your hand. You won't have any problem with him. In fact, I think you should go early, before something really does come up." He rubbed his finger softly around the top of the crystal glass and made it squeal.

"I'm happy you like my work, Mister Reilly."

Reilly took an envelope from his pocket and held it out.

Laurent smiled in appreciation and slid the envelope into the breast pocket of his suit jacket.

"Tomorrow, if it's all right with you, after I go to Intelligence headquarters I will return to the hotel and speak to the manager about a room. Is that all right with you?"

"Sure, Paris, it's fine with me. But be careful about being too close to me. If the Bolos catch on, they'll send assassins. You wouldn't want to be shot just because you know me, would you?" His eyes were playful and his body relaxed.

"On the other hand," Laurent said, "if the Bolsheviks send an assassin I might just save your life. I don't fear danger."

"Oh, it isn't that, Paris. I know how brave you are. But I wouldn't want to lose you just because we're working together. I don't know what I'd do."

Laurent smiled but turned serious. "I'll try the Astoria."

"It's not cheaper," Reilly said. "But what the devil, you're a professional. Live where you want. Damn the expenses."

"I told you I believe revolution is a time of opportunity. I should look as prosperous as I want to be," Laurent said.

Reilly got the documents. "I've got fourteen. There'll be fifteen or so more. Tell Sergei your superior will contact you in a week or so. I'll be away but I'll call when I get back."

Laurent sniffed the papers. "Oh, no," he said. "Do them over. They stink of cigarette smoke. Anyone would see that they were all produced at the same time."

Reilly sniffed the documents and said, "Right." *Damn it.*

The following day, Reilly saw Sergei, who delivered good news. "Our French friend checked out all right."

"What did he deliver?"

"Fourteen pieces. Big Bertha. The mother lode."

"Not bad."

"It confirms what another Russian said. A German agent."

Surprised, Reilly said, "An agent from Germany?"

Sergei Mikhailovich smiled. "No doubt about Lenin."

Reilly did not press Sergei as to the identity of the Russian-German agent because he was thinking about photographing everything for General Kornilov.

"I'll have them by this evening," Sergei told him. "Your tickets are for tomorrow night. I have the list of Okhrana agents you asked for." He took an envelope from his desk and gave it to Reilly. "By the way, there's more."

Reilly stopped.

Sergei said, "Some former Okhrana officers joined officers from disbanded units who've come back to the city. You should talk to them. Some are on that list."

Reilly opened the envelope and took out the list.

Sergei picked up the telephone receiver. "Cable Malibaev. We'll be there in the morning." He dropped the phone on the switch hook and said, "I'll go with you. I think I can get Lockhart to drive. Pick you up about five in the morning."

"Five?"

"It's a long drive out to Sosnovy Bor and I've got to get you back by six in the evening if you're going to Mogilev."

9. Remnants of the Tsar's Secret Police

At daybreak on a cool Petrograd morning in May of 1917 a black car made its way from the British Embassy past the Trinity Bridge, turned onto the Nevsky Prospect and came to a stop at a large block of flats. The engine idled until a man in a black leather jacket came through the entry arch.

"Dobrey Utra, Sergei Mikhail'ich," the driver said in Russian. "Good morning."

"Hello, Lockhart," Sergei Mikhailovich said.

The car slipped out onto the Nevsky, drove several blocks to Mikhailovsky Street and stopped in front of the Europe Hotel. The driver nodded to the doorman, a diminutive man in a blue uniform with brass buttons.

"I hope you know what you're doing," the driver said.

"Don't worry, Lockhart."

"But I am worried. This whole business makes me nervous. Why should I drive you out there at this hour? Why the devil couldn't you get a government car?"

Sergei smiled at Lockhart. "I have to protect the government from the Soviet until we're ready. I couldn't risk taking one of their cars. But surely you British wouldn't want us to leave you out. The French are already in, full-steam."

"It sounds like a big Russian fiasco if you ask me."

"If we left matters alone and Lenin's thugs took power over Russia, *that* would be a big Russian fiasco."

Reilly walked to the car, got in the back and said, "Hello."

Lockhart did not reply, but shook his head disapprovingly.

"Morning, Reilly," said Sergei Mikhailovich.

The car spun around onto the Nevsky and drove south. Sergei turned around to face Reilly, his elbows steadied on the back of his seat as the car rolled along.

"Our friend Lockhart seems to have reservations," he said to Reilly while looking at Lockhart with a subtle side glance. "If I didn't know better I'd say the British are afraid and would just as well leave it to the French."

"Oh, no," Reilly said, "we want in. Just need a nudge."

"The only reason I'm doing this," Lockhart said, his voice filled with forced severity, "is that we're allied against the Germans. But it's absurd to think you can discredit Lenin by peddling a handful of French decrypts on the Soviet and the newspapers. It's a lunatic scheme, bound to backfire. And bringing in a busload of disgruntled former police terrorists won't exactly reduce the risk. The two of you are crazy."

"Never talk to Lockhart early in the morning," Sergei said.

The car sped out onto a highway along the water, where forests and open fields filled the view on the left and the island of Kronstadt, where sailors were training to become revolutionaries, sat off the coast to the right. Past Kronstadt a few rowboats floated close to shore. Sergei went silent, rested his head and closed his eyes. Reilly leaned on the door and noticed an occasional smile tug on Lockhart's cheek. For a few hours Russia, was quiet and peaceful.

Ahead to the right a peninsula jutted out into the Gulf of Finland and hooked back toward the coast. A sign by the road said "Sosnovy Bor" and pointed to the left where the road veered away. On the right a smaller trail led out onto the peninsula, just wide enough for the car, which bounced onto it from the main highway and sent a cloud of dirt into the air. Shrubs and tree branches obstructed its path and brushed it on both sides. For the next few minutes the car rocked along the untended forest trail and jostled the occupants left and right. After a while Sergei motioned to Lockhart, who let the car roll to a stop in a small clearing near the water. Sergei pointed ahead to a house near the water.

The man they wanted to see was Yusepov, an ex-Okhrana officer in hiding with his colleagues and their former commander, Malibaev. Sergei Mikhailovich did most of the talking, and in trying to get the support of these men, exaggerated everything: the British were sending one-hundred thousand troops; White Russian divisions led by General Kornilov were all in; they had authentic documents proving Lenin a German agent. The Okhrana officers, by now desperate to hear someone with a plan, were hooked.

When the meeting ended, Sergei led the way to the car.

Lockhart slid into the seat. "How will you deliver all that?"

Reilly climbed in next to him and Sergei got into the back. Lockhart turned the ignition and the car rolled forward, sped up and raised a cloud of dirt and dust in its wake. In a few moments it turned onto the main road. Reilly lit a cigarette and stared through the window.

"You're the biggest liar I ever met," Lockhart said. "One hundred thousand British troops. Bloody rubbish."

"You might have tempered their expectations," Reilly said.

Sergei said, "Kornilov will think he has no choice."

"Bloodiest liar ever," Lockhart said and stepped on the gas pedal. The car sped toward the less tranquil city of Petrograd.

10. Mistrust

A few days later a long train arrived at the Mogilev station. Reilly held a small satchel as he made his way through the narrow corridor to the metal steps that led to the platform. Outside, a young man introduced himself as Semyenov. He worked for Filonenko, Savinkov's assistant at HQ. He said political intrigue had taken the officers. War Minister Kerensky was having difficulty with General Kornilov.

Upon arriving, Reilly heard shouting from an upstairs window. Semyenov gestured toward stone steps that led to the house. Savinkov appeared in the doorway, looking bewildered and anxious. He embraced Reilly and smiled.

Upstairs, Kornilov shouted, "You have the brain of a goat!"

Kerensky replied, "You don't!"

Savinkov said, "War Minister Kerensky is General Kornilov's boss. It's making Kornilov crazy. Kerensky is already crazy." Savinkov led Reilly along a road to a small house where a sign said, 'Officers' Club.' A soldier in a crisp khaki uniform greeted them at the door and escorted them to a table near a window where they sat.

"They're at each other's throats and it's getting worse."

"Did you tell them about my documents?"

"Your cable started the trouble," Savinkov said. "Kerensky saw it as an attack on the revolution and not just on Lenin."

"What about Kornilov? Did you tell him I was coming?"

"Well," Savinkov replied, "yes and no. I told him you had proof that Lenin is a traitor."

"What did he say?" Reilly said.

"That Kerensky is a traitor too."

The waiter brought a bottle of vodka and two glasses.

"We've got everything," Reilly said, "but military backup. The local troops are uncontrollable. The Bolos are agitating. We could discredit Lenin but lose at the last minute if the troops side with him. That's what this feud could lead to."

"We may not be able to get the backup we want," Savinkov said. "Even if Kornilov agrees, no one knows if troops from the front will obey orders to march on the city."

"I want to talk to Kornilov," Reilly said.

"You don't want to talk to him right now."

Reilly slept soundly until boots stomping across the wooden floor rocked him awake. He heard Savinkov's voice. Boot steps got closer. Abruptly the door to Reilly's room opened. General Kornilov, in uniform, stood in the doorway.

Kornilov walked with deliberate slowness to Reilly's bed and spoke in a firm but restrained, emotional voice. "Listen carefully, Reilly. I want nothing to do with politics. If the idiots in the government and the Soviet want or don't want a Constituent Assembly, it's fine with me either way. Just leave me out of it. I'm going to war against the German Army. I'm leaving now for the front. And this Kerensky is all yours."

With that, General Kornilov stormed out of the room.

Savinkov came in wearing a new army uniform.

"I'm going to the front with Kerensky. Filonenko will take you to the station. Sorry." He shrugged and hurried off.

Reilly buckled up and put on his boots. He brushed his hair and stuffed his night clothes and toiletries into a satchel.

Soon he boarded the train, found his private compartment and threw the satchel on the seat. He sat down and put his feet up. He glanced out the window at the station house and the barren street behind it, looked at the clear blue sky and wondered how long he would wait for the train to move out. But the train soon rolled out of Mogilev into the countryside.

Reilly thought back through the previous weeks and imagined that the result he had just obtained, which was no result at all, could have been different.

Damn it. Who will believe we're going anywhere without an army? Who will think their investments in Russia or Europe are any safer because of me? What the hell will I say to Ford, to Morgan. They'll all want their money back. What about the secret police agents who never asked for payment and are willing to die for my scheme? To Sasha; God, to Volodia and Anna.

Reilly stared at the Russian countryside, but the ghost of Kornilov, who had dismissed him so summarily, returned:

What an insult, Kornilov reporting to Kerensky. Can I get him if he's subordinate to Kerensky? He needs a battlefield victory first. While I'm fighting the Bolsheviks he'll be somewhere else fighting Germans.

I have forged proof that Lenin is a traitor. Can I win over a city with a short stack of forged documents and no army?

In the morning, Reilly carried his bag through a busy station, filled with crowds hoping to escape Petrograd. As he reached the entrance, a man in a grey suit shouted at him.

"Sidney!" Boris Suvorin, editor and owner of the city's most conservative paper, hurried to greet Reilly.

Suvorin said, "Is it true? About Lenin?"

"Is what true?" said Reilly.

"Evidence that Lenin is a traitor, a German spy."

"Where did you hear that?"

"A former Okhrana agent. Word's spreading. Is it true?"

Reilly said, "We can't speak now. Come to my hotel at five." Reilly walked to a taxi. Suvorin appeared at five.

"If you ask anyone in Russia who has any sense," the newspaper man said, "they'll tell you that the last good day they had was sometime in nineteen-fourteen. Hell of a long time since Russia had much to cheer about. Now you've got something that could make me smile. I want to see it." He read the first document and said, "Is it authentic?"

"I don't see why not," Reilly said.

Suvorin smiled and said, "We might be able to use this."

11. True Forgeries

Sergei again rebuffed Reilly's plea for an early release of the incriminating documents, concerned that the French would take it as a double-cross. However, he said he would try to persuade the Soviet to ban a demonstration until they could put a defensive plan in place. But even if the Soviet agreed, he said, only Kornilov's troops would stop a determined Lenin.

"Look, Reilly," Sergei said, "Savinkov can't divert troops to the city if Kerensky is sending them to the front."

At the Astoria, Laurent sat near the wall with a newspaper.

"Hello, Paris," Reilly said. "Fine place."

Laurent smiled and raised his eyebrows. Reilly sat down and a waiter came up to the table. "Something to drink, sir?"

"I'll take coffee, black with sugar."

"How was your visit with Kornilov?" Laurent said. He seemed a different man, with a cleaned and pressed suit, European cologne, his hair trimmed and nails filed.

"Don't know yet," Reilly said. "But Kornilov went off to fight the Germans. So we have no army and Lenin's going to go for checkmate tomorrow afternoon. Some fix."

"What are we going to do, Mister Reilly?"

The waiter brought coffee and sugar. Reilly took a sip and rested the cup in the saucer. "That's why I came to see you, Paris. I thought you might have an idea."

"You mean you came here just to see me? Nothing else?"

"That's right. You're the only reason I'm here."

"Then I'm yours, Mister Reilly. I'll help you if I can."

"Well, think of something. I'm running dry."

"I'll consider the problem. Let me digest it."

Reilly smiled and then chuckled. "All right, Paris."

"I have a question," Laurent said.

"Go ahead."

"What's all this to you? What kind of life do you want?"

"Don't know," Reilly replied. "What do you want?"

Laurent's smile turned shy. "A cottage in the countryside outside Paris, a lady to cook breakfast and make my bed."

"A beautiful French girl."

"She doesn't have to be beautiful and she doesn't have to be French. A Russian lady would be fine. Really, that's why I came to Petrograd, to find someone who might have use for me. So I won't be alone. So I'd have company. I'd be happy."

Reilly liked what Laurent had said and Laurent had said it in just the right way. His head rocked back as he laughed quietly to himself.

"Do you think I'm ridiculous, Mister Reilly?"

"It's your dream, Paris, and I hope you get it. Why not?"

"That's what I say. Mister Reilly. Why not? Now here is my idea: I could go to Bolshevik headquarters and warn them that French Intelligence is going to turn these incriminating letters over to the government. I'll say there's a rumour that preparations are now being made for arrests. They might cancel their plans if they think they're being watched."

"Bloody dangerous," Reilly said.

"Maybe," Laurent said, "but if I help you and we succeed, then both Russia and France will be free. My lady Svetochka and her friends can live a normal life. The more I think about it, the more I think it's the right thing for us to do."

Reilly sat up. "It'd give Lenin something to think about."

"Then I'd consider it an honour, Mister Reilly. It isn't about me. It's about saving Paris from the Germans, saving Russia from the Bolsheviks. It's about big things, even if it involves someone small like me. Should I take a letter?"

"Just information. You're a French socialist sympathizer."

Rumours about rebel forces were all over Petrograd. At the barracks, the Bolshevik Military Organization urged troops, anarchists and factory workers to demonstrate the next day. On Kronstadt Island, rabble-rousers pumped adrenaline through tens of thousands of radicalised sailors. The Bolshevik propaganda machine was going strong.

Volodia walked the corridors of the Military Palace with some of the others who had attended the day's session of the All Russian Congress. He hated hard seats, boring political speeches and dull company. Posters outside said:

"Demonstrate against the Tsarist Duma Saturday at two."

"All power to the Soviets! Demonstration Saturday!"

Volodia's stomach tightened. The Soviet delegates looked at one another bewildered. "What are they going to do?"

When they went inside for an emergency session, Volodia realized that if a demonstration came off in the next few days, and if the Bolsheviks tried to use it to attack, the government would have no defence. Neither would the Soviet nor the military. At Bolshevik headquarters he gave Derzhinsky his report, and hoped that a hint of military intervention might bring out Lenin's cautious side.

"How was it?" Derzhinsky said.

"The Congress brought up the issue of the government's seizing a house from anarchists. But when the session closed, I went outside and saw how we've blundered."

Derzhinsky glared into Volodia's eyes. "Blundered?"

"We intend to lead the demonstration. If the opportunity comes we'll use the Machine Gun units to physically seize power from the Provisional Government and place it in the hands of the Soviet, which we will then control. It will not be a trivial moment in history, but one that marks a turning point not just for Russia but for the entire world."

"How did we blunder?"

"We put announcements all over the city."

"What? The billboards for the demonstration?"

"People would have to be blind to miss them."

Then Peters opened the door and stuck his head inside the room. "Come down, Feliks. Men from the Soviet are here."

Derzhinsky left abruptly. Trotsky spoke to soldiers from the Machine Gun Battalion. A Soviet man said the government had banned the demonstration. The machine-gunners asked Derzhinsky to approve mobilization anyway.

"Trotsky," the Soviet man said, "something like that would be so big that even you couldn't contain it. The Soviet supports the government. Demonstrations are banned."

Derzhinsky started to argue that the Bolsheviks didn't start demonstrations, but just followed the people's will. But the Soviet representative refused to back down: "Public opinion is turning from the Opposition because Kerensky's drive against the Germans looks successful and the government is starting to believe in itself. So stay home."

Derzhinsky said, "If you mean that the demonstration would endanger the population, then we agree to a postponement. But no ban. We can't speak for the soldiers."

The Soviet man said. "You'll have no demonstration."

The Bolshevik Central Committee convened in the large first-floor room and after an excited debate agreed to postponement. Lenin said he would attend the next day's Congress session so his followers would not feel abandoned.

Everyone was relieved that the demonstration was off. At the All-Russian Congress, speaker after speaker proclaimed support for the coalition Provisional Government and suggested that the Soviet could never assume full power.

One speaker insisted that there was no political party

prepared to assume full power.

Lenin shouted, "There is!" and swaggered to the podium

"The citizen speakers have declared that there is no political party in Russia that would take the entire power on itself. I answer: there is! Our party is ready at any moment!"

Groans filled the hall. A Socialist Revolutionary member shouted from the audience, "You have no program! You are no more ready to assume power than any of us! You want to seize power but have no idea what to do with it!"

"But we do! Our first step would be to arrest the biggest capitalists and smash their intrigues. We'd announce to the nations independently of their governments, that we hold all capitalists to be plunderers, the ministers of the bourgeois government and the French and British capitalists and all.

"Where are we? What is this council of workers' and soldiers' delegates? Is there anything like it in the world? No, of course not. Nothing so absurd as this exists in any country today except in Russia. Then let us have one of two things, bourgeois government with plans for so-called social reform on paper, such as exists in every country now, or let us have that government which you long for but which you appear too frightened to bring into existence. A government of the proletariat, which had its historic parallel in 1792 in France.

"Look at this anarchy which we have now in Russia. What does it mean? Do you really think you can create an intermediate stage between capitalism and Socialism? Can you persuade the bourgeois governments of Western Europe to come to our point of view on the peace settlement? No, it will fail as long as power is out of the hands of the Russian proletariat. That power I and my party are prepared to take at any moment on their behalf."

Sarcastic laughter burst from all corners of the large hall.

"Look at what you are doing," he shouted, pointing his finger at some of the socialist ministers who had joined the Provisional Government. "Capitalists with eight-hundred per cent war profits? Why not arrest fifty of them, and lock them up for a bit, even though you may keep them under the same luxurious conditions as you keep Tsar Nicholas Romanov?"

"You talk about peace," said Lenin, "without annexations. Put that principle into practice in your own country, in Finland and in Ukraine. You talk about an advance on the front. We are not against war on principle. We are only against a capitalist war for capitalist ends. And until you take the government entirely into your hands and oust the bourgeois you are only the tools of those who have brought this disaster upon the world."

The hall buzzed as Lenin took his seat. Kerensky stood at the far side of the hall and stride to the podium.

"We have been given some historic parallels," Kerensky began. "We have been referred to 1792 as an example of how we should carry out the revolution of 1917. But how did the French Republic of 1792 end? It turned into imperialism and set back the progress of democracy. Our duty is to prevent that here, to strengthen our newly-won freedom so our comrades who have come back from exile in Siberia shall not be forced to go back, and so that the comrade," he pointed to Lenin, "who has been living comfortably all this time in Switzerland, shall not have to fly back there again!

"Lenin proposes to us a new and wonderful recipe for our revolution. Arrest a handful of Russian capitalists. Comrades, Brother Lenin: Marx never proposed such Oriental despotism."

Delegates applauded, though Bolsheviks cursed Kerensky.

"Our Bolshevik colleagues say it is a good thing for Russian soldiers to trade vodka for bread crumbs with German soldiers at the front, that comradely exchange will end the war. But, Bolshevik comrades, be careful. Or you'll find yourselves kissing the mailed fist of Kaiser Wilhelm!"

Kerensky turned red, his voice strained and harsh.

"You tell us that you fear reaction! You say that you love our newly-won freedom! But you propose to lead us the way of France in 1792. Instead of appealing for reconstruction, you clamour for further destruction! Like a Phoenix, out of the fiery chaos that you make a steely dictator will arise."

Kerensky stopped, and walked toward the Bolshevik delegation and Lenin, his steps deliberate and dramatic. A hush descended on the hall. "But I will not be the dictator you are trying to create!" He stomped back to his seat.

Lenin stroked his beard, turned to Trotsky and said, "This is true. But then Kerensky is not the dictator I had in mind."

Still, Kerensky was Minister for War, and this influenced Lenin's thinking about whether and how to attack. The government was optimistic. The militia was finally going after anarchists. Russian Intelligence put the Bolsheviks under surveillance with the help of the Soviet. For Lenin, any sign of confidence on the government side called for caution.

Word came that Kerensky's offensive had stalled, then that the German Army had turned it back and finally that Russian troops had fled with losses heavy and desertions.

Astonishingly, the Red machine gun units in Petrograd complained. "If I were you," Savinkov told Kerensky, "I'd take half of those little brats and send them to the front. Let the regulars hold ground behind them with fixed bayonets."

Lenin said, "We need to be cautious now."

Trotsky said, "You're trying to appease the government."

"Appeasement is no crime if it helps us succeed. We have to give them something, so give them what they're going to take anyway, a few machine gunners and their weapons."

Then word spread that Lenin's relationship with the Germans would appear in city newspapers. The government cancelled the demonstration. Lenin escaped.

12. A Family in Partial Repair

Reilly and Ilya shook hands and embraced. "How's Ilya?"

"Not bad," Ilya said. "School's almost out."

"What are your plans for the summer?"

"Who makes plans mid-revolution? I don't know."

Reilly took a book from his satchel. "Happy birthday."

Ilya smiled. "Thanks, Sidney. *Raw Youth*. Dostoevsky. Only

one of his that I haven't read. How'd you know?"

"I looked for it last time I was here but didn't see it."

Ilya flipped through a few pages of the book.

Reilly sat on the edge of the bed. "I've narrowed the list of your attackers to four. Describe him again for me."

"What'll you do if you find him?" said Ilya.

"I'll have charges brought against him," said Reilly.

"What'll they do to him?"

"Prison term, most likely."

"All right," said Ilya. "He was big. I don't think I came up to his chin. Dark eyes, thick eyebrows. Didn't look mean. But when he touched me I could feel the meanness. In my arm, my shoulder and then my stomach and legs when he threw me to the ground." Ilya absently stroked the scar.

He gave Ilya a calling card and stood. "How's mother?"

"Nervous. She wants me with her in July. I'll go crazy."

"Would you like to go to Moscow? I'll be spending some time there in late July. I could get you a job, a place to stay."

"It depends. I don't know. I'll have to think about it."

"All right. We'll talk about it another time."

They embraced. Reilly went downstairs.

Anna agreed to go to Moscow for the summer.

"How is it?" Reilly said.

"Interesting," Volodia said. "I'm assigned to observe the machine gunners. The proverbial tempest in a teapot."

"How many have gone over?" said Reilly.

"Impossible to say. They're all angry. Some have orders to go to the front. Others are afraid they'll be called next. But no one wants to die in a 'dirty capitalist war'."

"The Bolsheviks' propaganda is working," said Reilly.

"Working? They've lit a fire under them that nothing but a suicidal rampage through the city will douse. Their chant is 'Soviet, take power from the bourgeois bandits.' The word 'Bandits' is the only one they understand."

"Can the Bolsheviks restrain them?"

Volodia topped off the glasses with more vodka, drank some down and smacked his lips. "That, Sidney, is the big question. They might get out of control and have their own little revolution. Sink everything and leave rubble all over."

"What are the Bolsheviks doing about it?"

"The gunners don't know what to do. Lenin's in hiding. Compared to Trotsky Derzhinsky sounds like the voice of reason. Who will the gunners follow? They listen to the Military Organization, but that propaganda changes daily. One day they give Trotsky's pitch, 'Throw out the government!' Next day they follow Derzhinsky with, 'Do nothing until you are instructed by the Party leadership.' They're not clear, but where anger boils, action follows. How is Laurent doing?"

Reilly said, "He's convinced Government Intelligence that the forgeries are genuine French spy treasure. But Sergei Mikhailovich won't release anything to the papers until the six Soviets who joined the government agree. We may have to pass out the word with broadsheets, with the Okhranists working the crowds. Can you imagine?"

"Your margin is no more than two weeks," Volodia said.

"You said the Bolsheviks are undecided."

"They are," Volodia said. "But the Machine Gun units aren't. If the Bolos don't lead them against the government, they'll lead the Bolsheviks. Be prepared in any case."

Debate continued at Bolshevik headquarters, but without Lenin. Derzhinsky seemed a calming force against Trotsky's fiery rhetoric. Pressure mounted from the Machine Gunners and now Volodia sensed it from the sailors at Kronstadt.

Ilya recalled that the Okhrana officer who beat him had large hands, a thick dark moustache with a few grey whiskers and no beard. Reilly told them he had a list of three and needed just a detail to draw an accurate conclusion.

Reilly saw Katya in the kitchen and they brushed cheeks.

"Ilya seems better," said Reilly.

"Don't be fooled. One minute he's well, the next he's crazy.

He's obsessed with the old secret police. But then he makes excuses for them, for your making use of them."

"Katya, let me take him to Moscow and get him a job."

"He's got a girl, "Katya said. "Maybe if you speak to him."

"All right. How's Anna."

"I'm taking her to Moscow in a few days with her friend."

Reilly gave Katya money and said, "Get them a good place to stay. In the centre, but away from the Kremlin. Anna and Natasha can work at the Syndicate until their dancing school starts in September. How are you, Katya?"

"Lives are up in the air. No one knows what to do. You can't plan. You can only try to survive. It's lonely."

"You have friends," said Reilly.

"My friends have gone away."

"Are you getting out of the house?"

"For food lines. They're boarding up windows on Kamenostrovsky. The Fontanka is filled with junk and the neighbourhood stinks on hot days. Who wants to go out?"

"I'll take you to the countryside when school lets out."

"The loneliness would kill me," said Katya.

"It'll be safe."

"What'll I come back to? A house filled with anarchists?"

"We'll watch the house," said Reilly.

"Who'll watch Sasha?" said Katya.

"Sasha?"

"His drinking," Katya said. "I don't know what I'll do. Maybe I'll go and maybe I'll stay. I could use a swim. I could preserve the fruits and vegetables as usual. But the solitude will eat me up. I think I'd prefer to be here."

Reilly put his arm around her and felt moisture on her cheek.

"I'll be fine," she replied but the moisture spread. "I'm lonely. I'm going to die of loneliness." She broke away, walked to the doorway and stopped. "I can't talk. I can only survive if I keep all that down. Otherwise it'll consume me. Nothing personal, Sidney. I can't be around you right now."

Reilly met with the three former Okhranists, suspects in Ilya's beating. Each had dark eyes, thick eyebrows and big hands. Malibaev and Konstantinov wore full moustaches. Platnikov was cleanly-shaven, and admitted that just before the revolution- just before Ilya's beating- he had shaved the full beard he had cultivated for years. A clean face was his disguise. Reilly mentally scratched Platnikov off his list, leaving Konstantinov and Malibaev.

Then Reilly went to the café at the Astoria Hotel. Laurent was sitting with a woman in a black dress. He wore his hair trimmed and brushed back like Reilly's. He held an ivory cigarette holder with a foreign cigarette and wore a tailored suit. A brunette with bright red lipstick hung on his arm. Laurent smiled like a proud father.

"Mister Reilly, I'd like you to meet Svetochka. We're a sort of... sort of an item, you might say. Right baby?"

"That's right, babykins."

Laurent drank something from a champagne glass.

Reilly said, "Say, Paris, do you think you and I could have a little private talk, maybe go to your room?"

Svetochka patted her red lips with a linen napkin.

Laurent gave her the room key. She drew up her dress as she rose form the table, glanced again at Reilly and patted the Frenchman on the head. When she was through the door, Laurent smiled. "How do you like her, Mister Reilly?"

"I don't know, Paris. I can't imagine her keeping house in the countryside." Reilly's thumb and forefinger stroked his chin. "No," he said. "She's a city girl. More than one country day would kill the likes of her."

"I like her, Mister Reilly."

Reilly said, "Don't bet the farmhouse on a girl named Svetochka. Not this year, Paris, and not in this city."

Laurent's smile disappeared and his eyes opened wide. "What do you mean, Mister Reilly?"

Reilly had probably said too much. "Well, girls like that... I mean at this particular point in time... they want to escape from

Russia. If you paint her a picture of a house in the countryside near Paris, she'll think she's died and gone to heaven. Why, you're a prize catch, Paris. You keep your eyes open. Don't get hurt, or let her become disappointed."

Laurent looked wounded. "Why don't you give me the documents now and I'll go see to Sergei Mikhailovich?"

Reilly put his elbows on the table. "Oh come on, Paris," he said. "I'm only trying to protect you. Why, this city's filled with girls who'd do anything to get out with a fellow like you. They're lined up at the train stations. Russia's a wasteland right now, but you've got life ahead of you. I just want you to keep your eye on it and protect yourself."

"So go ahead and give me the envelope. I'll take it now, and Svetochka will be waiting in my room when I get back."

Reilly took the envelop from his suit pocket and tossed it on the table. Laurent took the money and then put it inside a wallet that was stuffed with cash.

"I hope you don't let anyone, see that," Reilly said, lighting a cigarette, "including Svetochka. "Why don't you give it to me and I'll have the hotel manager put it in a safe?"

"I'll be careful, Mister Reilly."

Reilly went to the train station to bid Katya, Anna and her friend Natasha good bye. Today the young women would leave for Moscow. With Katya standing in the ticket line and Natasha waiting not far away with luggage, Anna stopped Reilly as he bounded up the stairs at the Nevsky Prospect entrance. He gave her money, a list of contacts and papers that identified both as VIP officials at the British Consulate.

Anna threw the items in her bag. "I'm going to work for your people, Sidney. I know about what's happening and I don't like any of it and I'd give my life for Russia."

"Be careful of the men there. Don't trust anyone."

Anna hugged Reilly, kissed him and said, "Count on me."

Reilly watched them go to the platform. Anna smiled slightly as she looked back. He imagined that on practically any other occasion, had Anna been so assertive he would have thought her silly, patted her on the head and kissed her forehead. But this time he did not think her silly; rather, he was thinking of generals who wouldn't show up, newspaper editors who were too afraid to print the truth and bloodthirsty secret police hoodlums who wanted as much to trash the government as to stop the Bolsheviks. He thought of Laurent and Anna, risking their lives for Russia. Patriots. Reilly felt responsible for keeping them alive.

13. Preparing for July

Ilya told Reilly that his attacker had two gold teeth. For Reilly that left only Malibaev, who was critical to his plan to distribute broadsheets when the Bolsheviks made their move. He asked Sergei not to take action until after the attack.

"But why were you looking for him?" Sergei said.

"He beat a boy to within an inch of his life just before the revolution and then stuck him in the prison at Peter and Paul Fortress. The boy's got a scar about four inches long running down his cheek and a bad limp. I promised him justice."

"What are you going to do?" said Sergei. "Malibaev is in charge of a hundred men at Tauride. The demonstration is likely to come off in one or two days. We can't afford to lose him. Arrest him and the whole plan will go up in smoke."

"I know," said Reilly. "Call the Minister for Justice."

Sergei picked up the phone receiver. "Sergei Mikhailovich here, Minister. What is our policy on crimes committed by the secret police before the revolution?"

A groan came from the other end. "What is this?"

"One of the Okhrana officers in Vyborg beat a boy and threw him into the fortress just before the revolution. One of our friends wants justice. But nothing can be done until after the present situation with the Bolsheviks dies down."

"Who is the officer?"

"Malibaev."

"I see," said Justice Minister Pereversev. "Our friend?"

"Sidney Reilly."

"Send Reilly to my office in the morning," said Pereversev.

"I'll draw up the charges and save them."

"All right." Sergei hung up. "He'll see you."

"The demonstration is about to come off. Are you prepared to release the documents?"

"I don't know," said Sergei. "The Soviet is raising a stink. I'm getting threats. I don't know if Pereversev will go for it."

"I see," Reilly said.

"It's not my fault."

Reilly glanced at Sergei Mikhailovich and walked off.

Reilly found a message from Volodia at the safe flat the following morning, reporting that Lenin was still in hiding, and that this day's events would be a mere test of the government's ability and willingness to defend itself. The real push would come the following day. Probably.

Then he went to see Sergei Mikhailovich, who reported that the moderate press wouldn't touch the Lenin story.

"Suvorin may be our only ally," Reilly said.

"Maybe," Sergei said.

"What did Pereversev offer?"

Sergei Mikhailovich sighed. "He wants those documents held as trial evidence and is offering the publishers only the story about the other case, the Russian spy who told Sergei that Lenin is a German agent."

"Yermolenko?" Reilly said. "No wonder the papers won't touch it. Give them what Laurent gave you."

"I do what the Minister tells me to do," Sergei said.

Reilly held his temper. "Where's the Stalin letter?"

"I don't have it."

"Where is it?" said Reilly.

"I gave it to Laurent," said Sergei. "Payment for the second set of documents he gave me."

"Payment?"

"Don't sound so surprised, Reilly. I paid hard cash for the first fourteen letters. There was no need to pay him twice."

Reilly, loosening his tie, said with restraint, "Laurent won't know what to do with the document. If he shows it to the Bolsheviks it could get him killed. Give me the money, Sergei."

Sergei Mikhailovich drew back, his eyes wide open at the sight of the restrained anger on Reilly's face.

"Give it to you?"

"Yes! Unless you've got Laurent hidden somewhere in your office, of course, give it to me and I'll give it to him. I've got to get that letter away from him. How much?"

Sergei mumbled something inaudible.

"How much?" Reilly said and took Sergei by the collar.

"Five for the first and the letter as five for the second."

Reilly let go. "Give me the second five."

Sergei looked at Reilly with fear and uncertainty. "Why?"

"Turn it over."

"Who is Laurent to you?"

"He's just a little man with a little dream who deserves more than the bullet in the head that that letter's going to buy him. Now give it to me." Reilly held out his hand.

Sergei took out the money and dropped it on the desk.

Reilly counted it and shook it in front of Sergei's face. "I wouldn't mind you trying to steal from me, old man, but stealing from a little fellow like that, well, things like that help the Bolsheviks make their case against the capitalists."

Reilly put the envelope into his pocket. "Another thing," he said as he walked to the door, "those newspaper publishers will get the real story. It's up to them what to do with it. But I guarantee that by tomorrow night, if Lenin makes his move, everyone in this town will know he's a German grunt. I don't care what Pereversev says."

On the way to New Times, Reilly saw that most of the cars near the Central Post and the Telegraph station had weapons attached to their roofs. Nearby, armed soldiers had pinned red ribbons to their shoulders.

The facilities of New Times occupied the first floor of a warehouse and the offices filled the second. Reilly went in through the back door, worked his way around tons of idle machinery, found the stairs and sprinted up. Boris Suvorin studied a map similar to the one Reilly had shown to Yusepov. His desk was cluttered with papers and his wastebasket overflowed with shreds. He wore a white tunic, unbuttoned at the top. He had a newsman's peak of a hat and a pencil behind his ear. Four portraits hung on the wall behind him, his father, his brothers and himself. All newspaper men.

"Let's see the documents. How many have we got?"

"Twenty nine," said Reilly.

"What's Sergei Mikhailovich going to do?"

"The government doesn't have a plan," Reilly said. "They've known for at least a day that the Bolsheviks would make a move. They haven't cabled Savinkov for troops. Eyes closed, just hoping the Bolsheviks won't go through with it."

"Is Pereversev going to call the other papers?"

"The real story is right here. But the justice ministry wants to hold it back to use as evidence in court. Imagine, they think they'll get Lenin to stand trial."

"They'll need the evidence to get arrest warrants."

"A story somebody made up," said Reilly. "Sergei said the Russians arrested a man called Yermolenko, who went for bail with a story that Lenin's working for Germany."

"Any proof?" said Suvorin.

"No," said Reilly. "Just talk. And that's their whole case against Lenin, the one they'll peddle to the press. Nothing else."

Suvorin said, "If they expect other papers to run a story based on Yermolenko, they're more stupid than I thought."

"I know," Reilly said. "You'll have to call every newspaper publisher in the city. If we find just one we can force Pereversev to confirm the information with our documents."

"Then I have a big job to do," Suvorin said. "I can do the broadsheets and the paper, call the newspaper publishers and finish printing by noon tomorrow."

"I want the broadsheets first thing," said Reilly. "Before the Bolsheviks send over one of their factory goon squads. Can you work through the night?"

"We always do," said Suvorin.

"A man called Yusepov runs the ex-Okhrana men."

"I know him," Suvorin said.

"He'll be here before ten. So will I."

Reilly went to the street, where several black cars sped off toward the southern part of the city. Workers from a local factory walked by. "Are you fellows out for the day?" Reilly said. "Were going home. The Bolsheviks want workers to demonstrate against Kerensky. We want to get out of the way."

Reilly thought the same would be true at the other factories in the city and at the local barracks, and imagined that the Soviets would send men to try to keep them calm.

Cars with mounted machine guns idled in front of the State Bank. Soldiers with red ribbons stood around with rifles. Reilly wondered what Volodia might have to say. He walked to the Nevsky and got a tram.

Trotsky was headed to Tauride Palace to harass the socialists in the Soviet, to wear them down, he said, announce the transfer of power and arrest some of the ministers.

"Is that Lenin's plan?" said Volodia.

"No," Trotsky laughed. "It's my plan. I know it's crazy, stupid and probably a waste of time. But the politicians are such dimwits that it might just work. Anyway, Orlov, this is Russia and you never know what can happen." He walked out as though in step with his own private jazz.

Late in the afternoon Derzhinsky called Volodia.

"What do you think, Your Honour?"

"I think it's almost out of control," Volodia said. "We've had men from the Machine Gun Regiment come by to insist we vote on the demonstration. I did a hand count. It's going to be close. Stalin may be the key vote."

"Don't worry about Stalin," said Derzhinsky. "If we are successful, Lenin will appoint me president of the intelligence service. I would like you to accept a responsible position, reporting to me. What do you say?"

Volodia's heart skipped. "Good," he said.

The tram took forever to get across the Trinity Bridge, which was filling with all kinds of people— soldiers rushing around, businessmen and merchants heading home from their offices and workers in transit between their factories and their apartments. On both sides of the bridge soldiers stood guard, some directing traffic and others shouting at passers-by, cars on both sides with machine guns on top.

Reilly's tram stopped when the crowds were too thick for it to move further. The driver jumped out and walked away. Passengers grumbled, cursed and climbed off. Reilly slid through the rear door and stepped down. He glanced at Bolshevik headquarters and walked in the opposite direction, toward the Vyborg District and then to Sampsonievsky Prospect to the flat where he hoped to see Volodia. But the curtain blocked the front window: no messages.

The presence of entire regiments forced Reilly as far as Finland Station, where he approached a few soldiers. "Say, fellows," he said and took out a cigarette. "Got a light?"

A soldier lit the cigarette.

Reilly said, "Looks like today may be important."

One said, "Everyone's going over for a demonstration."

Reilly's watch said seven-thirty. "At night?" he said.

"Right now," replied the soldier.

"We're going to demonstrate tomorrow," Reilly said.

The soldier shrugged. "It was supposed to be tomorrow. But we were called out about an hour ago. We'll meet at Litany Bridge and then march to the government."

One of the soldiers crushed his cigarette on the ground. Another did the same. "Let's go," another said.

"Good luck, fellows," said Reilly.

They went off toward the bridge.

"Tonight?" Reilly thought. "Tonight we're not ready. The Okhrana men are probably drunk. Broadsheets won't be ready until the morning. Tonight? We have no defence tonight. If the Bolos move tonight, nothing will stop them."

Reilly followed the soldiers and quickly found himself in the midst of hundreds more, then thousands. Coming from every direction, they filled the street and buried Reilly in their midst. Behind and in front of him, as far as he could see, were uniforms and red flags. He thought of the cars with mounted machine guns at the State Bank, the Central Telegraph Station and the post office, both sides of the Trinity Bridge and every strategic location and bridge over the Neva.

Reilly thought, "It's been building since noon. Do they control the city? Have the Bolsheviks already seized power?"

He had to move with the crowds. In front and on both sides the men were young. Behind him someone started to sing the Internationale loudly, above the noise of the crowd:

"Arise, ye starvelings from your slumbers..."

It was not the voice of a young soldier, but of someone older, more directed. The Bolshevik Military Organization. Some of the younger men joined in, then more sang:

"Comrades, come rally, and the last fight let us face..."

They sang loudly with empty faces, angry and vile.

Reilly's head began to swim. He felt nauseous. He moved slowly to his right toward the edge of the procession, looking around quickly for the next opening and the next until he broke through. He stopped behind a tree to catch his breath. There, the Litany Bridge crossed the river; as Reilly reached it an officer climbed on top a car and held up both arms. The crowd quieted, and Reilly moved closer to the officer, who took a bullhorn and shouted: "Comrades, tonight we'll tell the government what we think about their stinking war, that the only political organization with authority is the Soviet!"

The officer stopped to give the crowd of soldiers time to applaud. But most had not heard what he said, and the applause was light until someone shouted, "Where are the Bolsheviks? Why aren't they here?"

A murmur went through the crowd and anger rose: "If the

Bolsheviks aren't going to go, why should we?"

The officer tried vainly to calm the crowd, patting his palms on thin air and nodding his agreement and finally conceding, "We'll appoint a delegation to go see them."

Soldiers moved to the side, formed a delegation and marched up the street to Bolshevik headquarters. Then the officer sent larger delegations to Tauride and Mariinskii palaces. Reilly hurried to get behind the delegation.

Have they taken power, or not?

Bolshevik leaders filled the sitting room on the first floor of the palace that had once belonged to ballerina Ksheshinskaya. The ones of stature, Trotsky, Zinoviev, Kamenev and Derzhinsky occupied comfortable chairs and sofas. Lenin sat in a regal high back cushioned chair that had belonged to Louis the Fourteenth and later to Napoleon. Other Central Committee members sat on the floor.

"What do we do?" Lenin said. "Do we move ahead?"

Zinoviev questioned Lenin's confident belief that he could safely assign local regiments the task of arresting government ministers? Could any be trusted?"

Lenin said, "The Military Organization will arrest them. It won't take more than twenty, and the 176th Regiment will arrest the Soviet. We're ahead of you, Comrade."

"Then what?" said Zinoviev.

Then someone entered the room and said: "There's a hundred or so soldiers outside, delegates of the First Machine Gun Brigade. They want to hear from Comrade Lenin."

Lenin said, "Feliks, work the crowds. Calm them down. We start at noon and they should get a good night's sleep."

Derzhinsky walked toward the door, gesturing to Volodia to follow. In the marble foyer he said, "Outside with me. Quietly, tell them we'll march on Tauride at noon."

Reilly stood at the edge, the air humid, the temperature too warm to be in a crowd filled with troops in a bad mood.

"Where's Lenin? Tell Lenin to come out!"

Someone appeared on the second floor balcony and said, "Comrade Lenin sends greetings. He's been ill and has a weak voice. But tomorrow his voice will be stronger."

"Tomorrow?" buzzed through the delegation.

"We're here tonight!" they shouted.

"*Tomorrow*," the man repeated. "Comrade Lenin thanks you for your support, and says his plans are complete and he will tell you more about that tomorrow."

Nearby Reilly heard someone say, "Tomorrow at noon we'll meet at Tauride Palace." Reilly looked to his right and saw Derzhinsky. Another voice spoke to him from the left.

"Tomorrow," Volodia said quietly. "Be prepared for the demonstration at Tauride. More than five thousand sailors from Kronstadt. We expect fifty thousand. And Lenin."

In moments the troops started talking aloud among themselves. "So it's tomorrow. Go back to the barracks."

Derzhinsky went up to Volodia as the crowd broke up.

"Good work, Your Honour. Go rest for tomorrow."

"Good night, comrade," Volodia said.

Volodia walked off and Reilly went to the Europa Hotel.

14. The July Days

Reilly looked into the mirror and thought, "If you think you're going to stop those people, the machine gun regiment, the workers from the Putilov, Nevka, Erickson, Siemans, Rozenkrantz and God knows how many other factories, the Kronstadt Naval Base, thousands of soldiers from local regiments, maybe ten thousand more from Peter and Paul, and the Bolsheviks themselves, if you think your little forgeries are going to throw a wrench into this massive wheel that already has as much momentum as the earth itself, then you are living in a strange world, Reilly. Volodia said fifty thousand, but it could be more. All you've got is tape and glue. No Army, one newspaper, some secret police bullies. Nothing else. Where are all the loyal Russians? Other than Anna, Sasha and Volodia. Patriots. Laurent is French and Lockhart British, but they'll risk their lives for Russia."

Reilly took several items from a dresser drawer and put them on top of the dresser under the mirror. He put a black strap over his bare chest, positioned the holster around just above his navel to the left and added a small pistol. He took it out quickly several times in front of the mirror, slid the holster an inch to the left, dropped the pistol into it again and left it there. He put on a clean grey tunic and black jodhpurs.

Inside, he pulled a pair of black boots half way up his calves, took a black belt from the closet and put it on over the tunic at his waist. The pistol bulged. He pulled the tunic out to keep his weapon unnoticed in the holster and left a button undone so his hand could slip inside.

He stood in front of the mirror for a time and studied his appearance. He guessed how far his hairline had receded since he left home for the first time, twenty-five years earlier, when he was not yet seventeen. He thought of his father, not usually a conscious presence in his mind, who had disowned him for having an affair with his cousin Elena. He mouthed the words his father had used:

You're not my son. I take back my name. Get out!

He wondered, "If I am successful, will he know? Or care?"

Reilly looked at his watch at seven forty five. He put a few things in his satchel, threw the satchel over his shoulder and went downstairs. A car turned onto Mikhailovsky Street. Inside, Sasha smiled. Reilly got in. The car drove to the end of the street and turned at the park near the Pushkin statue.

"Where do we start?" Sasha said.

"State Bank, then the Central Post and Telegraph Station."

The streets were almost deserted and the city eerily silent. At the State Bank, loyal government soldiers put up signs that said, "No Demonstrations Until Further Notice!" They had also posted signs at the Central Post and the Telegraph Station. Some had stayed to defend those locations.

Sergei and Reilly drove across the city and stopped at the Field of Mars, near the British Embassy. A guard stood in front of the Military Palace. Reilly got out and walked over.

"What does it look like?" Reilly said.

The guard shook his head. "They wanted garrison troops to preserve order, Commander Reilly. Only a few came."

"How few?"

"We've got about a hundred from the Preobrazhenskii Guards, two thousand Cossacks, a company from Vladimir Academy and a few dozen war invalids, sir."

"That's it?"

"Yes, sir," the young soldier said.

"Thank you," Reilly said as he turned and headed back.

"Let's go to Suvorin's paper. They should be ready."

In a few minutes the car stopped at the loading dock in the rear of the New Times building. Six cars were backed up to the dock and men loaded boxes into the cars. Reilly and Sasha went inside, where the press was running. Near the stairs several men stood at a table, folded the newspapers, put them in large piles and bound each pile together with twine. Headlines said: "Lenin a Proven Traitor." The sub-headline said: "Proof! Lenin A Paid German Agent, Financial Relationship established between Bolsheviks and Berlin."

"Great job," Reilly said to the workers.

Upstairs, Boris Suvorin was on the telephone. "Good," Suvorin said. Then, "Good morning, gentlemen."

"What's the news?" Reilly said.

"The news is good. I've got a partner. 'Word of Life' will run the story. I left some of the documents with them last night. Before they go, they want Pereversev to call them and offer some guarantees. Police, militia or government troops to protect them in case the Bolsheviks attack. I couldn't get through to Pereversev. I'll try him again in a little while."

"Good," said Sasha.

"Are the broadsheets finished?" Reilly said.

"The Okhrana men are already loading them."

Reilly said, "Let's call Pereversev and get the paper out."

Cars screeched to a stop outside.

"Is the front secure? " Reilly said.

"For a few minutes, unless they have axes. Bolsheviks?"

"Anarchists, I think," Reilly said, hurrying toward the back of the office. He tried to open a window but it was stuck. He took a chair, smashed out the glass and shouted to the Okhranists standing near their cars, "Raid! Go! Get out!"

They jumped into cars filled with broadsheets and sped off. Armed men rushed inside. Suvorin ran to a large window, opened it and jumped to a ledge and then headed across a rooftop. Sasha followed and said, "Hurry, Sidney!"

The attackers started up the stairs. Reilly drew his pistol and fired several shots into the stairwell. The attackers stopped momentarily, raised their weapons to the level of the floor and fired back as Reilly sped to the window, twisted around and fired another shot. He jumped onto the adjoining roof and ran the length to Sasha.

"What do they want?" Sasha said.

"A printing press," Suvorin said.

"They'll want more than that when they see the headline."

Suvorin nodded. "Where are my tradesmen?"

"Got out the back way," Reilly said. "And the Okhranists took the broadsheets and newspapers. We're still in business. Let's find out what Pereversev has decided."

They climbed down to the small lane behind the building and jumped into Sasha's car. Several cars were stopped in front of the State Bank, where armed soldiers with red ribbons stood looking suspiciously. A sign across the bank door said, "Closed." The posters banning demonstrations lay in shreds on the ground. A machine gun barrel hung over the edge of the roof. The Central Post, the Telegraph Station and the Trinity and Stock Exchange Bridges gave the same impression, as did every strategic location that they saw.

The car sped past the Winter Palace and along the Neva to the area where Fontanka Canal ended and the Gulf of Finland began. A fleet of warships sailed the Gulf toward Vasilievsky Island, probably carrying sailors from Kronstadt.

Sasha drove to Intelligence headquarters. Reilly would go to Mariinskii to see Pereversev at the Justice Ministry.

Sergei watched the scene through binoculars.

"What do you see?" said Reilly.

Sergei said, "Thousands of armed sailors marching across the island toward the Stock Exchange Bridge." He gave the binoculars to Reilly. "Where to?"

"I think it's Tauride Palace," Reilly said. "If they wanted to take Mariinskii they'd cross over on Dvortsoviye Bridge." He gave the binoculars to Sergei. "Did you speak to Pereversev?"

"Yes" said Sergei. "He's calling newspapers now."

"I've got one," said Reilly. "Word of Life. They've seen the papers, are going ahead and want protection."

"You showed them the documents?" said Sergei.

"Pereversev has to listen," Reilly said.

"If you paint him into a corner, he'll get more stubborn."

"I'll talk to him. Have you spoken to Yusepov?"

"His men are waiting near Tauride."

An explosion from outside shattered windows. "Bolshevik Militia," Reilly said. "Let's go."

They sped up the stairwell and jumped out onto the roof. They walked across to the adjacent building, found the stairs and went down to the street.

"What do you think, Reilly?" Sergei said.

"I'd get Pereversev out before the Reds get him."

They walked past the Admiralty to Saint Isaacs Square and came out near the cathedral and the Astoria Hotel. Troops concentrated at the far end of the square, near government headquarters at Mariinskii Palace. At the entrance to the palace, armed troops approached them.

"What's your business?" said one.

"I'm Rosenblum," Reilly said. "I work for the Soviet."

"All right," said the soldier. "Let them pass."

At the Justice Ministry, the Ministers hid under the implied protection of Pereversev.

"We're here to take you out, Minister," said Sergei.

"Oh, no, rescuers?" he replied. "Lord, no! I'm Minister for Justice. They won't arrest me because if their putsch fails, they know I'll get even. If I run they'll arrest the whole government."

"Minister," Reilly said, "have you called the papers?"

"Yes," he replied. "But so have Soviet deputies who don't want the story to go out. So the papers won't do it."

"I know one that will," said Reilly.

"Which one?"

"Word of Life."

"How do you know?"

"Suvorin talked with the publisher," Reilly said. "He'll do it."

Pereversev said, "They can only use the document that Yermolenko gave us. The documents from French Intelligence are legal evidence against Lenin."

Reilly glared at Pereversev. "I don't care what you use. Just tell the newspaper they can expect protection."

Pereversev made the call.

"We'll give out broadsheets at Tauride," Reilly said.

Pereversev glared at him. "Who authorized that?"

"It's all you've got. What are you going to do?"

"I'll stay here and wait for my telephone to ring."

"We're going to Tauride to get those broadsheets out."

"On foot?"

"Yes."

Pereversev gave Sergei a key. "Take The Ford."

"Thank you," Reilly said.

"Thank you," the ministers said, standing quietly by.

Reilly and Sergei got the car and drove to Tauride Palace.

At the same time, Peters took Derzhinsky and Volodia to Tauride. Ibrahim said he would bring a few young recruits.

They went through the rear door and walked to Derzhinsky's Rolls Royce, parked behind the palace. Peters waited. Derzhinsky and Volodia got into the rear:

"Take the Trinity Bridge," Derzhinsky said.

"Peters turned over the engine and then took the car along

the driveway to the street. In a moment he turned onto the bridge, drove out and then stopped.

"Do you see that, Feliks?" He pointed over to the Litany Bridge, filled with soldiers from the Vyborg District. "There must be ten thousand. All going to Tauride."

"They'll fill the embankment before we can get there," Volodia said. We should go down Sadovaya and past the Military palace. The back streets will be easier."

Peters drove over the bridge, passed the British Embassy and came out on Sadovaya Street. Ahead, the road was clear. But closer to Tauride Palace more people were in the streets. Soldiers, sailors and workers' detachments. They reached Litany Prospect, made another turn and approached Nevsky. Peters slowed to a stop. An armoured car turned onto Litany from Nevsky, and then another and another driving slowly. Behind them thousands of sailors and armoured cars tried to turn onto the Litany Prospect.

"Stop here," Derzhinsky said.

Volodia looked up at an open window near the corner and thought he saw someone with a rifle. Then he spied another.

"No!" said Volodia. "Drive, Peters! Drive!"

Derzhinsky looked at Volodia. "What is it?"

"It's an attack!"

Peters jerked the car forward, sped around the corner in front of an armoured car and drove down Nevsky Prospect.

"Good," Derzhinsky said. "We don't want to wait."

"The hell," Volodia said, "We don't want to be shot."

Sergei and Reilly drove along the Fontanka Embankment to Nevsky, where they got out ahead of a big armed procession on its way to Tauride Palace. Ahead, at the far end of Litany Prospect, the troops from Vyborg filled the street, on their way to Tauride along the embankment road, while behind them followed a huge contingent.

"We're short petrol," said Sergei, his hand thumping down on the steering wheel. They stepped out into an eerily quiet street. Ahead, men scurried around a corner. Across the street windows opened and rifle barrels protruded through.

"Look, Reilly," Sergei said, pointing to an open window.

"I see him."

Reilly drew his pistol.

"There's another," said Sergei.

A car sped by, slowed to a stop at the Nevsky and then roared out onto the road in front of an armoured car, which turned onto Litany Prospect, followed by several others and the first sailors. Something moved on a rooftop. In a third floor window someone held a photo camera ready. The armoured cars drove slowly with a massive crowd of sailors behind them. From a rooftop someone shouted, "Steady!"

The sound echoed. Reilly and Sergei looked all around.

"There!" said Sergei. "It's Malibaev!"

Reilly spun around and saw the face of the former Okhrana officer who held binoculars and a rifle.

"Steady!" Malibaev repeated.

"Malibaev!" Reilly shouted. "No!"

Sailors approached. Sergei pulled Reilly. "Let's go."

"Malibaev!" Reilly repeated. "No!"

"Get ready!" Malibaev screamed.

A dozen more windows opened wide and rifles appeared. Men stood on the rooftops. The armoured car passed by.

Reilly and Sergei sprinted around the corner and dove into the archway of a building as dozens of rifle blasts suddenly echoed in the wide Litany Prospect. The first armoured car stopped and the driver got out. A bloody haze filled the air around his head as it exploded with a rifle shot. Suddenly the huge contingent broke apart. Sailors scattered in every direction, firing wildly as they fled. The armoured cars drove further down the street and stopped. Gunshots continued to rain down on the sailors until, abruptly, it stopped.

Reilly walked back to the street. Several dozen men were down. Their comrades came back, slowly at first. But soon they ran to the wounded men, picked some up from the ground and stood them on their feet. Dozens were bloodied. Some did not get up at all. The angry sailors cursed, "Bourgeois bastards! You're finished!" The sailors came to formation. "March!" someone cried.

Reilly watched as they stomped ahead in fury, aching to use their rifles.

"Come on, Reilly," Sergei said. "Let's get to Tauride."

The sailors joined the soldiers at the Neva end of the street for the final leg of their march to Tauride. Rising above the sounds that came from this band of sailors and the units of machine-gunners at the far end of the street was the clamour of another crowd, much larger, already assembled at Tauride.

At Tauride Palace, Peters held a red flag high to open a path through the crowd and led Derzhinsky and Volodia inside. Trotsky said to Derzhinsky, "Lenin will speak soon. The central Committee are in the Catherine Hall."

Volodia, Derzhinsky and Peters went to a room where dozens of Party members stood. Lenin sat with his secretary reviewing troop strength. A man said, "We've just got eight thousand from Peter and Paul Fortress."

"What does that make?" Lenin said.

"More than fifty thousand."

"How many could the government send?" Lenin said.

"Maybe thirty under favourable circumstances," the man said, "and another fifty thousand from the front. But it would take time and preparation."

"Are *we* prepared?" Lenin said.

Peters said to Derzhinsky, "Lenin's wavering. Do you see?"

"Yes," Derzhinsky said.

Trotsky walked over to Lenin. "The announcement?"

"Soon," Lenin replied. "I think we'll do it very soon."

"Why not now?" said Trotsky.

"Let's be certain the government isn't up to anything."

Trotsky glared and left the room.

Ilya and Comrade Antonida came through the archway of the building on Suvorovsky as Ibrahim tossed a cigarette to the ground. Antonida fastened the top button of her tunic.

"I was starting to think you went without me," Ibrahim said.

"Hello, Ibrahim," Ilya said.

"Good to see you, pal," said Ibrahim. "Been a long time. You ready? I think we're going to see history today."

Crowds heading toward Tauride filled Suvorovsky Boulevard. Workers, clusters of soldiers and sailors and the curious. Ibrahim led Ilya and Antonida along the boulevard and then through some back streets as the clamour at the palace grew louder. They cut through the grounds of the cathedral, which had deteriorated since Ilya had last taken the same shortcut on his way to school. They came out on the garden behind the palace, an area the size of four square city blocks. Crowds of soldiers, sailors and factory workers filled the area and chanted, "Take power, Soviets!"

They squeezed along the edge of the crowd and got to the back of the palace, where the shouts were louder and angrier. Ibrahim gave Ilya and Comrade Antonida the history of the day. He pointed at some of the men in the crowd: "You got soldiers here, troops from local barracks and machine gun units all over, factory workers. It's all about Socialism."

"Why are they making so much noise?" Ilya said, though he suspected it wasn't about Socialism.

Ibrahim said, "The Soviet deputies inside the palace are all deaf. They're all afraid of us Bolsheviks."

Ilya thought, "It's not about Bolshevism."

"How many do you think are here?" Ilya shouted.

"Ten thousand," Comrade Antonida said. "Millions."

Ibrahim counted out the statistics on his fingers. "We got about twenty thousand sailors from Kronstadt, another forty thousand workers from the factories, we got..."

The soldiers shook their fists. "Soviets! Take power!"

Ilya thought, "It *is* about power.

Then from close to the building another chant started to spread, "Hang Pereversev! Hang Pereversev!" filled the air but was muffled when someone appeared in the doorway and spoke.

The crowd screamed, "What's wrong with you Soviets? We offer you power and you refuse it!"

The man seemed to be making a speech but the sound did not reach far. Suddenly a group of soldiers descended on him, pulled him from the doorway and beat him until others came over and stopped them. Ibrahim led Ilya and Comrade Antonida along the edge of the crowd to the palace.

"What did he say?" Ibrahim asked a soldier.

"A government man made a speech about farming. I think. Then someone resigned and went home. All we wanna know is when the Soviet's gonna take power. So Trotsky took him and put him in a car out front so he can think it over."

From the side of the building an anxious buzz swept through the crowd. Troops looked over, trying to see what was passing through the crowd. Broadsheets.

"That's Lenin's announcement," Comrade Antonida said.

Ilya and Ibrahim tried to look through the crowd to see what it was. Then Ilya stepped back, turned and saw a familiar face not fifty feet away. A man opened a box of leaflets and gave stacks to other men who took them to the crowd and passed them out. Ilya stood still, a feeling of rage boiling to the surface. Malibaev and his men had arrived.

Malibaev, the Monster. Ilya stood and then walked forward.

"Where are you going?" Comrade Antonida said.

"Lenin is a traitor!" Malibaev shouted.

"Lenin is a traitor!" rumbled through the crowd.

"Hey, Pal, where you going?" Ibrahim said.

"The man who beat me," he said, walking away entranced.

Ibrahim and Antonida raced after him.

"Ilya!" Antonida repeated, "Ilyushka! "Stop!"

Gunshots reverberated and then faded away. Reilly and Malibaev opened boxes, took out bundles and gave them to subordinates who quickly passed them out. Two men came close to Reilly. One nodded.

"In the black tunic," said Reilly.

"We'll wait for your signal, Reilly."

The men moved into position well behind Malibaev.
Malibaev shouted: "Lenin is a traitor! Read about it here!"
Malibaev's men repeated: "Lenin is a German spy!"
A buzz swelled in the crowd: "Lenin's a traitor!"

Trotsky looked at his watch and said to Lenin, "It's time."

Lenin said, "Call our men at Mariinskii Palace and ask them if they are ready to arrest the government ministers."

Someone got on the phone, said a few words and then said, "They're all in Pereversev's office. Just give the word."

"Keep them on the line," said Lenin. "Are the guards ready to arrest the Soviet deputies?"

"We're ready for the order," said the captain of the regiment assigned to protect the Soviet deputies.

Lenin looked at Derzhinsky. "Now?" he said.

"Now," Derzhinsky said.

Then someone marched up to Lenin and showed him a newspaper. Lenin looked at the headlines and said to Trotsky, "See? Trouble. I told you so."

"Should I order the arrest of the government?" the man on the telephone said.

"Should I order the arrest of the Soviet deputies?" the captain of the guard said.

Lenin put the newspaper in Trotsky's face. The headline said: 'Lenin Unmasked as German Agent and Traitor!'

"What?!" Trotsky screamed. "Lies! Slander! Forgeries!"

Lenin turned to his secretary. "Well, *could* be forgeries."

"A scandal!" said Trotsky. "A government provocation!"

"There could be arrests," said Derzhinsky.

"Arrests!" said Trotsky. "If there's arrests, arrest me first!"

"Well they're not going to arrest me," Lenin said.

"I'll get the car," his secretary said.

"Let's go together," Lenin replied.

Derzhinsky took Peters away. Volodia followed.

Outside people said, "Lenin's a traitor! Troops are coming to save the government! They'll be here any minute!"

"The Bolsheviks deserve whatever happens to them!"

The troops at Tauride, Bolshevik supporters, looked frightened. Sailors dropped their weapons and ran away.

"But we haven't transferred power to the Soviet!"

"They've sent troops from the front." "Kornilov is coming!"

"The officers hate the Bolsheviks! We're as good as dead!"

The policemen standing behind Reilly looked surprised. Reilly looked around to see Ilya approached Malibaev, uttering threats and obscenities. Then Ilya hit Malibaev on the head.

Malibaev turned around, looked at Ilya, slapped him hard and knocked him to the ground. "Stupid Bolshevik," he said.

Reilly sprinted toward Ilya.

Antonida put her hands to her cheeks: "Ilyushka!"

Ibrahim drew his pistol.

Malibaev kicked Ilya in the head, hopped and drew his leg back, prepared to kick again. Ilya writhed in pain and shock on the ground.

The crowd chanted, "Lenin is a traitor!"

As Reilly approached Malibaev, Ibrahim raised his pistol and fired. Malibaev fell back and crashed on the ground, a bullet having blown away part of his skull. Reilly rushed to Ilya, but just as quickly Ibrahim stepped in with his pistol.

"Get away, pal. The boy don't belong to you."

Reilly stood straight for a moment. Ibrahim kept the pistol aimed. Ilya jumped to his feet, holding his head.

"Put down the gun," said Reilly.

"Get away, pal," Ibrahim said. "I'll blow your head off."

"No," said Ilya. His hand gently lowered Ibrahim's pistol.

Reilly glared at Ibrahim. "Ilya, come with me," he said.

Ibrahim glared back. "I'll kill you first."

"No!" shouted Ilya. He snatched the pistol from Ibrahim's hand, aimed the pistol at Malibaev's body and fired.

The two policemen came up behind Reilly with pistols

drawn. "Put down the weapon, son," one said.

The crimson scar on Ilya's cheek twisted with anger as he glared at Reilly. "Malibaev's your man. I'm not with you."

"Drop the weapon, boy," the policeman said.

Ilya put the pistol on the ground and said, "I'm going with Comrade Ibrahim." He turned his back and limped away slowly. Ibrahim followed. Antonida took Ilya's arm.

An official came up to the two men behind Reilly. "They've issued arrest orders for Lenin and Derzhinsky."

Reilly watched Ilya limp away from the palace.

"Lenin is a traitor!" the crowd chanted.

As Reilly digested what had just transpired he noticed three men coming from the side exit of the palace: Volodia, Derzhinsky and Peters. They approached quickly until a policeman identified Derzhinsky and yelled: "Arrest him!"

Peters shouted to Derzhinsky and then rushed to the left to disappear into the crowd. Derzhinsky ran to the right and vanished among the troops. There stood Volodia and the policemen, who said, "Arrest him!"

The police slapped the handcuffs on Volodia's wrists.

"Let's go," said a policeman.

Reilly looked at Volodia who subtly shook his head.

"Where are you taking him?" said Reilly.

"Municipal jail," said the policeman, who twisted Volodia around and then marched him to the front of the palace.

From the front of the building came the music of a military band playing a Sousa march, and loud cheering:

"The troops are here! Hurrah! The government is saved!"

"It's Kornilov! The Bolsheviks are doomed!"

Yusepov walked up to Reilly and saw Malibaev's body.

"Couple of Bolsheviks killed him," Reilly said. "One disappeared. The police arrested another one."

Yusepov looked at the body and took off his hat. "I knew one day he'd get himself shot. He loved his country. But he thought that made him better than anyone else. He had more pride in his patriotism than in his country. I always thought that would get him in trouble. Too bad."

"Pity," Reilly said.

They walked toward the front as the crowd thinned out. "I can't believe it," Yusepov said. "It worked as you said."

In front of the Tauride Palace, the veterans military band played another Sousa march.

"Where are the troops?" Yusepov said.

"Right there," Reilly said, pointing to the marching band.

"That's it?" said Yusepov. He laughed quietly. "A perfect finish for a lunatic scheme. This could only work once, Reilly, and only in Russia."

Reilly dug into his pocket and got a cigarette. He lit it, inhaled deeply and blew the smoke slowly into the air. With the cigarette between his teeth, he dropped his hands into his pockets and walked along slowly.

"Did you hear, comrade?" a soldier said. "Lenin's a traitor."

"Yeah," Reilly said. "I heard."

"Who would have believed it?" said the soldier.

"These days, nothing's sacred." He went toward Litany Prospect and the hotel as the brigades marched to their barracks and Bolsheviks scattered to avoid arrest.

The cost of stopping Lenin struck him. The trade-off, if it stuck, was spurious: a temporary defeat of the Bolsheviks at the cost of losing Ilya. He probably would have succeeded in his political quest even if he had tended to it less and involved himself more in Ilya's leap into manhood. He might have balanced his priorities had his sponsors and their money not weighed on his thinking so heavily.

Reilly had not shut down this moment of self-examination when he reached the Litany Bridge and Savinkov approached.

"Your cousin Elena came to me," Savinkov said. "She joined Lenin. She asked me to give you this letter."

"Elena?" Reilly said in a rush of emotion. He read.

"Elena's explanation?" Savinkov asked.

"No," Reilly answered. "Word of my father's death."

"I never saw you react like that," Savinkov said.

"I haven't seen her in years. She was my first lover."

Then Savinkov noticed another first: a tear in Reilly's eye.

"My sympathies for your father, Sidney."

"Quiet, damn you!" Reilly said and walked off abruptly.

And all the while Volodia waited inside the municipal jail.

Part III: Logic, Passion and Madness

July – August, 1917

15. An Honourable Scheme

The jailer at the Petrograd Municipal Police Facility gave no explanation for releasing Volodia later that day. Nor did Volodia ask questions. He simply walked to the door and rushed out into quiet, empty streets.

He might have exalted in his sudden freedom. But it was likely that the authorities were shooting Bolsheviks, and Volodia had made no small effort to convince everyone that he really was a Leninist. Bolsheviks were shooting spies and informers too. A nervous sense of license hung in the air, as though inevitably, some crackpot would fire blindly and kill a poor wanderer on city streets.

Why was he free? Had Reilly somehow intervened to secure his release? Perhaps Derzhinsky had paid a bribe. Maybe Peters had done something. But what if?

What if someone were watching, following, checking up on him, writing a report on where he went? Perhaps someone did not trust him- the Bolsheviks trusted no one- and wanted to use the chaos or the escape to discredit him. Perhaps the jailer was a Bolshevik agent, reporting back to...whom? Perhaps Ibrahim, the weasel. Perhaps anyone.

At that moment Volodia *was* a wanderer. Where could he go? Ksheshenskaya's palace, for the latest few months Lenin's headquarters, was no doubt occupied by the police. His own flat had to be off limits. The safe flat he shared with Reilly? Perhaps, but in truth it was safe only because he was usually not there. More than one night spent in that flat would seem strange to anyone who noticed, some potential informer. Where could Volodia go, so lost and anxious?

To the British Embassy.

At the same time Savinkov brought news to Reilly's flat.

"I'm the new Deputy Minister for War."

"Says who?" Reilly said.

"Kerensky. He's the new Prime Minister."

"Oh, Lord," Reilly said, his voice dropping in quick descent. "Oh, well. Come to the embassy. Lockhart has money for General Kornilov."

"He has something for me too," Savinkov said. "A British officer's uniform. The Provisional Government had none."

The money was enough to fill a small suitcase, half a million sterling. The uniform came with greater difficulty. It was too large, so Lockhart measured Savinkov, chalk-marked the jacket and trousers and promised to have them altered.

"You mean 'tailored,'" Savinkov said. "Hand-stitched to the eighth of an inch. Shoulders roped, with epaulets, sleeves with working buttonholes. When can I pick it up?"

"Your bloody choice, damn it," Lockhart said. "We can send it over to the French Embassy, where they have a Russian tailor. Or I can cable the Foreign Office and have them send the man from Chesterton. But if you want them favourably disposed to assisting Kerensky, I suggest you just let the Russian tailor do the work."

Captain Cromie brought a new man, fresh from London, delivered from the Kazan Station by the embassy driver.

"Somerville," the new man said.

"I'm Savinkov, Minister for War."

"You don't say," Somerville said.

"Deputy Mins, anyway," Reilly said. "In from the north?"

"No, Vladivostok. Four days of Czechs and anarchists taking pot-shots every few hours. For sport, you know?"

"A moving target always attracts its own peculiar fate," Reilly said. "C send you?" Silence.

Cromie took Somerville's arm and hustled him upstairs.

The others went to the rear of the building to a smaller meeting room. Lockhart poured vodka and disappeared.

"A bit thin, no?" Volodia said. "No army, no Kornilov, just a newspaper and some broadsheets. Best you could do?"

"Fickle crowd," Reilly said. "Don't know who's who."

"Bloody good luck, if you ask me, Sidney. That's twice."

"I hear Lenin went into hiding," Reilly said.

"Lenin is cautious. But he can be pushed. Even worse, he could have been pulled. If the machine gun units had gone off on their own, Lenin would have followed. Your flyers would have been confetti for a city full of people waving red flags."

"What do you advise?" Reilly said.

"Derzhinsky will find a way to co-opt the hangers-on near Kerensky and Kornilov. The ones looking for work."

"Derzhinsky and Lenin are in hiding," Savinkov said, "we can persuade Kornilov to cooperate with Kerensky."

"Seriously," Volodia said, "Kornilov? Have you forgotten our little tussle in May? He let his temper call a retreat back to the front, where he could fight the German army while Lenin tested the Provisional Government's defences. And he stayed there the whole time. Almost didn't have a government to come back to and defend. So much for Kornilov. Your strategy frightens me."

"We can do it," Savinkov said.

"How?" Volodia said.

"Patriotism," Reilly said. "The Allied Powers are going to back Kornilov and Kerensky, once we get them to sit at the same table. Boris is meeting with Kerensky first thing in the morning. Then we're taking a suitcase of cash to General Headquarters with a promise to send troops and supplies."

"Cash sounds like bribery," Volodia said. "But bribery probably trumps patriotism."

"Britain is investing in Russian patriots," Savinkov said.

"That sounds more like gambling."

"No," Reilly said. "Investing. Kornilov will inspire his men with the Russian flag. I proved it could be done, with newspaper headlines calling Lenin a German agent. That was patriotism you saw at Tauride Palace, even in the regiments' retreat back to their barracks. Russian patriotism."

"And where was General Kornilov?" Volodia said.

"That's my point," Reilly insisted. "The citizens put Kornilov to shame. We're going to show him the only way he can get his name back is to come back himself."

"I can read your mind, Sidney," Volodia said. "Will the patriots who were absent today come the next time the balloon goes up? Today you're the only one left. Will you be the only one next time? Is that why I'm sleeping in Lenin's basement?"

Reilly and Savinkov went silent.

"Do keep me informed," Volodia said. "But now go find me a pistol or two and some bullets. The police have mine. I feel naked walking around unarmed. They're shooting people out there. Or haven't you heard?"

Tall crimson curtains were drawn to the sides of a window that stretched almost from floor to ceiling. Through the window to the north, across the River Neva, the cathedral spire of the Peter and Paul Fortress glistened in the sunlight. Just south of the fortress the Stock Exchange Bridge carried a few carriages and pedestrians to and from Vasilievsky Island. Across the Neva students walked among university buildings. Kerensky saw no sign of revolution: he himself was the new occupant of the Winter Palace, home of Russian monarchs.

"We're going to save Russia," he said, "as I promised."

"Yes," Savinkov said, "everything is possible. But we have a million obstacles. The Bolsheviks have just started. The war in Europe isn't over. The Soviet won't be easy to deal with. And we've got to get the military..."

"Yes, yes," Kerensky said. "A good start, that's what we need. Make it impossible for anything to interfere."

Outside a unit of troops marched in front of the Palace,

turned to Kerensky's window and saluted. Kerensky waved back. The troops turned, snapped their rifles to their sides and guarded the home of the new Prime Minister of Russia.

"The soldiers like you," Savinkov said. "Let's get the officers back on our side too."

"Back on our side?" Kerensky said. "What do you mean?"

"It's important to remember that military men often have difficulty with civilian leadership. General Kornilov, for example, could be a great help if we approach him right."

"I don't trust him."

"Never mind," Savinkov said. "He doesn't trust you either. But to the troops and the other officers Kornilov is a man among men, a war hero and patriot. So we need him."

"Kornilov will have to wait," Kerensky said. "I haven't even picked the ministers for my new government yet."

"Make Kornilov a priority. We have enemies, after all."

"I'm only one man. I can't do everything at once."

"Perhaps your new *Deputy* Minister for War could help."

"You?"

"Kornilov is back at General Headquarters," Savinkov said. "Let me speak to him on your behalf and tell him you want to make him your Commander-in-Chief."

"What?" said Kerensky.

"Get the military on your side with a single bold move."

Kerensky glanced into the clear blue sky above the cathedral spire across the River Neva. "Yes," he replied, in a visionary tone. "Go to Mogilev and get Kornilov's support."

Savinkov looked down and wrinkled his nose. "It might take some convincing, Alexander Fyodor'ich," he said quietly.

"Like what?" said Kerensky.

"An agreement of some kind," Savinkov said. "A commitment to restore army discipline. The Death Penalty."

"I don't know," Kerensky said, but then, "yes, restore army discipline. I like it. Go tomorrow."

Savinkov returned Kerensky's salute and departed in a state of euphoria. Kerensky had not argued that empowering

Kornilov would be to encourage the military's ambitions, but had agreed to Savinkov's idea, an alliance with Russia's great general. And Kerensky had ordered Savinkov *himself* to implement that agreement. Savinkov's first act as Deputy Minister was a *smashing* success. He *knew* he could manage Kerensky and this new, crucial relationship with Kornilov.

But inside the Winter Palace Kerensky's uncertainty surfaced. He stared absently through the window toward the Stock Exchange Bridge as a large unit of soldiers marched across to the city from Vasilievsky Island.

"What have I done?" he said quietly to himself. "Have I empowered the right wing and the military?"

Across the River Neva Embankment, troops guarding the Winter Palace sat barefoot on the stone ledge, smoking cigarettes and dangling their legs over the water.

"What've I done?" Kerensky thought. "How could I give Kornilov a chance to take power? Oh, Kerensky, you fool."

The sun sparkled on the tall silver spire across the river. In the distant sky a rain cloud hung over the Gulf of Finland. And from the ledge on the other side of the embankment a soldier threw an empty vodka bottle into the River Neva.

Oh, Kerensky! You fool!

16. Kornilov, the Believer

Savinkov's second act as Deputy Minister for War seemed successful too. At first reticent, General Kornilov smiled as he listened to Savinkov read Kerensky's Command Agreement, which contained a promise to restore the death penalty. Reilly gave the general a suitcase filled with money as proof that the British still believed in Russia. Then he sent a cable to the British Embassy requesting contact with Henry Ford to arrange an emergency delivery of seven hundred trucks via Vladivostok in the east. He did not mention that he had sealed that deal months earlier with Ford in New York.

As Kornilov spoke, his assistant, Zavoiko, gave Savinkov a cable. It had just reached the GHQ cipher room from Petrograd and bore the signature and code of Kerensky's assistant, Nekrasov. Savinkov slipped it into his pocket and tested Kornilov's opinion of the Command Agreement.

Kornilov said, "It's precisely what we need."

The meeting *was* a success. General Kornilov ordered Zavoiko to drive Savinkov and Reilly back to the station.

At the station Zavoiko took Savinkov and Reilly to the platform. "Listen to me, Reilly," Zavoiko said. "If Kerensky crosses General Kornilov, I'll have your head on a stick."

Reilly said, "Don't worry. No one will cross the general."

Once aboard, Reilly said, "You promised a lot, Boris, some of it unrealistic. What if Kerensky rejects concessions you told Kornilov he favoured?"

"I said what was necessary. I'll manage Kerensky myself. It's an honourable scheme. Without Kornilov, the government and Russia will fail. We'll have a civil war."

"What was in the cable?" Reilly said.

"Kerensky's little helper, Nekrasov, says Kornilov wants to take power. He ordered me to make no promises."

"Does Kerensky know about it?"

"Nekrasov sent the cable. I don't work for Nekrasov."

Then Reilly said, "Who was our driver, the man who interrupted General Kornilov and then threatened me?."

Savinkov answered, "Name is Zavoiko, a civilian who works for Kornilov. That's all I know."

Reilly closed his eyes and leaned back into his seat, his head on a soft cushion and a tense expression on his face.

Savinkov said, "What are you thinking?"

"About the command agreement. About people like Nekrasov in Petrograd and Zavoiko at GHQ. About how much influence they may have over Kerensky and Kornilov."

Savinkov said two agents were already there as Soviet representatives to GHQ. His personal spies.

"Who are they?" Reilly said.

"Two of my best men," Savinkov said without mentioning names or the fact that he had obtained them from C, the one-legged spymaster, who was Reilly's superior officer.

Reilly lay his head back. "Mercy," he said. "My head on a stick. Now *there's* a man with a mission."

17. Anna in the Game

Dark grey clouds hung over Moscow. A bolt of lightning shot from the sky and echoed through the streets. Rain cascaded over everything. A few pedestrians ran for cover. Anna put a newspaper on her head, hunched over and hurried to the edge of the wide street close to the trees.

"Hurry Natasha!"

Natasha came running after her. Another lightning bolt flashed in the sky. They ran to the intersection, Anna with the newspaper still pressed against her head and Natasha without cover. They crossed the street and slipped behind a wooden fence and into a yellow mansion where a grey-haired man with dark eyebrows saw them. "Good morning, ladies."

"Good morning, Mister Tretyakov," Anna said.

"Good morning, sir," Natasha said.

Anna smiled. "I'm afraid we're both rather soaked."

Tretyakov said, "I'll have some things brought down."

"Thank you," Anna said, lifting the bottom of her dress as she followed Natasha toward their office. Moments after they arrived, a maid appeared in the doorway with two folded dresses, some underwear and several towels. The women dried, changed clothes and began typing coded messages.

Several messages later, after the rain had stopped, the door to the office opened and a man entered the room. He wore a black patch over his left eye, carried a file under his arm and a document in his hand. "I have something for you to do."

A small, quiet man stood behind him.

Natasha put another sheet in her typewriter.

Anna stood up. "Give it to me," she said.

He walked to Anna's desk. "I want messages coded, typed and delivered to the people on this list. By foot, not post."

He opened the file and gave her official-looking stationary.

"When do you need them delivered?"

"By tomorrow night," he said. "And each must go from your hand to the recipient. If someone's not home, find out when they'll return and go back. Don't leave it with anyone but the recipient. I'll stop back later."

Anna put the first letterhead in the typewriter and began.

He said, "Krepov, Yuri Alexandrovich."

She smiled. "Anna," she replied. "Just plain Anna."

The smaller man added, "Lvov, Vladimir Nicholae'ich."

Krepov pulled Lvov from the doorway, pushed him away and said, "You idiot. No one wants to hear from you."

"Goodbye, Vladimir Nicholae'ich," Anna said.

In a while, Anna walked through Tretyakov's library and left the mansion by the side door. She squeezed behind a fence and walked out onto Big Nikita Street, and from there to Tverskaya to catch a tram. She reached the Zamoskvorechie District by two o'clock; and made most of her deliveries by five. At six she was back at the mansion. When she arrived at her office, Krepov was waiting at her desk.

"Oh," she said.

"I knew you'd be back," Krepov said. "Dinner?"

Anna thought, 'no.' Yuri was good-looking, tall and not more than fifty, his hair silver and black, cut short with a moustache to match. He had perfect teeth, a straight nose and a jaw that reminded Anna of her brother's. He smiled with a curled, sneer of a lip. His speech commanded. His eye was blue, unfocused and shifted quickly around the room.

"Let's go," he said.

"I'm not hungry," she replied, feeling danger though she did not want to offend him.

He rolled his head back, insulted. "Another time, then."

"Tomorrow, perhaps," she said.

He stopped in the doorway, pursed his lips as though he had something more to say but instead said nothing, swung around and walked out into the library, pulling the door with a finger as he passed through. It floated shut.

Anna cleaned off her desk, put the remaining letters in a drawer and locked it. Then she left through the side door, made her way to Big Nikita Street and walked to her flat.

He came to her office late the next day.

She was prepared. "They're all delivered," she said.

"Good," Krepov said as though he had doubted she would complete the assignment on time. "Are you coming?"

"Where are you going?"

"To the Arts Café."

"All right."

Outside they crossed what Anna thought was the widest street in the city, Tverskoi Boulevard, a highway with opposite lanes separated by a park filled with trees. Lovers walked there, old men sat on benches and played chess and elderly women sat nearby and fed pigeons. On the far side they went along quiet streets where stately homes sat empty, abandoned by owners who had moved to their countryside dachas for the summer, or farther away for an indefinite period. They came upon a pond with wooden benches.

"Let's sit there a while," Anna said.

"Fine," he said.

They sat down.

She said she was lucky to have found an apartment that faced the street and had a view of life. He said he liked his flat, which was in the rear of his building and offered both privacy and a view over the trees.

The late afternoon sunlight struck Yuri's face. Anna smiled. "Your profile reminds me of my younger brother."

He smiled back. "I hope that's in my favour."

"Of course." There were two swans nuzzling one another gently, and two others nearby. "I like swans," she said.

He moved closer; when he put his arm near her shoulder, Anna moved away, though not abruptly.

"Swans?"

"Yes" she said. "One day I'll dance at the Bolshoi."

"So you want to be a dancer," said Yuri.

"I like gracefulness," Anna said. "Not just in dancing, but how we live our lives. Some people move through life awkwardly, always agitated, finding fault with everything. But some people live gracefully, taking good with bad without changing who they are. That's how I want to be. Dancing keeps me balanced and graceful. What do you like?"

"Antiques," he replied. "I'm connected to the past. To the depths of Russian history. In antiques I see the power of the Tsars, of Peter, Catherine and Ivan. In icons I see the glory of The Church, the exquisite blood-suffering of the Russian people. In ancient armour and weaponry I see the power of the Russian Empire and the glory of the Third Rome. I have something, if you would like to see it."

"What?" she asked.

He opened his briefcase and withdrew an old pistol with a long barrel. He held it in front of her with one finger at the bottom of the handle and one finger at the end of the barrel. "Sixteenth Century. Tsar's Guards. Care to hold it?"

She studied it carefully, surprised, an eerie sensation coming over her. He grasped the handle and slid his finger slowly along the barrel and then offered it to her. She took it with both hands. Her finger caressed the trigger.

"It seems to fit naturally into your hand," he said.

She pointed the pistol across the pond and gave it back.

"You're a very aware young lady," he said, "not afraid of life. Yes, very graceful."

"I've grown a lot in the last year," she said.

"What did you think of the revolution?"

"I don't know what to think. What do you think?"

"It came from neglect, from too much liberal thinking and from fear of using force. The militia could have prevented it. But their hands were tied."

"There were questions of police brutality," Anna said.

"They weren't brutal enough."

"Were they right to attack people?" Anna said.

"They had a duty to use force to stop Russia's decline. But

they were prevented by people who didn't know any better. We couldn't go far enough."

"We?" said Anna. "You were in the militia."

"The Okhrana."

"Ah." *Ahah.*

"I'll tell you what I think, Anna. I think there are two classes of people. One rules, the other is ruled. Ruler and ruled. The ruler is wise and must exercise his duty over the other, who cannot survive without him.

"That's why I laugh when I hear the socialists talk about democracy in Russia. Power cannot be given to the masses because they don't know what to do with it. It belongs to special men with God-given knowledge, who understand the people's interest better than the people themselves."

"Special God-given knowledge?" she said. "A class of people appointed by God to rule, to make decisions for everyone else. How simple. And to think I was confused."

"But you understand exactly."

"Do you think this is always true?" she said, her brow feigning curiosity, a seduction that suddenly gave her pleasure and seemed to empower her. "Does the class with special knowledge always rule? For example, in marriage..."

"Ah, Anna!" he said. "Yes, of course the same is true in marriage. Man dominates because he has special knowledge necessary to woman's existence."

"Goodness," she said, glancing at him from the corner of her eye. "That's profound. The class of people called the Okhrana were among the special class of people called men, but with an even greater special God-given knowledge."

"Oh," he said. "Not 'were,' but 'are.' We're not a public presence yet. That would be too dangerous. At the moment we are in exile. Internal. Temporarily."

"When will the Okhrana come out of exile."

"Very soon, Anna. We won't let Russia's decline continue. The next changes will be for the better. We'll have a dictator instead of a two-headed clown for a leader."

"A dictator?"

"Oh, yes," he said. "Only a dictator can save Russia."

"Tell me."

Krepov leaned toward Anna. He said breathily, "A general such as Kornilov, a hero."

"When will they save us?" she said, glancing at the pond, where the swans had flown to the far side.

"When?" he repeated.

"Yes," she said with a half-smile.

Yuri leaned toward Anna. "You may not believe me yet, but we'll be in control by September. Twenty seventh or twenty eighth of this month."

His answer sent a chill through Anna and his unflinching certainty and bitter tone told his story. She said, "I'll be away at the end of August and won't see the papers until I get home." She smiled tentatively. "Yuri, I ran all over Moscow today and I'm exhausted." She rose from the bench. "I've got to go home now." In seconds she was half a block away.

Anna went directly to the British Consulate and wrote a letter. A member of the British legation had it encrypted and forwarded to Reilly in Petrograd. It read: "New arrivals here, Rightists Y. A. Krepov (Okhrana), A. F. Aladin, V. N. Lvov. Krepov predicts Right attack 27-28 August."

Reilly received Anna's cable the next day. He did not know Krepov or Lvov. He knew Aladin as a Russian spy with ties both to extremists and conservatives.

Reilly went to Sergei Mikhailovich at Intelligence Headquarters and requested reports on the men. Sergei calmly replied that in his opinion Aladin could be trusted, Krepov could probably be trusted but that Lvov was a down-and-out former government bureaucrat who performed favours for men in power, hoping to find employment.

"Favours?" Reilly said.

"He was Malibaev's best boy. Give him no responsibility. He isn't dangerous but he just might try to find a higher bidder."

18. Kornilov in Petrograd

Boris Savinkov glanced into the mirror on the wall of Kerensky's suite and noticed that the door to the adjoining bathroom was slightly ajar. He thought he heard the sounds of whispers coming from the room. He reached behind his chair and pulled the door shut. When Kerensky came into the suite Savinkov forgot about that and said, "Congratulations, Prime Minister. Kornilov agreed."

Kerensky sat opposite Savinkov, pensive, perhaps pressed by something. He rapped his fingers on his belt buckle, stuck his hand inside his tunic and scratched his chest.

"You know," Kerensky said, "the right-wing plotting against this government is very thick and very deep. I hope you are as concerned with it as I am."

"Yes," said Savinkov. "That's why we need Kornilov. He gives our government an identity quite distinct from the Soviet and the Bolsheviks. Without him, the generals wouldn't know you from Lenin. With him, you look right."

"What did you discuss with the general?" Kerensky said.

Savinkov drew a paper from his valise and put it on a small table that separated the two men.

"An end to the death penalty?" Kerensky said mournfully.

"It's necessary in order to reduce the number of battlefield desertions. If we fail on this score the army will collapse."

"I hate to give up the gains of the revolution. The death penalty is barbaric. Do you know I was the one who sponsored the resolution against it in March?"

"Yes, Prime Minister. Everyone is proud of that."

"I don't suppose we could take a half-way position."

"No. But we could invite Kornilov to Petrograd to discuss the agreement and let him speak to the Soviet ministers. Say you'll sign it once the details are fleshed out."

"These things will come but details need to be decided."

"Right," Savinkov said, "but eventually you'll have to sign it. Kornilov has no patience left for politics. And he has to pay attention to the Germans, who are about to move on Riga. I wouldn't make him wait too long."

"Cable the general, Savinkov. Invite him to come here to brief the ministers on the war and take up the agreement."

"You'll sign it, then?" said Savinkov.

"Yes, yes," said Kerensky.

"I'll say you've given your word."

Savinkov left the suite. Nekrasov came from the WC.

"Did you hear?" said Kerensky.

"Some," said Nekrasov. "He's too right-wing in his thinking." Nekrasov picked up the agreement. "This won't go down well with your ministers, much less the Soviet. I wouldn't touch the death penalty. Lenin will say you took both sides, that you don't believe in anything. You'll lose."

"But if I refuse the military will think I'm like Lenin."

"Buy time. Make Savinkov focus on the details instead of the whole agreement. Let Kornilov think eventually you'll sign it. Let the Soviet think you never will."

"I miss the old days," said Kerensky, shaking his head. "Everything was so clear."

"What? The university days?"

"The first days of revolution, when they listened to me."

"They still listen, Prime Minister. Most of them."

But at that moment Kerensky himself stopped listening and veered off into a private world. Nekrasov waited to regain the Prime Minister's attention. He looked again at the Command Agreement, glanced at Kerensky and then walked from the suite and down the corridor of the Winter Palace.

The train coasted into the station, came to a stop, hissed and sent out a cloud of smoke from its underbelly. General Kornilov stood in the open doorway. He appeared nervous despite the escort troops standing in front of him and behind, as though the pressure of events had worn him down. The troops climbed down the steps and stood on either side with rifles at their chests.

"Welcome to Petrograd, sir," Savinkov said

Kornilov nodded, waiting for Savinkov to lead the way. "I don't like cities," he said, looking agitated. "This one in particular. It upsets my stomach."

"Why?" Savinkov said and gestured with an open palm toward a row of parked cars.

"I'm the son of a Cossack farmer," he said, walking toward the street. "To me it's not natural for men to live so tightly packed inside one place." His eyes seemed to take in the whole city, though he could see only a small part of the Nevsky Prospect and Znamensky Square.

"No," said Savinkov.

"It changes people," Kornilov said. "Men do things they'd never do if they lived on the land. That's why Russia's such a wreck. The city turns people into rats."

"This way, General," Savinkov said and led to a car.

Kornilov got in; Savinkov followed. The escort troops went to cars parked before and after Kornilov's. A dozen engines started. The lead car swung out onto the main street and the others followed closely behind.

"We're glad you came," Savinkov said. "We hope you will show the ministers the importance of the death penalty."

"I'm a soldier, not a salesman," Kornilov replied, a little nervous. "I'll give them plain facts. If they can't draw good conclusions, then something's wrong with them."

The car passed a factory, where workers were holding banners and loitering in the yard with soldiers who wore red ribbons pinned to their uniforms.

"What do those signs say?" Kornilov said.

"A slogan. 'Worker control of factories.'"

"Imbeciles," said Kornilov. "All Kerensky's ministers really need to look at is desertions and disbanded army units. Or Latvia, where those stupid Soviet committees want to give the German Army a beachhead near Petrograd. That's all they need for a good opinion of the death penalty."

The cars turned off the Nevsky Prospect to a small street that led under an archway into a big square. On the far side of the square sat the Winter Palace. The cars sped across the square and stopped at the stone steps of the entrance. The escort troops jumped out first, formed a cordon to the steps, stood at attention and held their rifles across their chests as Savinkov and Kornilov went inside.

They walked through a long, ornate corridor of rich coloured walls trimmed in gold, past suites lighted by chandeliers, filled with luxurious paintings, ornaments and vases. At the end of the corridor was a brass sign with black letters that spelled, 'Chamber of Ministers.' Savinkov opened the doors. The escort troops moved to the sides and held weapons ready. Kornilov stopped in the middle of the doorway. Kerensky, seated at the end of a table that was partially covered by a relief map of the western front, looked up, stood and saluted him. Kornilov stood in the doorway and returned Kerensky's salute.

"Come in, General," Kerensky said.

Kornilov stepped inside the room. Most of the ministers rose from their seats. Kerensky pulled a chair from the table next to his own and gestured for the general to seat himself there. Savinkov sat on Kornilov's right and Kerensky on the general's left. The escort troops remained outside.

Kornilov began with a review of the status of the armed forces. Then after a few minutes he said, "Now I'll discuss some reforms that are badly needed by the army."

Savinkov interrupted: "Those questions are under review now. But we'd like to hear about the situation in Latvia."

"I'll start," Kornilov said, "in the occupied areas."

The ministers leaned forward or stood up to see the relief map and the area to which Kornilov pointed-- from Galicia up to the Baltic. He drew an imaginary line about a hundred miles to the west of the one on the map, near the Front.

"This is what one million deserters have cost us," Kornilov said, "in land and resources that belonged to Russia but are now in German hands." He stopped and examined the eyes of each minister one by one until he got to Kerensky, whose eyes were somewhere else. He pointed to Latvia, northeast of the occupied territories. "The German Army is preparing an offensive. If they succeed, we'll lose Petrograd."

One of the ministers said, "What are their chances?"

"Ordinarily I'd say our forces would push them back easily. But there is a certain negative influence..."

Just at that moment Kerensky uncrossed his legs under the table and kicked Kornilov in the knee. Kornilov glanced briefly at Kerensky, who tapped his fingers rapidly on his chest and cleared his throat. Kornilov continued, "But in this case, as I was saying, the negative influence of the..."

Again Kerensky's foot cracked into Kornilov's knee. Kornilov reached under the table to rub it and then glanced at Kerensky, who smiled sheepishly as his fingers continued to tap nervously on his chest. Kornilov kept an eye on Kerensky, speaking rapidly as though under a deadline: "The influence of the committees on the troops..."

Kerensky's lips and jaw twitched as Kornilov spoke, as though he were having a mild seizure.

"Unless discipline is restored," he continued, pointing to Riga on the map but looking at Kerensky, "the German Army will take Riga and then attack Petrograd."

"How will we counter-attack?" a minister said.

"The next offensives against the enemy will be..."

Kerensky leaned in and whispered, "No details."

Kornilov said, "...in the area of central difficulty."

Kerensky nodded, as though everyone understood.

Kornilov added, "The German Army will attack Riga on August twentieth. If you can't control the political committees, we'll have German troops on our streets."

Savinkov whispered to Kornilov, "Tell him in private."

Kornilov's face reddened. He covered it with his hand and squeezed his cheeks. He said, "Are there questions?"

A few questions came out. Kornilov tried to answer them. Kerensky called a recess and the meeting broke up. Kerensky took Kornilov and Savinkov back to his suite.

"What were you trying to do?" Kornilov said anxiously.

Kerensky fidgeted with the top button of his tunic.

Savinkov replied, "We aren't sure who to trust."

"It's your government," Kornilov said.

"Six of them are from the Soviet," said Savinkov. "We aren't certain who is loyal or where information might go."

"Go?" said Kornilov. "Where would it go?"

"The Soviet, to Bolsheviks, to Germans," Savinkov said.

"Through the papers," Kerensky said.

"You don't know where information might go?"

"There is the possibility of a leak," Kerensky said.

"What about the death penalty?" Kornilov said.

"We're working on that," Savinkov said.

Kornilov squeezed his forehead, his face crimson and his voice raspy. "And the Command Agreement?"

"We're fleshing out the details now, General," Kerensky said as he looked at his watch. "The Deputy Minister for War will have it all worked out very soon."

"When are we going to discuss the Command Agreement, and in particular, the death penalty?"

"How would next week be?" Savinkov said.

"Say, August tenth," Kerensky said.

"August tenth?" said Kornilov.

"Yes. Tenth of August," Savinkov said.

"I'll be back on August tenth." Kornilov walked from Kerensky's office, snapped his fingers in the corridor and led the escort troops to the square. Savinkov asked Kornilov what he could do to help him against the German Army.

Kornilov replied, "Issue an order to move about fifteen thousand regulars from Mogilev to Velikiye Luki."

"Velikiye Luki?"

"That's right," said Kornilov. "Halfway between here and headquarters, equidistant to Moscow, Petrograd and Riga. Close enough if the Germans attack Riga or the Bolsheviks stage an uprising in Petrograd. I'll be able to act in any case."

"Good," Savinkov said. "Move the troops as required."

Kornilov walked past the escort troops, who held their rifles at their chests. He opened his own door and then turned around as Savinkov followed behind him. "You know, Savinkov," he said, "this is a very strange government."

"I know," Savinkov said.

"It isn't worthy of leading the nation. It's not capable."

"I know that too, General. It's just getting started."

"It's off to a bad start."

Kornilov climbed into the back seat of the car. The escort troops went ahead and behind. The motorcade swung out into the Palace Square and sped under the Triumphal Arch and away from the Winter Palace.

Savinkov walked back to the building, embarrassed and angry at Kerensky who had let himself be caught unprepared for a meeting with the one man who could save him. But Savinkov realized that he himself had failed to live up to his sworn responsibility to safeguard the Kerensky-Kornilov relationship. It was, he thought, his own bloody fault.

19. Kornilov and Kerensky: August Tenth

Once back in Mogilev, Kornilov received a telegram from Savinkov confirming arrangements for the meeting in Petrograd set for August tenth. At the same time the assistant Zavoiko warned the general that the next visit could be a set-up for a Bolshevik attack, with or without Kerensky's participation. Savinkov's own new GHQ representative, Filonenko, had said as much. Kornilov accepted Zavoiko's opinion and gave him full responsibility for making all necessary defensive precautions.

Filonenko cabled the information to Savinkov. The cable went to his Tauride office, where it was logged and copied.

Reilly said, "That was stupid. Communication between you and your agents *must* go through the British Embassy. If you haven't spoken to Lockhart or Buchanan, I'll do it. Unless you want everyone in Russia reading your mail."

"Oh, damn!" Savinkov said, stomping his boot. "I'm a fool!"

On August tenth a special train from Mogilev pulled into the station shortly after nine in the morning. It consisted of three passenger cars, one staff car that bore the imperial seal and two flat freight cars carrying armoured automobiles. From the last passenger car a dozen mechanics set up special equipment to help the armoured cars to the ground. When that was done they mounted machine guns along the sides of the two armoured cars, four weapons in all. Special troops climbed onto the running boards behind the wheel-covers, where mechanics strapped them in place with their weapons.

Dozens of soldiers marched to a few automobiles, climbed inside and hung their weapons through the windows. Kornilov came from a railcar that bore the imperial seal and took the back seat of a limousine; in moments the motorcade raced up Nevsky Prospect to the Winter Palace. Along the street, people on the walkways stopped to see what appeared to be a parade of royalty, or a military occupation by a foreign potentate and his troops. Entire food queues broke apart as people rushed to the edge of the street to see.

"Look!" a woman shouted. "It's Tsar Nicholas!"

"The King of England!" others said. "The British!"

"No!" someone yelled. "It's Lenin!"

Kerensky's telephone rang. "Kerensky here."

The caller identified himself as a member of the Soviet and said, "Alexander Fyodor'ich, it appears that Kornilov has arrived in Petrograd with a military contingent. At the same time sources report troop movements between Mogilev and Velikiye Luki. They could be positioning themselves for an advance on Petrograd. A military coup could be underway."

"Are you certain?" Kerensky said.

"We don't know Kornilov's intentions, only the facts I've related to you. But be on guard."

Kerensky put the telephone on the switch hook and took it up again. "Provisional Guard to the Winter Palace. Now."

"What is it?" Nekrasov said.

"It's Kornilov. He may be about to stage his putsch."

"What are we going to do?"

"Do?" said Kerensky. "What can I do? Call headquarters for troops? They'd laugh in my face. I'll have to confront Kornilov myself. He won't get away with this."

Kerensky looked through his office window as his trusted Provisional Guard hurried into place outside the palace. Kornilov's motorcade sped through the Triumphal Arch into Palace Square and roared to a stop in front of the stone steps where Kerensky's guards were standing. Kornilov's troops unbound the machine guns and their operators from the armed cars. Then a contingent of soldiers took the weaponry into the palace. Kerensky's guards formed a cordon to the steps. Kornilov appeared from his car; the Provisional Guard stood at attention and saluted him.

"Oh, no," said Kerensky. "My own men have gone over."

The special troops of the Tekinzy Regiment formed a barrier around Kornilov and marched up and into the palace.

Nekrasov stood next to Kerensky. "Unbelievable."

The Prime Minister strode to the doorway and looked into the corridor. His troops stood at attention with their backs against the wall as Kornilov's guards took up positions right outside Kerensky's door and put their machine guns in place. Then Kornilov himself strode down the corridor, his armed Tekinzy Regiment passing right by Kerensky's guards who stood erect and gave a prolonged salute. Kerensky returned to his suite as Nekrasov slipped into the corridor.

Kornilov marched into Kerensky's office.

Kerensky's arms nervously flew into the air.

Kornilov stopped. "What's wrong, Prime Minister?"

"I s-see you've brought your ... army," Kerensky said.

"Just my Tekinzy Regiment."

"And your m-machine guns."

"There are reports that the Bolsheviks plan to attack."

"Who?" said Kerensky.

"The Bolsheviks," Kornilov said.

"There are no Bolsheviks here, general." Kerensky pulled the tails of his tunic under his wide black belt and scratched his chest. "W-what are you doing here?"

"What?" said Kornilov.

"What are you d-doing here?" Kerensky said.

"What am I doing here?" said Kornilov. "I've come to address the cabinet ministers."

Kerensky's eyes bulged. He went to the door and looked outside. "Nekrasov!" he said. "Tereshenko! Come in here!"

Kerensky's two close advisors stepped into the suite.

"General Kornilov says he is here to address the cabinet," Kerensky said in a panicky voice. "You are witnesses. He wants to address the cabinet."

"That's correct, Prime Minister," Tereshenko said.

"What do you know about this?" Kerensky said.

"I've known about it for a week," Tereshenko said.

"A week? Yet you said nothing to me."

"You've known about it for a week too, Prime Minister."

"What?" said Kerensky.

Kornilov said, "You asked me to address the cabinet and said you would sign the agreement and read the bill on the death penalty. Have you forgotten, Prime Minister?"

"No, no," Kerensky said, his fingers rubbing against his tunic just over his heart. "Of course not. It's just that your arrival was a bit dramatic. When I saw machine guns, I lost track. But now I've had a chance to gather my thoughts."

Kornilov said, "I've come here to help you defend the government against a Bolshevik attack. I am your ally, Prime Minister, not your enemy. What's come over you?"

"Of course," Kerensky said. "Sit down, please. We'll talk."

"I didn't come here to talk," Kornilov said. "You said you needed my help, so I came. You promised to put these issues to the government today. That hasn't changed, has it Prime Minister? Where is Deputy Minister Savinkov?"

"General," Kerensky said, his head shaking in every direction, "these things take time. All the details are being worked out now, even as we speak, and we'll have everything tied up just as it should be in no time. That's why I had Savinkov finalize the details this morning."

"You don't want me to speak to the cabinet? You won't sign the Command Agreement today? You won't read the bill on the death penalty? You kept the Deputy Minister away?"

Nekrasov interrupted. "General. The pressure from the Soviet to ditch the Command Agreement makes the bill on the death penalty impossible right now. The only way we'll succeed is if we can deal with one issue at a time until everything is in place. If the Prime Minister pushes the Soviet now they will oppose it. That's why the Prime Minister says we need time."

"It's a dilemma, general," Kerensky said, his voice slightly less strained and his body somewhat more under control and relaxed. "There's pressure from the right to put you in power, whether you want it or not. There's pressure on me to stave off a right wing coup attempt. I can't do that without your help.

"You already know about the pressure from the left. I'm walking a thin line, general, and if I veer too far in either direction the result could be civil war. I need your help to stay on course and protect the government."

"What should I do?" Kornilov said in a calm voice.

"Let me do my job," said Kerensky.

"And the cabinet?"

"I can get some of the ministers for this afternoon, but let's not raise these issues in front of the six who are from the Soviet.

Kornilov rose from his seat. "Very well, Prime Minister." He marched through the room and passed the heavily armed guards in the corridor. Outside, Kornilov said to his men, "I'm going to call on Savinkov. I'll be back at one o'clock."

Kornilov climbed into the back seat of the limousine, which sped through the square under the Triumphal Arch and then disappeared into the city of Petrograd.

Kornilov surprised Savinkov and Reilly when he walked alone into the office of the War Ministry at the Tauride Palace. They expected the meeting later in the afternoon.

"I saw the Prime Minister," Kornilov said and walked up to

Savinkov's desk. "He'd forgotten that I was coming. Why did you insist that he had agreed to the terms of the Command Agreement?" He glared at Savinkov.

Savinkov cursed under his breath. "The Prime Minister himself asked for the meeting, General," he said slowly with obvious restraint in his voice. "He has agreed to the terms of the Command Agreement and will sign it today."

"I'm completely confused," Kornilov said. "The document is exactly what I hoped for. Kerensky insisted he could not go ahead with it. Now you say he will."

"Sign the document, General," said Savinkov. "Sign it in good faith as a commitment to serve the Provisional Government and Russia. Go ahead. Sign it."

Kornilov put the paper on Savinkov's blotter and signed it.

"Now give it to Kerensky and let him sign it."

Kornilov picked up the document and folded it. As he put it into his pocket he looked at Savinkov. "I don't know what to make of all this, Boris Viktor'ich," he said.

Savinkov took up his telephone receiver. "Kerensky," he said. "Prime Minister. Greetings. Savinkov here. I am with General Kornilov. He signed the agreement and will give it to you. If you refuse to sign it I will go to the ministers and call upon them to demand your resignation."

As Kornilov walked out, Savinkov walked to the window and stared at the statues in the courtyard outside. "Oh, Russia," he said, "what can I say to you? You are crazy."

But Savinkov knew that the point was to save Russia, not to cast blame. His job was to guide Kerensky to a critical partnership with the general. He should have managed Kerensky's attention to every detail in order to keep Kornilov's confidence. He had assumed that Kerensky would remember the meeting and why it was important. Now, out of frustration, Savinkov had threatened and humiliated Kerensky in the general's presence. Savinkov was in agony. It was his most despairing moment.

20. The Command Agreement

Kerensky signed the agreement. But when Kornilov returned to Mogilev, self-doubt overtook Kerensky again. "What have I done?" he said, pacing the floor, his arms waving in the air in despair as Nekrasov backed out of his way. "What have I done?"

"You've done just what Kornilov and Savinkov wanted you to do," Nekrasov said.

"I had no choice. The Tekinzy Regiment, machine guns, unauthorized troop movements near the city! Kornilov is a conniver, an intimidator, a pretender!"

"Kornilov?" Nekrasov said. "Kornilov's not smart enough to think up all this connivance by himself. Savinkov's the one. Savinkov's behind it all."

"Yes, Savinkov! He's behind it all. It was Savinkov who set up that meeting and the whole bloody Command Agreement and abused my good faith."

"It's outrageous," said Nekrasov. "A cabinet minister organizing a putsch. A general dictating to a Prime Minister."

"Well they won't get away with it," Kerensky said.

"No," said Nekrasov. "I don't trust them."

"Liars and scoundrels," Kerensky said, "that's what."

"I certainly wouldn't trust them if I were you."

"I'm on my guard," Kerensky said. "Call Savinkov's secretary. Tell her to get him here in the morning."

Nekrasov bowed his head and disappeared.

"It's all Savinkov's fault," Kerensky said to himself, "and I'm not going to let them get away with it." At this moment, Kerensky hated Savinkov as much as Savinkov hated himself.

On the next day the morning sun broke through the white of the night. Footsteps shuffled on the stone steps of the palace. Savinkov opened the door and went inside to quiet corridors. A door opened and closed silently, a click echoed along the walls. From outside came a dog's bark. Distant typewriter keys tapped from behind a closed door and the aroma of freshly cooked sausage slipped under another and wafted into the stilted warm air. Savinkov opened the door to Kerensky's suite.

The room was dark. The sky over the River Neva was bright. Kerensky's silhouette loomed small in front of the tall window. He wore his uniform.

"Good morning, Prime Minister," Savinkov said.

"Greetings, Boris Viktor'ich. Do you drink coffee?"

Savinkov loved the aroma. "Yes. Thank you."

Kerensky walked to the side of the room near the bathroom door, where a porcelain carafe sat on a silver serving platter with several cups and saucers.

"Cream?" he said.

"Please," Savinkov said.

Kerensky poured coffee into a cup, took a small pitcher and added cream. He lifted two lumps of sugar from a silver bowl, dropped them into the cup and put a spoon on the saucer. He walked across the room and gave it to Savinkov.

"From Tsar Nicholas' personal stores," Kerensky said. "There's so much in the vault downstairs. Dried meat, vegetables and fruit, everything one dreams about."

"Umm," Savinkov said as he sipped his coffee.

"I'd give it all up in a flash if I thought it would save Russia and the revolution."

"Um-hmm," Savinkov said.

"What do you think, Boris? Would it benefit the revolution if I gave it up? Should I give it all up?"

"Dried meat and vegetables?" said Savinkov. "Deserts?"

"Everything I have worked for. My life and position."

"I certainly wouldn't. Why should you?"

"That's interesting," said Kerensky. "You say you would not and you advise me to follow your lead. It seems that I should follow your lead in many things."

"Like what?" Savinkov stirred his coffee and sipped.

Kerensky ripped open his jacket, drew a document from his breast and threw it on the table. "Like that!"

Savinkov moved it away from his saucer and said, "This?"

"That. The so-called Command Agreement. The Dictum

Militarium. The declaration of Kornilov's independence. The blueprint for dictatorship."

"This?" Savinkov said with a snarl.

"That," said Kerensky.

"What's wrong with it?"

"It's a de facto putsch. A plot masked as a treaty. Subterfuge disguised as a handshake. Total capitulation."

"What?" said Savinkov.

"You, *Deputy* Minister for War, are its author. You, who have wanted to put Kornilov in my place ever since I came to this office. This is your doing. You have sold Russia to the counter-revolution. You have betrayed me."

"No," Savinkov said. "You know as well as I do that this document is our only chance to prevent a coup and maybe a civil war. You think I want Kornilov to replace you? Don't be crazy. I want the alliance to succeed."

"You've schemed and plotted behind my back. You've encouraged General Kornilov and made my own position more and more impossible each day. You badgered me, twisted my arm and seduced me. You've betrayed me, *Deputy* Minister!"

"You *are* crazy," Savinkov said.

"Very well," said Kerensky. "I withdraw your portfolio."

"Stuff your portfolio."

Kerensky's face turned bright red and his eyes bulged. He shook his head uncontrollably, glanced at Savinkov's shoulder, took the corner of his subordinate's gold-starred red epaulet and tore it away from his uniform. Then he took the epaulet from the left side and ripped it away too.

Shocked, Savinkov slowly, silently felt his left shoulder and glanced at the tear in the cloth of his British made officers' uniform. He examined the material and turned to his right shoulder, where the other tear made his heart palpitate.

"What do you say to that, betrayer?" Kerensky said.

Savinkov held an epaulet gently with both hands, eyes moist, he said, "My uniform. Oh, bloody hell."

"Yes," Kerensky said. "Now get out."

"Bloody hell," Savinkov said.

Kerensky raised his arm and pointed to the door.

Savinkov stomped off and slammed the door behind him even as his grief plummeted to new depths. His anger had taken him out of play and breached the possibility of absolution for his earlier sins of blood. Now, unless he did something drastic, his soul would be eternally corrupt, his patriotism tainted and Russia forever lost.

21. Reilly's Fix

At the safe flat, Volodia told Reilly what he had discovered about Aladin, Krepov, Nekrasov, Zavoiko and Lvov. "Derzhinsky's strategy," Volodia said, "is to seduce certain agents close to the principals, Kerensky and Kornilov. The intended result is to change the principals' behaviour in some way that causes mistrust and ultimately separation. What's most interesting here is that he has left execution of the strategy to Ibrahim, whom we thought a nobody. Ibrahim is targeting people who may have indirect or direct influence over the principals. That means practically everyone is in play. But I have little information beyond that.

"Of the names you asked me to look into, each of them would likely be involved in a coup to overthrow Kerensky and install Kornilov as Dictator. That is, if a practical scheme existed. But Kornilov has forbidden his generals to participate in anything subversive, and that makes efforts to go behind his back completely futile. So for those men the question is not how to replace Kerensky, but how to keep him in power. That's the only way to keep Kornilov as head of the Army. So they will all be on your side, not because they love you but because they need you. Do you agree?"

"Yes," Reilly said. "My challenge is to get Kerensky to focus on Lenin. He fired Savinkov this morning. Everyone will attend a conference in Moscow starting in a few days. I'm looking for a way to spread the fear of Lenin among the Ministers so that Kerensky won't be able to avoid it."

Reilly gave Volodia a typed document. Volodia studied it,

smiled and said, "Better than I could have done."

"Good enough for Savinkov to get his job back?"

"Not if he knows it's a forgery. Better not tell him."

"No," Reilly said and went back to his hotel.

"You worked all night," Laurent said, his snub nose wrinkled and his nostrils stretched open. "Yes, the thick cigarette smoke in your suite tells me you are contemplating another complex project that will require my services."

"Why don't you come in and let me tell you why I sent for you? Or, fine, stand here and explain me to myself."

"I would prefer the former, if you don't mind, Mister Reilly." Laurent had reverted to his pre-Svetochka period, his suit neither cleaned nor pressed and his hair afloat with oily tonic. He stepped into Reilly's suite.

"It's early for brandy," Reilly said. "I have fresh coffee."

"Black," Laurent said, "if you don't mind."

Reilly led Laurent to the small bar in the centre of the room, where a rich aroma rose from a porcelain pot. He poured coffee for Laurent, who held the cup near his nose. Reilly led to the terrace and opened the double doors.

"Let me guess why you sent for me, Mister Reilly, and what your project is about." The Frenchman cradled his cup.

Reilly leaned with his elbow against the iron railing, his legs crossed at the ankles and the top button of his white tunic unfastened. He grinned. "Sure, Paris, go ahead."

"Just before I got your message, Sergei asked me if French Intelligence had anything else on Lenin."

"You're warm."

Laurent sipped his coffee and squinted as the sun broke through a cloud above the palace across from the hotel. "He wanted to know if the French had any information about when the Bolsheviks might make their attack."

"Warmer," said Reilly. "What did you say?"

"I said we might have something, but that I'd have to confirm it with my superiors first. I imagine you have a way to provide that very same information. No?" Laurent kissed the rim of his cup, tipped it and gulped the coffee.

"It's something like that," said Reilly. "But it's a bit more complicated. We want to get information about Lenin to Kerensky, so he can protect himself. But we can't just deliver the information to him and leave it at that. He's got to get it from several sources, so he's forced to think about it."

"Of course," said Laurent. "And one of those sources should be the Intelligence Department. But you can't rely on Sergei at Justice. So you'll give the information to other people too, people who would react strongly to it and pressure Sergei to report it to Kerensky or show it to him."

"That's not bad, Paris. In fact, that's pretty good. That's just the way I want to handle it. Kerensky is going to Moscow today for a conference. Everyone will be there. I will as well. But I can't show up with the documents."

"No," said Laurent. "You're not French."

"Well, that's exactly my point. So here's what I want to do. The first person to see them should be Sergei. He won't care that they're forgeries. And of course he'll bury them for a few days until he can decide how to make money on them."

"We should get them to some of the ministers," Laurent said. "They'll pester Kerensky until he does something."

"You're on the right track. Savinkov is the one to do that. But he'll get nervous if he suspects forgery. But if he believes they're authentic he'll get them to Kerensky's ministers. They'll tell Kerensky."

"Kerensky will be surrounded by people telling him about Lenin's next coup attempt." Laurent shook his head.

"That's the idea," said Reilly.

"Poor fellow," said Laurent.

"It's his job," said Reilly.

"I suspect I will be asked to go to Moscow."

"Don't volunteer," Reilly said. "Let Savinkov ask you and then tell him you've got to get clearance first."

"Then where do I go? Who do I see?"

"If I'm right, Savinkov will send you to certain ministers and maybe give you an introduction to make your job easier."

"Is that all?" said Laurent.

"No. Open a different channel before seeing any of the ministers. The right wing."

"I see. And then the ministers on Savinkov's list."

Reilly gave the document to Laurent.

"Yours?" Laurent said. Meaning forgeries.

"I don't suppose I could hide that from you, Paris." He put several copies into a separate envelope. "This is a priority," he said. "For the Right Wing factions."

Laurent tucked it into his pocket.

"For Savinkov," Reilly said and gave him the other set.

"Then," Reilly began and gave Laurent a third envelope.

Laurent looked at it. "Who is Anna?" he said.

"Just deliver it."

"Just a simple question. Don't be offended."

"I know you're a straight-up fellow. But I don't want to get my friends killed. Anna's important to me. Special."

Laurent turned to the door.

"By the way," Reilly said. "How's Svetochka?"

Laurent turned back to him and raised an eyebrow. "Thank you for asking, Mister Reilly. Svetochka is well. She's returned from Estonia after visiting her mother."

Laurent went to Savinkov's room.

Savinkov put his hand to his temple and moaned as he sat up. He threw his legs over the side of the bed, braced himself with his fists and slowly stood. "I'm coming," he tried to shout, but the sounds were low and probably inaudible. He went to the door. "Yes?" he said, blurry eyed.

"My name is Laurent. I have something. May I come in?"

Savinkov felt a small pistol inside his robe. "Who?"

"Laurent."

"What do you want?"

"To come inside."

Savinkov backed up and waved the little pistol toward the inside of the suite. Laurent raised his hands to shoulder height, looked up at Savinkov and walked in.

"Now," Savinkov said, "who sent you?"

"I work with French Intelligence. I'll put my hand in my jacket to show you what I brought with me. All right?"

"Go ahead."

Laurent took the thinnest of the three envelopes from his pocket and gave it to Savinkov. Savinkov put the pistol back into the pocket of his robe and opened the envelope. He took out a letter that was several pages long and read each page. "Christ," he said. "Where did you get this?"

"From my colleagues."

"The French?"

Laurent nodded.

"Who else has seen this?"

"Government Intelligence. Some of our own agents."

"Sergei Mikhailovich? What did he say about it?"

"He asked me who else had seen it."

"And no one else has seen it?"

"No one. But I think Kerensky should see it."

Savinkov glanced at the documents and looked up at Laurent. "I don't believe you," he said.

"What?" Laurent said.

"The documents are too good to be true."

"We don't want a Bolshevik attack, do we?" Laurent said.

"We don't."

"Then documentation about it must be helpful."

"It's probably a forgery," Savinkov said.

Laurent, feigning impatience, said, "if I've misjudged the situation I'll go back to Government Intelligence. Someone has to tell Kerensky about these papers."

Savinkov said, "Right."

Laurent stood quietly, his lips pressed together.

Savinkov glanced at the document, slid his middle finger along the scabbard and said, "Can you go to Moscow?"

"I'll have to get clearance from my superiors first."

"How long will that take?"

"I can call you at lunchtime."

"When can you leave?"

"On the evening train."

"And no one else has seen this?"

"Just Sergei and some other French agents."

Savinkov looked out the window at the palace across the street from the hotel, tapped his fingers on his robe and ran his fingers along the barrel of his small pistol.

"How much would you want to go to Moscow?"

"I'd be honoured to do whatever you want me to do," he said. "I'm not here for money. I want Russia to honour her commitment to France. After all, I couldn't go back to Paris if it were occupied by German troops."

Savinkov scratched his left calf with his right foot, his big toe adjusting a leather holster with a second pistol that was attached to his leg. "I'm glad you're on our side."

Laurent nodded modestly.

"Now here's what I'd like you to do," Savinkov said. "I'll give you a list of government ministers who should see the letter. I'll give you a letter of introduction."

22. The Great Conciliator

Kerensky drove a black limousine along a dirt road through a forest, came out onto a hilltop clearing that looked down upon Moscow and said, "It looks peaceful from here." He turned the limousine around and went down the dirt road. "I'd better get back to prepare for my meetings."

"When do you expect Kornilov?" Nekrasov said.

"Who knows?" Kerensky said. "Late, I hope. I should have kept him in Mogilev."

"The right wing would have hanged you."

"I know."

"Will you let him speak at the conference?" said Nekrasov.

"No," said Kerensky. "I don't need to have Kornilov work up his lunatic followers while I'm trying to build consensus and broaden my base. He'd ruin everything. I won't allow him to disrupt the proceedings."

The limousine pulled out onto a highway and sped toward the city. In a few minutes, it crossed a bridge over the Moscow River and went down to an embankment road at the river's edge. A mile down the road Kerensky turned, drove for a few more minutes to an intersection where several cars idled, a militiaman standing with his arm raised. Hundreds lined the street, waved flags and threw flowers.

"What's this?" Nekrasov said.

"They can't keep us here for long," said Kerensky.

A cheer went up from the crowd: "Hurrah!"

Kerensky pulled the hand brake and opened the door. "I'll get them out of the way." He stepped out of the limousine and walked toward the militiaman.

"I'm Kerensky!" he shouted. "Kerensky here!"

The militiaman looked at him and waved him back to his car. The cheering grew louder. Then Kerensky heard a brass band coming down the intersecting street, playing a march. At first there seemed to be only a few. But soon Kerensky saw that the band was large enough to fill the street, and that its members wore the uniforms of a high school for cadets. He walked back to the car and leaned through the window.

"It's a parade," he said.

At the head of the band a soldier carried the Russian flag. Men and women threw flowers onto the street and cheered enthusiastically. "Hurrah! Russia forever!"

"They're government supporters," Kerensky said, smiling. "They don't even know I'm here; they're cheering for me."

"Hurrah!" the crowd said.

Then an automobile filled with dignitaries appeared behind the band, and behind it came another and another. Hundreds of women followed the automobiles with children, all of them throwing flowers onto the road. Flags flew everywhere. Then, cruising slowly behind the women and children came a car with a convertible top drawn down. A military officer stood in the front seat, waving to the crowd.

"Hurrah, Kornilov!" the crowd cried.

Kerensky sank into his seat.

"Oh, no," said Nekrasov.

"Bloody hell," said Kerensky.

The procession crawled by. Kornilov waved to the crowd. He caught a flower and put it between his teeth as everyone surrounded the car, some on their knees.

"Kornilov, save Russia!"

Women with their arms in the air screamed, "Ohhh!"

Kerensky's body trembled. His hands began to shake and his eyes opened wide. He grabbed the steering wheel, squeezed it, let it go and then released the hand brake.

Nekrasov reclaimed the brake. "Relax, Prime Minister."

"Relax, you say!" Kerensky attacked the horn with his fist. The horn blared, "Vooba! Voot!"

Some in the crowd turned around.

"Vooba! Voot!"

Kornilov looked at Kerensky, smiled and waved.

"Vooba! Vooba! Voot!"

"Bloody hell!" Kerensky shouted.

"Damn," Nekrasov said.

The motorcade finally disappeared down the street, followed by the members of the crowd. The militiaman lowered his arm. The cars ahead of Kerensky crossed the street and drove off. The limousine rolled forward. Kerensky glared at the militiaman, who looked back blankly.

"Let's go," said Nekrasov.

Kerensky stepped on the accelerator. The limousine screeched, jerked forward and then sped through the intersection, leaving a cloud of flower petals in its wake.

In the evening, Kornilov requested permission to speak at the conference. After Reilly's forged document arrived, the Prime Minister personally invited Kornilov to speak.

Reilly stood up and stretched his muscles as the train jerked into the station at Moscow. On the platform, guards checked documents. Familiar spies walked through the crowd. One came his way.

"Ah, Aladin," Reilly said.

"We'll go to the Metropol," Aladin said.

"Did Laurent come?" Reilly said, fighting the crowd.

"Yes, we have the document."

They stopped at the side of the street.

"How does it look?"

"Seems to be an authentic outline of Lenin's plan to attack, with dates. Already worked its way up to Kerensky."

A cab rolled up. They jumped in. Reilly looked out the window and grinned as the car turned a corner onto the Theatre Square near the Metropol and Bolshoi.

"And Kornilov?" Reilly said.

"Yes," Aladin said.

"What'd he say?"

"He already knew it."

"Ha! He knew it! What do you think Kerensky will say?"

"That he knew it too."

Aladin took Reilly to the Metropol Hotel. Reilly dressed in a British Officer's uniform, walked to the Bolshoi Theatre and sat in the front section of a box reserved for foreign diplomats.

The new government had kept the wide stage trimmed in crimson and gold. In years past, Opera singers performed where a long table now rested in center stage. Today the ministers of the Provisional Government were there, sandwiched between two huge red curtains tied to each side of the stage. The delegates were seated in the main section of the Theatre. On the right sat Duma members and middle-class political parties, army officers and respectable-looking people dressed in fashionable suits or uniforms. On the left were delegates of the Soviet, workers and soldiers in common clothes. In the middle section sat the professional associations, then officers of the Russian High Command and Allied diplomats. A box reserved for the Soviet Executive Committee was empty.

Nekrasov looked at the agenda and said to Kerensky, "What? Why did you gave Kornilov permission to speak?"

Kerensky replied, "This business about a Bolshevik uprising has got the other ministers by the gonads. I had to do it. They threatened to walk out. So I called Kornilov and dealt. He can speak, but just military matters, no politics."

"Will he keep the agreement?" said Nekrasov.

Kerensky did not answer.

"Look," said Nekrasov. "Kornilov and General Kaledin are talking. Did you give Kaledin permission to speak too?"

"Should I have?"

Nekrasov could see the typed agenda of the session. "He's there, a fanatic, after Kornilov. Kornilov will do military issues and Kaledin the politics. Better talk to him."

Kerensky rushed down the stairs from the stage to the main seating area, where Kornilov and some other military people sat in a private box. He shook Kornilov's hand. "We're looking forward to your speech, General," he said.

"I'm not much for speeches," Kornilov said. "Just facts."

Kerensky introduced himself to Kaledin.

Kaledin looked up, smiled and shook Kerensky's hand.

"I'm happy you're on the agenda," said Kerensky. "Did General Kornilov tell you about our agreement? Military Staff speak only about military matters."

"Good thing I'm not on your military staff," Kaledin replied. "But no matter. I support Kornilov one-hundred per cent. His politics are my politics. Whatever he says, I agree."

"Good," Kerensky replied. "We want to be sure that our messages are consistent, to build policy consensus.

Kaledin said, "Consensus?" He nodded toward the Soviet delegates. "Do you believe you'll get consensus with them? Throw them out and you'll have consensus."

The officers began a chant: "Korn-i-lov, Korn-i-lov."

Tereshenko slammed down a gavel. Kerensky sat down.

"The Moscow Conference on Political Consensus is convened," Tereshenko said. "The first speaker will be Prime

Minister Alexander Fyodor'ich Kerensky."

Kerensky stepped to the stage to some polite applause from the centre. But no sooner did the applause begin than jeers came from the left and right. His brow filled with beads of sweat. He started strongly but soon his voice weakened.

"Is it better to save Russia," he said, "or the Revolution?"

From the left, the Soviet delegates shouted, "Revolution!"

From the right came cries of, "Russia!"

"I say we cannot save one without saving the other. That is why we need the state, why I serve the state. That is our mission, to protect the state and save Russia and our revolution. So, today I speak in the name of the state.

"I say the state must re-build the Army, honour its war commitments and never cede to impossible territorial demands. Bless our Allies for not abandoning Russia in our hour of greatest need! To the enemy I say: destruction!"

The men on the right jumped to their feet and applauded. Murmurs spread across the left side of the hall.

"To the mutinous I say: Iron and blood!"

The men on the right cried out: "Hurrah! Kerensky!"

The delegates on the left sat silently, their arms folded.

"As Minister for Justice, I abolished the death penalty."

The Left applauded and shouted, "Hurrah!"

"And as Prime Minister, in order to preserve our army and save our nation, it was also I who introduced the partial restoration of capital punishment."

From the right came, "Hurrah! Kerensky!"

"But who can applaud when the death penalty is at issue?"

The hall fell silent.

"At that moment, at that hour, a part of our human heart was killed. If the State's survival demands the death penalty, if our warnings do not reach those who pervert our army and mock the state, we must use the death penalty to save both."

Sympathetic applause spread like a wave through the hall. Kerensky spoke for a few more minutes, until his voice lost more of its remaining strength, fell off into a whisper and disappeared.

Kerensky returned to his seat. Tereshenko stepped to the podium and introduced General Kornilov. The right exploded into cheers and foot-stomping. The delegates on the left remained seated quietly.

"Stand up! Stand up!" the Right chanted, taunting the Left.

Kornilov put a handwritten speech on the podium and looked down. He glanced at the delegates and at the speech. The delegates on the right chanted quietly, "Kornilov..."

"I'll give you some facts," Kornilov began slowly in a low monotone. "First, along the corridor that we now call the front, the news is not favourable."

The chants became quieter: "Korn-i-lov, Korn-i-lov."

"There is also the situation in Latvia, where it's likely that the German Army will try to take control. I'm afraid the news from that sector is no more encouraging than..."

"Korn-i-lov, Korn-i-lov."

"In Ukraine, held by Germans, the government threatens to turn Kiev over to..."

"We want Korn-i-lov. We want Korn-i-lov."

Kornilov kept to his prepared text. His voice was dull and his presentation uninspiring. He left the podium to general applause, enthusiasm on the right and relief on the left. Then the Cossack General took the stage with no prepared text, nodded to the right and glared at the left.

"Did you get his agreement?" Nekrasov said to Kerensky.

"I don't know."

"What's he going to say?"

"I don't know."

"There is a disease of fear in the land," Kaledin began. "Our citizens are afraid to speak, to listen, to act. They're afraid to fight to stop Russia's slide into oblivion."

The left remained silent. The right began to buzz.

"But some are not afraid. Some are ready today at this very moment to do anything necessary to save our country."

The buzzing on the right began to grow.

"From this we will not be deterred by any man, political

party, any idea or theory, or any enemy whatsoever."

On the right men stood, applauded and cheered.

"You know, it's outrageous when a group of hooligans can destroy a monarchy and an established way of life, throw people out of their homes and murder army officers and the police who guarded their streets. You know what they deserve, these hooligans, no matter what name they give their so-called political parties, Bolsheviks or Mensheviks or Revolutionary Socialists. They deserve the back of the hand, the gallows or the firing squad. That's what we'll give them."

On the left, hundreds of seats thumped as the socialists jumped up with raised fists: "Reactionary swine!"

On the right men cheered, "Korn-i-lov, Kaledin..."

On the left, the army of Left SRs stomped to the exits.

"Bloody hell," Kerensky said.

"I told you so," said Nekrasov.

Kaledin turned toward the officers. "You have our support, General Kornilov." Then to the ministers: "You have our support, Prime Minister." He left the stage.

Kerensky stared absently at the seats vacated by his revolutionary allies, the democrats. He glanced at the men on the right, applauding and shouting. "Now what can I do?"

"Well, you've got to do something," said Nekrasov.

Kerensky made another appearance at the end of the following day's session, looking exhausted, worn and sad. He walked to the stage head down, shoulders slumped, his steps short and slow. He was not as the same man who had led the revolution in February, but one beaten and bruised by a brutal history. Yet when he spoke, his hoarse and jagged voice resounded through the quiet hall:

"I asked you to meet with me here for I have always had faith in man. I dreamed that together we could build a consensus that would unite and restore our country and our people. You and I. Left, centre and right. All who share my dream of a Russia united, peaceful and strong.

"Have I failed? I have not succeeded but am not willing to

accept defeat. I will not let Russia die.

"I am often told that I have too much faith in man, that I dream too much. Now, I can dream no more. I have less faith. The Government is blamed for having boundless faith in man's soul, in his conscience and reason. What is the value of Russia's soul if we let her die?

"If each one of you could glance for just a moment at everything that is happening in this country, see and understand, you would not speak the way you do. You'd cooperate and work together and not attack one another and perhaps even share my dream. But each sticks to his own view, argues, fights with the rest as though the fate of Russia has no meaning, as though there is no point to lowering our voices and moving ahead together. Will we let Russia die?

"Do you remember the revolution, when for the first time we met on common ground and understood that we were members of a public? We were citizens then. But where is our sense of the public today? It has dissolved into private ownership of ideas, philosophies and personal interests. That is neither public nor private, but chaos, a war of all against all. Is it necessary? Yes, judging from the speeches made, it is necessary. But if this is so, must Russia also die? I say no. I will not let Russia die.

"If we can no longer dream, no longer have faith in man, then let my heart be stone. Let my faith in man die and all the flowers of my dreams for man wither away."

"No, Alexander!" men shouted. "Don't let this happen!"

"These have been scorned and shredded at this rostrum. So I must stomp on them myself. They must cease to be."

"Prime Minister! Your heart will not let you do this!"

"So now I cast out the keys to this heart that loved people, to think only of the state. Only the state can save Russia."

Kerensky returned to his seat, gathered his documents, shook a few hands and left the hall.

23. The Answer to Savinkov's Prayers

Kerensky called Savinkov immediately upon his return. Savinkov arrived at his office the following morning, just after the sun had risen. Kerensky had not slept. His dark figure bathed in the brilliant morning sky, hunched over a desk at a tall window that stretched floor to ceiling. He faced the outside, his hands resting on the desk and his arms extended, pushing up his shoulders almost over his neck.

"Good morning, Prime Minister," Savinkov said.

Kerensky turned around. "Good morning, Boris."

Savinkov went to the window and shook Kerensky's hand. "How was Moscow?"

"Terrible," said Kerensky. "I went there to build consensus but failed. How long ago it seems, when I told you we would save Russia together. I made two speeches. I promised I wouldn't let Russia die. But Russia is obsessed with suicide. What do you think? Can we save Russia?"

"We can," Savinkov said.

"I apologize," Kerensky said.

"I also apologize," Savinkov said.

"The government, the cabinet and Russia all need you."

"And you?" said Savinkov.

"Yes, yes," said Kerensky in a faltering voice. He added, "But I do not need Filonenko."

"Filonenko?"

"I don't trust him."

"Filonenko?"

"I'm sorry," Kerensky said.

"What's wrong? He's our eyes and ears at headquarters. He gives me reports on Kornilov. You don't want him?"

"He warned Kornilov that there could be trouble when the general came to Petrograd. Assassination attempts. He's a nobody trying to influence policy and I don't want him!"

Savinkov replied, "Oh, no. That wasn't Filonenko. It was one of Kornilov's hangers on. Zavoiko."

"But Filonenko agreed with Zavoiko," Kerensky said. "He

confirmed Zavoiko's opinion to the general. He had no reason that I know of to do that."

Savinkov quietly shook his head and thought. Why would his agent have agreed with Zavoiko's claim that the Bolsheviks were preparing to attack Kornilov in Petrograd? Savinkov and Filonenko both knew this was false. Had Filonenko goaded Zavoiko into giving Kornilov an incorrect impression? Was it possible that Filonenko or his lieutenant, Semyenov, had tried to disrupt the Kornilov-Kerensky alliance? No, Savinkov thought. After all, they were C's men.

Savinkov explained his concerns calmly to the Prime Minister, and then added, "It's not Filonenko, I promise you, but one of Kornilov's boot lickers. They're all over General Headquarters spreading rumours in the hope of obtaining a paying job or some graft. If Kornilov has a weakness, it's Zavoiko or one of the others. Not Filonenko."

Was Kerensky listening? Uncertain, Savinkov said, "Have you forgotten that you accused me of treason?"

Kerensky smiled weakly: "Yes, I have forgotten all, it seems. I am a sick man. No, not quite. I have died. I am no more. At that conference I died. I cannot offend anyone; no one can offend me. But don't worry. Keep your Filonenko. A dead man doesn't need to worry about enemies."

Savinkov was uncertain how to interpret Kerensky's quick shifts from weakness to strength and then to what appeared to be despair. He waited for Kerensky to continue and hopefully offer some clue to the sudden changes in his disposition. But Kerensky seemed preoccupied with his truism about dead men and said nothing more.

Hoping to bring him back a step from the edge, Savinkov said, "Do you know about the Lenin document?"

Kerensky threw his hand up to his face as though he intended to slap himself, but then threw it down just as quickly and whacked his leg. "Oh, oh," he said, his voice once again falling into a pit of self-indulgence. "Everyone knows about the Lenin document. At the Conference it seemed I was to be replaced by a military dictator. Now the Intelligence Services say it will be a Bolshevik dictator. Which is worse? A military dictator or a Bolshevik dictator?"

"I know," Savinkov said.

"Friends have deserted me. Russia wants to abandon me. I must throw my ideals to the ground and stomp on them. There will be nothing left of me. They won't need a coup."

As Kerensky talked, Savinkov stood quietly, becoming more and more concerned about the Prime Minister's emotional health, resolved again to do everything possible to help him. When Kerensky finished, Savinkov embraced him.

"I promise, Alexander," Savinkov said. "I won't abandon you. Let them all run off. I won't abandon you."

"We can't let Russia die," Kerensky said.

"We won't let Russia die," Savinkov said.

Savinkov slapped Kerensky on the shoulder, looked at him and nodded in a brotherly way. But Kerensky offered only a weak half-smile in return. Savinkov was uncertain whether Kerensky was indulging in self-pity. Perhaps, he thought, the impossible strain of Kerensky's position had snapped him in half and changed him in some unhealthy way.

24. Whispers of Insurrection

"How is he?" Reilly said and put his glasses on a table.

"I don't know," said Savinkov. "Weakened, Nervous. Terrified. Defeated. Perhaps weary from the conference. But it could be more. I'm concerned about his judgment and his ability to resolve conflict. About his capacity to continue treading that fine line between Left and Right. But maybe I'm imagining something. Maybe it's not as bad as I think."

"It's worse," Reilly said. "Derzhinsky has an inside man."

"Where?" Savinkov said.

"Close to the top."

"I'm not surprised," Savinkov said. "No question but that he wants to break up the Kerensky-Kornilov alliance."

"What should I say to Kerensky?"

"Just that. Lenin wants to disrupt the alliance."

Reilly went back to his room. Savinkov sat for a while at his typewriter and drafted the bill on the death penalty. In the morning, he delivered the document to Kerensky, who took it right out of Savinkov's hand and signed it.

Savinkov said, "Derzhinsky has a spy close to you. He wants to undermine our relationship with General Kornilov."

"No doubt as prelude to their coup," said Kerensky.

"He is visiting local battalions and offering Bolshevik support in case of a military coup. We should review the plan to defend the government."

"I have a meeting. Come back in two hours."

At the same time advisor Nekrasov entertained a man who claimed that the entire government was faltering so dangerously that men on the Right whom he represented were concerned to protect Kerensky. He said to expect a military coup on August twenty seventh or twenty eighth. But, unable to reveal more without his associates' permission, he requested Nekrasov's approval to obtain it.

Nekrasov went to Kerensky and repeated the claim that a coup was likely on the twenty seventh or twenty eighth.

"Which coup?" Kerensky said.

"Military."

At this, Kerensky laughed a self-effacing laugh. "No, no, Nekrasov," he said. "You've got it all wrong. Those are the dates for the Bolshevik coup."

"Maybe so," Nekrasov said, "But I mean one run by the generals to put Kornilov in as Dictator."

Kerensky looked at the ceiling and exploded in laughter. "That's perfect! Two coups in one day! We'll let the generals and the Bolsheviks slaughter each other!" His face turned bright red. "Hah! They're scheduling coups like opera performances!"

"We have to take action now, Prime Minister."

"What's your remedy, Nekrasov? What's your answer?"

Nekrasov offered Kerensky a fresh document.

"By order of Kerensky, Commander-in-Chief," Kerensky read aloud and looked at Nekrasov. "So, martial law in Petrograd.

Headquarters will move fifteen thousand troops to Petrograd to serve directly under the Commander-in-Chief. The officers' conspiracy at General Staff Headquarters will be liquidated." He gave the paper to Nekrasov.

"There is your remedy, Prime Minister."

"What would Kornilov say?" said Kerensky.

"Let Savinkov give it to him," Nekrasov said. "Decisive action. Kornilov will love it."

Kerensky paced the room. "By God, Nekrasov. It has a good sound: 'Kerensky is in control'. A peaceful pre-emptive strike. The generals' strategy in shambles. Lenin, powerless to act. 'Kerensky's coup'. I like it!"

"Put Savinkov on the train to Mogilev."

Nekrasov went away. Savinkov came in and saluted. Kerensky wore a determined look. He gave Nekrasov's document to Savinkov and, in a deep theatrical voice said, "Now sounds the death-knell of Bolshevism."

Savinkov looked at the document. He took Kerensky by the shoulders and with a broad smile said, "First, the death penalty. Now this. Bless you, Prime Minister."

"Take the train to Mogilev at seven. My best to Kornilov."

"Yes," Savinkov said shakily, his voice filled with awe.

"Very well," Kerensky said with a casual flick of the wrist.

"It's a coup," said Savinkov. "A brilliant coup."

Savinkov marched out and Kerensky smiled. Outside, Savinkov soaked up the sun as his own. Kerensky had signed the document. But Savinkov thought his own genius the author.

The idea, however, of two possible coups set for approximately the same time and place bothered Kerensky. Never mind that either or both could be lies. Savinkov was right to have said, "Trust no one." Kerensky needed to do something unexpected and pre-emptive. But what could he do?

General Kornilov sat amazed. His lips parted slightly and then closed. He swallowed, tried to speak and could not. His face blushed. He covered his mouth.

"You understand what this means?" Savinkov said.

Again Kornilov opened his mouth to speak but said nothing. He shook his head slowly, as though in disbelief. "I'm astounded," he said weakly. Our long winter may finally be over." He sighed, took a deep breath and then quietly laughed, involuntarily, in a self-mocking way. "I knew there was something brave in him. His situation has been intolerable. Does he have the strength to do all this?"

"Who knows?" Savinkov said. "But this is a start. I want you to respond immediately, so Kerensky knows you are on his side. Start with the officers' conspiracy. Move the Officers' Union to Moscow. Tell Kerensky now."

"All right," said Kornilov.

"Then move the Special Army to Petrograd. Presently those troops are headed for Velikiye Luki. Cable their commander, General Krymov, with Kerensky's orders. Copy Kerensky so they know you're acting on Kerensky's orders."

"Yes," Kornilov said.

"I'll take him a formal resolution demonstrating the support of every officer at headquarters. I'll go back to the city as soon as we've worked out the details."

"You've actually done it," Kornilov said.

Savinkov barely restrained a smile, saluted and thought, "Yes, General Kornilov. Yes I have!"

25. A Visitor from Moscow

At the same time another visitor sat with Nekrasov. He was Vladimir Lvov, a discarded Kerensky bureaucrat whose face bore the black and blue marks of a brawl.

"What happened to you?" Nekrasov said.

"Misunderstanding in Moscow. Big deal former Okhranist. Never mind. There will be payback."

"Why did you come here?" Nekrasov said.

"Your friends in Moscow sent me. Aladin and Ibrahim."

Nekrasov, now imagining himself as a powerful minister in a new government, took Lvov to Kerensky. The visitor, he said, had information vital to the safety of the government.

Kerensky replied, "Vital, is it? You know, Lvov, every day a dozen men tell me how to save Russia. They mean well, but say nothing new. Tell me something different."

Lvov cleared his throat. "I represent a group of industrialists and military men who understand what will happen to Russia if the officer's conspiracy is not squelched."

"What do you know of this 'officers' conspiracy, Lvov?"

"Word from GHQ says a military coup is in preparation."

"And when will this coup take place, Lvov?"

"On the twenty-seventh or twenty-eighth of August."

"Ah, yes," said Kerensky. "I know that coup. It seems the officers have not coordinated putsches with Lenin. Those are the dates of the Bolshevik coup too. But never mind. You're here to talk about the officers' coup. Very well. Is this yet a third coup, or another description an existing one. Did you bring any names? No, I think not."

"What I can tell you is that my associates would not ordinarily be disposed to look to this government for leadership. But under the present circumstances, they are."

"And the alternative to me?" said Kerensky.

"Civil war," he said. "May I tell them we've spoken and that I have your permission to request more information?"

"Very well, Lvov," Kerensky said sarcastically. "You'll find out, then, if they want to release their names."

"Yes," said Lvov. "May I say that you've authorized me to speak to them, to obtain further clarification?"

"Tell these mysterious people whatever you like," Kerensky said. "If they have something to say to me, you can deliver their message. How's that, Lvov?"

"That's very kind of you, sir," Lvov said.

"Think nothing of it," Kerensky said. "Good day."

Kerensky turned to some papers on his desk as Lvov walked from the room. He glanced up at Nekrasov and said, "Idiot. Nekrasov, keep these fools out of my office."

"He may have good information, Prime Minister."

Kerensky sighed. "All right, then."

Nekrasov walked out. Kerensky signed a few documents and glanced at the grey sky hovering low over the Neva. Then he opened a paper and looked at his horoscope, which said, "Woe be to great men in whose shadow lurk petty tyrants."

In Moscow, Anna heard voices coming from Tretyakov's nearby library. She recognized only Aladin's voice, but remembered the name of Vladimir Nicholaevich Lvov, to whom Aladin offered enthusiastic congratulations.

"Come with me, Vladimir Nicholae'ich," she heard Aladin say. "I'll drive you to the train and then cable Zavoiko to get a driver in Mogilev to take you to General Headquarters."

After the two drove off, Anna rode a bicycle to the British Consulate to cable Reilly in Petrograd.

In Petrograd Reilly went to Sergei and explained that Lvov, whom both had considered merely a disgruntled ex-government bureaucrat, might create a problem by virtue of his own stupidity. He was headed for Mogilev. Anything could happen. Sergei cabled Savinkov at GHQ and wired Savinkov's agent, Filonenko. The cables were identical: "Possible danger Vladimir Lvov now entrained to Mogilev. Keep him away from Kornilov and hold for Reilly, now en route. Please confirm receipt of this message, etc."

Sergei took Reilly to the station and left a trusted agent to receive confirmation. Sergei would wait there for Savinkov. Reilly boarded the last train for Mogilev. A system was in place to cable certain rail stations along the route to Mogilev with any news for Reilly. Half way to Mogilev the train stopped and a stationmaster boarded with a cable from Sergei for Reilly: "No contact from BVS."

26. Russia is Saved!

While these events were unfolding, Savinkov, Kornilov and officers of the General Staff celebrated the Command Agreement and exchanged toasts for a new Russia. The soldiers and officers shouted hurrahs. They signed and sealed the document.

Kornilov held it high for his men to see. "God bless the Prime Minister," he said. "Russia is saved!"

Savinkov, now determined not to let anything interfere with his success on the Command Agreement, wore a disguise to detrain in Petrograd. He jumped into his car and told his driver to go full speed to the Winter Palace. He and Sergei did not meet at the station.

Savinkov hurried to Kerensky's office and gave the Prime Minister the document that the generals had approved, restating their understanding of Kerensky's orders.

Kerensky took the document, set it down on his desk next to a newspaper. The newspaper headline said, "Conspiracy!"

Kerensky said, "It's not news, really. Just more about my relationship with Kornilov and the coming right wing coup."

"The right wing coup has been cancelled," Savinkov said.

"What?"

"That story is Bolshevik propaganda. Just look at that." Savinkov pointed to Kornilov's signature on the document.

"He signed it?" Kerensky said.

"Of course," Savinkov said.

"My God."

"All the generals signed it," Savinkov said.

"What did he say?" Kerensky said incredulously.

"That you have defeated Lenin and saved Russia."

Kerensky's eyes popped wide open and his jaw dropped. He walked slowly toward the window with the document in his hand, looked at it again and turned to Savinkov. "My God," he said in a low voice, "I was wrong about him."

Savinkov said, "You did the right thing and the generals are all on your side. There will be no generals' conspiracy."

"Then it's true," Kerensky said. "Russia is saved."

Savinkov glowed with warmth. It was his finest moment. "Yes, Prime Minister," he said. "Russia is saved at last."

27. Kornilov Meets Lvov

At Mogilev headquarters, Lvov gave Zavoiko a sealed letter from Aladin. Zavoiko then took Lvov to see General Kornilov and introduced him as Kerensky's representative. Lvov sat down and squeezed his hands together on his lap.

Perhaps concerned that Lvov would be intimidated by his rank, General Kornilov said, "How was your train ride?"

"Good, General Kornilov. It was very good."

"You know," said Kornilov, leaning back in his seat and casually putting his hands behind his head, "I love that ride. The farther away I get from the city the more I love it. I love the countryside. The fields, the green forests, the blue sky, pure and untouched by industry. It gives me peace of mind."

"Yes," Lvov said. "The countryside is very good."

"Now, Lvov, tell me what brings you to Mogilev. I understand you have met with the Prime Minister."

"Yes," said Lvov.

"What can I do for our Prime Minister?"

"What is your opinion on the question of a new government?" said Lvov. "How can we build the strongest possible government to protect Russia."

Kornilov said, "This is the Prime Minister's wish?"

"It's definitely his business," said Lvov. "They won't do anything until they understand your preferences."

"I think," Kornilov answered, "the strength of the country depends on the strength of its leaders. They should stand up, both to Lenin and to the German Army. I am very satisfied with the actions taken by the Prime Minister."

"I see," said Lvov. "How durable do you think these accomplishments will be? Could they be strengthened?"

"What do you mean?" Kornilov said.

"For example," Lvov said, "the Prime Minister himself could assume dictatorial powers. Or a directorate of yourself, Kerensky and Savinkov. Or you could become dictator, with Kerensky and Savinkov holding ministerial portfolios. What do you think? Which of these would best serve Russia?"

"What about Savinkov? He could be dictator while Kerensky and I hold portfolios."

"What do you think of the other alternatives?" Lvov said.

"I suppose," Kornilov replied, "that a Kerensky dictatorship is possible. A directorate won't work. People need a single leader they can look up to."

"Military experience would help to establish authority."

"It might."

"So you would favour the latter option, that is, a strong government with Savinkov and Kerensky holding top positions with you in charge as dictator."

"On a temporary basis," Kornilov said. "Only until elections and the establishment of a Constituent Assembly."

"But which of the three would you prefer?"

"I will always subordinate myself to the head of the Russian Government. But if the Prime Minister is asking me to take on the main responsibility, I would accept."

Lvov said, "That's the third alternative. Is there anything else to say about this arrangement?"

"I think the whole subject needs to be developed. Kerensky, Savinkov and I should meet to work it out. I'll go back to Petrograd with you to begin the talks immediately."

"With me?" Lvov said with a look of extreme discomfort.

"Why not?" Kornilov wrinkled his brow. "You know, Lvov, there are indications that Lenin could try something soon. Is the Prime Minister confident in his own security?"

"Not at all," Lvov said.

"Then let's meet here. please extend my invitation for both to come here at their earliest convenience."

"I'll tell them it's a command performance," Lvov said.

Kornilov said, "Will there be anything else, Lvov?"

Lvov looked at his watch. "I'd like a ride to the train."

28. The "Kornilov Plot" Reaches Kerensky

Savinkov stood in the doorway to Kerensky's office. "Hello, Prime Minister," he said. Kerensky led Savinkov to his desk, shuffled through some papers and then handed him a typed document. "This is the bill on the death penalty, the one you drafted. I'm calling a cabinet meeting for tonight. I'll read it officially. It goes into effect at midnight."

"Thank you, Prime Minister. And congratulations."

"Thank you," said Kerensky. "You've done much to help. I'm very much in your debt. The country is in your debt."

"What can I do now?" Savinkov said, feeling victorious.

"Go rest," said Kerensky. "I'll see you tonight."

They smiled and shook hands. Savinkov returned to Tauride. Moments later Nekrasov announced Vladimir Lvov.

"Do you remember me, sir?" Lvov said.

"You're the man who wants to save me from my officers."

"I followed your orders and met with the principals. I can now say that Kornilov is the key man involved."

"Involved?" said Kerensky. "Involved in what?"

"He's one of the men I've met with," Lvov said.

"You met with Kornilov?" Kerensky said.

"You told me to meet my associates and report back."

"All right. What does the general have to say?"

"Kornilov demands dictatorial power, sir."

"Dictatorial power?" Kerensky said. "Heh heh."

"Dictatorial power over the government."

Now the separate reports of a planned military coup jumped into Kerensky's mind. He had laughed at them. But now *this*. Kerensky twisted his fingers and said, "What?"

"I mean," said Lvov, "that during my meeting with General Kornilov we discussed political alternatives that might strengthen the government. The only alternative acceptable to him is dictatorial power and he wants it now."

Kerensky, his voice shaking, said, "What *is* this?"

"I am re-stating Kornilov's demands."

Nekrasov sat down and said, "Kornilov has deceived us."

"It looks that way to me, too," said Lvov.

"What else did he say?" said Kerensky, his face crimson.

"He commands you and Savinkov to go to Mogilev now to surrender."

"What?" said Kerensky.

"Commands?" said Nekrasov.

"It looks like a trap to me, sir," Lvov said.

"What else do you have to tell us?" Kerensky said.

"Nothing," Lvov said.

"Perhaps you'd be so kind as to write it out."

Lvov took a writing pad and pen, scribbled his testimony and gave it to Kerensky, who read it aloud:

"General Kornilov demands that martial law be proclaimed in Petrograd, that military and civilian authority be placed in the hands of the Commander-in-Chief, that all ministers resign, including the Prime Minister and that provisional executive authority be transferred to deputy ministers until the Commander-in-Chief forms a cabinet."

"Come back later," Kerensky said. "Eight o'clock."

"All right," Lvov replied and rose from his seat.

"Good bye then, Lvov," Kerensky said with a weak smile.

"Good bye, Prime Minister," said Lvov.

Lvov walked from the room. Nekrasov shut the door.

"I'll go to my room," Kerensky said. "Do not disturb me."

29. Kerensky Responds

"What am I going to do now?" Kerensky said, holding his hands to his temple. "Kornilov tricked me. What'll I do?"

"Well," said Nekrasov, "you have to do something."

"Two can play this game, Nekrasov!"

"What game?"

"Deception!" Kerensky said.

"Ah," said Nekrasov.

"That's what!" Kerensky said with a mad gleam in his eye.

"Deception," Nekrasov repeated.

"When I get done with Kornilov, no one in Russia will have any doubt who I am. Everyone will know who he is."

"How are you going to do that?"

"Superior strategy," Kerensky said.

"What?" said Nekrasov.

"Obfuscation, divide and conquer. Decoys."

"I don't understand," Nekrasov said.

"I'll smoke him out into the open and then strike a death-blow. He'll never know what hit him. Dictatorship. Hah."

"To think we trusted him," said Nekrasov.

"I never trusted him," said Kerensky. "Is the Hughes apparatus working? Let's go to the wire room. You'll see. I'll get Kornilov to say to me just what he said to Lvov, and the transcript of our exchange will be proof at his trial."

"Why not wait until Lvov comes back? Then you could direct the conversation, they would talk and Kornilov would be cornered. Let's wait a half hour."

Kerensky looked at his watch. "I have a better idea."

"What's that?"

"Acting!" Kerensky said.

"Acting?" said Nekrasov.

"The Great Kerensky as Kerensky and Lvov as idiot!"

"Ahah," said Nekrasov. "A play."

"The Awful Tragedy of Kornilov the Pretender."

"I see," Nekrasov said, his jaw grinding from side to side.

Kerensky took Lvov's written testimony, swirled around to face the door, sped through and raised his right arm high as though carrying an invisible flag into battle. Nekrasov followed and almost sprinted to keep up with The Great Kerensky. They zoomed through the corridors and slid the last ten feet on the thin layer of dust that covered the floor. At the wire room Kerensky said to the operator, "Where do you keep the Hughes Apparatus?"

"In a separate room, Prime Minister."

"Is it complicated to use?"

"Not if you understand code."

"Ahah," said Kerensky. Kerensky looked at the wire operator and shook his head.

"That's my job," said the operator. "I can set it up so you and another party can send messages back and forth almost instantly, just like a telephone conversation but without voices. The limit is my ability to write down the code as characters in the Russian language. You won't notice me."

"How long does it take to set up?" Kerensky said.

"Five minutes. Follow me, Sir."

They followed the wire operator to a table in the centre of the small room. The Hughes apparatus provided direct communication. It seemed simple enough: the operator typed letters on a device that that looked like a piano keyboard. On the receiving side, the message came out as full words.

"I'll be your stenographer," said the operator. "Who do you want me to call?"

"General Kornilov," Kerensky said. "In Mogilev."

The wire operator nodded. "Do you want to take a minute to gather your thoughts?"

"Should I?" said Kerensky.

"It depends," said the operator. "The communication is immediate. You won't have much time to think on your feet unless delays are acceptable."

"Delays are acceptable," said Kerensky.

The operator hit one more switch. A single light flashed and then remained on. The operator wrote something on his pad. "They're getting the general now."

Kerensky glanced away as sweat beaded up on his brow.

"General Kornilov on the line," said the operator.

Kerensky said, "Prime Minister on the line. We are waiting for General Kornilov."

"General Kornilov on the line."

"How do you do, General? V. N. Lvov and Kerensky are on the line." He wore a devilish smile. "We ask you to confirm that Kerensky can act as conveyed to him by Lvov."

The wire operator read: "How do you do, Prime Minister? How do you do, Lvov? To confirm once again the outline of the situation I believe the country and the army are in, an outline which I sketched out to Lvov with the request that he should report it to you, let me declare once more that events in the offing make it imperative to quickly reach a decision."

Kerensky's teeth glistened as a sinister but delighted smile stretched across his face and his head bobbed rhythmically up and down. Then he said, "Lvov, here, general."

The operator glanced curiously at Kerensky.

"I inquire about this definite decision which has to be taken, of which you asked me to inform Prime Minister Kerensky strictly in private. Without personal confirmation the Prime Minister hesitates to trust me completely."

Kerensky looked at Nekrasov with determination.

"Kornilov says, 'I confirm that I asked you to transmit my request to the Prime Minister to come to Mogilev.'"

"I, Kerensky, take your reply to confirm the words reported to me by Vladimir Lvov. It is impossible for me to leave here today. But I hope to leave tomorrow."

The wire operator hesitated. Kerensky and Nekrasov looked at him. "What are you waiting for?" said Kerensky.

The operator said, "Prime Minister, you haven't confirmed anything. You haven't told General Kornilov what words Lvov reported to you that you are confirming."

Kerensky nodded, looked at Nekrasov and said, "I confirm the words of Vladimir Lvov. I cannot leave today but hope to leave tomorrow. Will Savinkov be needed?"

The operator shrugged, looked back at his equipment and turned Kerensky's words into electrical signals. Kerensky leaned forward nervously on the edge of his seat.

The operator said, "Kornilov says, 'I urgently request that Savinkov come with you. What I said to Lvov applies equally to Savinkov. I would beg you most sincerely not to postpone your departure.'" The operator looked at Kerensky.

Kerensky nodded. "Are we to come only if there are demonstrations or in any case?"

"In any case," Kornilov replied.

"Goodbye," Kerensky said as he shook his finger above his head in a triumphal manner. "We shall meet soon."

"Goodbye," said Kornilov.

Nekrasov said, "Type a transcript and bring it to me."

"What should I say to Lvov if he returns?" Kerensky said.

"Have him repeat everything he said in front of a witness," Nekrasov replied and went away with the wire operator.

Kerensky walked alone back to his office, where a guard

stood at ease. Lvov arrived there at the same time, forty minutes late for his meeting with the Prime Minister.

Kerensky turned to the guard. "I want you to witness something. Come inside." Lvov was waiting there.

"Vladimir Nicholae'ich, repeat what you said earlier."

Lvov said, "Very well" and then repeated his assertions.

Kerensky presented the guard with Lvov's written summary. The guard looked it over. "Yes," he replied, "this was said."

"Sign it at the top, please."

The guard signed the document. Kerensky gave it to Lvov. "Sign at the bottom."

Lvov signed the document and then asked Kerensky if he had served well. Kerensky did not reply but told the guard to arrest Lvov and to take him to the inner prison.

General Kornilov bounded into the officers' dining hall and sat with several colleagues, rubbing his hands together.

"You're looking chipper today," said one of the officers.

"Why shouldn't I? The Prime Minister and Savinkov are coming here to strengthen the government."

Kornilov jumped up and went over to Zavoiko. "Take care of the arrangements. Best of everything. Put them in the apartments in the officers' quarters, top floor. Make sure each room has writing materials and clean sheets."

"Yes sir," said Zavoiko.

"Can you think of anything else we can do for them?"

"I'll take care of everything, General."

To an officer, he said, "Think about a new government, and what roles should be reserved for Kerensky and Savinkov. I like Kerensky as Prime Minister and Savinkov for War Minister." He said to another officer, "Cable General Krymov and the Special Army at Velikiye Luki. Kerensky wants no delay relocating Krymov's troops to Petrograd to protect the Provisional Government." He wondered what else he should do before he allowed himself to eat.

30. Kerensky in Control

Kerensky and Nekrasov hurried through the corridor. Savinkov followed, but Kerensky's door closed before he could enter. He knocked on the door, waited for several moments and knocked again. Nekrasov opened the door.

"Where is Kerensky?" Savinkov said.

"Busy," Nekrasov said.

"When will he be free?"

Nekrasov looked at Savinkov condescendingly and gave him two documents, the first a copy of Lvov's statement, the other a transcript of the communication with Kornilov.

"What is this?" said Savinkov.

"Isn't it obvious?" said Nekrasov.

"Not at all. What is it? What happened?"

"Kornilov demands dictatorship," said Nekrasov. "He'll be indicted, tried and imprisoned. Proof is in your hands."

Savinkov anxiously scratched his head and glanced down at the transcript. "This is an invitation for Kerensky and me to visit Kornilov in Mogilev. Who is Lvov?"

"Lvov is one of the conspirators."

"What conspirators?"

Nekrasov said, "Just wait for Kerensky to announce it."

"This is crazy," said Savinkov.

"It's final."

"It can't be!" said Savinkov.

"It is," said Nekrasov.

"What the hell are you doing? Where is Kerensky?"

"Kerensky will see you in the Chamber of Ministers."

Savinkov looked inside Kerensky's office and saw no one. He shoved Nekrasov aside and went to the Chamber of Ministers. Kerensky came from another direction.

"There's been a terrible mistake, Alexander Fyodor'ich!"

"Get out of my way, Savinkov."

"There's been a misunderstanding!"

"Your portfolio is withdrawn."

"What is this document?" Savinkov persisted, waving Lvov's

statement in Kerensky's face. "Who the hell is Lvov? Who told him to speak for Kornilov? Or for you?"

"Kornilov's demands are clear."

"Did you confirm any demands with Kornilov?"

"Everything is clear."

"It's just generalities except for an invitation to go to Mogilev. Did Kornilov tell *you* he wanted a dictatorship?"

"Kornilov sent Krymov to occupy Petrograd!"

"No," Savinkov said. "*You* ordered those troops here to defend you against a Bolshevik uprising. If Kornilov wanted to attack, his army would be here. He wouldn't warn us in advance."

Kerensky stared absently into the Ministers' Chamber.

"What are you thinking?" Savinkov said. "Lvov's statement means nothing. Did you authorize him to speak with Kornilov? Hold off until I can speak with the general."

"Very well," Kerensky said. "Go ahead." He walked into the Chamber of Ministers as Savinkov went to the wire room.

The Ministers of the Provisional Government sat solemnly at the table. Kerensky walked to the and held up two documents.

"I am going to read these to you," he said, and gave Lvov's statement as a representation of Kornilov's demands.

The ministers said were aghast, disbelieving.

Kerensky raised his hand to silence them.

"Tereshenko," he said, "will you please come here."

Minister Tereshenko got up and went to the head of the table. Kerensky gave him the Kornilov transcript. "Read."

Tereshenko said, "So, Kornilov invited you to Mogilev."

"Kornilov sent his army to take the city," Kerensky said.

"No," said Tereshenko. "*You* yourself ordered the troops here to protect the government against a Bolshevik attack."

"Ahah!" said Kerensky. "I meant *this* government, not one taken forcefully by Kornilov! It's treason! They will not take the government, and I will not give them the revolution."

"Doesn't look like General Kornilov wants either one."

"Kornilov isn't the enemy," the Ministers shouted.

Kerensky waved them aside. "I assume full dictatorial power

in order to deal with this crisis. Kornilov is relieved."

"You want to be dictator?" they said.

"I order General Krymov, commander of troops advancing against Petrograd to reverse his action and report to me here The ministers will stay as advisors until the crisis passes."

At four AM, Kerensky dictated a cable restating his words and sent it to all officers, officials and the Soviet.

Meanwhile, Soviet troops, mostly from the Bolshevik Military Organization, moved into positions near the Winter Palace with orders to protect the government from an attack by General Kornilov's troops. "To protect the Prime Minister."

At General Headquarters in Mogilev, Kornilov rested for only half an hour before returning to his office, dictated several new cables and issued more orders. To Savinkov, he wrote at two-forty AM, "Per PM's orders, General Krymov is assembling the Corps of the Special Army in the environs of Petrograd toward evening, August 28. Request PM place Petrograd under martial law August twenty-nine. Kornilov."

The general went back to his quarters and was soon awakened by Zavoiko, who had Kerensky's latest telegram.

Kornilov rubbed his eyes and looked at the telegram. "My God!" he exclaimed. "The Bolsheviks have attacked!"

"Kerensky has relieved you."

"Don't you see?" Kornilov said, "Kerensky is captured!"

"He has ordered your arrest."

"No," Kornilov said. "It's a Bolshevik provocation intended to divide us. Order a full alert. Cable Generals Krymov and Kaledin. Order the General Staff to assemble. Kerensky's in trouble and needs our help."

Kornilov took up the telegram again, studied it and told himself why it was a forgery. It was improperly formatted and bore no serial number. Kerensky's signature could have been sent by anyone. It had no title and carried no legal authority since the cabinet were the only body authorized to relieve a Commander-in-Chief. He was sure it was a Bolshevik forgery and that Kerensky had been taken.

The General Staff were already assembled when Kornilov arrived at his office. He strode to the front of the room.

"Gentlemen, the Bolsheviks have taken Petrograd. I've received a pack of lies from their forgers. They've captured Kerensky, dictated this message over his signature and forced him to send it to us. But Kerensky used the wrong format in order to tell us in secret code that he is their prisoner. I have ordered General Krymov to speed up the advance of his troops on Petrograd. A state of civil war exists in Russia. Prepare to liberate Kerensky and restore him to power!"

In Petrograd, Savinkov looked through the window at the great Palace Square, which had filled up with Soviet troops. "Kerensky is a fool," he said. "Where are Krymov's troops?"

"Outside the city," Tereshenko said. "The Soviet troop trains led by Derzhinsky are out to stop them."

The wire operator gave Savinkov telegrams from Generals Lukomskiy and Kornilov.

"Kornilov wants martial law in Petrograd," said Savinkov, "but told Lukomskiy to confirm that they're doing what we want. They have no idea what's happening here."

Savinkov dictated a cable asking Kornilov to confirm that, he knew of no meeting at which politics or changing the government came under discussion. In addition, "What could explain the opinion of the government, that it is threatened by the General Staff or by yourself?"

Kornilov and his men studied Savinkov's telegram. It appeared genuine, containing an appropriate serial number. But it did not contain any title or any reference to Savinkov's position as Minister for War. Kornilov answered directly, insisting that Savinkov's recollection was correct, that their discussions had never ventured into politics or conspiracy. Then he described Lvov's recent visit: he thought Lvov represented Kerensky, who was offering him a dictatorship, in the government.

Savinkov read Kornilov's reply. He studied Kornilov's invitation to Kerensky and Savinkov at GHQ. The offer was genuine, sincere and not a demand. He considered the movement of the Third Cavalry Corps. He himself had given the order and knew Kornilov had no motive other than to defend Kerensky and his government.

Kornilov stated his intentions: "I will not leave my post but restate my invitation to you and to the Prime Minister to meet with me here, confident that any misunderstanding may be dispelled through explanations. -Kornilov."

Savinkov knew Kornilov had been tricked. But by whom?

"You'd better talk to Kerensky," Tereshenko said.

Nekrasov again rebuffed Savinkov at Kerensky's office.

"It's not too late," he said excitedly. "There's been a misunderstanding. We can save the alliance. Get Kerensky!"

Nekrasov replied, "It's too late. Believe me, Savinkov."

"There's been a mistake."

"The Prime Minister ordered me to draft a statement of Kornilov's treason. I've delivered it to the newspapers along with the incriminating evidence. You've lost."

"What?!" Savinkov said. "Kerensky promised he'd withhold those documents until I spoke to Kornilov, who doesn't know what is happening here. We've been had!"

Nekrasov went into the office and locked the door.

Savinkov pounded on the door. "Open up, Nekrasov!!"

Other ministers were gathering at the end of the corridor. Savinkov approached them. "What is this?" he said.

A minister looked at him sadly. "Kerensky is broken. The palace is surrounded by Soviet troops, most of them Bolsheviks. Derzhinsky is taking a whole division to attack Krymov's forces outside the city."

One gave Savinkov a newspaper. "It's on the streets. 'HQ Conspiracy. Kornilov Plot Smashed. The General Arrested.'"

Lvov, the story said, had come to Kerensky as Kornilov's agent to convey the general's demand for dictatorial powers. It held out as evidence the odd exchange between Kornilov and

Kerensky, in which Kerensky had pretended to be Lvov.

Savinkov suspected the story had been concocted by Nekrasov. Or perhaps Zavoiko, or Aladin or even Lvov himself.

In Mogilev, doubts began to overtake Kornilov. "I was wrong. Kerensky is not a prisoner of the Bolsheviks but of his own fear. He tried to discredit me and my patriotism."

The General Staff officers urged him to tell the generals in the field that Kerensky was lying. He ordered Zavoiko to send a cable to all officers asserting his innocence and patriotism.

Then Kornilov retired to his quarters while Zavoiko wrote a scathing condemnation of Kerensky and sent it out over the general's name. He restated Kornilov's version of the Lvov visit, called Kerensky's version a lie and cursed the government as a tool of the Bolsheviks and the German General Staff. "I swear to lead the people to the Constituent Assembly, where Russia will decide its own destiny and choose a new political system."

Kerensky replied to the military officers with accusations.

In Savinkov's view, both men believed their own stories because neither had trusted the other to begin with. To what extent, he wondered, were the words issued over their names in fact their own, and how much the work of smaller men. But that did not really matter. He felt a sinking sensation that had two faces, one of himself, the other of Russia.

Is this my fault?

31. Reilly in Mogilev

"What happened?" Reilly said to Filonenko as the staff car drove away from the Mogilev station.

Filonenko said, "Kornilov and the Prime Minister aren't getting along. Kerensky accused Kornilov of conspiring to become Dictator. Kornilov called Kerensky a liar."

Reilly said, "Has Kornilov issued orders to mobilize? Anything about taking Petrograd?"

Filonenko said, "No. The general had Zavoiko cable the officers with his denial. His cable sounded ominous. But Kerensky had already cabled everyone with his accusations.

Kornilov stationed troops outside Petrograd to safeguard Kerensky. But Kerensky sent them away. Who knows?"

"Is there anything to Kerensky's claim?"

"Someone named Lvov claimed to speak for Kerensky and offered Kornilov dictatorial power. Kornilov concurred." Reilly asked Filonenko to take him to Kornilov's office and then said, "Where's Savinkov?"

"He went back to Petrograd just as Lvov arrived. He's probably spoken to Kerensky by now. Look, Reilly, the truth is that no one here really knows what's happening."

Reilly went into the general's office. Kornilov stood looking out of the window. "General Kornilov," Reilly said.

Kornilov turned around and said, "I'm sorry, Reilly. I've done my best. I've failed. I don't know what's got into the Prime Minister. But I can't imagine how we'll repair the breach." He went to a closet, unlocked a safe and filled a suitcase with cash. "Take custody of this until you can sort things out." He gave the suitcase to Reilly as someone knocked on the office door.

Two adjutants entered and saluted. "General, sir," one said, "it is my duty to inform you that you are under arrest. Will you come with us please, sir?"

"Yes, of course," Kornilov replied. Then to Reilly he said, "Do what you can to help Kerensky. He needs it."

32. Enter General Alexeyev

Where does a Prime Minister turn when he fires a popular Commander-in-Chief only to discover that he has no army? To the Prime Minister's credit, Kerensky did not choose the first option, in which the political leader appoints himself military leader. He had by this time discovered that the two jobs required quite different skills, and chose to retain for himself the better match to his abilities. That left him with the obvious option of selecting a new Commander-in-Chief from the existing field of candidates, his General Staff.

Thus Kerensky sent Nekrasov and Savinkov to communicate with the officers to find the best candidate for the job. But no one stepped forward. Kerensky, by now having shed his procedural liberalism in favour of pure utility, ordered Kornilov back to his post as Commander pro temp. Kornilov, the same man whom Kerensky had charged with treason and put under house arrest, agreed to come out of retirement. Temporarily.

Also to the Prime Minister's credit, the final selection of a military leader went to former Commander Mikhail Alexeyev, who was rumoured in certain places to have been involved in a "Kornilov Plot." Kerensky, aware that no such plot had existed, forgave the vague accusation. In early September, General Alexeyev became the government's top military advisor with the unanimous support of the General Staff.

While that was playing out, General Krymov reported as ordered to Kerensky's office. He stepped into the room, stood at attention and saluted. Kerensky waved his hand in front of his face and said nothing. Krymov lowered his arm.

"What can you tell me about the movement of the Third Cavalry?" Kerensky said, his eyes avoiding contact as he referred to the troops he himself had ordered to Petrograd. "Why did you move your troops, General?"

"On your orders, sir, I understood that the government was under attack by the Bolsheviks."

"Did the Bolsheviks attack?" said Kerensky.

"Apparently not, sir," Krymov said.

"General, you knew this business about the Bolsheviks was just a rumour intended to provoke the Bolsheviks and give Kornilov a pretext to march on Petrograd to subjugate the government. Isn't that so?"

"No, sir."

"You knew all about it, General. You're Kornilov's great pal. You were privy to the whole conspiracy. In fact, I'll bet you were in on it. Isn't that correct, General?"

"No, sir," replied Krymov.

Kerensky glared at Krymov. "Is there any point in this conversation, General?"

Krymov said, "I hope so, sir."

"Do you know what the penalty is for treason?"

"Yes, sir."

"You are guilty of treason. You will pay the penalty. What do you think of that?"

Krymov answered, "I acted on behalf of the Russian Government and the Prime Minister. I neither knew about nor participated in a conspiracy of any kind and I honestly believe General Kornilov didn't either. Both of us acted on your direct orders in your service."

"Both of us?! You presume to speak for the chief defendant?! Both of you?! I'll tell you what! We'll arrest both of you! We'll court-martial both of you! We'll put both of you in prison. Both of you, unless the courts-martial decide to execute both of you! Now, General, report directly to Military Administration."

General Krymov saluted.

Kerensky said, "Bah! Court Martial!"

General Krymov, unwilling to admit to false accusations of treason, did not report to Military Administration for a Court Martial. Instead he went to a friend's home and, in a private room, killed himself.

Reilly arrived at the hotel nearly thirty-six hours after setting out by train. Exhausted, he went to Savinkov's room and found the ex-Deputy Minister for War in a drunken haze, stretched out on his bed. Savinkov moaned:

"It's my fault. Let me die. Put a pistol to my head."

Reilly said, "Where *is* your pistol?"

Savinkov pointed to a table next to the bed. Reilly took the pistol and put it into his pocket.

"It's my fault," Savinkov repeated. "We've lost. Russia's lost and it's all on me. I want to die."

"You idiot!" Reilly said. "We're not done. Sober up and stop this infantile self-pity. We have work to do, and even more now that Kerensky has lost his mind. Get up, damn you! Get the hell out of bed!"

Part IV: Waiting for Kerensky

August – November, 1917

33. Authority and Honour

A small dining table rested near an open window. A branch brushed gently against the glass and a breeze blew across the small table. The trees on Sheremetyevsky Street had begun to yellow. Through the leaves, past the rooftops of the neighbouring buildings, the coloured onion domes of Saint Basil's Cathedral and golden spires over the Kremlin twinkled in the twilight. Above, the early evening sky had a grey and reddish hue. Below, the street was empty, dark and tentatively quiet, the Moscow air chilly. Anna shivered.

"Are you allowing Krepov to visit you?" said Sasha, who now ran Reilly's organization in Moscow, despite the fact that his enemy Krepov worked there.

"Krepov?" said Anna. "No. Why?"

"I see him in the doorway to your office often."

"I can't get rid of him."

"You must."

"How?" said Anna. "Could you talk to him?"

Sasha leaned forward. "Let me tell you about him, Anna."

Anna sat back, an unlit cigarette between her fingers.

"I remember a few months ago, when you and Ilya asked me about how your grandmother Nadezhda died. I didn't tell you who was responsible. But now that you are working not far from him, I must tell you it was Krepov."

"What?!"

"Yes. He ordered an attack on civilians during the Bloody Sunday demonstration."

Anna sat up in her chair, covered her face with her hand and looked around the room frantically, as though in shock. She jumped up, stumbled through the room, found the bathroom and slammed the door behind her. Sasha raced after her and heard the sounds of vomiting. The sounds stopped. Anna moaned. Sasha stood outside.

"Anna?" he said gently. "Are you all right?"

"I'm all right," she said in a voice that was not all right.

Sasha heard the sound of running water. In a moment the door opened. Anna looked out and said, "He's alive. He's out there. Why isn't he in jail? Why didn't you kill him?"

Sasha took her by the arm and walked to the table.

"Krepov had powerful friends in the Interior Ministry. When I went to press charges, Krepov's commander said, 'Yes, we can charge him. But.' He gave me Sidney's file, which showed that he had spied for several countries."

"Blackmail?" said Anna.

"Had I acted against Krepov, the files would have gone to all those intelligence services. One would have executed Sidney. I've had a reluctant truce with Krepov since then.

"Anna, no one at the Syndicate knows that you and I are related. We have to keep it that way, or lose everything. Just stay away from Krepov. Keep your door closed. Come and go when he's not around. Stay away from him."

She twisted the unlit cigarette between her fingers and then put it to her lips. "What was he?" she said, taking a match to the cigarette. "What kind of man?"

"He loved himself and had absolute contempt for everyone else. You could see it in his eyes."

"It's still there," she said.

"There were many like him in the Okhrana. Cruel and indifferent men who manipulated circumstances and used people. They relished abuse, built their own dynasty inside the monarchy and did bad things to stay in power. Krepov was among the most cruel. No one could stop them."

"I hate him," said Anna.

"Listen to me," said Sasha. "Put your feelings aside. If you can't do that, then you'll have to go back to Petrograd."

"I want to strangle him."

"If you do, everyone will know that Sidney put us there because he didn't trust the ex-Okhrana officers. Including

Krepov. Sidney would lose control of the organization and the whole anti-Bolshevik alliance. Not a word, Anna, to anyone. Even Sidney."

"Even Sidney?" said Anna.

"He doesn't know anything about Krepov," said Sasha.

She stared through the window past the colourless leaves at the golden domes of the Kremlin in the distance. "What is it about us Russians?" she asked quietly. "What is this vicious streak I see, this urge to strike out against everything human, to manipulate and control? How can we hurt one another so easily? How can we have such contempt for our own humanity? And how can we ignore justice?"

Sasha glanced through the window into the darkness. Anna looked at him with tired eyes. She rested her elbow on the table, and her chin on her hand. "You should have done it, Sasha," she said. "You should have killed him."

General Alexeyev returned to Petrograd and called Savinkov, who went with Reilly to the General's flat. The General Staff polled their peers about making demands on Kerensky, one of which was Alexeyev's candidacy as Commander-in-Chief. Alexeyev thought he could keep the generals on the government's side and asked Savinkov to tell Kerensky. Savinkov put the telegrams in his pocket.

"Would the generals support Kerensky?"

"No," said Alexeyev. "Their opinions vary. Some would like to hang him. Others don't see any difference between Kerensky and Lenin. He has little support."

"Would they obey you as Commander?"

"'Commander' would be a satisfactory title to start. I suppose in the long run, given the Prime Minister's fickle character, officers should simply consider me their advocate and Kerensky's military advisor. Let's not dwell on titles. Under those conditions I believe I would have authority."

"And if the Bolsheviks were to attack, then what?"

Alexeyev said, "The army would follow my orders. But I

could act only if Kerensky issued orders. Otherwise my hands would be tied."

"Otherwise, how would you defend the government?"

"I'd try persuasion," Alexeyev said. "I'd plead with him. I'd even threaten him with resignation. But nothing more without authority. I'll be damned if I'm going to go down in history as the man who started a Russian Civil War."

"What would you do if he refused you?" said Savinkov.

"I'd try to get an alternative authority like the cabinet to twist his arm. But honestly, unless the cabinet made an emergency declaration, I'd lack the authority."

"I don't know about the cabinet," said Savinkov.

"It's a question we need to answer," said Reilly. "And I think I may have an alternative. My organization has several thousand former Okhrana officers and army officers whose units were disbanded because of desertion or heavy losses. Ten to fifteen thousand troops at our disposal. They would place themselves under your command."

"My authority is subject to the Prime Minister's direction."

"General," said Reilly. "Your formal authority would extend to the military but not to civilians who feel that the government, the army or Russia itself has abandoned them. They are under no command. You might not feel you have the authority to order troops from Mogilev to the city. But it would be different to order these men to defend the government if we had no other defence against an attack."

Alexeyev said with a wry smile, "A Russian general is not permitted to command his own private army."

"But he could ask the general citizenry to help in an emergency. These men are of the general citizenry."

Alexeyev shook his head. "Snake oil, Reilly."

Reilly said, "How else can we defend Russia, General?"

"Please," Alexeyev said. "What is the source of my authority to act? The answer, in every case, is bigger than I am. I don't know how else to work it out."

"What is honour if it demands surrender?" Savinkov said.

Alexeyev shook his head and said, "Nothing."

"Then we need to look at the source of your authority," Reilly said, "and to find an answer that doesn't allow Russia to fall without even mounting a defence."

"You want me to rationalize the question," Alexeyev said.

"Of course I do!" Reilly said in an unpleasantly loud voice. "Normal rules don't work here. Lenin isn't waiting for authority. He's organizing an uprising that may succeed."

Alexeyev promised to keep an open mind. Reilly and Savinkov left unsatisfied with the discussion.

"What the hell's his problem?" Savinkov said.

"He's afraid of what people will think. It's going around."

"He's got medals all over his chest," Savinkov said.

"Look at Kornilov and Krymov," Reilly said. "Loyal to the end and paid the price. Can you blame Alexeyev?"

Savinkov said, "No. But I know the difference between honour and cowardice."

Anna was deep in thought, the dull lamp next to her bed casting dark shadows across most of the room. As she slowly rolled a cigarette between her fingers, a fantasy that had come to dominate her imagination replayed itself in her mind:

I take a pistol from my handbag in the desk drawer. I wait until Krepov is outside my door, in the library, and leaves the house. I go out and look through the window and see no one except that ugly shape walking from the house. I take my bag, go through the library and leave by the side door. I run through the back yard, slip between the fence and the thick tree, slink along the wall at the building next door and get to Big Nikita Street. He took the long way. I'm ahead of him.

The streetlamps are out and evening is pitch dark. I look left, to the street he'll take to his flat off Tverskaya. I race across Big Nikita and hide near the corner house. I see his silhouette approaching Tverskoi Boulevard. I sprint up the street and hide behind a tree. He approaches from the end of the street. I flatten myself against the tree, open my bag, take the pistol and raise it to eye-level. I wait. I'm nervous. My mission is sacred. God will forgive me. He passes. I spin around, aim and pull the trigger. He falls. I walk closer and fire three more shots. I throw the pistol in the shrubbery.

She sat up in bed and lit the cigarette. She puffed, exhaled, and chafed at the idea that she could shoot anyone.

Even Krepov.

But can I let him live?

Savinkov and Reilly went to General Alexeyev's flat with an idea: if Kerensky failed to act in the face of a Bolshevik attack, Alexeyev could look to one body for authority, the Syndicate that Reilly had invented. After all, it boasted many respected, successful and powerful Russians.

In the early evening they crossed the Nevsky Prospect and made their way past the Kazan Cathedral to Morskaya Street. The air was filled with tension, the quiet a thin and fragile veneer. A few beggars stood on street corners. Young radical troops harassed passers-by. Reilly and Savinkov walked quickly with their eyes fixed to the ground.

Morskaya was empty and the Moika Canal filthy, the reflections of the stately mansions on the street coloured in a dark green haze. General Alexeyev opened one lock on his door, then another and another. He opened the door a crack, just widely enough for his visitors to squeeze through before he re-shut it and fastened the locks.

They followed Alexeyev to his library, where many rows of bookshelves covered two walls. Alexeyev and Reilly seated themselves in comfortable chairs. Savinkov stood and examined the titles of the books. Every Russian writer was represented. The philosophers of The Enlightenment were there with de Custine, de Tocqueville, revolutionary tracts and a small book by Marx. Savinkov sat in a wooden chair.

"How is Kerensky?" Reilly asked Alexeyev.

"He met me wearing a bathrobe with a handshake like water. Barely got up from the divan to greet me."

After a short discussion of Kerensky's condition, Reilly said, "On the question of authority, let's imagine that the Prime

Minister falters in an emergency. The government falls. Imagine that loyal citizens, in anticipation, have organized a government-in-waiting and are ready to step in. They form the new government, draft the former commander and order insurrection put down by any means necessary."

Reilly stopped. Savinkov opened his mouth but before he spoke, Reilly gently raised his hand and the room was silent.

Alexeyev leaned forward in his high-back chair and rested his arms on his legs. "We'd look like the Bolsheviks."

"These men would act in Russia's interest," Reilly said.

"That's what Lenin would say," Alexeyev said.

"Imagine there is no government," said Savinkov, "or law or rights. It's all survival of the fittest and most determined."

"Just because Kerensky failed to act doesn't mean we'd have no government," said Alexeyev. "We'd simply have a government that failed to protect itself."

Savinkov looked to Reilly for help.

"What I'm getting at," Reilly said, "is that either you or Lenin will fill the vacuum of Kerensky's possible inaction."

"The question, Sidney, is also what is intended. From your description, once our government-in-waiting announces itself, Kerensky and his cabinet will be kaput. We'd still have the problem of authority. And for me the problem of treason. I won't involve myself in anything intended to replace the government. I will only be involved in something that defends the government. A protectorate, if you like."

Reilly looked at Alexeyev and said, "Yes. It would be an organization set up to save the government and not to become a government itself. Yes, a protectorate."

"Like a regent and a young king," Alexeyev said. "Someone takes care of business until the king comes of age. To preserve a government that is temporarily dysfunctional."

"A protectorate would do everything necessary to save the government and its leaders," Savinkov said, "including mobilization of troops and civilians, and ultimately the possible establishment of a Constituent Assembly."

"Not bad, Reilly. Who would your protectorate include?"

"People with a stake in the government's survival, who can manage details, organize elections and a Constituent Assembly. Tretyakov, Putilov, the industrialists and bankers, then Churchill, Britain and the Allied Powers."

"I think they'd buy it," Alexeyev said.

"I'll go to Moscow," Reilly said.

Alexeyev glanced at the wall of books. He squeezed his hands together, took a deep breath and looked back at Reilly.

"Strict procedures, Reilly. What will constitute an attack? How many times will I go to Kerensky for orders when the uprising begins? How many times can he refuse to act before the protectorate takes over and orders troops to defend the city? I want a statement signed by those involved, delivered only *after* an attack has begun. Otherwise, we're only conspirators against the government and our actions have no legitimacy at all. All of this must be specifically enumerated."

"We won't have time once the uprising starts."

"Nevertheless," Alexeyev said. "Unless we follow procedure, we're traitors, just like the Bolsheviks."

"We could get prior approval without sacrificing an ounce of authority. A wait would cost the battle and the country."

"No, Reilly," Alexeyev said. "Your plan can only work in the face of an immediate threat and Kerensky's clear failure to respond. I know this will give Lenin an edge but if we follow real procedure I should be able to activate ten thousand troops. That's the only way. Procedure means honour. Every Russian officer would see it that way."

Reilly and Savinkov looked blankly at one another.

"When will you go to Moscow?" said Alexeyev.

"Tonight, if I can make the train," Reilly answered.

Tretyakov was a gentleman. He spoke with warmth and looked at people with soft eyes. His firm handshake left people feeling that he respected their opinions and did not have too much respect for his own. He was slightly hard of hearing and sometimes when listening to others would cup his hand to his ear, lean forward and smile with embarrassment, almost a caricature of himself. He said 'yes' with enthusiasm and 'no' with authority. He never raised his voice. He lifted everyone with a nod and disarmed opponents with gentle questions.

Reilly opened the French doors to the garden and waited. Tretyakov saw him and walked over with a pink flower in one hand and water pitcher in the other.

"I'd shake hands but don't want to upset Eucomis nana."

"I certainly don't need another enemy," Reilly said.

"Very rare," said Tretyakov. "They call it 'purpureocaulis.' I don't know what it means but it's a very rare specimen. I grew it from seeds imported from South America. My dream was to build an arboretum. And perhaps someday I will." He walked back to a table on which he kept other flowers. He carefully put his potted purpureocaulis with other flowers, sprinkled water on it, blew on the leaves and then gestured toward a glass table at the far side of the enclosed garden.

"Your Consulate's message was urgent," Tretyakov said.

Reilly said, "General Alexeyev is Kerensky's new Commander. We are concerned about Kerensky's ability to defend against Lenin's next attack. He appears to be suffering from some mental or emotional difficulty. We don't know how he'll react in an emergency. I have an idea that might help."

"Kerensky is a sad figure," Tretyakov said. "He was given an impossible task, to walk that line between Left and Right."

"I know," Reilly said.

"Can he recover?"

"I don't know," Reilly said. "But even if he does, he won't trust the military and they won't trust him. In the end, when the Bolsheviks attack, that fact alone could doom all of us. No strength, no will or trust."

"What can we do about it?" said Tretyakov.

"Persuade General Alexeyev to use troops if Kerensky fails. Otherwise there will be no authority. But a protectorate will satisfy General Alexeyev's need for authority."

"What would a protectorate do?" Tretyakov said.

"It would be an organization that can defend the government when the government fails to defend itself. It would claim temporary rule and empower Alexeyev to order his troops against the attackers in Petrograd."

"That's treason, you know," said Tretyakov.

"No," said Reilly. "We would take action only if the government fails to act in an emergency. The protectorate would not be a government, but an authority determined to save Kerensky and the government with military action. Kerensky would be restored to power in the near term."

"Shaky ground, Sidney. What would Kerensky say?"

"We can't have another February. It'd be a civil war."

Tretyakov said. "Who would the protectorate include?"

"The board of the Syndicate, industrialists, bankers and a few officers. You as chairman and chief executive. During an interim period your word would be law."

"For how long?"

"Until Kerensky recovered or the government convened a Constituent Assembly."

"And the Allies?"

"As soon as the protectorate is declared, the Allies will announce their support. Churchill in particular and the Russian Church. But Alexeyev insists on procedure."

"What procedure?"

"He won't act until the Bolsheviks attack. Then he'll go to Kerensky and request permission to use force to defend the government. If Kerensky issues that order, Alexeyev will act on it. If not, Alexeyev will repeat his request. If Kerensky fails to respond, Alexeyev will call the British Embassy, who will cable me here at the Moscow Consulate with his instructions.

"I'll bring the request. You'll sign papers announcing that the Provisional Government is temporarily incapacitated and that a protectorate has taken interim power. You'll issue signed orders drafting Alexeyev as Commander-in-Chief of the armed forces, directing him to use all available means to defend Petrograd and

Russia on the government's behalf. I will cable instructions back to Alexeyev. Then he will act. That should be enough."

"He's an idiot. Does he expect Lenin to wait?"

"It's the best we've got."

Tretyakov smiled. "You know," he said, "I like Kerensky because he believes in the human spirit. Even though he's a socialist. He's had a rough time."

"And this won't be easy," said Reilly.

"Easy?" Tretyakov replied. "It's not easy to get rare flowers to bloom in Moscow, but I've done that. We can do anything we put our mind to."

Tretyakov agreed to speak with his associates and wire the results to Reilly via the British Consulate. They shook hands. Reilly walked through the enclosed garden to the library and stopped outside Anna's office. He knocked lightly and slipped inside when Anna opened the door.

Anna went through her concerns about the secret police.

Reilly said only, "I understand."

Anna waited for more; when more did not come she said, "I've missed you, Sidney."

"I'll be here again soon," he said. "For now, I can't stay."

She threw her arms around him, kissed him on the cheek and lingered on his lips. He hesitated, pulled back, brushed her cheek and said, "Look out the door and make sure no one can see us. I've got to go. Sorry."

Anna opened the door, looked out and said, "Go ahead."

When he passed by she closed the door and muttered, "Is that all you brought me, Sidney Reilly? Is that it?"

Volodia returned to the safe flat with news. The Bolsheviks were divided on how to take power. Lenin wanted an attack involving everyone the Bolsheviks considered loyal. But no one thought even a thousand would show up.

Trotsky favoured an approach with less risk, one that could allow the Bolsheviks to deny any ill intent should the plan fail. Take over the Petrograd Soviet. Pretend to peaceful intentions, occupy key areas but in a peaceful way, perhaps make it look like a takeover was far down the road in Bolshevik capability. Win a majority in the Soviet by seducing SR Party delegates. With a majority achieved, Trotsky would simply declare power to have been transferred from the government to a neutral Soviet in which the Bolsheviks were an incidental majority.

"The city is exhausted," Volodia said. "People might accept a bloodless coup. They're too tired to fight."

"How are you," Reilly said.

"Older," Volodia replied, "constantly on the verge of getting ill. But not quite. The knot in my stomach doesn't go away but I notice it less."

"Do you want to come out?" Reilly said.

"How would you get information if I did?"

"I don't know," said Reilly. "I can't let you die there."

"We are all dying. I'll keep you informed."

They went to the kitchen door. Volodia left first, after agreeing to take Ilya to Moscow the following day.

Early the next morning, troops filled the train station along with vagabonds and potential exiles, standing in lines that barely moved. Volodia and Ilya waded slowly through the crowds to a long line at a ticket window. They dropped Ilya's luggage on the wooden floor. Volodia lit a cigarette and counted the cash in his pocket, prepared to pay almost any price for tickets. Someone spoke to him from behind.

"Good morning, Your Honour." It was Derzhinsky.

Volodia turned. "Good morning, comrade," he said.

"Where are you going, Your Honour?" Derzhinsky said.

"Ah," said Volodia, his heart suddenly thumping loudly inside his chest. "To Moscow, a quick fix for some family difficulties." His voice was weak and nervous.

Derzhinsky held Volodia's shoulder. "We need you here."

Volodia turned around. "It's a family emergency. People will be hurt if I don't go."

"Everything will be clear. I need you. You must stay."

"This young fellow is my nephew," Volodia replied. "He's had some problems at home and I promised his mother I'd take him. I'll be on the first train back."

"Ah," Derzhinsky replied sympathetically, "No more tickets. They're telling the people to go away."

"Oh," said Volodia, his voice trailing away.

"But you're in luck," Derzhinsky said, standing aside to reveal Ibrahim. "The comrade has two tickets for a private compartment but needs only one."

"Whaddya know, pal?" Ibrahim said with a leer.

"Ibrahim!" Ilya said as a smile creased his scar.

"Comrade Ibrahim will see that your nephew gets safely to Moscow." Derzhinsky extended his hand. "Feliks Edmundovich, Feliks. An honour to meet you, comrade."

"Uh...Ilya. Hello."

"And it appears you already know comrade Ibrahim."

"Sure," said Ibrahim. "Ilya and I are old pals, right?"

"That's right," said Ilya.

"There, then," Derzhinsky said and leaned close to Volodia. "Everything will be taken care of." He looked at Ilya and said, "Ilya, where will you stay in Moscow?"

Ilya shrugged. "They found a place for me."

Derzhinsky looked at Ibrahim. "See that our young comrade is well provided for."

"That's a deal," Ibrahim said with grin.

Derzhinsky said, "The boy will be fine in Moscow."

Ibrahim took one of Ilya's suitcases. Derzhinsky patted Volodia on the back. Volodia handed Ilya his cash. Then the four men went their own ways. Volodia walked from the station entrance with a dour look on his face.

"Volodia!" came a woman's frantic whisper. He looked to his right. It was Reilly's cousin, Elena. In July, she had delivered Reilly the news of his father's death. Volodia could not remember when he had last seen her.

She said, "Did you let Ilya go with that monster, Ibriham?"

"Lena!" he said, surprised, "I had no choice."

"He's a horrible little man," Elena said. "I don't know him well, but I can tell you that he's the lowest form of life. Even if he is a Bolshevik. Where are they going?"

"Moscow."

"Does Katya know who Ilya's traveling with?"

"She thinks I'm taking him," Volodia said.

"You'll have to tell her," said Elena.

"I can't," said Volodia.

"Why not?"

"I can't go back to the house."

"Why not?"

"Because I work for Derzhinsky," he said, quietly.

Elena stopped in surprise. A trace of a comradely smile seemed close. But suddenly she looked suspicious. "I don't know what you're up to, Volodia, and I don't want to know. But if you can't go to the house, I will."

"Good."

"If you and Sidney are playing some game you'd better understand it's a dangerous one. They shoot informers."

He smiled gently. "Go well, Lena," he said and went away.

Elena went to Katya's. Katya quickly left for Moscow.

34. Anna's Father

Anna left Syndicate headquarters late in the dark Moscow afternoon and walked with Sasha together to her flat. "I like Mister Tretyakov," she said. "He has a gentle face. He could have been the grandfather I never had."

"He would have been a good father," said Sasha.

"Sasha," she said quite matter-of-factly, "who was my father?" She surprised herself with her words.

Sasha seemed befuddled, unable to offer a coherent reply. Seeing this response, Anna tried to refine her question and said, "I mean, is Sidney my father?"

Sasha stopped and cleared his throat. "Sidney? Why?"

"It might be true," she replied. "No one will tell me about my father. When I asked my mother, she got upset with me. When I asked Sidney he changed the subject and you almost choked. I need to know who my father was, who I am."

"It certainly wasn't Sidney."

"Then who was it?"

Sasha said, "You're old enough to know about this. But promise me you'll never mention it to your mother. After I tell you, you will understand why."

"All right," she said.

"When I was at the university, Katya fell for a man who turned out to be much the opposite of a gentleman. He promised to marry her, got her pregnant and disappeared."

"She had a daughter out of wedlock. Me."

"He returned later, demanding to see you. Katya refused."

"She had a bastard son. Ilya."

"I got out of school. I moved back in with your grandmother, Nadezhda and Katya, Volodia and Sidney too."

"Was that all?"

Sasha said, "That's enough."

"What happened to my mother?"

"She was abused. He may have raped her."

"Did she tell you that?"

"No. But she suffered and never had another man."

They walked slowly near a large pond and sat on a wooden bench. The streets were empty, the evening dark but the moon full. Some gas lamps off the street glowed.

"Did you ever meet him, Sasha?"

"Yes."

"What was he like?"

"Arrogant. Contempt in his eyes for everything. He loved only himself. He didn't care about anyone."

"What did you say to him?"

"I told him to leave us alone."

"Who was he?" she said nervously. "Tell me his name."

Sasha sighed. "That would be dangerous, Anna. Anyway it is not important. You are who you are. A good woman who inherited nothing from her father. Let it rest."

Then came silence. The door of a nearby house opened and

closed. Footsteps shuffled along a street and faded away. Blocks away an automobile started up and drove off.

"Thank you for telling me," she said.

"I'm sorry," he replied.

"No. I know there are good Russian men. But so many are beaten up by fate. They drink too much and fear responsibility, commitment or sacrifice. They brutalize us, de-value human life and destroy themselves. It makes relationships impossible. I wonder why."

Anna knew Katya was waiting for her, but could not resist the urge to follow Krepov after work. She slipped out the side door moments after he left one evening. She raced behind the house next door and squeezed around the tree. She crossed Big Nikita Street in a flash, rounded the corner and waited until he reached the same street. She sprinted the full block and across the next street, where she knew he would come. The lamps were out. The low clouds hid the moon. She crawled behind a wide tree in the lawn in front of a nearby house, a few feet from the walkway. Her heart pounded. The pistol in her handbag would be useless if she were seen. It had no bullets.

Krepov appeared at the end of the street, started in her direction and came closer and closer. As he approached she slipped around the tree. She held up her handbag and pointed it. Krepov walked by without turning his head.

"Bang," she whispered. "You're dead."

Krepov went along the street and turned the corner. Anna stepped from behind the tree and heard her heart pound. She had never felt so nervous or exhilarated.

After Anna went back to her flat and climbed into bed, she fell off into a deep sleep. She awoke in a cold sweat, as agitated as she could be, plagued by that same familiar, horrifying fantasy of murder.

How could I imagine such a thing? Is it better to shoot him as he walks home after work, or to seduce him and at the moment of his greatest vulnerability stab him with a knife? Have I given myself away?

Can I get control? Am I crazy? I'm like one of Dostoevsky's crazy young men. But they're made from real people, people just like me. They ask themselves the same questions I ask and then commit murders, even after terrorizing themselves with the possibility. Am I another Raskolnikov? A sane person driven crazy by the devil himself?

Why test myself? I'll go back to Petrograd with Mama. This has no place in my life. I want my life to be mine, as sane as possible.

A cool breeze drifted through the small opening beneath the window that looked out onto Sheremetyevsky Street. Katya glanced at the buildings in the distance.

Sasha said, "I have some unpleasant news for you, Katya. Krepov works at the Syndicate, where Anna works."

Katya leaned back and cried, "God, no!"

"Anna's met him and hates him."

Katya's eyes opened wide in horror. "Oh, God," she said.

"And I told her about Nadezhda's death."

At this, Katya collapsed open-eyed onto her outstretched arms on the table. Sasha stroked her hair and she looked up with glassy eyes. "What else does she know?"

"Nothing, I promise."

"What did she say?"

"She wants to kill him," Sasha said.

"So do I," Katya said. "Does he know who she is?"

"No."

"Get her out."

"She won't come," Sasha said.

"I'll talk to her," Katya said.

"She wants to stay."

"Then get him out."

"You know I can't do that," Sasha said.

"She needs protection," Katya said.

"She's a woman now. We can trust her good judgment."

"I'll talk to her."

"She'll be back this evening."

"I need a bed," said Katya, her eyes red and tired.

Sasha took her into Anna's room. She lay down on her daughter's bed and closed her eyes. Sasha tiptoed away.

35. Somerville

The Germans were on the move in the north, and Russian Army regulars now took orders from the Soviet. But the Soviet saw no difference between Kerensky and Kornilov, and refused to follow either. The generals loved Kornilov, saw Kerensky and Lenin as the same and ignored orders from the Prime Minister. Kerensky was almost shut out.

As Savinkov explained, "Since the Kornilov affair, the Bolsheviks have controlled most of the Soviet and all of the Soviet Military Committee. We are the enemy."

But men of substance remained. One, a British agent called Somerville, was a famous writer sent by the one-legged British spymaster to report on Kerensky's progress. Somerville and Kerensky had become trusting friends. Kerensky, now in despair, invited Somerville to an afternoon tea.

"Good day, P-Prime Minister," Somerville said.

Kerensky rose, his grief written in his face and demeanour.

"How are you, sir?" the agent said, not as a formality.

"I am defeated, Somerville," Kerensky said. "We are defeated. Soon we will have a Bolshevik insurrection. The Russian Army cannot defend against it because the generals would seize the opportunity to stage their military coup. I can mobilize some troops from the Petrograd garrisons. But the Bolsheviks can bring out ten thousand on short notice."

"I see," Somerville said.

"The Bolsheviks now control the Soviet and will soon be able to do what they like. Lenin has escaped for the moment, so I am granted temporary reprieve. But they will attack as soon as he returns. So I am limited in what I can do.

Kerensky continued, "There remains for me and for Russia but one hope. And that is you. If your Prime Minister could send a small detachment of troops from Archangel or

Murmansk, Petrograd would unite against a Bolshevik putsch. That, dear Somerville, is our last chance."

"Do you want me to cable London, P-Prime Minister?"

"Ciphers may not be secure. If your message were intercepted, the Bolsheviks would use it as proof that I am part of Kornilov's plan for military dictatorship. We'd have an uprising. Please deliver my request in person."

"Oh dear," Somerville said nervously. "You know, I came to Russia in the hope of serving my country and yours. In the back of my mind I sup-pose I also hoped to come across some good material for my novels. I never imagined...".

"I'm sorry to burden you with Russia's fate, my friend."

"Not at all, Prime Minister," Somerville said and reached into his briefcase to take out a notepad and pencil.

"Your hand is shaking," Kerensky said. "Believe me, your part in this is minor. All you need do is deliver a message. But imagine how I feel. I'm ready to jump off a bridge."

"A b-bridge, sir?"

"Not really," said Kerensky, half smiling. "Relax, my friend. Sit next to me on this divan and write a few words."

He took Somerville's arm, went to the divan and sat beside him. "Now then, Somerville, you are a writer of consummate skill. Tell me how it plays out best in English."

"I beg your p-pardon, P-Prime Minister," Somerville said. "But p-perhaps you'd tell me just what you want me to say."

Whereupon Alexander Fyodorovich Kerensky, Prime Minister of the Provisional Government of Russia, addressed David Lloyd George, Prime Minister of Great Britain:

"Prime Minister, Greetings. At this moment, fate reposes in you the hope of millions of Russians who yearn for freedom, hate tyranny and love Britain. A ruthless attack by merciless enemies of humanity is imminent. Our armies are tired, weak and hardly up to the task. Our people are ill and confused. But one thousand men in British cloth could rally our people and move our nation. We have little time, but time enough. You are our only hope and Russia's last chance. Can you do it?"

Somerville took out a handkerchief, held it to his eyes and then to his nose. "Shall I read it back to you, Prime Minister?"

Kerensky smiled gently, took the notepad and said, "You've got it right, Somerville. We'll get you to Helsinki. My gratitude. Good luck. God speed."

36. The Bolshevik Housing Committee

"Hiya, pal," Ibrahim said, saluting with a few fingers.

Ilya opened the door and stood aside as Ibrahim entered.

"Say, decent place you got here."

"My sister's."

"Too bad," said Ibrahim. "Young men need privacy."

"Well," said Ilya, "It's what I've got for now."

"That's why I came. I got my eye on something good, furniture, a view. Big place. I think I can get it for you free."

Ilya smiled. "Really, comrade Ibrahim, I don't need so big a place. I'm fine here, at least for now. But thanks."

"Oh," said Ibrahim, "that's the point. You'll need a bigger place. Privacy too."

"Why's that?" said Ilya.

"Because Comrade Antonida's in the city now." He smiled a lecherous, crooked little smile that made his pencil-thin moustache ride up under his nose and raised his lip to reveal a mouthful of yellow and brown teeth and a few empty spaces.

"That's good," said Ilya. "Where is she staying?"

"They got her a small place. She said she wants to see you as soon as you can go there. I'll give you the address. Or, hey, why not? I gotta go myself. Come with me."

Ilya grinned. "I'll have to meet you there, pal," he said. "No problem."

"See? I told you ol' Ibrahim would take care of you."

Three men strode along a Moscow street, where tree branches with golden leaves filled the space overhead. Three and four-story houses lined the street, most with windows covered by boards. Ibrahim walked between two men who might have earned their brutish physiques through years of factory toil. The three stopped. Ibrahim studied a document. "This is the house," he said.

They went up the walkway and inside, climbed up some stairs.. Ibrahim banged on the door with his fist. From inside came, "Who is it?"

"Bolshevik Housing Committee!" Ibrahim said.

In a moment the door opened a crack. Frightened, tired eyes that belonged to an older gentleman peered out. Ibrahim stepped aside. One of the workers stepped up, raised his leg and kicked the door in. The older man fell back against a wall. Ibrahim went in, brandishing a document, and said, "Orders from the Bolshevik Housing Committee to vacate the premises immediately. Penalty for non-compliance is death."

An old woman appeared in the foyer. Her skin was wrinkled, her bones small and fragile and thick blue veins covered her hands. Her silver hair was neatly set over a stern brow. Her eyes were clear and betrayed no fear. "I don't care who you are, sonny," she said. "We won't go without a fight. So go away."

The older man reappeared in the foyer. He was tall and silver. He might have commanded a battalion of soldiers or run a bank in his younger years. Now his hand shook and his chest expanded and contracted rapidly.

"Get the old lady's coat. You got a minute to vacate."

"We're not going anywhere. "We'll call the authorities."

Ibrahim gestured to the two workers, who stepped forward and aimed pistols at the old couple. A loud flurry of gunshots filled the flat. The old man and woman fell.

Ibrahim stepped over the bodies and blood and said to the two men who stood in the doorway, "Clean it up. I'm going to see my young pal. Yeah, if this don't impress him, nothing will."

37. Raw Youth

At the same time, Sasha had fallen under Volodia's influence. His bravery in Reilly's service seemed super-human.

Near the Kremlin, a banner said, "Citizens! The Soviet is Your Voice!" Comrade Artur Artuzov welcomed Sasha, who made a boiler-plate speech, brief and noticeable. After the meeting Artuzov proposed a drink at the Tramble café.

They met the following day. After a conversation in which Sasha was able to position himself as a practical revolutionary, Artuzov invited him into the Bolshevik spy service and changed Sasha's name, which he did not know, to "Timor Lipkin."

Comrade Timor Lipkin. Artuzov sent him to 'Yekobsen' at the Tsar's stable, just outside the Kremlin.

Reilly now had two agents on the inside.

"You said he'd be here. Where is Ilya?" Katya held her arms around her shoulders, trying to warm herself.

"He's usually back by this hour, Mama," Anna said. "I can't imagine where he is."

Katya stood near the window, her eyes on the walkway outside. "I've been here a week and haven't seen him."

"I know," said Anna. She looked at her watch and rose from the table. "I'm tired, Mama. I'm going to bed."

"I'll stay up," said Katya. "I've got to speak to him."

"All right, Mama, good night," Anna said.

Katya stayed at the window for a few minutes. As she took her overcoat from the closet she looked through the hallway to see Anna lying in her bed, facing the window, motionless. She opened the door quietly and in moments was on Big Nikita and then Tverskoi Boulevar, where some streetlamps still worked. She passed the yellow mansion that was Reilly's headquarters and saw a few lights burning on the higher floors, where Anna said Krepov sometimes stayed.

Katya stopped and remembered old images of her own hatred for Krepov. Standing next to a wide tree, she closed her eyes and imagined Krepov strutting through the front entrance of the yellow mansion, having seduced a maid or a secretary with his lies. She imagined aiming a pistol at him, her finger squeezing the trigger and Krepov falling hard to the ground. She continued up the boulevard toward Tverskaya Street, looked in all directions and gazed incessantly into the park to her left in the hope that some shape would be familiar. A limp, two youthful arms swinging in a pseudo-manly gait, quiet whistling of an old Russian tune. Ilya.

The intersection at Tverskaya was dark and quiet. The taller building on the far side blocked the only source of light, the sinking moon. She crossed Tverskaya and continued along the boulevard, whose name changed every so often as it circled the centre of Moscow. She knew this section was not called Tverskoi, but could not recall its name. Farther down the street some traditional Russian homes mixed with some of European style that had replaced those destroyed by fire a century earlier. Interspersed were shops and markets with glass windows covered by boards just days earlier now sat naked, uncovered, smashed open by the wood-thieves.

Katya shivered. It was a good area, where good people lived or stood in food queues. But apprehension filled her. The street was quiet and most of the houses unlit. Abruptly, from a house on her right came loud claps that sounded like building construction, though no one was building in Moscow, certainly not at ten in the evening. A respectable-looking man went away carrying pieces of wood he had torn from the house or from the fence that encircled it. In a moment two other men came away carrying wood.

Not construction. De-construction. People are cold. They have no confidence in the future. They're cannibalizing houses so they won't freeze to death. I'm amazed. The revolution has destroyed everything. Hope. Civility. The basic stuff that always held us together as Russians has melted away. It's like war. You against your neighbour, your brother against your friend. Cannibalizing houses, their own houses. They're devouring Russia. Russia is devouring itself.

From close by came the sound of a gunshot. Its echo died. The neighbourhood fell into a ghoulish silence.

Will we kill each other? Will we starve? What will we do?

Farther along the street were the remains of another house. A chimney and steps that had once led to a door, the wooden skeletal studs of a room not yet dismembered, lit in the orange glow of a fire in the lot just behind. *Firewood.*

Children hurried past. Curious, she walked by the remnants of the house to the lot, where children stood around, played games or guarded possessions.

"Why are you here?" she said to one who stood close by.

The child backed away suspiciously. Quickly another appeared to take his place, this one eleven or twelve and not shy, if the pistol in his hand was any indication.

"The question is, what're *you* doing here?"

"I'm curious," she replied. "I saw a vacant lot and a few kids ran past me. So I thought I'd take a look. That's all."

The child raised his arm and aimed the pistol. "This is our place," he said. "Nobody else is allowed here. Go away."

"I don't mean any harm," she replied.

The child dropped his arm and let the pistol point to the ground. On the edge of the lot was an object guarded by a dozen or so boys near a metal drum in which wood was burning. The object was a dead horse. Several boys hacked at the carcass and others held sticks of meat over the fire.

"It's ours," the boy insisted. "Don't get any ideas."

"I don't want food," she replied. "I have a question."

"What?"

"Isn't it late for you boys to be out? Isn't it dangerous? When do you go home?"

The boy looked at Katya in amazement. "Home? Lady, this is our home. That horse is our dinner. The warmth of the fire is ours too, and we'll fight for it if we have to."

"What about your parents?" said Katya.

"Parents? Lady, we've got no parents. We all had folks once, but not now. My mother and father left last winter. But some of the others don't remember their parents."

"That's terrible," she said.

"What, lady? You never saw kids like us? Well, there's plenty of us. Who knows where our parents are? Some are dead. Some escaped when the revolution came."

"And you?" said Katya.

"My father went to Kiev during the revolution and sent for my mother. I lost her in the crowds at the station. I thought she would come back for me but she never did. Never mind. Now I have my own army and we stick together and help each another. If anyone gives us trouble," he said, holding the pistol up as though pointing at someone, "then 'pop,' and everything's fixed. Who needs parents?"

"But your future," said Katya. "What will you do?"

"What future?" said the boy. "There's no future here."

Katya shook her head.

"You want to eat? You can eat something if you like."

"No thank you," Katya said.

"You want to buy something? We got things to sell."

"What are you selling?" she said.

"Come here," he said and led her toward the fire. On a slab of stone sat dozens of objects found in the streets or left in houses otherwise turned into firewood. Silver spoons, a coloured metal samovar and books. A small opened box with two bullets. Behind the box, a small pistol.

"See there?" he said, picking up one of the books. "War and Peace, Tolstoy. Ten kopecks." He handed her the book.

"Why don't you read it?" she said.

"I did," he said. "We all did. One guy can recite it almost by heart. We can get ten kopecks for it. Want it?"

Katya shook her head. "No thanks."

"Here is some solid silver," he said, taking a sterling silver spoon in hand and holding it between his two forefingers. "Four of 'em. A matched set. Two rubles." Then he took the small pistol and box with two bullets. "But this is what you really need, lady. Self-defence. It'll fit in your pocket and no one will be any wiser."

"You'll shoot yourself or one of your friends," she said.

The boy said, "No one touches the weapon. Except me, when I have a customer."

"What about the one you carry?" she said.

"That's different. It's our army's defence. The first chamber's empty. So there's no mistakes. But this one here," he said, holding up the small one, "it's not loaded."

Kids with guns. My God. I'll take it off his hands. "How much?"

"Five rubles," he said.

Katya reached between two buttons of the overcoat and stuck her hand into her dress. She took out two banknotes and handed them over. The boy stashed them in his pocket and put the bullets inside the chamber.

"What are you doing?" said Katya.

"You don't want to carry an unloaded gun around, lady," said the boy. "Because that makes you a target. You might really have to use it someday and so you gotta have it ready. But look," he said, pointing to a sliding metal button. "When it's back like this you can't shoot. If you want to shoot you gotta push it up, like this." He pressed the safety mechanism with his thumb to the 'ready' position and pushed it back down to lock it again. He gave her the pistol handle first.

"Thank you," she said.

"Thank you," the boy said. One more thing. When you want to shoot it keep your feet on the ground, your shoulders square and your arms straight and tense. Otherwise it'll throw you backwards. You'll shoot into the trees."

"Thanks," Katya said and put the pistol inside her overcoat, turned and started back to the street. In the park across the boulevard the moonlight revealed a passing figure that seemed to be walking with a limp.

It's Ilya, heading home. Thank God.

She hurried to the street; but by the time she got there the figure was gone. She hurried along the boulevard to Anna's flat. But when she arrived Ilya was not there. She took off her overcoat, put it into the closet and promised herself she would not forget to dispose of the pistol the following day. Then she walked to the window, sat down at the small table and looked at the street. She sat there alone for several hours. When the sun rose, she gave up and went to bed.

In the morning Anna's first words were, "I've never seen you with a cigarette." She rubbed her eyes, fixed the hook on the back of her dress, stepped into her slippers and walked to the stove to pour tea.

Katya blew an awkward puff of smoke into the air. It formed a small cloud that dispersed in the draft coming through the opening at the bottom of the window.

"When did you get up?" said Anna.

"Early," said Katya.

"You look so tired, Mama. Why don't you get some rest?"

"There is no rest for me. My brother has become a spy. My son is hiding somewhere. I should rest? Where?"

"Your daughter is here," Anna said, bringing her teacup. She rested the cup on the table, stood behind Katya and put her hands on her shoulders.

Katya put her hand on top of Anna's. "I don't know what to do," she said. "My family's half-gone. I'm afraid."

"Of the dangers?" said Anna.

"Of the loneliness," said Katya.

Anna kneaded her mother's shoulders.

"Where is Ilya?" said Katya. "Why is he avoiding me?"

"He wants his own life," said Anna. "Besides, he can't see anyone's needs but his own. Something's happened to him."

"What can I do?" Katya sighed.

"Let him go, Mama, that's all. If he's ours, he'll come back to us. If he's not, he won't. That's all you can do."

"I have to speak to him."

"I have to go to work," Anna said and finished her tea.

"I'll stay here and wait," said Katya. "His clothes are here. He's got to come back."

"I'll see you tonight." Anna slipped on her overcoat.

"I'll speak with him, then go to Petrograd. Come with me?"

Anna sighed. "I don't know. I could go, but not for long. My dancing is here."

"Lord. You can't imagine a mother's loneliness."

Anna took a few steps toward Katya. "All right," she said.

"I'll come but not for too long. When will you go?"

"I'll get train tickets for tomorrow," Katya said.

"All right, Maman," Anna said. "I'll see you tonight."

Anna left the flat. Katya returned to the table and sat down. She opened the window slightly, lit another cigarette and watched Anna walk under the arch. Some time went by before she looked through the barren tree branches and saw a single figure moving along the sidewalk. It was a young man with long hair, an arrogant stride and an uneven gait.

He's limping.

The figure turned from the street and came through the arch. The door to the building slammed shut. Footsteps came up the stairwell, one loud and one soft, one loud, one soft. A key rattled in the door lock. The door opened.

Ilya's face seemed older and his expression severe. A crimson scar ran from his eye to his chin. His body seemed wound up, about to spring into the air or shoot across the room as he hurried into the flat.

"Ilya!" said Katya. "Where have you been?"

Ilya walked nervously to the far end of the room, his eyes looking all over before falling on Katya, though he had not missed her upon entering. He paced quickly back and forth, agitated, perhaps carrying guilt but defiant, taunting and ready to fly off at a moment's notice. A scared young man at the point of a critical decision.

"What do you want from me?" he said hurriedly.

"I have to talk to you," said Katya.

"What about? To change me? Do you think you can make me a child again? Why are you haunting me like this?"

"I love you. I'm your mother. I worry about you."

"You want me to be a child but I'm a man now. You have to leave me alone. Let me live my life. Let me be a man."

"I want you to come home."

"You can't control me."

"I love you."

"You want to tyrannize me."

"I want to protect you."

"You can't save me."

Footsteps came from the landing outside the door. Katya got up abruptly. Ilya said, "Sit down," and went to the door.

Outside, a voice said, "Hey, Ilya, pal. Got a minute?"

"No. Later," he replied, opening the door slightly.

"Ok, pal," Ibrahim said. "Look, I got that place for you."

"Uh-huh."

"So when you got time, you could just come there."

Katya listened closely, her heart pounding in fright.

"Where?" Ilya said.

"Sixty two, Spiridonovka. First floor. Great place. I'll wait there."

"No problem," Ilya replied, still agitated. He closed the door, turned quickly around and stripped the room with his eyes in search of something. He took a suitcase from the closet. He went to Anna's bedroom, opened the bottom drawer of the dresser and threw his clothes into the suitcase. "My life is changing, Mama," he said as he went through the room toward the door. "There's nothing you can do about it. Maybe there's nothing I can do."

"Oh, Ilya," Katya moaned. "You were always so good."

"No," he said. "You always wanted me to be good. You always thought I was good. You had me convinced of it. But your world's a dream. It doesn't exist and maybe never did exist. This is a new world and I intend to survive it."

"You're such a good boy," said Katya.

"Good?" he said. "What good is good? Good is weak. Good is vulnerable. I'll take my place without pretending to anything but what I am. Mixed. Good and bad. And which will rule? I won't tell you what I think."

"I love you," she said, taking his arm, "no matter what."

"Leave me alone!" he said and broke away with a twist.

Katya sat in shock as Ilya glared at her, left the flat and slammed the door behind him.

But Ilya had not yet gone over. There remained one person who would listen, probe, understand and finally say that he loved Ilya no matter what the circumstances were, no matter what Ilya might have done. That was Reilly, whose presence had sustained Ilya even in his worst moments. Ilya took as evidence of this devotion the fact that Reilly had given him the address of one of his safe apartments near the Moscow centre that no one else knew. A secret place, a special connection between them.

Ilya put his suitcase down, sat on the floor waited in the unlit flat. Reilly came but, having stopped at Anna's flat, was in a hurry. He hardly looked at Ilya until finally, clearly angry, he said, "What did you say to your mother?"

Ilya backed away from the language and tone he had used.

"I wanted her to know that I'm not a child anymore."

"You hurt her. You were rude and abusive."

"She deserved it. She owes me an apology. She never respected me." Ilya scratched the scar under his eye.

"Respect?" Reilly said, remembering for an instant the ugly circumstances in which he had broken from his father. He recognized in Ilya's behaviour the same impudence he had shown then. But the recognition flew off quickly, leaving behind only Reilly's self-directed anger, which had little to do with Ilya and much to do with how he thought he had hurt his father. Perhaps as the boy had hurt his mother.

"Respect, yes!" Ilya said.

"Be worthy of it."

A conversation that might have helped became a shouting match, lengthy and repetitive, until Ilya screamed:

"She had me out of wedlock! Does she deserve my respect?"

Reilly responded with a slap across Ilya's cheek that stunned the boy and turned his expression venomous.

Reilly spoke as though he were a different man in a different time and place when he said, "Get out. Stay out."

These words shook Ilya as badly as anything had ever shaken him, as badly as Reilly had been hurt when his father uttered them to him twenty-five years earlier. The boy threw himself to the door, stumbling, and barely found his way to the stairs.

Ilya walked around the block a few times before containing himself. The sum of the feelings from his meetings with his mother and Reilly merged into a nervous trembling and complete uncertainty about everything, especially the very strange thought that now his last hope for salvation might lie in Ibrahim. After a few blocks he stopped a passer-by and said, "This is Spiridonovka. Isn't this Spiridonovka?" The passer-by nodded, looked strangely at Ilya and hurried away.

Farther down the street he checked the address again. A few minutes later he found number sixty-two, walked the path to the front door and went inside. He stopped, glanced down and noticed a dark red patch on the floor. He looked away. The next door was open just an inch or so and a voice that sounded like Ibrahim's came from behind it. He noticed another fresh red smear in the wooden floor. He knocked. Ibrahim answered.

"Hey, Ilya, pal! Good to see you. C'mon in and tell me what you think of your flat."

Ilya walked slowly, apprehensively into the apartment, uncertain what lay ahead of him but aware that his very presence represented a decision about his life, character and soul. In the foyer two small dark red spots remained of a larger one that had been partially wiped away. He stepped over them. In the sitting room old furniture and the stale smell of old age told him that people had lived there for a long time. He imagined grandparents he had never known.

A suit jacket lay on the floor, ancient but sturdy except for a tear. Clean but for a red stain, worn with pride but cast off quickly in fear. It covered a pink sweater that had buttons like pearls, distinctively Russian and from an older time, torn at the neck with a few strands of grey hair at the top seam.

"Hey, pal," Ibrahim said, "take a look at the other rooms."

Ilya walked to the hallway on the left and found two bedrooms, a library filled with books and a bath. He went to the right past a bath and wandered into a large kitchen. In the kitchen a woman kneeled on the floor with a wet rag. She looked up and said, "Ilyushka."

"Hello, Comrade Antonida."

Ibrahim followed Ilya to the kitchen and produced a bottle of champagne and glasses. "Whaddaya think, pal?"

Comrade Antonida got to her feet and nodded at Ibrahim, who left the room. She said, "I hope you like it. We put ourselves on the line with Derzhinsky to get it."

"Why is it so important?"

"We like you," she said.

"It isn't just that," said Ilya. "There has to be more."

"Well, sure," she said. "When a comrade brings a boy like you, I mean a kid from a family like that, and helps him see the light. Well, it's a victory. Somebody young and smart and good looking. Maybe a leader. It makes us look good."

"Is that all?"

"It's up to you, comrade," she said. "Take a look around."

Ilya walked back through the hallway, glanced through the window at the street below and went into one of the bedrooms. He came back into the living room and stared at the dried blood, the old woman's sweater and the old man's jacket. Ibrahim and Antonida appeared in the hallway. They looked at each other and then at him. She nudged Ibrahim.

"Whaddaya think?" Ibrahim said.

Ilya walked to the window and looked out. Images of the jacket, sweater and blood stains stayed in his mind. He thought of going back to Anna's flat, apologizing to everyone and staying there. "Where are the former owners?"

"Moved," said Comrade Antonida. "Bolshevik Housing Committee helped them out."

Ilya imagined moving back to home to live with Katya. He glanced at the houses across the street, recalled the view from his old room that overlooked Fontanka Canal and imagined the young men and ladies who often held hands and tossed pebbles into the canal.

"It's a once in a lifetime deal," Ibrahim said.

It is a lifetime deal. If I take it I can't go back.

Ilya remembered silly messages he and Anna wrote to one another on the inside of the closet door that opened and closed next to an oak table. Once when he was a very young boy Grandmother Nadezhda Petrova baked cookies and left them to cool on that table. Ilya and Anna stuffed themselves with hot cookies and hid under the table when Nadezhda came back. She smiled, pretended not to know where they were and said, "My, my. Two little mice ate half of the cookies." Katya later spanked them.

What kind of future would I have if I went back?

"Think of what kind of place you'll wind up with if you let your family make your decisions," said Comrade Antonida. "What kind of life?" She looked at Ibrahim.

On Saturdays Nadezhda took Ilya and Anna around the house, let them wind up the clocks and promised they could wind them again the next day as well. But one Sunday Nadezhda went out early and never came back.

"The Tsar's police used to live in places like this," said Ibrahim. "Some of 'em probably still do. It's up to us to make sure only guys like us live like that now."

Ilya had not wound the clocks again. Much later Sasha told him why Nadezhda had not come home, though Ilya had only gradually come to understand. A peaceful woman, Nadezhda had been murdered because her presence threatened to deprive the militia of its pretext for brutality. An officer ordered her shot; that shot was followed by hundreds of others. That Bloody Sunday was burned into the Russian mind forever.

I'll never forgive them. They killed my grandmother and beat me.

"It's our job to bury all of 'em," Ibrahim said nervously. "That rat who beat you, why, he's dead but he ain't buried. Nah, he won't be buried until you say, 'This place is mine. I'm takin' it from you and your kind.' That's what's gonna bury every one of them, until there's only guys like us left."

Malibaev deserved what he got.

"Well?" Antonida said. "You want to bury them or not? The

guy who beat you. The one who killed Baba Nadia."

All the Tsar's henchman deserve it.

"The spy who got rich off a deal with the secret police to keep Lenin out of power. You ought to kill him yourself. You want to bury the past?" Antonida said.

Ilya turned around. "I want to bury it."

Ibrahim seemed to relax. He threw his hands into the air, palms up, shrugged and said, "Otherwise, well, it wouldn't be smart to give it away. It's your future. Where would you go?"

"Yeah," said Antonida.

"All right," said Ilya.

With a gleam in his eye, Ibrahim opened the bottle of champagne and poured three glasses. "Our new comrade," he said, exposing his yellow teeth and a crooked smile.

Ilya and Antonida raised their glassed, sipped and then gulped down the rest. Ilya put his glass down and marched through the other side of the flat and back. "I like it," he said.

Clouds drifted over Moscow and the air grew colder. On the streets a few people shuffled quickly along, their eyes to the ground. Katya waited well into the evening for Anna to come back from work. When she arrived, Katya embraced her and announced that she had bought train tickets.

Anna took off her overcoat, put it in the closet and noticed something missing. "Was Ilya here?" she said.

Katya nodded.

"What did he say?"

"He's lost, Anna. But I'll find him tomorrow and get him to open up to me, maybe get him to come home with us."

"You're dreaming," Anna said.

"I *am* tired. I think I'll go to bed." She walked to the closet and took out her overcoat. "Brrr," she said. "It's cold in the bedroom. No extra blankets. I'll cover myself with this."

"I'll stay up for a bit," Anna said. "I want to get ready for tomorrow. I'll clean up."

"Good night," said Katya. She carried her overcoat into the

bedroom closed the door behind her. She covered herself with the overcoat, lay down and turned off the lamp. Then for a while everything was silent. But cigarette smoke drifted under the door and spread into Katya's nostrils. She sneezed and then lay awake with her thoughts, unable to sleep.

38. Krepov

Anna sat in her robe, her head buried in her arms, her heart pounding with apprehension at the uncertainty of everything. Reilly's resistance movement, her family, her dancing, her future. Everyone's future. Russia's future.

It's the hour. I'm tired. Everyone's tired.

She imagined the Petrograd she had known before revolution had changed, smothered and starved it. Once it was a city of colours, of life, conversation, perpetual movement and more than anything, engagement. Now Petrograd was a city of greys where people moved quickly without so much as looking at the eyes of passers-by, terrified into their most private selves, although private life was gone.

Outside, someone swished through a pile of leaves. Anna sat up and looked outside, where a man came through the arch and headed for the building. She heard boot steps on the stairs and stumbling outside her door. She dropped down, looked under the door and saw what appeared to be boots. She held the two sides of her nightshirt together.

Ilya? Sidney? Sasha?

Someone pounded on the door. Anna silently cried, "Stop!" She took a deep breath and floated dreamlike toward the door, resisting but not able to stop, drawn irresistibly. She put her hand on the doorknob, twisted it and undid the latch. She opened the door slightly. Before she could see who was there, an arm stretched out and sent the door crashing into her. She pulled back and clutched her robe.

Krepov!

"What?!" she said in a low guttural voice that she hoped Katya would not hear.

He pushed his way through the doorway.

"You can't come in at this hour," she said, terrified, her hands squeezing both sides of her robe across her body.

He leered at her and said, "You don't like me, do you?" His eyes were red, his posture arrogant and his lips curled. He ran his fingers through his hair. He stank of alcohol.

"It's too late for a visit," she said. "You have to go."

He sneered. His eyes examined the dark flat. He took a step forward, moving as though drunk. She stepped back.

"You know," he said, "we have something in common."

What could I have in common with a murderer?

"Yes," he said. "Something in common."

"Get out."

"Are you related to Sasha Grammatikov?" he said, taking a step back. "I just want to know. Are you related to him?"

Don't provoke him. He's dangerous.

"No," she answered coldly.

"If you are," he said with a smirk, "I should kiss you."

"You'll have to leave," she said. "Get out."

"You are his niece." He moved toward her, stretched out his arms and swiped at her as she slipped back. He lunged forward, caught her arm and pulled her near.

"Get away!" said Anna. "Get back! Get out!"

He shook her back and forth. "You think you're so perfect?! You little slut!"

Anna twisted her body, spun around and broke away. "Get out!" she cried. "You filthy drunk!" He slapped at the air as she drew away from him. "Don't you touch me!" she cried and pushed him toward the door. "Get out!"

"You harlot!" he shouted and stood in the doorway. "A harlot who won't even kiss her own father!"

The bedroom door swung open. Katya stood in the doorway. She walked to him with a pistol raised and pointed it at his chest, just out of his reach. She slid the release button up, unlocking the weapon and planted her bare feet. "Give me an excuse to pull the trigger."

"He says he's my father," Anna cried, shaking. "He's not. Mama, tell me he's not!"

Katya kept her eyes on Krepov and said, "He's not your father, Anna. You have no father. Shall I kill you, Yuri? As you killed our Nadezhda? As you murdered my heart years ago? Tell me, Yuri, what should I do?"

"Oh!" Anna said.

Krepov slipped back, shifted his eyes nervously between mother and daughter and said, "The daughter's a whore, just like the mother. What should you do? Don't make me laugh. You'll do nothing." He moved closer to the door.

Katya held the pistol, aimed at him. "If you ever come back, Yuri Alexandrovich Krepov, I'll kill you."

Krepov opened the door and backed into the hallway. "You're a harlot, Katya, but beautiful. I'd take you now."

The crack of a gunshot interrupted Krepov. A bullet ripped into the door near his hand. He looked at the hole in absolute surprise, glanced again at Katya and then stumbled into the landing and down the stairs.

Katya closed the door and fastened the latch.

"Oh, God," Anna whimpered and covered her face.

Katya went to her. "Never mind, darling," she said. "You won't see him again."

"Why didn't you kill him?"

"I love myself more than I hate him. If I'd killed him, I'd have been his prisoner forever."

Anna broke away. "Maybe so," she said. "But if that pistol had been in my hand I'd have put a bullet in his head. My father, my blood. Now I hate a part of me."

"No," said Katya. "We've got tickets for tomorrow."

Anna walked to the window, looked outside and saw Krepov stumble through the archway to the street. "He is pathetic," she said. "Every part of him. I can't imagine what you were thinking or what you were doing with him."

Katya glanced at Anna and said, "It isn't your place to ask. But really, I don't know either."

They went to bed but neither slept much. In the morning Katya had tea. Anna dressed and prepared for work.

"Are you angry with me?" Anna said.

"No, but don't ask me about him again," Katya said.

"Are we going to Petrograd tonight?"

"Yes," said Katya. "I'll see you at seven. Train's at nine."

Anna confirmed, "You'll be by at seven?"

"Yes," Katya said. "At seven."

Anna packed, put on her overcoat and went to work.

39. What Would People Say?

Cold and dangerous was Petrograd in the early hours of the twenty-fourth of October, 1917. An impenetrable blackness hid the stars and moon. Clouds of fog swept mercilessly from the River Neva through the city streets. A church bell chimed and echoed through the darkness. River waves splashed against a ship, rocked it and crashed against the embankment of stone that seemed to stretch forever. The golden spires of the Peter and Paul Fortress were lost in fog.

In the early morning, in secret locations scattered through the city, men lit lamps, spoke in low voices over maps and tucked pistols inside leather jackets. They uttered oaths, vows and promises and made solemn embraces.

From one haven Volodia slipped quietly away into the quiet streets, his black leather jacket buttoned high with its collar turned up. He approached the Neva from a small lane, turned to the mansion that was the British Embassy and stopped, his vision limited to a few meters by the thick fog.

In a second-story window at the British Embassy a properly dressed naval officer peered through a spyglass into the darkness, unable to see more than a dim light that looked like a moon in hiding atop the Admiralty Tower. He opened his window to listen to the city but a cold, moist breeze forced him to close it. He kept his spyglass up, waiting. When he heard a knock at the rear door, dropped the spyglass on his bed and ran down to answer it.

Volodia stumbled. Between deep breaths he said, "Today."

Cromie pulled back.

Volodia said, "Tell them. Militia at the telegraph and telephone exchanges. Close down the Bolshevik press and guard the newspapers."

"I never quite imagined they'd really do it."

"Never mind," Volodia said. "The Winter Palace and the ministers are the prize. Tell Kerensky to fortify the palace immediately or the Bolsheviks will just walk in."

"What else?"

"Blockades with armed guards at the bridges."

"I'll call Savinkov. Where will you be?"

"With Derzhinsky, Trotsky, Lenin," Volodia said.

Cromie went to his office, called Savinkov and then sent a cipher to Reilly in Moscow.

Alexeyev and Savinkov arrived at the Winter Palace before daylight. Savinkov pounded on the door. "Get up!"

Kerensky answered the door in his bathrobe. He rubbed his eyes and said, "What?"

A pillow on the red divan told Savinkov that Kerensky had spent the night there, probably sleeplessly.

"Today," Savinkov said.

"What?"

Alexeyev said, "Minister, the Bolsheviks are attacking."

Kerensky ran his fingers through his short hair and put his hands on his hips. "What details can you give me?" He put his bare feet into his slippers, walked toward the bathroom and waved Savinkov and Alexeyev along behind him.

"First the Winter Palace and then telephone and telegraph exchanges," Savinkov said, following Kerensky through the bathroom as the Prime Minister peeled off his bathrobe, hung it carefully on a door hook and went into a bedroom.

"Then the newspapers," Alexeyev continued.

"What's Lenin's troop strength?" Kerensky said as he reached into a dresser drawer for a clean shirt.

"Few thousand at most," Savinkov said.

"If we act now and act smartly," said Alexeyev, "you can put

Lenin out of business."

"All right," Kerensky said as his hands fumbled through a closet and came out with an officers' uniform. He compared the colours of the tunic and the trousers, threw back the tunic and took out a different one. "How we are going to beat Lenin?" He slipped on his trousers. "Well?"

"Move troops in from Velikiye Luki," Alexeyev said.

"Velikiye Luki?" said Kerensky. "I ordered General Krymov to send those troops to Narva. What are they doing in Velikiye Luki?" He found a belt on the closet doorknob and a chest strap nearby on the floor. "Well, Boris?"

"Krymov killed himself. You were berserk, so I rescinded the order. The troops are still there."

Kerensky buttoned his tunic, tucked it into his trousers and threw on the chest strap and belt. "There you go again, Boris." He spotted his boots, hurried by his four-post bed and took the boots to a stool. "I told you I wouldn't let those men into the city because," he said, struggling to get the first boot on his leg, "a right wing coup is as bad as a Bolshevik coup."

The left boot was stubborn. Alexeyev kneeled down and helped him while Savinkov took charge of the right boot. As they fastened the buckles Kerensky continued, "You said I still have support in the local regiments. Send them where they are needed most. How many can you get?" He stood.

Alexeyev said, "A few hundred."

"You have to protect the premises," Savinkov said. "You need hundreds more."

"We have hundreds here already," Kerensky said.

Savinkov shook his head. "You have a few dozen military school cadets and a handful of women. Maybe a score more volunteers. That won't do."

"The Woman's Shock Battalion will be here in an hour."

"That won't do either," said Alexeyev.

"General, won't a few more from the garrisons come over?"

"I have five thousand who can crush Lenin's little army."

"Not from Velikiye Luki," said Kerensky.

"No," Alexeyev replied. "The irregulars here in the city. They'd die for you."

"Hah! They're ready to die for the chance to overthrow my government. No."

"You're not using your resources!" Savinkov said fighting his anger and frustration, "Or protecting the government!"

"I will defeat the Bolsheviks without subjecting the government to another attack."

"No," Alexeyev said. "Bring a thousand from Velikiye Luki or let me activate as many in the city. Or you've lost."

Savinkov said. "They'll take orders from the general."

"That's what you think!" Kerensky said as he put on his officer's hat and stood in the bathroom doorway. "Who do you think you're talking to? You're talking to Kerensky! That's who! I'll take decisive action! And I will still have my government and the revolution at the end of the day." He sped through the WC.

"All right," said Savinkov. "How long will you need?"

"Hours," said Kerensky. "By noon I'll have them."

Alexeyev said, "It's seven o'clock. I'll call you at ten."

"Very well," said Kerensky. "Go make your calls. Reconnoitre. Check in at ten." He strode through the door.

"Are we going to waste three hours?" said Savinkov.

"Is Reilly ready in Moscow?"

Savinkov nodded.

"Tell Cromie I'll wait 'til ten to see what Kerensky does."

They walked into the corridor, where mattresses and palace defenders' personal effects nearly filled the wide space. A few young men slept, and others were up and in various stages of dress. Fog and quiet sealed the tall windows.

"Are you sure it's today?" Alexeyev said.

"Reilly has a man on the inside," Savinkov said.

"Could he have been wrong?"

"He works for Derzhinsky."

"A man you trust?"

"One of our closest friends."

"Brave fellow," said Alexeyev. "Too bad we're wasting him

behind enemy lines."

"We're not wasting him. He's kept us in the game."

It was half-past seven. Savinkov said nothing more. He glanced at the centre of the square, with the top of the tall Column of Alexander almost visible through the fog. A pigeon flew through the mist, landed on a windowsill and squawked. Savinkov went inside. Alexeyev drove off.

As the sun burned its way into the sky, people appeared on the streets, went to work or looked for food queues. Petrograd seemed calm, peaceful and like any other day.

At eight-thirty small military vehicles brought one hundred forty women soldiers to the Winter Palace to stand guard with sixty cadets from a local military school. At the same time, reserve troops went to the newspaper buildings to protect the loyal papers and to close those with ties to Lenin. Others went to the telephone and telegraph exchanges. Lightly armed militia took up positions at bridges connecting central Petrograd with the other districts. By ten-thirty Kerensky thought he had thwarted the attack.

General Alexeyev returned. "What are my orders, Prime Minister?" he said.

In Moscow Reilly called members of the Syndicate with information and got assurance that they would remain there.

During the day of twenty-four October, 1917, no divisions of Bolshevik troops appeared on the streets of Petrograd. But at ten-forty in the morning, small groups of men began to approach the loyal militiamen at bridges and exchanges.

"Comrades!" they said. "We're reinforcements. Don't worry. We'll secure this bridge. We'll need your weapons."

Most of the militia guards turned over their weapons and walked away. By eleven o'clock, Lenin's Red Guards had almost all of the bridges and telephone exchanges in Petrograd; the Bolshevik newspaper, "Pravda," had reopened. At the bridges, Red Guards dismissed the militia troops.

"How many does Lenin have?" Alexeyev said.

Savinkov had received specific numbers from Volodia. "Six

hundred," he said.

At two-thirty, the city took on a strange apprehensiveness as people left their offices and the streets emptied.

At three o'clock Alexeyev went to the Military Palace to reassure the officers that reinforcements would come.

At three-thirty, members of the Soviet Military Committee arrived at the Military Palace and told the officers in charge that the building was now Soviet property and that they should go. The officers in charge called the Winter Palace for instructions. Savinkov told them to arrest the Soviet Military Committee members if they returned. When he went to check, the palace stood abandoned and its doors were open.

At five o'clock, Katya went out to make a final attempt to get Ilya back. She went up Tverskoi to Tverskaya Street, crossed over to Spiridonovka where Ilya lived and found the building without much trouble. She went up to the front door, knocked several times but got no response. She waited an hour, until six forty-five, and then went outside, afraid she might miss Anna at seven. She had fifteen minutes for a five minute walk. But once outside, the walk from the rear of the building to the house front left her disoriented. She went left on Spiridonovka and when she did not see Tverskaya, the familiar cross-street, she panicked and guessed wrong.

A pedestrian approached from the opposite way, and Katya asked directions. But the man hurried away without answering, as though she posed some immediate threat. Her heart thumped. She ran ahead, no street familiar, every intersection foreign and unfriendly. She entered an abandoned neighbourhood that was dark and quiet, and moved through it cautiously. A nearby gunshot sent her running back. "Anna," she cried. "Stay where you are. I'm late. I'm lost. God help me."

Late in the afternoon small units of Red guards occupied the Central Post Office and the banks, and secured bridges still guarded by the local militia. At the same time, Alexeyev and

Savinkov tried to stay the tempers of the loyal troops in Petrograd, pleading with undecided local reservists, though many were drunk. A handful offered their services on the condition that the Soviet issue orders.

"The Bolsheviks control the Soviets," Savinkov said.

The officers shrugged and said, "Our hands are tied."

Alexeyev returned to the Winter Palace as Savinkov briefly visited other local military regiments. They met at Kerensky's office to find the American Ambassador staring out the window.

"Where's Kerensky?" Savinkov said.

"Went out for reinforcements," the ambassador said.

"When?"

"Oh, a while ago. Lent him my embassy automobile."

"Where'd he go?"Alexeyev said.

"Tsarskoe Selo," the ambassador said. "Or Velikiye Luki."

Savinkov said, "Did Kerensky give you a brief, General?"

Alexeyev shook his head. "I have no orders."

"Oh, it's safe," the American Ambassador said. "I had them put little American flags on the car so everyone would know it's ours. Kerensky won't have any trouble."

"The reds are attacking," Alexeyev said.

"Yes, I understand that they are," the ambassador said.

"Idiot!" Savinkov said.

The ambassador did not reply.

Savinkov said, "Here is your brief, General: call Cromie at the British Embassy."

Savinkov rushed Alexeyev to one of the few phone lines that the Bolsheviks had failed to cut. First, on impulse, Savinkov tried Velikie Luki but failed to get through. Then he called the embassy.

"Cromie here," said the voice on the other end.

"Savinkov."

"How long?" Cromie said.

"We have an hour, maybe two."

Cromie went to the cipher room and at 8:30 sent the cable to Reilly over Savinkov's signature. It read, "Bolshevik attack underway. General Alexeyev requests authorization to use force to defend the Provisional Government of Russia. Estimate one-to-two hours remain. Reply British Embassy, Petrograd. (signed) Savinkov, Minister Without Portfolio."

Reilly took the cable to Syndicate Headquarters in Moscow and went to the meeting room where some were laughing at those who had moved the cars to safer grounds.

"You really think these clowns can defeat Alexeyev?"

"No," Reilly said, "not if we finish this business quickly."

At the same time, in Petrograd, General Alexeyev again called his officers and assured them that the approval process would be swift and was worth upholding.

"If we move now, we're traitors. Kerensky could have us shot, win or lose. Stay ready. Procedure is in process now."

"Bloody procedure," Savinkov muttered and walked off.

At Syndicate Headquarters in Moscow, Anna watched anxiously as the clock on her office wall ticked closer to seven. By seven thirty Katya had not arrived. Anna was impatient, squirming in her seat and tapping her fingers on her desk. She glanced at the clock again, and as it struck eight someone outside her door asked Tretyakov, "Where is Reilly? What's holding things up? We can't stay here forever. What if the Reds attack?"

Come on, Mama, you're late. Let's go. Take me home. Why are you late? Did you take a nap? Did you sleep through the alarm? Are you coming? Should I go out and try to find you?

Anna's thoughts flew in every direction. Where were Katya and Reilly? What pleasure it would be to kill Krepov!

Can a bullet kill a devil?

She glanced at her purse, where she'd put the pistol that rebels had given her that February day.

Katya will come soon. We'll go to Petrograd. The trains never leave on time. I'll have a life in Petrograd. I'll ignore this and keep what's good in me. I'll kill him.

Katya's words jumped to the fore of Anna's mind: "I'll be by at seven and we can go to the station."

Did she mean she would come here? No, she meant she'd get back to the flat by seven. No! She'll think I changed my mind and go without me!

Anna took her overcoat and purse, went through the library to the back door and ran across the lawn. She squeezed through a space between a fence and the adjacent building, ran across Big Nikita Street and hurried up several blocks. She stopped one block short of her home and glanced across the street at the block of apartments where Krepov lived. She rested against a thick tree, put her hand in her pocket and toyed with the safety lock on her pistol.

As one of the Syndicate leaders signed a document, he said to Reilly, "If you see General Alexeyev, tell him I think this whole thing is idiotic. The Bolsheviks want to take power and Alexeyev ought to have them shot."

Reilly took the document without comment and gave it to Tretyakov to sign.

"Excuse me," the telegraph operator said. "But the line has been cut. We won't be able to send that telegram."

Reilly cursed. "Cut."

"Yes, sir, sliced."

"Cars?"

"We moved them out to the suburbs."

"No telephone lines, no cars, no bicycles. The British Consulate's a half hour run. Give me the bloody documents."

Reilly hurried to the rear door and slammed it shut behind him. He was racing across through the back yard when an adolescent voice cracked out, "Sidney!" Reilly stopped.

Ilya came running up to him. "There was no answer at the door," he said. "I have to speak to you. It's the most important decision of my life. I don't know what to do."

"You'll have to make your decision without me, or wait here. I can't stop. Not now."

"I'll go with you," Ilya said.

"I'm not walking. I'm running. And I have to go now."

"Where are you going that's more important than me?"

Reilly was losing patience. "I've got twenty minutes to get to the British Consulate. And you're still limping."

"I'll keep up with you," Ilya pleaded, coming close. "I'll help. The short way?"

"Yes," Reilly said, pushing Ilya away by the shoulders. "But not with you. You go around front, knock and introduce yourself. I'll be back later."

Reilly twisted away and ignored Ilya's protests even as they turned ugly and obscene. His moment of patience had passed. He was focused on his mission and cared only about getting to the British Consulate. Quickly. The short way.

Fortune, meanwhile, crossed Katya's path as she stumbled along in panic. It came in successive waves: the familiar frame of the burned out structure where children lived; the crossing that led down Tverskoi Boulevard; the wide grassy park that separated two sides of the street, where older men played chess in warmer weather. Big Nikita Street gave her bearings: she realized she had spent the past hour going around the inner ring road but that somehow she had reversed her course. The relief she felt at familiar settings lulled her into a surreal cloud and released her only when an automobile ripped along Big Nikita, tore around the next corner and a few moments later screeched to a stop in the distance. She started up the next street, which after a few twists and turns would lead to Anna's flat.

Anna leaned against the thick tree across from Krepov's flat, the only sound the screeching wheels of a car on the other side of Krepov's building. Her heart raced. She thought of her fantasy of killing Krepov right there as he arrived at his flat. Then her obsession came alive and played the murderous scenario. She mimicked the physical actions, taking the pistol from her pocket, putting a bullet in the chamber and removing the safety catch. She leaned back against the tree and imagined his footsteps approaching. She raised her arms parallel to the ground and, as her imaginary victim came into her mind's view, took aim and squeezed a silent shot.

Bang.

Anna's heart thumped. She aimed again, this time at a silhouette behind a window shade in Krepov's building. But then the silhouette began to take Krepov's shape as it moved around the dimly lit room. She focused on the figure, certain it was he; and abruptly her blood ran cold.

All you have to do is aim and squeeze.

The street was silent, dark and empty. The light in the flat across the street went out. Anna kept her eye on that window and held her pistol ready.

Then at the far end of the street another silhouette appeared, running in her direction. Her heart beat faster.

Of course! The man in the window wasn't Krepov. He said his flat faced toward the Kremlin. The other way. But this one has the right silhouette. This is Krepov!

Anna held back against the tree and twisted around with slow, cat-like steps. She waited as his footsteps got closer. She took a step, spun around and extended both arms with the pistol firmly in her grip. When he vanished behind the tree, her finger tightened around the trigger. He appeared.

"God forgive me!" she said and awkwardly squeezed the trigger. A shot exploded; the victim crashed to the ground.

Did I shoot him? Am I a murderer?

In that same moment, as a new horror screamed inside her, she fell back against the tree and relived the sound of death, which had an unfamiliar ring. Then she pulled herself away, and as she approached the body her senses betrayed her. She stood confused, unsure of anything. A puff of smoke hung in the air across the street and the tall bushes around Krepov's building rustled as someone hurried away.

Nor was Krepov the man lying in blood on the ground.

It was Reilly.

"Sidney!" she shrieked, her hands at her temple.

Blood trickled from Reilly's head and coloured her dress, which touched the pavement. Reilly moaned, still alive.

"Help!" she said, now oblivious to everything but the horror that possessed her for what seemed an eternity. To everything, almost, until a man's voice said:

"What have you done to Reilly? What have you done?"

It might have been a moment of consciousness, of recognition of hope suddenly resurrected, a springboard to action. Instead it was one that compounded her horror as she realized that Reilly was on the brink of death, and that without him the Bolsheviks would seize Petrograd, her dream of love would die and Russia would fall to Lenin.

The masculine sound of the voice and the physical presence of the man towering above her could only have been the design of a demonic fate that had set the cruellest of terms for Reilly's survival, perhaps even for the survival of Russia. For the man who towered above her, the saviour named by fate, was Krepov.

I am insane.

"What did you do?" he said when he recognized Reilly. He picked up Anna's gun and tossed it away. When Anna cried, Krepov slapped her, held her by the wrists and said, "Stop. Help me get him inside. I know what to do."

"Someone should go," she said in a daze.

"The others have gone. I'm the only one left who knows what to do. I must go. It's up to me now." Krepov looked around desperately and said, "We can't attract attention."

Anna cried. Krepov shook her by the shoulders and said, "Get hold of yourself. Help me! Now!"

Anna watched Krepov rifle through Reilly's pockets, find a document and stuff it in his pocket. Then everything changed, and the physical reality of what happened next lagged behind, as though in a slow-motion cinema.

First came a small moment of comprehension, not just of Katya's sudden presence but also of the pistol in her mother's hand and of the years of suffering and hate in her mother's voice. Of course the recognition did not preclude Anna's shock as the blast shook the air, sent a small metal bullet moving toward Krepov's temple, blew out a piece of his head and felled him helplessly to the ground where he lay still with horror written in his open but unmoving eyes.

Katya rushed to Anna and said, "Darling! Did he hurt you? Are you all right?"

Anna looked at Reilly, who seemed to be breathing.

"It's Sidney!" Katya said.

Anna did not hear Katya. "Something important."

"What?" Katya said.

"Something important about stopping Lenin. But he never told me what it was. But Krepov knew. Only Krepov knew."

Reilly opened his eyes and tried to speak. Anna leaned over and put her ear near his lips and heard only a whisper, "General Alexeyev," before he closed his eyes and moaned.

"What are we going to do?" Katya said.

Anna said, "We'll take him back to the house where I work."

They lifted Reilly up, though he was semi-unconscious and limp. Katya turned to Krepov's body and said:

"The devil take you, Yuri Alexandrovich."

A cold wind roared up the street, howling like cruel laughter. Clumsily, Katya and Anna dragged Reilly through the cold October night toward the yellow mansion on Tverskoi Boulevard that in the present circumstances, seemed very far away. And in the heavy mist, a single streak of lightening cracked through the dark Moscow sky.

Book Two: Assassination and Terror

Characters Introduced in Book 2

Representatives of the German Government

Rudolph Bauer – Intelligence Chief
Lt. Mueller – Embassy adjutant
Count von Mirbach – Ambassador
Helferrich – Mirbach's successor as ambassador

SRs, Socialist Revolutionary Party Oppositionists

Alexandrovich- leader of SR faction in the Moscow Cheka
Colonel Popov – SR Cheka Officer
Jacob Blyumkin – SR Chekist, Assassin
Andreyev – Blyumkin's minder
Fanny Kaplan – SR, alleged assassin
Maria Spiridonova – SR
Semyenov – SR

Bolsheviks

Peters, Chekist second to Derzhinsky

References

London Centre –London Spy Service headquarters
Cheka – Derzhinsky's terrorist secret police
SR Chekists – SRs inside the Cheka who oppose Derzhinsky.

Part V: The Mirbach Incident

Moscow, January-July, 1918

40. After the Putsch

As soon as Anna and Katya brought the semi-conscious Reilly to the yellow house on Tverskoi Boulevard, the patriots of the Syndicate gave up hope and went out to the suburbs for their cars. Some drove to Tsarskoe Selo or Gatchina to seek protection under the shield of Russian Army units stationed there. Others tried to escape to Kiev and south, where divisions of the White Army had encamped. Only Tretyakov and Doctor Kostin remained in the house. Kostin treated Reilly for superficial wounds, though at first there was some concern for his vision. He stayed for a week at Anna's flat and then went back to London with one Major Fothergil, whom the one-legged spy master at London Centre had sent to retrieve him. Katya went back to Petrograd, leaving Anna to wait impatiently for Reilly to return.

A notepad-size journal sat on the table near the window in Anna's apartment, opened with the front cover and just a few pages pressed back. The two open pages were unused, but at the top of the left one the date was printed in black publisher's ink in classical Cyrillic type-face. It said '10 January 1918'. Between the two pages was a thin black ribbon, attached to the binding. A mahogany capped fountain-pen rested in the same crack and a small jar of blue ink sat close to the edge of the table. Near the jar was an ashtray with a single, crushed cigarette butt, and beyond the ashtray the bottom of the white window frame hung suspended about an inch from the sill. A cool breeze came through the space and sent some cigarette ashes swirling into the air and onto the table. Anna lifted the ashtray, wiped the table with a cloth and leaned down to blow a few straggling ashes through the small window opening.

From outside came the sounds of boots stomping through

the snow, dim thumps at first but then loud squeaking noises as someone approached the building, crunching the top layer of snow into the bottom one. They moved on and faded out somewhere near the end of the lane or across the street.

In the opposite direction, a few houses up the lane, a man's laughter preceded the delighted cries of children. In a moment he appeared in the street, pulling a sled that carried several youngsters. A snowball flew through the air and exploded into a tree. The children on the small sleigh cheered. Anna smiled. The father laughed as a snowball exploded into the back of his overcoat and sent a cloud of flurries into the air. They reached the end of the street, turned around and repeated their journey in the opposite direction. From somewhere nearby a single gunshot echoed through the neighbourhood with more children's laughter and delight.

Anna took the fountain pen from the open diary and put it in her overcoat pocket with some papers and a pencil. She glanced at Reilly's photograph. Men from the British Embassy had taken him to London after his recovery. Volodia said he had received a message. Reilly would return. The British were coming to save Russia.

She opened the front door, locked it from the outside and glanced at the avant garde paintings on the yellow walls of the hallway as she slid her hand along the black cast iron railings and descended the wide staircase to the street. The lobby was dark with shadows. The sun was blinding and the sky a magical turquoise blue, pure as the white snow on the street and clear as the water that dripped slowly from trees covered with icicles that were doomed by a January thaw.

Anna loosened her scarf and unbuttoned the top of her overcoat as she walked through the arch into the street. She went to the corner and then to Tverskaya Street. Some of the buildings on the right side of Big Nikita Street had windows partly open. Anna gazed at them with astonishment. In Moscow, January was a month of near imprisonment and temperatures above freezing were rare. On the left she passed a salon and through its glass-front window saw people sitting at small round tables that had red and white checked table cloths. They smoked cigarettes, drank tea, immersed themselves in conversation and even laughed.

What has come over Moscow?

She opened the door, went inside and spied a free seat at a table otherwise occupied by two older men. She glanced at the empty chair. One of the men gestured to the seat and smiled at her. "Please, child," he said. "Take a seat."

Anna sat down. "Is there a waiter?"

"No," one of the men said. "Tea?" he said, rising up.

Anna smiled. The man skirted through the crowded café, said something to the proprietor and made his way back. In a moment the proprietor brought a cup of tea and a pinch of sugar, a silver demitasse spoon and a small, wrinkled linen napkin. He filled the little space on the table in front of her. She said "Thank you" to the proprietor and then smiled at the two men seated at the table who were too wrapped up in their conversation to notice her gesture. She took the newspaper, opened it and pretended to read. Then she folded it, put it away and took out her journal and pencil.

I don't want news, but just to be here with real people. It's been so long. Everyone is in such a good mood.

At a table behind her someone spoke loudly enough to be heard above the other voices in the café. "We've been moping around long enough! Do they have vodka?"

"What does it matter anyhow?" someone said. "This so-called government won't last another two weeks."

"Right," said another. "The Germans will invade soon enough anyway, and we'll be rid of these Bolshie clowns."

"I heard the French or British were coming."

"The Bolsheviks will destroy themselves."

At another table a woman spoke almost loudly enough to compete with the others. "My nephew got out with his wife and daughter. They went south, to Kiev. My sister sold all their things on the street. It'll be no time before the Bolsheviks take their house. Ours too. But we can eat."

"When the Allies come, they'll bring food for everyone."

"One way or another, someone will come to save us."

"Yes, we're too important for Europe to forget. They'll come. You just wait. They'll come and we'll all be saved."

"I heard the Japanese are coming. That they're already in Vladivostok, and they're taking the Trans-Siberian railway. They'll be in Moscow in a week."

"The Allies will get here first."

Then a man stood up and shouted, "They'll come! They'll all come! But the Reds will shoot all of us before that!"

The conversations died down but no one looked at him. Anna finished her tea, held the newspaper in front of her face, put it down and wrote a few lines in her journal.

Someone said, "We need the Constituent Assembly and elections for a real government. I heard it was coming soon."

"The Constituent Assembly is our last hope."

"Our last chance to save the revolution."

"Our last chance for democracy."

"Our only hope."

"You fools!" someone said. "Don't you know? Didn't anyone tell you? Lenin cancelled the Constituent Assembly. The SRs protested and Lenin had them shot."

"That's not in the papers!"

"It was blacked out!"

"So much for your democracy! You'd better pray the Allies or the Japanese come to save you. Because that fellow is right. The Bolsheviks are going to shoot all of us!"

The Russian mood's as fickle as the Russian weather.

Anna folded the paper, got up and put it back on the seat. She tucked her pencil and journal into her overcoat, smiled at the two men who looked up and smiled back, and left the salon. She headed to Tverskaya, half a block away, crossed through the snow that was melting into slush and noticed neither horse carriages nor cars in any direction.

The Kremlin stood near the bottom of Tverskaya Street.

Ahead, several blocks away, she saw the top of the Bolshoi Theatre. She took her journal and the other documents from her overcoat and paged through them until she found the right one. She studied it for a moment, glanced up at the building, went to the entrance and walked inside.

The foyer was long, wide and filthy. Drapes hung over the walls, which a few open spaces told her were blue with gold trim. A canvas cover hid the ceiling and four chandeliers that made impressions but did not poke through. An electric lamp hung suspended on a wooden pole. Behind the pole was a door. Anna knocked. It opened, revealing a tall, slim man in a black tunic and black trousers.

"Who are you?" he said.

She handed him the documents, put the journal back inside her overcoat and said, "I'm Anna. I was accepted for the spring term. I've come to register."

"I'm Daniel Sergeiivich," he said, returning the documents. "I remember. Ksheshinskaya sent a letter. No one has heard from her since."

"The Bolsheviks took her house. She escaped."

"A common practice these days," he said. "They took this one too. I'm just cleaning out my desk." He looked at her sympathetically. "The spring term's been cancelled."

"What about the dancing school? Won't it be open?"

"That depends on moon-man, or whatever he's called, the Bolshevik Commissar of Culture. I've been dismissed with the faculty for having a bourgeois background."

"No," said Anna.

"Yes," said Daniel Sergeiivich.

"What should I do?" Anna said.

"Go to America," he said. "They still have dancers there."

"I want to dance at the Bolshoi Theatre," she said.

"Perhaps. But don't say anything about Ksheshinskaya."

"What are you going to do?"

"I'm leaving."

"Where will you go?"

"Where there are no Bolsheviks. I suggest you do it too."

"I'm not leaving," she said. "I want to dance in Moscow."

Daniel Sergeiivich reached out to a clothing rack, took a black overcoat and put it on. He nodded in a friendly and sympathetic way as he took a black fur hat from the top of his desk. "Maybe one of these days I'll pick up a magazine in some Paris café and read about you." He smiled, put the hat on his head and stepped around Anna. "Goodbye," he said. "Maybe you'll turn out the lamp when you leave." He walked through the dreary foyer, opened the door and left.

Now what will I do?

An explosion sounded from outside. Anna turned off the lamp, opened the door and peeked through the crack. The sky had turned dark grey. Another explosion sounded from somewhere nearby. She put on her hat as lightening flashed in the sky. She stepped outside, stood on the covered steps and lit a cigarette. The skies opened and rain poured down.

It's January. It's not weather or mood. Life's fickle.

She leaned against the front door, sucked on the cigarette and watched the top layers of snow melt away under the rain.

Now it's just strange. But later it'll all be ice. The streets of Moscow will have no snow but everything will be covered with six inches of ice.

Several cigarettes later, the rain turned to snow. Anna left the former Moscow Dance School and went to Big Nikita Street. She saw a rainbow over the Bolshoi Theatre. The Theatre's huge Corinthian columns were filthy. A few black cars were parked in front. The door opened and a man came out. "Excuse me." she said, "I'm here to see the director."

The man stopped. "Bourgeoisie?" he said.

"No," she said. "Dancer."

"I can't do anything for you. You have to go to the employment department, near the Kremlin. Tell them you want to dance. Maybe they can do something."

"Are people still coming to the Theatre?"

"Yes," he said. "In fact, we've had full houses recently."

"Then there's hope," she said.

"For some of us," he replied and walked off.

Anna looked around. The snow had stopped and the clouds were breaking up. Down the street, at Lubyanka Square, people were milling around. She walked past the Metropol Hotel toward the square, where the scene was familiar and yet not. On one side high school girls, older women and former officers were selling things. Clothing, expensive knick knacks, silverware, army overcoats and hats, a stack of books, a pair of black knee-high boots. At the Lubyanka Insurance Building, older women sold food. They had dried meat, preserved vegetables and fruit, some tea, most of which had been produced the previous summer and stashed in a cellar or separate area in a country house.

An officer took a few kopeks he'd received in exchange for a heavy military jacket, gave them to one of the old women and walked off with a bag of millet and a handful of sesame seeds. A woman in a cloth coat took five kopecks and gave them to a peasant lady for a half-jar of preserves. Anna looked at the foods. "What is it?" she said.

"Strawberries."

"How much?"

The peasant woman looked her over. "Five rubles."

"You sold the other jar for five kopeks," said Anna.

"That was half a jar, dearie," the old woman said. "Besides, you could get a few rubles for that nice bourgeois overcoat and fur hat. What's an old lady supposed to do?"

"Two rubles," Anna said.

"Four," the woman said.

"Three," Anna countered.

"You look like you could use a bite to eat, dearie," the woman said. "Four's a favour, a good deal."

Anna gave the woman four rubles. The woman handed her the jar. Nearby a group of men and a few women gathered noisily around an empty blanket. Anna walked to the edge of the crowd. "Where's the employment office?"

"It's all the fault of the old government!" someone shouted. A woman shook her finger. "Well, I can't see much good coming from the Bolsheviks," she said. "I was a piano teacher but I had to sell my piano." Everyone joined in an argument. A small man stood by, a worker or a peasant. His smile was cynical and condescending.

"Who cares whose fault it is," said a man who seemed educated. "The point is, what are we going to do? Are we going to take responsibility or give way to the Germans?"

"Yes," one said. "The Germans will lock everyone up."

"The Germans will bring order," someone else said.

"Who's going to pay for what's happened to us?"

"We're paying now!"

"We'll pay the Germans!"

The small man with the cynical smile raised his fist. "The Germans are coming! But before they get here we'll kill all of you! That'll show you who's in control!"

The educated man tried to reason with him. A bourgeois woman cursed. The man with the cynical smile put his fist into the pocket of his filthy overcoat. Anna thought the pocket bulged more than it should for a mere fist. She skirted away from the crowd. In front of the Lubyanka Insurance Building someone gave her directions to the employment office. She set out toward the Kremlin.

It took half an hour. The building was tall and wooden with shutters covering the windows. The paint was light green and the earlier layer, exposed in numerous areas, was a darker blue. A line filled the street in front, twisted around a corner and broke into various clusters of debate. Anna went up wooden steps, twisted the knob and pulled.

"It's locked," someone in the line said. "Start at the end."

Anna pursed her lips and nodded. As she turned to go down the steps the door opened behind her, a young officer came out wearing a ragged grey military overcoat, his hat and a paper in his hand. His eyes were empty and his face sallow but rugged and handsome. He might have commanded a unit at the front. The obvious but failed attempts to keep his beard trimmed suggested aristocracy and a dull razor. He was alive, so he was lucky. That he looked defeated made him seem completely normal. Anna walked next to him.

"Looking for work?" she said.

He stared quietly at her, frightened, and nodded.

"What's your line of work?" she said.

He shook his head.

"What did the officials say?"

"Officials?"

"The people you spoke to about a job."

"They weren't officials," he said. "Just police hooligans."

"Wouldn't expect Lenin's secret police to be much help."

He put on his hat, unfolded the paper and offered it.

"What is it?" she said. At the top it said, 'Search Warrant'.

"What does it look like?" he said.

"It looks like a search warrant," Anna said.

"They laughed at me when I asked for a job. They said there was nothing for a class enemy like me. I told them I was hungry and would do anything. They gave me a search warrant and said, 'Go steal something. Just shake down a few bourgeoisie. That should teach you how to make an honest living.' Probably still laughing."

"What will you do?"

The young officer tore up the warrant, wiped something from the corner of his eye and said in a shaky voice, "I don't know." Anna followed the line around the corner. The young officer continued on without speaking or looking back.

As Anna stood in line the clouds again filled the skies and the day got darker until, in mid-afternoon, evening came to Moscow. The door to the employment office remained locked. Some in the queue, unwilling to relinquish their rank in line, hunkered down for an all-night wait. Again snow fell, at first flurries but soon in persistent squalls. Most of the line dissolved. Anna walked off among numerous others, her legs tired and her throat sore. As she stood with a small cluster of people waiting for a tram, the snow came in full force, pushing and pulling, blinding, the air chilling and soon bitterly cold. After a while, through the foggy grey-white sheets of snow, a tram moved toward the stop with agonizing slowness, the front appearing first, surreal and mystical, revealing its body gradually, in slow-motion. Anna climbed aboard, paid her fare and squeezed into a seat near the front as someone abruptly got up and jumped off.

The tram jerked forward and slowly wound its way from the Kremlin. It stopped at each of the next few blocks and exchanged passengers for pedestrians. At Big Nikita Street Anna rose from her seat, walked a few feet toward the door and stood behind several other women waiting to disembark.

The tram slowed to a stop at the next block. Anna moved forward when the door opened and jumped from the steps to the street. She stopped at a kiosk on the corner and bought a paper. She walked back to Big Nikita and her street, glanced at her building and saw that the lamp in the window was lit.

The smell of cooked sausage came from under the door of the flat. She nervously put the key into the door lock, quietly twisted it and nudged the door open. She stepped into the flat, where the odour of sausage was thick and mouth-watering. "Who's there?" she said assertively.

"Anna!" It was a woman's voice. In a moment Natasha emerged from the bedroom. Their embrace was long, filled with smiles, laughter and tears. Natasha had gone home to Petrograd before the Bolshevik putsch. Anna had not heard from her since and had feared for her safety.

"How is Petrograd?"

"Bad," said Natasha. "Cold, hungry and afraid."

"How are your parents?"

Natasha closed her eyes. "They're arresting people who worked for the old government. Mama and Papa were terrified. They packed what they could, locked up the house, took their money from the bank and left the city for Kiev."

Anna threw her hands over her mouth. "No!"

"They're taking over houses in Petrograd. They come in the

morning and tell you to get out by night. They shoot resisters. Secret police, the Cheka. Lenin let them out of jail. Men with a grudge. You can't deal with them. They enjoy hurting people. They enjoy killing."

"Did you see my mother?"

"Go back, Anna. Katya's a wreck. She looks years older."

"Is she still in the house?"

"She's still there," said Natasha. She gave Anna a letter.

"She doesn't sound too bad. She still has some hope."

"Until they take her house. Then what will she do?"

"No," said Anna. "She says the house is on a protected list. She's a registered house tenant. So are you and I. You must have told her about your parents."

"Just before I left..."

"She got Sasha, Volodia, Sidney and Ilya on the list as tenants too. We can go back there and be safe if we need to. For some reason our house is protected."

Volodia did this. God bless him.

The young women sat down at the small table and shared a meal of sausage and preserves. Natasha told her story. Anna told hers. Late in the evening, they agreed to continue their conversation in the morning. Then Natasha said, "You haven't said a word about your brother. Is Ilya all right?"

Anna shook her head. "We lost him to the Bolsheviks."

The lights went out. Through the night the windows rattled. Iced branches cracked against the side of the building; bits of shattered ice and clumps of hardened snow exploded on the caked surface below. The moon hid and the wind howled, haunting screams, dream-like. But on this January night there was no gunfire on the streets of Moscow.

"I need rubles," Anna said and sipped tea. "All I have is the British money that Sidney gave me."

"They shoot speculators, you know," Natasha said, resting a cup in a saucer. "But maybe there's someone who'll buy it. At Izmaelavo Park, or the market at Lubyanka."

"I've been by Lubyanka a few times," said Anna. "A regular

zoo. They come in from the countryside with bags of food to sell to the city people. Maybe one of them."

"Peasant women? Don't be crazy. They'd sell you out in a minute. They'd go to the Cheka and collect a reward."

But the peasant women would be there. Neither the snow that filled the streets nor the cold wind that gusted through the square could stop them from coming to Moscow. They stood bundled behind their produce with thick scarves wrapped around their heads. Their dresses hung beneath the bottoms of their patchwork woollen coats and flirted with snowdrifts as the early afternoon shadows of the Metropol Hotel and Bolshoi Theatre rolled slowly by. Mixed among them were bourgeoisie who brought their remaining silverware or engraved volumes or blue French overcoats or British shirts. A line of older officers offered newspapers or Army hats or blouses replete with ribbons of valour won against the Germans or the Turks.

Anna and Natasha passed by the Bolshoi Theatre, skirted the hotel and came into the square from the Petrovsky side, where most of the peasants had set up their blanket-shops.

"Let's just walk around and see if we can figure out how the system works," said Natasha. They separated. Anna passed by the officers and some school girls.

Everywhere I look the faces are filled with hopelessness. Those officers were the pride of Russia. Now their eyes are empty. These young ones should be in school? Have the schools closed? The old men have no future. But what about these young girls? From good families but now beggars or prostitutes. What do they think of their future?

"Here, child," said an old soldier who had a few newspapers. He reached into his overcoat pocket, brought out sunflower seeds held out his palm. "Just ten kopecks."

"No thank you," she said. "But is that today's paper?"

He smiled through his military moustache and said, "So you're a modern girl. Yes, I have Russian News. Today's. And I have yesterday's Russian Word."

"Which one would tell me about the British?"

"The British?" he said.

"About when the British will come to save us."

"You're dreaming, child. That would be the Russian Word. But the British aren't coming to save us. If we're lucky the Germans will come and conquer us. Then maybe we'll be saved." He leaned forward. "You know, I hear the Germans really are coming. Taking the train from the south. Can you imagine it? A railroad war. They buy tickets, jump on the train and come north to Petrograd. It's all in here," he said, pointing to the newspaper called 'Russian Word.'

"I'll take both," Anna said and gave the man a rouble. "I'll give you another rouble for some advice."

"What's that, child?"

"How would you exchange British money for rubles?"

Who would trade British money for rubles?"

"You, if you wanted food but had only foreign money."

Natasha returned. Anna found the money-changer and swapped her British money for rubles. She turned to the old soldier, who nodded his approval and said, "Papers and sunflower seeds! I've got newspapers and sunflower seeds!"

They walked arm in arm toward Tverskaya Street as the afternoon clouds coughed up their hourly attack of snow. They went a few blocks up and found a kiosk that had cigarettes. Anna bought a pack and they walked home.

Upstairs, the flat was cold. The women sat at the small table bundled up, the window next to it closed and locked and the room filled with a thin cloud of smoke from British cigarettes. They drank warm tea, read books and talked.

Anna took out the newspapers she had bought and opened the one called 'Russian Word.' She read reports of fighting at the front, of Lenin's scheme for a separate peace treaty with Germany, of soldiers fleeing from Moscow and Petrograd because according to rumours German troops were approaching from the south by rail.

She read all the stories and wondered what the censors had replaced with black blotches on some pages. She read headlines such as "General Yanushkov Executed by Soviet Counsel of

Pokrovskoye Village." Or "Allied Imperialists Will Try to Topple People's Government!"

Anna put the paper down and shuddered. Natasha went to bed. Anna turned off the lamp, sat by the window and looked out at the quiet night. The streetlamps were out but the moon, partly visible through small openings in the clouds, lit portions of the night. Anna got up, folded the newspaper and slid it under the small table. Shivering, she drew the curtain and walked quietly to her bedroom.

In late February Anna went to Petrograd in a train filled with soldiers, most of whom did not make it all the way. Seats began to empty just forty miles outside Moscow, at the village of Klin, as troops detrained in small clusters and disappeared into the countryside. So too, at the next stop and the one after that. The train stopped at all the stations, at locations were there were no stations and at each stage the number of available seats grew. A certain nervousness floated in the railcar, as though to go further on was to tempt fate. Anna looked at a soldier seated nearby, across the aisle.

"Where are the soldiers going?" she said. "To a battle?"

The soldier smiled. "They want to avoid battles."

"They're running?"

The soldier shrugged. "The Germans are going to attack."

"They got on in Moscow. It's a long time to Petrograd."

"They say Germans will attack both cities. So the troops want to avoid both cities."

"I thought they were going to sign a peace treaty. Why fight if there's going to be a peace treaty? If there's a peace treaty the Germans won't attack."

"Maybe not," he said, "but then again they might."

"Then who's going to defend the cities?"

"Maybe the Bolsheviks," he said. "It's their peace treaty."

"Nonsense," said someone else. "Lenin's moving his government to Moscow. Nobody will defend Petrograd and no one's waiting in Moscow for the Germans to attack. No one's defending anything."

The train passed encampments outside the city, where little was happening. Likewise the Moscow Train Station in Petrograd had no more soldiers than usual, though large numbers of civilians waited to board the train to the south. They carried suitcases, canvas bags or even sheets and pillow cases filled with possessions while men who looked prosperous enough to be Bolshevik government officials carried boxes of documents and office supplies. It was the same as the other excursions she had taken through railroad stations in the last year, with the addition of the officials.

But this time, in Petrograd, something was different. The people waiting to depart did not have the hopeful look of the travellers she had seen before, men and women to whom the prospect of leaving Petrograd or Russia meant the possibility of a new life somewhere else. Their pride was gone and their expressions filled with neither hope nor despair but with pity. Anna stopped a woman near the entrance. "What is it?" she said. "What emptiness on all these faces!"

"Haven't you heard?" said the lady. "The Bolsheviks are moving the capital to Moscow. They've abandoned Petrograd. Abandoned her to the German Army or to starvation. We're dying." She covered her face and ran off.

Abandoned Petrograd? St. Petersburg? Our city?

Anna bought a paper at a kiosk and went to the street. The Nevsky Prospect was cold and empty, swept by cruel winds from the River Neva, its grandeur buried under boards that covered the shop windows and doors and by the food queues. Rain had melted the snow and ice and in places the sun might have been trying to break through the dark grey clouds, but Petrograd seemed a city without colours.

Anna walked to the Fontanka Canal and stood at the stone wall. The ice on the water was grey and partly covered by debris and junk, items that would not burn in a fireplace or could not be dissembled for any other use.

Junk, in my Fontanka Canal!

A few people passed by, talking quietly about the Germans and how the Bolsheviks had abandoned the city to their army. But she saw no German soldiers. Across the canal, to the right, pale green paint was peeling away from the mansion that nearly filled the block. The yellow mansion on the left side was less yellow than Anna remembered. Workers came and went through the wide front door. The occupants had gone away.

There were a few boards over the windows of the mansion on the corner at Fontanka: glass and glassmakers were impossible to find. Large parts of the roof looked ready to fall in or slide off into the street. But the red stone house to its right seemed solid and well cared-for. Curtains were parted in the windows, which were clean and had no boards. Smoke rose from a chimney. Branches of giant spruces towered over the roof as lower ones brushed gently against the windows.

"I've seen only Volodia," Katya said. "Our friends are gone."

"Petrograd looks like a dying city," Anna said.

"Does Moscow look any better?" Katya said.

"No. Sasha's still on the inside. I see him several nights a week, but only for a few minutes. He sends love. And Sidney went to London. He'll be back."

A ray of sun broke through the kitchen window. The top of the faucet over the sink glistened. Outside the clouds dispersed and the sky turned blue. The kitchen lit up.

"They say the Germans are coming," Katya said. "I hear it every time I go out. Coming by train. Coming by air. I'm tempted to go to the countryside to live. But I'd die of loneliness. Of course, it's lonely but we still have people."

Anna nodded. "I'd die out there too. But the Germans? I hear Lenin's going to sign a peace agreement. For us the war's over. At least for now. Believe me, the Germans aren't coming. They're sending their troops to France. They're not interested in Russia or in hurting anyone here. Don't worry."

"Do you want something to eat?"

"Brought some things and ate on the train," Anna said. "Go

ahead. Eat, if you like."

"We'll go for a walk," Katya said and went upstairs.

Anna looked at her newspaper, lit a cigarette and sipped her tea. The headline said, "Lockhart, British Envoy, Returns." Anna knew the name. "The British diplomat has been granted official unofficial consular status with diplomatic privileges in a possible first step in Britain's recognition of Soviets." *No!*

"Soviet representative Litvinov, based in London, has equal consular status." Anna shook her head.

"Lockhart has spent most of this week in meetings with Trotsky and will go to Moscow soon to assume his position at the British Consulate. Meanwhile, the British Embassy in Petrograd will remain open with a reduced staff."

What is this? The British can't recognize the Soviet Government. Sidney's coming back to Russia.

Katya appeared in the doorway. They got their boots and went out the back door. They stopped at the Nevsky crossed the empty street. They strolled to a bridge; on the far side was a Palace that the Bolsheviks had taken, and ahead the canal opened up into the River Neva. On the right was their own street, the Fontanka Embankment, and nearby the building that once housed the Tsar's secret police. They went to the centre of the bridge over the canal, leaned against the stone and iron railing under a cool blue sky.

"You know, Mama," said Anna. "Russia is beautiful but such a wreck. Our life is always such a struggle." She gazed at the wide River Neva and across it to the Vyborg side. "Was I wrong about the war? Germany couldn't have done worse than the Bolsheviks." In the distance a speck appeared in the sky and glistened in the sun.

"No, darling," said Katya. "You were always right. No one could've done worse than the Bolsheviks, that's true. But my greatest fear hasn't been the Bolsheviks, but German bombs falling on our city. I'm glad the war is over for us."

The speck glistened again in the distance. "Look," said Anna. "An airplane? Or a kite?"

"I haven't seen an airplane in the sky for ages," said Katya. "I think it's a kite or a bird." She looked at Anna gazing into the distance. "I'm worried about Sasha," she said. "It's dangerous for him to work near Derzhinsky. When Sidney comes I want him to get Sasha out of the Cheka."

The speck grew closer. It might have been an eagle on the descent, or an airplane about to fly low across the city. But it was flying too fast to be a kite.

"You know, Mama, I miss Sidney." She watched the object approach and said, "It's an airplane."

"I miss Sidney too," said Katya, shielding her eyes with her hand as she studied the approaching airplane. Then, when the plane was almost overhead, not more than a few hundred feet in the air, she said, "Look, a German sign on the wing."

The airplane engine filled the Fontanka Canal with loud mechanical noise and, suddenly, as it flew overhead something fell from its underside.

"A bomb!" Katya took Anna's arm and said, "Run!"

They rushed toward the far side of the canal as the bomb exploded near the headquarters of the old Okhrana secret police. They ducked down as chunks of cement and stone flew into the air, into the water and even across the canal, shattering nearby windows and crashing everywhere. A cloud of debris hovered overhead and the echo of the blast reverberated far down the length of the Fontanka Canal. Dust and debris showered down on them. They stood up, dusted one another off and looked at the scene in amazement. The German airplane vanished over the city.

Tears came to Katya's eyes.

Anna caressed her. "It's all right, Mama."

"The Germans just blew up our street. It's not all right."

Anna looked into the distance. "I know it's not, Mama."

"I want to go home," Katya whimpered.

Anna clutched Katya and led her over the stone bridge.

They walked toward the Nevsky as curious residents came out to see the small crater that the bomb had left behind, some staring absently at the shattered windows.

"Don't worry, Mama," Anna said. "We'll get Sasha away from Derzhinsky. We'll bring everyone back. Our house will be full again. Just wait 'til Sidney comes home."

"Are you sure?" Katya said. "When will he come?"

"Soon," Anna said. "A British diplomat called Lockhart is in Russia. The British will help. Sidney will come back."

When they arrived at the station, Anna saw Lockhart standing with Peters and a woman. She edged closer and witnessed the interplay of the three: Peters said, "You're a sport, Lockhart. Thanks for taking Moura to Moscow." Anna saw Moura smile at the touch of Peter's cheek. When Lockhart put his arm around Moura, Peters grinned and walked off. Lockhart was looking at Moura with more than passing interest. Had Peters planted a spy on Lockhart?

In Moscow, a letter from Reilly waited at Anna's flat.

41. Moscow, April, 1918

A red flag twisted high in the wind under a layer of dark grey clouds that joined the horizon in every direction. Beneath the flag a red stone turret shaped like a cone pointed to the dark sky and overlooked a high wall. Men stood with rifles on the ancient turret. Churches and cathedrals rose behind the wall, and stone towers capped with gold onion-shaped pinnacles. Muscovites knew it as 'The Kremlin;' Russians thought it was the centre of their history. Now it housed the new Bolshevik Government.

Just across the River Moscow, a black car waited in front of the Hotel Elite. Sasha sat behind the wheel. Reilly, in a British officer's uniform, came through the hotel entrance and got into the car. The car drove over a bridge to the Kremlin. It stopped at a white gate where a guard examined Sasha's Cheka card, which bore Derzhinsky's signature.

"Wait," said the guard. He spoke into a telephone receiver: "A British diplomatic representative called Sidney Reilly claims to have a message for Lenin from the British Prime Minister." He put the receiver back on the switch hook, looked quietly out at the empty Moscow night and shuffled some papers as string from the overhead lamp dangled near his ear. Reilly waited for twenty minutes before two armed guards came from a door that led to the long red stone building and took him inside.

Within an hour or so, two men went through the corridor of the National Hotel and stopped at the modest flat occupied by Vladimir Lenin. One was a slightly built man with light facial hair. Dressed in a military uniform, he was Derzhinsky, president of Lenin's feared Cheka police. The other, rougher-looking, wore a leather jacket. He was Jacob Peters. Derzhinsky knocked on Lenin's door.

The room was small and sparsely furnished: a writing table, some bookcases and a collection of books, a typewriter and a stack of papers and envelopes, some opened, some not. Lenin seated himself behind the writing table, took a pencil, turned to a document on his desk and without looking up said, "Well?"

"I told you so," said Derzhinsky.

"Told me what, Feliks?"

"That the British would try to overthrow us."

"So you did, Feliks." Lenin turned the document over.

"That they'd conceal their scheme inside an offer to defend us against Germany."

"Yes, Feliks, you said that too."

"You had a visitor this evening."

Lenin glanced up at Derzhinsky and said, "I rejected the British offer." He glanced back at his desk.

"Sidney Reilly. A British spy."

"Of course he is a spy. I rejected the offer."

"He's dangerous," Derzhinsky said. "He's here to arrange a coup. He has friends. He's creating an alliance between the Socialist Revolutionary Party and monarchists. Where would we be if the SRs joined the Whites against us?"

Lenin turned back to his document. "That's impossible. What do you want? Permission to shoot him? Shoot him."

"Just think. The SRs that *you* forced me to take into the Cheka. Our opposition. *My* opposition. In *my* Cheka."

"It was a political decision. I needed SR Party support."

"That was months ago. Now they want to kill you and take over the Cheka. They want the revolution for themselves."

Peters interrupted. "Look," he said. "We can reduce the SR threat without political sacrifices. An SR Cheka commander named Popov controls the troops that would form the core of any uprising against us. Just re-deploy them to Siberia."

Lenin agreed.

As they went away, Derzhinsky said, "Well done, Peters. But we still need a demonstration to change his view."

"The SRs will provide one."

Outside, Peters said, "Were you serious about Reilly?"

"No," said Derzhinsky. "He just a way to illustrate the dangers for Lenin. I must say his timing was perfect. But how seriously can I take a spy who knocks on Lenin's door and leaves his calling card?"

"You certainly persuaded Lenin he was dangerous. I barely kept a straight face."

"I thought my delivery quite good, if I do say so. Now," Derzhinsky said, "Go to Cheka headquarters and tell the SR Alexandrovich that Lenin wants Popov and his men on the train to Omsk this afternoon. They will stand guard over the Czech Legion along the Trans-Siberian."

At the same time, near a lake in the small but regal enclave of Gatchina, Reilly's allies met to make plans to overthrow Lenin in July at the All-Russian Congress in Moscow.

Boris Savinkov brought Latvian Commander Bredis, whose unit guarded Lenin but wanted to switch sides.

The SR Colonel Popov paced the floors, aware that when he returned to his barracks he would find orders to take his men to Siberia. He would return to Moscow by July.

Last to arrive was the White General Yudenich, loyal to the Tsar though friendly to the German Army. Yudenich commanded ten thousand men who would take Moscow when Bredis' Latvians arrested Lenin.

Yudenich meant order, as long as he could control his men. But they were the deposed Tsar's army and hated the SRs, their allies against Lenin.

Reilly could not have assembled a more diverse group. They hated each other but hated Lenin more. Savinkov, Bredis, Popov and Yudenich. SRs, Monarchists, Latvians, White Russians—all in the same room and no one shooting.

General Yudenich of the old Russian Army.

Savinkov, an ex-terrorist.

Latvian Colonel Bredis, Lenin's bodyguard.

Colonel Popov, the commander of a brigade of opposition SRs in Derzhinsky's feared secret Cheka police.

Sworn enemies, sworn to cooperate. For now.

In the evening Reilly reunited with Anna and took her to the Prague restaurant on Arbat Street and after dinner to a place called Strel'na to enjoy a Gypsy chorus and dancers. In the morning he received a message from the Germans, who believed he was their own: led by a Brit named Weber, SRs were planning to assassinate the German Ambassador. Lockhart and his British Consulate denied any knowledge of a plot. No one, including Reilly, knew Weber. The Germans asked Derzhinsky to investigate, and ordered Reilly, whom they knew as their own "Colonel Schaefer," to look into it too. Everyone was searching for British citizen Weber.

It was a beautiful June Sunday. Everyone wanted to meet with Reilly on Monday. Anna took a bottle of wine from the cupboard. "Picnic in the countryside," she said.

"A picnic?" he repeated in surprise and a half-laugh.

"A picnic," she said. "With wine and some sausage, and a loaf of bread." Procured for Colonel Schaefer by Colonel Bauer of the German Embassy.

"I don't know what to say," he said, scratching his head.

"Say nothing," said Anna. She went to her bedroom, brought back a small basket and put the food and wine inside. She went to the closet for something as Reilly watched curiously from the kitchen doorway. She picked up the basket and said, “Let’s go.”

“Where are we going?” Reilly said, opening the door.

“Somewhere romantic,” she said. “The Sparrow Hills.”

“You’re fearless,” he said, enjoying their exchange.

Downstairs, at the archway, he said, “Wait. I’ll get a car.”

“Hurry,” she said and put the basket on the ground.

Five minutes later a black car came around the corner from Big Nikita Street and slowed to a stop at the archway. Anna hurried to the door and jumped inside. “Drive!” she said, getting as close as she could to Reilly.

Reilly laughed quietly and put his foot to the floor. The car crawled to the end of Sheremetyevsky Lane, turned right, made a quick left and headed toward the bottom of a hill. Near the river road Anna said, “There’s another car.”

“Don’t worry,” said Reilly. “Only the Cheka have cars.”

“Are we the Cheka?”

The car raced up behind them. Reilly slowed down. “We are,” he said, taking a red card from his pocket and holding it out the window. The other car sped around and went away.

“Where did you get that?”

“Volodia.”

They crossed a bridge over the river and came out on a road that led up a hill. Reilly turned at an old grey stone wall, obscured behind shrubbery. The car rolled through the thickest part of the wooded area and slowed into a clearing. He stopped. Anna held the basket, got out and took Reilly’s arm. They walked past an old wooden sign with a picture of a bear and went to the edge of the clearing. Below, in the distance, was the city of Moscow.

Anna took a thin blanket from the basket. Reilly took one edge. They unfolded and sat on it. Reilly leaned back on his elbows. Anna lay on her side and faced him, bracing her head with her arm. She lifted her leg up and ran her foot across his knee. Her dress was blue with beige flowers.

“I’ll tell you a secret,” she said. “One of my favourite memories. When you came back from New York with those

American tunes. Mama played the piano. We sang and danced. I was young."

"That was four years ago," said Reilly.

"Never mind," she said. "I'll drink to it. The best day of year 1914." She sat up, opened the basket and took out the wine bottle and two glasses. She gave the bottle to Reilly, who pulled out the cork and poured the wine.

Anna held up her glass and said, "To the best day of year 1918." After a pause, she said, "What would it be like to live in a place without revolution and war? Where would you take me if we lived in London? Take me to Brighton?"

"I'd take you to Brighton," Reilly said.

"What if we lived in New York? We'd go to the ocean?"

"We would."

"I want to live in London and see New York again. And Moscow and Petrograd without war or revolution. Lord, I'd love to live in a place that didn't have war or revolution."

"You will, one day," said Reilly. "We both will."

"Can we live together?" she said, lying flat on her back and looking straight up.

"Why would you want to live with an old dog like me?" he said and breathed out something like a chuckle.

Anna sat up and sipped her wine. "On a beautiful day like today," she said softly, "I can't imagine not being with you."

"I'm not so good for women," he said.

"I'd fix that," Anna said.

"It's been tried," Reilly said.

"Sidney," she said quietly, leaning toward his neck, her lips near his ear, "What do you see when you look at me?"

"The most beautiful girl in the world."

"Girl?" Anna said. "I'm a woman."

"Of course you are," he said. "But I've known you since you were a baby. In a way I'll always think of you that way."

"Baby?" she said and sat up. She opened the basket, took out her pistol, aimed it at the wooden sign and fired six shots. Bullet holes encircled the bear on the sign. She came close to

Reilly. "Still want to call me 'baby,' baby?"

Reilly looked at the sign, sat up straight and laughed. "Where did you learn that?"

Reilly relaxed but kept Anna in his arms. They closed their eyes. The shadows of a nearby cluster of trees snuck slowly across the clearing and covered them as they slept. Hours passed before Reilly opened his eyes. Anna opened her eyes.

"I'm peaceful," he said. "I'm glad we came here."

"But we have to leave?" she said.

"I have to talk to Laurent."

"All right," she said, bringing her head closer to his. She kissed his lips again. She did not wait for him to slip back from her, but instead pulled away gently and rested on her knees. She put the cork in the bottle, the bottle in the basket and her shoes on her feet. She stood up and reached down for his hand with both of hers. When he took them she pulled him up. They folded the blanket together. She held his arm and walked close by as they went to the car.

Reilly was in no hurry to get back. He kept his foot on the brake all the way down the winding hill to the river road. A mirror image of the late afternoon sun in the river rode slowly along with them. They saw no cars along the way. But a few moments after Reilly turned onto Big Nikita Street, directly ahead a limousine slowed to a stop as it approached Arbat Street. A young man raced in front of Reilly's car and sprinted to the limousine. He slowed slightly, dropped low and tossed a package under it. He ran off and disappeared around the corner as flames and smoke shot out from under the limousine and an explosion blasted through the streets.

Anna said later, "Who threw the bomb under their car?"

"SRs, I think," Reilly said. "But could have been anyone. Mirbach isn't very popular."

Laurent said Lieutenant Mueller had called from the German Embassy. He said that German spy-chief Bauer thought the bombing of the ambassador's car was unrelated to the so-called

Weber-plot. What was Reilly's view?

"Why not?" Reilly said, cradling his cup.

A German agent called Ginch had penetrated the SRs and reported that the real SR plot was being organized for early July. He agreed that the bombing of Ambassador Mirbach's limousine could have been initiated by anyone, since everyone hated him.

Reilly, Hill, Lockhart and Station Chief Boyce thought they knew every British agent in town. If Britain were involved, one of them would know.

Laurent asked Reilly what he planned to say to Bauer.

"Nothing has turned up," Reilly answered. "There's no evidence. That's my conclusion."

But Laurent said that Bauer believed his man had real information and that there could be a Brit in the city that worked as a phantom, unknown to other agents. Back channel, like Reilly's friend, White. Would the Director at London Centre run two missions simultaneously? Maybe, if the Director thought he might need a contingency. Or a blind.

That evening, two of Anna's friends were evicted by Bolsheviks and came to stay at her flat.

42. The Phantom Agent, Late June, 1918

The Cheka had taken over Lubyanka Building; the market at Lubyanka square had disappeared. Close by, the Metropol Hotel was open and occupied largely by Bolsheviks. Adjacent to it, the Bolshoi Theatre was in business. Between the two buildings lay Petrovka Street. Sasha and the Chekist Artuzov stopped at building number nineteen. Artuzov ordered the commissar, Doctor Andrianov, to provide a list of tenants in the building.

After the visit by Sasha and Artuzov, Derzhinsky called the Germans to his office.

The dimly-lit room had several old grey pictures of Marx and Engels on the walls over the desk, where Derzhinsky sat. On the other side of the desk sat German officer Mueller. Peters sat nearby. Ibrahim came in with a document and placed it in front of Derzhinsky. The Cheka president glanced at the document and gave it to Mueller.

"Here is a list of people who live at nineteen Petrovka."

Mueller read the names on the document. He said, "This one. Vayber. He might be the man." Mueller insisted that the man be questioned and investigated. Derzhinsky ordered Peters to bring Vayber back. Vayber, Ouiber. English or German name Weber. A brief and superficial interview.

A cable arrived at the Consulate from London: "We know no one named Weber, etc. Give Captain Reilly all possible support for his enterprise and apprise me, etc. – C."

"Weber might be German," Lockhart said.

"Or a real English teacher," Hill said, "as he claimed."

"Possibly the SRs started a rumour to agitate the Germans in Ukraine," Reilly said. "Or Derzhinsky."

"Let's confirm that from the inside?" Lockhart said.

"Ask your Kremlin contact about it," Reilly said. "Tell him we're taking bets at the Consulate. Half believe there's really a scheme to kill Mirbach and the other half think it's a rumour by Derzhinsky to divert the German Embassy from the SR terrorists in the Ukraine. A bottle of consulate champagne hangs in the balance."

Lockhart said, "Just the sort of thing they'd believe."

"When can you do it?" Reilly said.

"Tonight," Lockhart said.

Later, Lockhart said, "He laughed when I asked the question and complemented me on being intuitive. I think you're right. There's no SR scheme to kill Mirbach. The rumours were started by Derzhinsky as a diversion."

"Thank you, Lockhart." Reilly put down the telephone. "It's a blind by Derzhinsky, as I thought. There's no plot."

"Good," said Laurent. "Let's go to the German Embassy."

But the spies at the German Embassy didn't buy it.

Reilly, speaking as German Colonel Schaefer, said: "The German Army in Ukraine is under attack by SR terrorists, the occupation is not going well and we can't control Bolshevik activity. Ukraine is our treaty prize because its wheat can feed us for generations. The Bolsheviks want to make our occupation temporary, so they support SRs."

Bauer said, "You think the Weber plot does not exist."

Reilly said, "I think the rumours were put out by Derzhinsky, and that it's all about wheat, Herr Bauer."

Bauer said, "Perhaps, but stay involved, Colonel."

"Javohl, Herr Kommandant," Reilly said.

43. Colonel Popov, the SR Chekist Military Commander

Colonel Popov raised a shot of vodka and said, "We're in business. The SRs will stage an uprising on the sixth, the final day of the Congress."

"They didn't object to the Tsarist General?" Reilly said.

"It's all their own idea. The balloon goes up at two, when Lenin starts his speech. If you can get the Latvians to arrest Lenin and the rest, good. But the SRs will move regardless."

Reilly said, "Are we in this together or not?"

"Yes, you and I are. But the SR Executive Committee's objective is just to create enough chaos to get Lenin to change his policies. Remember, they want to make a statement, not to take power. But if Lenin gets bumped off his seat, that's all right too. It's up to you to take control. I'll support you."

"Just what was approved by the Executive Committee?"

"An attack," said Popov, "an uprising signal."

"What signal?" said Reilly.

"I have an oath of secrecy, Reilly."

"What's the signal?"

Popov put his hand on Reilly's shoulder. "In the end it doesn't matter, does it? You'll hear it if you're at the Bolshoi Theatre with your Latvians. There will be no doubt that the uprising's started. More than that--don't ask. Just be there."

Reilly looked carefully at Popov. The colonel was sober.

Reilly thought, "Lead the SR Party off in a direction they haven't authorized but don't betray their signal? Should I insist? It would just anger Popov and do no good. Should I be concerned? Yes, if they're going to throw a bomb or start shooting inside the Theatre and we lose control. But Popov wouldn't be so sanguine if that were the case. Would he? It's just one of those stupid situations. I've made myself responsible for uniting the SRs, the Whites, the Latvians and the Allies against Bolshevism. But on how the starting gate will open, I have to take Popov on faith. How smart am I?"

"All right," Reilly said. "I'll be there."

Popov held up his glass, spilled some vodka onto the table and wiped it away with his sleeve. "You're all right, Reilly. If we trust each other we can do it. We can throw them from power and put some sanity back in Russia. We can do it."

Reilly held up his glass of vodka, tapped it gently against Popov's and drank it down. "We can do it," he repeated.

44: Latvian Officer Bredis

Reilly's face was plain in the moonlight. "How many Latvians will guard Lenin?"

Colonel Bredis wore his officer's hat low over his eyes and put a cigarette between his lips. The engine of Lockhart's car revved as though to speed up the meeting. The car was hidden among the trees just off the path to the main road. Bredis tipped his hat back and looked at the starry sky.

"Forty," he said.

"What is your job for the final session," Reilly said.

"Outside the Theatre and on the stage with Lenin," Bredis said, "behind the curtain."

"The stage?" Reilly said. "Does Lenin expect an attack?"

"Derzhinsky fears losing control with Lenin there."

"Why would he lose control?"

"SRs hate Mirbach, who will be in the second tier."

"Everyone hates Mirbach," said Reilly.

"Derzhinsky has warned me that Mirbach's presence could provoke the SRs to disrupt the proceedings. Everyone's particularly nervous about Lenin's speech."

"How many guards will be on the stage as Lenin goes on?"

"All forty," said Bredis.

"How many are with us?" said Reilly.

"All of them," said Bredis.

"Could Derzhinsky make any last-minute changes?"

"I don't know," Bredis said. "The Cheka will guard Mirbach. Derzhinsky could move some Chekists to the floor when Lenin goes on. But he doesn't want the SRs to see his concern. My men will be hidden behind the curtain."

Bredis asked Reilly to describe his planned scenario.

"I'll be at the Bolshoi Theatre at one thirty," Reilly said. "I'll wait outside. Come to me at one-forty five and we'll go backstage. The Bolshevik Central Committee will be seated on the stage. Lenin will speak from the podium. At that moment a signal will be given. Two o'clock."

"What signal?" said Bredis.

Reilly said, "Something to draw attention away from the stage. You and your men will come from behind and encircle the Central Committee, pretending at first to guard them but quickly taking them captive. I'll cuff Lenin and bring him to you. Two trucks will be waiting to take them away."

"What about the SRs and the city of Moscow?" he said.

"When the signal is given Laurent will call Colonel Popov at Pokrovsky Barracks. He will send his men to attack Derzhinsky's Chekists. Having subdued them, he'll take half his men to the centre in order to capture the Kremlin. At the same time we'll call General Yudenich. With ten thousand troops, he'll take Moscow within hours."

"You're sure?" Bredis said.

"I'm sure."

"The SRs and Whites will work together?"

"They both want a Constituent Assembly," Reilly said. "Can I count on you?"

"Yes." Bredis followed a path into the woods. A motor turned over; brush crackled as he walked to the main road.

The lights on Lockhart's car flickered on and off and the engine revved again, this time more assertively. Reilly walked toward the woods and got in the car.

"What did he say?" Lockhart said.

"He'll do it," Reilly said.

"And his men?"

"All forty."

The car rolled slowly through the brush. Lockhart twisted the wheel, drove up the path through the forest and headed out to the main road to Moscow.

45. The All Russian Congress of Soviets, July, 1918

A few days before the counter revolution would take place, Reilly drove to Viazma. General Yudenich was unusually excited by Reilly's message: Lenin's Latvian body guards were all in. Yudenich had shown discomfort about fighting alongside Socialist Revolutionaries. But if the SRs and the Latvians fought together alongside Russian Army regulars, that was a different story, likely to have a good ending. He agreed to move his troops close to Moscow in the early hours of July sixth and to take Reilly's call at a nearby dacha. From there it would be a short ride to the Kremlin.

On the night of the third Anna brought a message from Sasha, whom Reilly found sitting on the floor away from the window blowing smoke rings into the moonlight.

"You asked me if we had any information on an SR plot to kill Mirbach. I was in on the investigation and the interrogation of one of the principals, Weber, an Englishman who knew nothing. I think it's a ruse set up by Derzhinsky. He wants the Germans to believe Mirbach's a target. The implication that the British are involved is designed to make the Germans more nervous. The investigation was a farce."

"What do you think?" said Reilly.

"There's no plot, except for Derzhinsky's manipulation of the Germans. Hell, he even apologized to Weber for having him brought in. I'm sure he's doing it to scare Mirbach away from the Congress." Sasha said, "What about Savinkov?"

"His group will take Jaroslavl as we take Moscow. He'll hold the ammunition depots for the Allied troops who will arrive a few days after that. He's set."

"You're sure about the Allied landing?" Sasha said. "I do worry about Savinkov. The whole area between Moscow and Petrograd is swarming with Red Army."

Reilly explained the plan. Yudenich's White Russian troops, the Latvian guards, the Allied troop landing at Archangel in the north, the SRs and their signal to start the uprising. "Timing is critical. If the SRs, the Latvians and Yudenich are in, the only potential problem is timing."

"It's solid. You've run circles around Derzhinsky."

"Have I?"

"He hasn't said a word about you since you went to the Kremlin to see Lenin. He's convinced you're an incompetent foreigner he doesn't need to take seriously."

The All-Russian Congress of Soviets opened on July fourth. Reilly, dressed in his officers' uniform, attended as a representative of the British Government and sat in a special box with Lockhart and a few other observers. The session was uneventful, somewhat contentious and boring, as was the second session on the fifth. Reilly left early and drove to the suburbs to examine the launching base for General Yudenich's troops, who would arrive later from Viazma. Then he found the riverside dacha where Yudenich would be waiting for Reilly's call with the signal to march on Moscow. He called Anna just to test telephone equipment.

Reilly awoke early on July sixth. He sent Anna to Sasha. At eight he called Laurent for a review. But Laurent's phone was out so he went to Laurent's flat.

"It's nearly nine. I'll go to the consulate and then see you at the Theatre at one-thirty."

Laurent said, "I'll be here until one-fifteen."

"Your phone doesn't work," Reilly said. "I can't call you. Come with me."

They took Reilly's car to the British Consulate, where a staffer gave them an office with a telephone and brought tea. Laurent took a newspaper and sat at a desk. Reilly took the telephone and confirmed details with Yudenich and Bredis.

Lockhart came in. "Reilly, I have a cable coming in. You may want to wait before you make any more calls."

"What is it?" said Reilly.

"Something from Cromie at the embassy in Petrograd," Lockhart said. "They should have it cleared in a minute. "

Soon Lockhart returned with an anxious expression. "Bad news, Sidney."

Laurent folded the newspaper and put it on the desk.

"The American president is out," said Lockhart.

"Out what?" said Reilly.

"Out of Allied intervention in Russia," Lockhart said.

"So what?" said Reilly. "Who needs the Americans?"

"The Prime Minister needs them. He doesn't want to go ahead without President Wilson. The Americans could pull the plug in Europe. He says it's not worth the risk."

"What about us?!" Reilly shouted. "What about Russia?!"

"I know," Lockhart said. "But the British and French need the American Army. So the PM won't take a chance. There will be no landing at Archangel. Can you cable Savinkov?"

"They've taken down the telegraph lines. His men will be slaughtered without the Allied troops at Archangel."

Lockhart nodded.

"Christ!" Reilly slammed his fist on the desk.

"Sidney," Lockhart said. "The Americans are important. If Wilson backs out we'll lose the war. The PM is right."

Reilly shook his head in disgust. "I know it," he said.

"What does this do to our plans?" said Laurent.

"What *does* this do to our plans?" said Reilly.

"Cromie didn't say he had orders to stop, just that there would be no landing at Archangel," Lockhart said.

"All right," Reilly said.

"But," Lockhart said, "it might not be a good idea to call from here. If the Russians are listening we'll get egg on our faces and frankly I can't afford it."

"What do you suggest?"

"Let's go to my place and call from there."

"Is your telephone working?" said Reilly.

"Yes," said Lockhart.

"I want to call Popov," said Reilly.

"Go ahead," said Lockhart. "But then let's go."

Reilly picked up the phone. Lockhart went down the hall.

"I'm sorry, comrade," the operator said. "No answer."

"Try it again, will you?"

"One moment, comrade."

The operator came back on the line and said, "There's still no answer, comrade."

Lockhart appeared. "Let's go. Call him from my place."

"Paris, drive over to the barracks and see Popov."

"I don't have a car, Mister Reilly, and you need yours."

Lockhart looked at his watch. "Take a consulate car."

"Yes," Laurent said, "I'll call you from Popov's office."

"Let's go," Lockhart said and headed to the stairs. Reilly and Laurent followed him out the rear door of the consulate. Lockhart gave Laurent a key and said, "Be bloody careful."

The Frenchman drove out straining his neck with his head just above the steering wheel.

"Should have given him a pillow to sit on," Lockhart said.

"Get in," Reilly said, opening the car door.

They got in and drove to the Hotel Elite. At Lockhart's flat they sat at the dining table. Moura quietly got up, took her coffee to the kitchen and sat on a stool with an open book.

"Bring me up to date," Lockhart said.

"Yudenich is ready. Bredis will meet me at one-forty-five behind the Bolshoi." He sipped his coffee and glanced into the kitchen, where Moura closed her book.

"And Derzhinsky's Cheka?" Lockhart said.

"My inside man says we've run circles around him. He thinks I'm a clown. Not even worth following."

"Hah!" Lockhart said in surprise.

"When are you going?" Reilly said.

"Before it starts, half-past noon or so."

"God damn the Prime Minister," said Reilly. "He has no idea how close we are."

Lockhart said, "What *are* your chances?"

"If nothing disrupts the timing, Lenin will be helpless."

Lockhart answered the telephone and called for Reilly.

"Paris?" Reilly said.

"Something's odd, Mister Reilly," Laurent said.

"Popov?" Reilly said.

"No, the SRs. Blyumkin, the SR Chekist in charge of security at the German Embassy, strutted in and demanded a meeting with the SR Central Committee, including the head man, Alexandrovich. Insisted he sign a paper, probably a promise not to attack the German Ambassador. They had a shouting match."

Reilly said. "Who cares about Blyumkin?"

"He's in charge of security at the German Embassy. If he's here it's because Derzhinsky sent him. He would only do that if he thought there was some danger."

"Derzhinsky's nervous," Reilly said. "He doesn't want anything left to chance. Don't worry."

"All right," said Laurent.

"And you're sure Popov is on schedule?"

"He said to tell you."

"Take the car to the consulate and come over to Lockhart's." Reilly hung up, went into the dining room and repeated Laurent's commentary.

Lockhart laughed. "Blyumkin insisted that Alexandrovich, the Chairman of the SR Executive Committee, sign a document promising not to kill Mirbach? Alexandrovich actually signed it? Derzhinsky must be having fits! Hah!"

Reilly laughed. "That's how it looks to me."

Moura got up and put her book on the counter. "I'll head back," she said, standing in the doorway.

Lockhart got up, walked Moura to the door with his arm around her and kissed her. "Be careful today," he said. She brushed his cheek and hurried off.

Reilly checked his watch: twelve-fifteen. Lockhart came back to the dining room and said he wanted to dress for the afternoon session of the Congress in order to get to the Bolshoi Theatre by one o'clock. Laurent called a while later to report that Moscow was still quiet.

Cheka guards stood watch outside the Lubyanka Building, which was now their headquarters, although the SR faction stayed mostly at Pokrovsky Barracks. Just up the street the tram stop was closed and barricaded as extra security for the afternoon session of the All-Russian Congress, which would take place just across the Square at the Bolshoi Theatre. The area outside the Theatre was thick with Red Guards who stopped everyone and checked documents.

The session would open at one o'clock. Lockhart would be in his box with other Allied representatives. Reilly would meet Colonel Bredis at one-forty-five on the Pokrovsky side. Lenin would make his closing speech at two. A signal would be given, then the attack. Soon the city would be in the hands of Reilly's allies and Lenin would be their prisoner.

46. The German Embassy, July 1918

Laurent had sensed urgency at the meeting between the SR Chekist Blyumkin and the SRs. He correctly stated that Blyumkin had virtually forced the SR Cheka leader Alexandrovich to sign a document. He was also correct that Derzhinsky had sent Blyumkin there because he had discovered imminent danger. It was not simply nervousness, as Reilly had thought. But it had caused a frantic response.

Earlier, a Rolls Royce roared past the guard's gate, turned into Red Square and screeched to a stop at a small Kremlin door. Peters and Artuzov jumped out and hurried to Derzhinsky's office. Peters took Derzhinsky aside and said, "I need you alone." Derzhinsky waved Ibrahim from the room. Peters sat with Derzhinsky. Artuzov stood quietly.

"It's about Reilly," Peters said.

"Who?"

"Reilly, the British agent we thought was a buffoon. The one who came to see Lenin a few months ago."

"Reilly?" Derzhinsky said sourly.

"Well, of course," Peters said. "But Artuzov's team now reports that Reilly has enough support to outweigh his own incompetence. He is at the centre of a plot against us and our preliminary assessment is that he could succeed."

"Reilly?" Derzhinsky said.

"Yes."

"You don't believe it, do you?"

"I do," said Peters.

"You?" he said to Artuzov.

Artuzov nodded. "Comrade."

Derzhinsky's head jerked back.

"Reilly!"

Artuzov said, "He has ten thousand White troops outside the city. He has SR agents and the Latvian Brigade. The Allies plan to land troops at Archangel. It's the attack we've been talking about. The very same one. But it's real."

Derzhinsky's eyes opened wide in fury. He jumped to his feet, threw out his chest and raised his fists into the air.

"There's more, Feliks. He has enough support in the SR camp to wreck our plans. Everything. He has enough to put us out. He could, conceivably, take control."

"When?"

"Today, at the Congress. At two o'clock."

"That's our time! Two o'clock!"

"The assassination of Mirbach will be the signal for a general SR uprising, a simultaneous White Army attack on the city and the arrest of the Central Committee."

"That's our time!" Derzhinsky shouted. "Inconceivable! Reilly's got the SRs taking our plan and using it to trigger his own attack! We'll be crushed."

Peters took Derzhinsky by the shoulders. "We can do something to hurt his timing. We can pick him up."

Derzhinsky spoke quietly. "I will speak with Lenin. I will call the German Embassy and keep Mirbach away from the Congress." But with these words he began to growl again and said, "Not Reilly. I can't believe it. A nobody!"

He breathed deeply again, turned and took Peters by the shoulders. "Get Blyumkin to the German Embassy. But before that he's got to get the SR Alexandrovich to sign and seal a document authorizing entry. The last thing we want is the Germans to call us out on protocol and refuse to let Blyumkin in. Smooth and fast. We'll wreck Reilly's timing."

He looked at a clock. "It's twelve thirty. I'll call the embassy and then see Lenin. Go on! Tell them to get Blyumkin! Only Blyumkin." He twisted Peters around and sent him sprawling toward the door.

That is what landed Blyumkin at SR Headquarters, got him arguing with the SR Chekist Alexandrovich and finally produced an official Cheka document authorizing entry into the German Embassy for security purposes. Laurent was standing close by and heard practically everything. That is why he called Reilly. But he could not have understood the full picture or know what followed.

Derzhinsky, more controlled after Peters departed, stared for a moment at the coloured onion domes of Saint Basil's Cathedral. Then he rang the German Embassy for Herr Bauer.

Bauer came on the line. "Derzhinsky?"

"Yes. Your reports of an attempt on the ambassador's life were correct. You cannot allow him to attend Congress today."

"We told you so," Bauer said contemptuously.

"So you did," said Derzhinsky.

"I imagine the Allied Powers are involved."

"They are."

"We told you so," said Bauer.

"Keep the Ambassador away from the Congress," Derzhinsky said. "We will send the embassy security specialist. The ambassador must speak with him. Otherwise there will be confusion and danger. The treaty is at stake. Blyumkin has official permission to enter the Embassy."

"With the Cheka seal, signed by the proper authorities?"

"Yes, signed by Alexandrovich, Cheka Joint Commissar."

"Your man will show his identification at the front door?"

"Yes. Please speak to the ambassador."

Derzhinsky sped out to Lenin's office and found him at his desk with notes for the speech he would make in less than two hours. He gnawed at the pencil, tapped it a few times on the desk and mumbled a few words as though practicing the cadence of a particular line. Derzhinsky burst in.

"What is it?"

"You can't go to the Congress today."

"What?" Lenin said.

"Reilly plans to attack at the Congress this afternoon."

"How do you know?" Lenin said.

"The Whites are about to enter the city. The SRs plan an uprising. SRs that *you* insisted we take into the Cheka."

Lenin slammed his palm on the desktop.

"Damn you, Feliks! Why do you always come crying to me about the SRs I ordered you to take into the Cheka? We're *always* under attack! The imperialists will *never* accept us! So we must create the appearance of democracy in the Cheka and include Alexandrovich and his SRs!"

"I told you Reilly could unite the Whites and Socialists against us and he has done it. The attack is imminent. The enemy is real. You must stay away from the Congress."

Lenin stood, strode to the window and marched up to Derzhinsky. "Do you realize what you are asking me to do? To make a public announcement that we are not in control, that our enemies have forced us to cancel the Congress and that we are, in effect, not a government at all but merely pretenders to the Russian State. Is that what you want?"

"No," said Derzhinsky.

"But that is how my absence would be taken," said Lenin. "And that is certainly how a postponement would be taken. Our enemies would feast on it, whether they are involved in this so-called attack or not. They would derive enormous strength from it. In the end it would give them the energy to mount a true attack on us. One that we would not survive."

"You cannot attend the Congress," said Derzhinsky.

"To the contrary," said Lenin, "I must go to the Congress. Or you must convince me not to go, Feliks."

Derzhinsky spoke in a soft, quiet voice, his head low and his eyes gentle. "I don't mean to say I told you so, comrade. But the SRs are deeply implicated in this. We don't have all the details yet. But at least we've discovered it in time to prevent disaster. The SRs plan to kill Mirbach at the Congress. That will be their signal for general insurrection."

Lenin leaned back. "I see," he said.

"I've insisted the embassy keep Mirbach there. Peters sent agents responsible for embassy security to review everything with Mirbach in order to preserve the treaty."

"What I said remains true," Lenin said. "With Mirbach away the SRs will get no signal. That should make it safe."

"Anything could happen," said Derzhinsky.

"All right, Feliks. I'll compromise. We'll postpone my speech until later in the day. Go on with the Congress. If nothing happens I'll go. If we have a problem I won't go."

Derzhinsky agreed.

At one o'clock, just minutes after Blyumkin's meeting with the SR leader Alexandrovich, a black Ford screeched to a stop in front of the German Embassy. Blyumkin and another man jumped out of the car and hurried to the guard behind the black iron fence that encircled the house. They held up their Cheka documents and the guard took them to the front door. One of the men rang a buzzer. The front door opened. Lieutenant Mueller stood there.

"Well, Comrade Blyumkin," he said.

"Good afternoon, comrade," Blyumkin said. "This is comrade Andreyev. We've come to see the ambassador."

"Let me see your orders," Mueller said.

Blyumkin showed the document that he had just persuaded Alexandrovich to sign and seal.

Mueller leaned forward. "Signed by Derzhinsky?"

"No," Blyumkin said. "Derzhinsky sent me, but the document was signed by his deputy, Alexandrovich and bears the official seal of the Cheka."

Mueller squinted again. "Very well, Blyumkin. Come in."

Blyumkin put the document back in his briefcase. Mueller motioned the men through the door, escorted them to a small ante-chamber near the ambassador's office and went away. Blyumkin seated himself as Andreyev walked through the hallway and admired paintings on the wall. In a moment the ambassador's door opened and a man came out and went down the stairs. The ambassador appeared at the door and said, "Blyumkin, I understand you have something for me."

Blyumkin followed Mirbach into the office. The ambassador sat behind a long mahogany desk and gestured to a thick arm-chair next to it. Blyumkin sat down and rested the briefcase on his lap. He removed the document that SR Chekist Alexandrovich had signed and sealed.

Blyumkin said, "It says here, Your Honour, that the Cheka have information about an attempt on your life."

"Who will make this attempt, Blyumkin? Does it say?"

"Well," Blyumkin replied in a mumble, "SR assassins."

"Blyumkin, let me ask your opinion. Is it just possible, that there is no assassination and that these charges have been concocted by your own Derzhinsky to distract the German Government from terrorist attacks in Ukraine, made by members of the SR Party against the German Army? Attacks that are sponsored by Comrade Lenin?"

Blyumkin glanced at the document. "I see nothing about that, Your Honour. No."

Mirbach smiled sarcastically and adjusted the Pince-nez under his eyebrow. "Well, Blyumkin, tell me, then. What are the details of this supposed conspiracy? Who's behind it?"

"Members of the SR Party, Your Honour."

"And when will the assassination attempt occur? Today? Afternoon? Evening? Tonight?"

"Today, Your Honour," the SR Chekist said.

"Can you be more specific, Blyumkin? How is an ambassador supposed to feel, knowing he could be shot at any time? When will the attempt be made?"

Blyumkin put the document on the desk.

"When, Blyumkin?"

"Why, at this very moment, Your Honour," Blyumkin said, took a revolver from his briefcase and stood.

Shock covered Mirbach's face as Blyumkin aimed his revolver and then shot blindly into the wall behind the ambassador. Mirbach ducked under his desk, taking a pistol from a desk drawer on his way down. Blyumkin fired again. Mirbach sprang from the desk, waved his pistol and fired blindly. Blyumkin spilled backward and knocked a tall, colourful Oriental vase to the floor where it shattered.

Mirbach aimed, fired several shots into the floor and screamed, "You have no respect for property, you Bolshevik! That was a priceless piece, a rarity, you fool!"

Blyumkin rolled quickly away from Mirbach's line of fire as the shots ripped through the thick Persian carpet and the oak floor beneath it. Mirbach crept step by step to counter Blyumkin's manoeuvres in carefully controlled movement.

Blyumkin, in front of full-length windows that sparkled with brilliant afternoon sunlight, took aim, fired twice but once again missed, his bullets ripping through the Kaiser's portrait. Mirbach twisted through the room in an evasive serpentine pattern. Blyumkin stopped, fired again but missed as a porcelain bust of a Greek god burst into tiny fragments. Mirbach cursed and stomped his foot on the floor.

Suddenly both men faced one another across the room, each with his weapon aimed at the other. In a flash, both fired and missed. Again each took aim and squeezed the triggers of their pistols. But both pistols clicked but neither fired. Mirbach raised his hands over his shoulders, lurched across the room and prepared to strangle his assailant. A look of terror spread across Blyumkin's face. He turned, opened the window behind him and, just as Mirbach was about to pounce, leaped through the second-floor window to the ground below and cried out in pain.

Mirbach glared through the window, breathed heavily and

growled, "That'll teach you, you filthy little Bolshevik."

Then another shot rang out behind the ambassador, blew open his skull and sent part of his brain into the wall. He crashed onto the floor and blood gushed all over the rich Persian carpet. Another shot filled the room. A pool of blood filled Mirbach's chest. "That'll teach *you*," Andreyev said, "you filthy little German."

At one thirty-five, Reilly emerged from Petrovka Street in a black tunic, carrying Petrograd Cheka identification. The documents were signed by Commissars Uritsky and Orlov, two names well known inside the Cheka, even in Moscow. He passed the columns of the Bolshoi, walked toward the rear of the Theatre and approached one of the Latvians.

"Where is Commander Bredis?" He flashed a Cheka card.

"On his way," the guard replied. "You can wait here."

Reilly nodded. At one-fifty he looked at his watch. Bredis' assistant walked quickly from Petrovka, passed by and did not speak to him. Then Bredis came along looking nervous and upset. "Reilly," he said in a low voice. The SRs killed Mirbach. Our timing's shot."

"When?"

"Half hour ago. Forty five minutes. I don't know."

"What are you going to do?" Reilly said.

"The shooting was the signal for the SR uprising. Lenin stayed at the Kremlin. There'll be no Congress."

"Where did you get your information?"

"Savinkov's man, Semyenov. Called me from Pokrovsky Barracks. Two SRs had just arrived, announced that they'd shot Mirbach and said that that was the signal. Popov is trying to take control of the barracks but the Bolshevik Chekists are resisting. If you're going to act, do it now."

"And you?"

"My troops won't fight the Bolsheviks like this. They wouldn't stand a chance." Bredis went to a waiting motorcar.

Reilly hurried across the square to the Metropol Hotel. Not

far off, the doors to the Cheka headquarters opened suddenly and men poured through.

In a small office at the Metropol Hotel, Reilly cupped his hand over a telephone receiver as he spoke. The voice on the other end of the line said, "Popov here, Reilly. I assume you know the insurrection has started. My troops are fighting the Bolsheviks here. We've killed several thousand and have taken many prisoners. We'll control the barracks very soon. I can leave half of my troops here to hold the barracks and guard the munitions. Do you still need men at the Bolshoi?"

"No," Reilly said loudly, trying to be heard over the gunshots and shouting. "No, take them, take half to the Central Post and Telegraph station on Tverskaya and the rest to the Kremlin. I'll call General Yudenich. Good luck." He waited for an operator and then gave her a number.

"General Yudenich, please... General, Reilly. The SRs started the uprising a few minutes early."

"When?" the general said.

"Forty-five minutes ago. Popov has taken Pokrovsky Barracks and is moving half his troops to the Kremlin. Are your men ready to take the city?"

"One hour early?" said Yudenich. "What is the situation?"

"The SRs have taken the Pokrovsky Barracks, the telegraph and telephone exchange and have taken up positions all over the city. Twenty-five hundreds of Popov's men are moving in. We have to move up our schedule."

"What about the Latvian Brigade?"

"They've kept Lenin at the Kremlin," Reilly said. "That's where Popov's men are headed. Move your troops in now!"

"Were are the Latvians?" Yudenich said.

Reilly sighed with equal impatience, trying to slow himself down. "Returning to the Kremlin," he said more quietly.

"I see," General Yudenich said. "Which side will they take when they get there?"

"They'll guard Lenin," he answered. "For now."

"But they were going to *arrest* Lenin and his men."

"General, we need action and we need it now."

"Reilly. The plan we bargained for was a well-organized attack against the Bolsheviks that depended on the capture of Lenin and Trotsky by you and the Latvian sharpshooters. But with Lenin on the loose and the Latvians at his side, who is to say that the SRs won't just put down their arms or even switch sides against the White Army? My men would be slaughtered and the Whites set back. That's too much to risk."

"General, if you don't order your troops to the Kremlin, it'll just be the SRs against the Bolsheviks!"

After a few moments of silence General Yudenich said, "So, the Social Revolutionaries and the Bolsheviks will be shooting one another. Wouldn't that be a pity, Reilly? A real pity."

Then the telephone fell silent.

A flatbed truck screeched to a stop close to others scattered near Red Square at the Kremlin. A dozen armed men jumped from the rear and over the sides. Gunfire came from everywhere. From inside Saint Basil's Cathedral, SR snipers fired as the Red troops scurried for cover, blasting back at unseen enemies as they ran. In the Kremlin tower machine-guns pounded out staccato bursts.

Suddenly, blood covered Sasha's face as a bullet thumped into someone running in front of him. To his right, another Chekist screamed and crashed to the ground. He followed several others, raced to the closest barricade and dove over it as Cheka troops stood and fired to give him protection. For a moment he sat against the barricade with his back to the fighting. Artuzov came up to him, squatting all the while.

"There are SR snipers inside Saint Basil's, heavily armed but trapped. I'll send the younger guys to take the place."

"Good," Sasha replied.

"I want you to move behind the cathedral on the ground. None of our men are over there. Shoot everything that moves." Artuzov ran off to another group of Chekists.

Sasha took his position, aimed his rifle above the heads of the

SR fighters and fired. No one seemed to notice. He fired his rifle until the last bullet was spent. He took some ammunition from his belt, reloaded and resumed his charade.

Artuzov shouted, "Comrades! We're going to move our position closer to the embankment, to the left of the cathedral! Wait until the barricade is in place!"

Several Chekists ran across the square carrying a wooden barricade as a loud report came from Bolshevik positions in the Kremlin tower, deafening and terrifying. "Let's go!" Artuzov shouted, running ahead with his troops close behind him. Sasha ran in their midst, his head low, as machine gun and rifle fire tore into everything around him. Two Chekists fell. Others stopped to help them. Sasha reached the wooden barricade not too far from the SR troops. He peered over the barricade, and raised his rifle as an SR appeared. A voice behind him said, "Lower, Lipkin! Or you'll miss!"

Sasha lowered the barrel of his rifle and shot into the dirt.

"What are you doing?" the voice screamed at him. "You won't hit anyone like that!"

Sasha turned his head around and glared at a Cheka officer. He turned back to the embankment as someone moved into his sights- a blond-haired boy with blue eyes, a defector no doubt from the propertied classes. Sasha felt the barrel of a pistol on his neck. He took careful aim and shot just over the young man's shoulder.

"Not good enough, Comrade," a voice from behind said.

Sasha braced his rifle firmly in the socket of his arm. He fired again but his target fell away from view and resurfaced.

"Now!" came the voice from behind. "Now!"

He hesitated, felt steel pressing into the base of his neck and squeezed his finger around the trigger.

My God, what a fool I am. I can never forgive myself.

Sasha fired. Then his world stopped in time as a spark lit the barrel of his SR "enemy's" rifle, a puff of smoke billowed into the small space on the embankment near the cathedral and a blast that would have otherwise blended into the chaos drowned out every other sound and drove every other sensation from his consciousness. The blue eyes of his enemy were fixed on him, blazing, screaming and pleading. But Sasha could only wait as a small, hot and deadly piece of metal streaked invisibly through space. Then he felt sudden pressure on his neck, head and shoulders. A veil of red and pink blurred his vision and he fell under a terrible weight. He twisted himself, disengaged from the body of the man behind him and peered over the barrier.

The young SR had fired and disappeared. Sasha did not know whether or not he had shot him.

Artuzov led a small team into the cathedral, fired at the embankment and went inside.

An SR commander screamed, "Retreat! Move back!" The SR troops disappeared. Shouting came from the cathedral. Two bodies crashed from the heights to the ground with a single loud thud. Then silence. Artuzov and his men walked from the cathedral. Faces appeared in the open windows of the Kremlin and men waved their arms and shouted to one another: "The Cheka have saved the Kremlin!"

Reilly went to the Metropol Hotel, found a telephone and made several calls to get reports from around the city. SR losses were high. But they had taken many important locations. Lenin had only a few Latvian sharpshooters and no more than two thousand troops. Reilly went out to see whether the SRs had any strength left, or whether he would have to start over again.

The flatbed truck slowed to a stop outside the Bolshoi Theatre. A few Chekists jumped to the ground and ran into the building, Sasha among them. A few men and one woman sat on the stage. Fewer than half of the seats in the grand hall were occupied. The SRs were absent but thirty or so Bolsheviks were present. The members of the German Legation were absent.

Several members of the Allied Legations were near the front of the hall to the left of the stage. The Chekists arrived and the allied officers looked up in surprise. Someone from another

Cheka unit said. "Make the arrest now."

Then Sasha noticed Reilly among the Allied representatives, discussing something with Laurent and Lockhart. The latter tapped Reilly on the shoulder as the Chekists started down the long aisle. Reilly did not look up but reached into his pockets, tore up small pieces of paper and stuffed them into his mouth. The Frenchman did the same. Lockhart rocked back and forth on his feet and seemed amused. A Cheka guard approached them and said something. Everyone nodded and smiled.

Sasha was puzzled but relieved. The Cheka contingent went to the stage, handcuffed a woman with long black hair and marched her to the rear of the Theatre. She shouted something at the guards that Sasha did not understand.

"Who is that?" he asked one of his fellow Chekists.

"That's Maria Spiridonova. An SR leader."

"What did she say?"

"She said that she killed Mirbach."

In a few moments Reilly walked out with Laurent. Lockhart stayed with the Allies. Artuzov approached Sasha. "I need someone to search the basement. There's a rehearsal area and a few dressing rooms. Just to be sure. Why don't you go down, comrade. We'll be in the truck. No danger."

In a minute Sasha came from the basement, nodded casually as he passed Reilly and walked outside.

The Socialist Revolutionary Party controlled the Central Post and Telegraph Exchange on Tverskaya Street. Alexandrovich, Derzhinsky's renegade SR deputy, had made it his field headquarters for SR troops and called in Popov's men to guard it. Now the building and the surrounding area were filled with armed rebels loyal to Popov and Reilly. The first floor was a field hospital where the wounded and dying lay across the floor, filled the long room with groans and pleas aimed at a few women nurses and a doctor. Outside, sniper-fire rang out every few seconds. Everywhere men shouted orders and stomped up and down a wide wooden staircase that led to a weapons cache on the second floor.

Alexandrovich and Popov huddled in the rear of the building. "Lenin has no strength," Alexandrovich said. "Only Latvians untested in battle. He can't be sure what they'll do. If we guarantee his life he might surrender."

"He wouldn't guarantee your life!" Popov said. "Take control! Throw Lenin out!"

"It is not SR policy to overthrow the Bolsheviks," said Alexandrovich. "We only want to influence their policies and to destroy their treaty with Germany."

"That strategy failed when your man shot Mirbach. You have no choice. Get Lenin and the others or they'll get you."

"We want to negotiate."

"Derzhinsky will make minced meat of you and your diplomats! You have no choice! The lines are drawn! You've lost your chance to negotiate."

Alexandrovich looked away as soldiers marched across the floor with someone in their midst. A light-haired man with a blond beard and a military uniform. The guards had pistols to his head. Though they knocked him left and right he walked steadily and showed no fear. His eyes were blue, cold and steely, his gait imposing. He was Feliks Derzhinsky.

The room fell silent. Men and women spoke quietly as Derzhinsky went up the staircase with weapons at his skull.

Popov looked at Alexandrovich, who closed his eyes, as though in prayer. "What will you do?" Popov said.

Alexandrovich bit his lip. "Order his arrest," he said resignedly and followed Popov up the stairs.

SR troops surrounded their prisoner in the large second-floor room. The air was hot and dusty. Soldiers coughed. Dust peppered the wooden floor unevenly and formed clouds every time someone moved. Popov walked slowly into the room ahead of Alexandrovich. The troops turned Derzhinsky around to face them. No one spoke until he glanced at Alexandrovich, softened his eyes and said, "Do you know why I came here, Comrade?"

"Why did you come, Comrade?"

"Your so-called allies have abandoned you. Many of your men are already dead. Comrade Spiridonova is arrested."

Some of the troops gasped.

"Oh, yes," Derzhinsky continued. "Even now voices in the Kremlin urge Lenin to send the Latvian Brigade to blow up this building, kill everyone and end this senseless uprising right away." He searched the room with wide, steely blue eyes that spoke to every soldier one to one, intimidated, weakened and seduced their spirits.

"Oh, yes," he continued, "I knew you might execute me, but I came because we are brothers. Where are *they* now, the White generals who promised to come to your side to defeat us? They are in the countryside, laughing at you and at all of us while we murder each other and the revolution."

A few feet shuffled quietly and sent a thin cloud of dust into the air. A few coughs echoed through the room.

"So I have come here at my own risk, not as your enemy but as your brother. Because I don't care whether you are a Bolshevik or an SR or a Menshevik. I care only that you love the revolution as I love it and serve the peasants and the workers as I serve them. Execute me if you wish. I will not resist. I will not raise my hand against my brothers."

Alexandrovich surveyed the eyes of his SRs.

"Or you may choose to send me back to the Kremlin with a message of peace. I will be your barrister in the Kremlin and fight for you and plead for you. If that's what you choose then we will be one again. Together we will save the revolution, crush the White imperialists who want to send all of us to our graves here and now. Or later, against the German Army. The revolution needs you, comrades. Will you save the revolution? Or abandon it? What will you do?"

"Save the revolution! Let the revolution live!"

When Colonel Popov stepped forward, his thick military boots sent up a thick cloud of dust. He drew two pistols, raised them to the air and fired six blasts into the ceiling.

"Put cuffs on him!" he shouted at the troops: "Or I'll just blow his damned brains out!"

The crowd of young soldiers drew back. A guard took Derzhinsky's wrists and put handcuffs on them.

Popov turned to the crowd. "Now get the hell back to work if you don't want to stand in front of a firing squad!"

The soldiers hurried down the stairs. Popov motioned to Alexandrovich to go with them. Then he put Derzhinsky on a barrel turned on its side and said, "You can sit on this until I come back." Two guards stayed. Popov went downstairs.

After leaving the Bolshoi Theatre, Reilly visited locations controlled by SR troops who all seemed apprehensive.

"If we don't see reinforcements by nightfall," one of the commanders said, "I'm going to get my troops out of here."

"What will happen then?" said Reilly.

"I don't care," he said. "I want my men alive."

Other officers expressed similar sentiments. On one street the Bolsheviks had taken control of an important building early on in the fighting. Popov's men had arrived shortly thereafter. But when Reilly got there, hours later, the SRs were still outside. Inside the Bolsheviks had taken on the role of snipers and had been picking them off all afternoon.

"Why don't you take the building?" said Reilly.

"We have no officers here. Nobody to give us orders."

They had waited as time dwindled and their comrades were gradually killed off. Reilly was discouraged. Nothing had gone as planned. Yudenich was still in the suburbs or on his way back to Viazma. Lenin had the Latvians. The SRs would not be able to hold their positions for another day. Sooner or later they'd walk away.

He chastised himself for not pursuing rumours about SRs killing Mirbach. He'd known it was possible. He hadn't pushed Popov about the SR signal. If he had followed either of those lines he could have made some minor adjustments and used circumstances to his advantage instead of being forced to react after the fact. He should have seen it coming.

Tverskaya Street was almost quiet at seven o'clock. A few snipers remained in some buildings and every so often one shot at a pedestrian or at nothing in particular. A few cars filled with Chekists sped by on their way to or from the Kremlin. At SR headquarters guards stood outside smoking, their old grey uniforms filthy and torn. Reilly asked a guard to take him to Colonel Popov. The guard pointed to the rear of the building. Farther along, Popov approached him.

"Is there any good news?" Reilly asked.

"We've got Derzhinsky," Popov said.

"Where is he?"

"Upstairs. Handcuffed."

"What are you going to do with him?"

"Your call, Reilly. It's your game. Personally, I think we should execute him."

Reilly took Popov aside, put his arm around his shoulder and said, "I'd like to shoot the whole lot. But I don't think your gains will hold. What will you do after this?"

"I agree," Popov said. "But whatever we do, Derzhinsky will launch a reign of terror. It's better to execute him and let someone else try to get control of the Cheka."

"There is something else to consider. I have two men inside the Cheka. They are close to the top of the Moscow and Petrograd organizations and are extremely valuable. If we eliminate him now their usefulness will diminish. But if we let him live, they'll continue to provide good information."

"All right, Reilly. Glad someone is thinking about the future." Popov gave Reilly a pair of keys. "Here," he said. "Go up and take off his cuffs. Good luck."

"Goodbye," Reilly said and offered his hand.

Reilly climbed the stairs to the second story, which was filled with dust and haze. Derzhinsky sat on a barrel near the far wall beneath the windows. Reilly waited at the top of the stairs, told the guards to go slowly walked across the room. He stood in front of Derzhinsky.

"Give me your hands," he said quietly.

Derzhinsky raised his hands. Reilly took off the cuffs.

"Who are you?" Derzhinsky said, looking away.

"I'm Reilly."

Derzhinsky jerked back, almost lost his balance and growled in surprise, "Reilly!"

Reilly took a pack of cigarettes from his pocked and offered one to Derzhinsky. The Chekist took it and put it between his teeth. When Reilly struck a match Derzhinsky leaned forward, inhaled and blew smoke into the air.

"What are you doing here?" Derzhinsky said.

"Please," Reilly said. "No questions."

"No," Derzhinsky said.

Reilly said, "You attended university at Warsaw."

"I don't remember you," Derzhinsky said.

"Nor I you. But I remember a student named Petrov who was murdered by the secret police. I remember the talk about revolution, overthrowing the established order, how we hated the Tsar and his Okhrana and the bribes and the pay-offs, the endless suffering of Russians and the suffering inflicted by Russians on other people."

"Yes," Derzhinsky replied pensively, "I remember these things as well." He blew a long stream of smoke into the air. "Reilly, I really didn't think you were capable of doing this. You came very close. I'm very surprised. Congratulations."

Reilly nodded.

"You know, Reilly, your reasons for hating the Tsar and the injustice in the world, those reasons still exist and will exist for a long time. I don't know anyone other than our party who is really interested in changing them. But I think you want to change them, or you wouldn't be here. Consider what we might accomplish together. Can you imagine what our combined will could do to change the world?"

"I've always believed in the power of will," said Reilly.

"Men are tigers who will either tear the world apart or be

tamed and live peacefully. Consider how we could change the world, tame the tiger and transform the nature of man."

Reilly blew cigarette smoke over Derzhinsky's head.

Derzhinsky said matter-of-factly, "I have a son in Berlin. Perhaps you would honour my request to deliver a letter to him after the war has stopped, a note to say good bye and to express my regrets and love."

"No, comrade," Reilly said. "You'll tell him yourself."

"You will not execute me?"

"No," Reilly said, looking into his eyes. "It will be more interesting to defeat you."

Reilly walked away. Derzhinsky sucked on his cigarette and crushed it forcefully into the floor. He rose, walked to the window and studied the troops on the street below. He buttoned his military jacket, brushed the dust from his sleeves and walked to the stairs. He started down with his body erect and stepped in dress rhythm. SR troops stopped what they were doing and stood quietly as he reached the first floor and started through the long room toward the street. His eyes looked straight ahead and did not glance to either side.

"Look at him," they said.

Some of the troops raised their fists into the air. "Hurrah, Derzhinsky!" As he marched the crowd of soldiers spread open before him, wave-like. "Hurrah, Derzhinsky!" several young soldiers shouted. Others turned away and covered their faces, as though in shame. "Hurrah, Derzhinsky!" Some threw themselves at his feet as he passed them by with his shoulders back and his eyes fixed ahead. He walked as soldiers left and right backed away and shouted, "Feliks!" He did not acknowledge them but moved by quickly. Two soldiers opened the exit doors. He marched into the street.

Outside several hundred troops stood in a dense crowd but fell into sudden silence when he appeared in the doorway and then headed straight for them. In an instant the crowd split in two, fell back and opened up a wide path.

"Feliks!" they cried. "Hurrah, Comrade!"

He strode through the crowd, cut a military turn to the right and marched down Tverskaya Street into the Kremlin.

A black Rolls Royce tore through the streets of Moscow from the Arbat District, careened around a corner at Tverskaya and roared toward the Kremlin. It screeched through an intersection, stopped and then sped off again. Lenin, sitting next to Peters, the driver, spewed forth a barrage of obscenity and epithet, cursing everyone: the Germans, whom he had just persuaded not to take retaliatory action for the murder of their ambassador by two lunatic SRs. The British, helping the SRs to organize an uprising that almost wrecked the revolution. The Russians, for never wavering from their determination to self-destruct. And Derzhinsky, for the stupidest act in the history of diplomacy, sending two SRs to secure a German Embassy that the SR Party was committed to destroying.

"It's impossible! I can't believe he could do something so stupid. How could he not know that Blyumkin was an SR?"

The wheels of the Rolls Royce squealed as the car slid at the bottom of the hill, headed toward the Kremlin guardhouse and veered off at the last possible moment before accelerating toward a livery stable in the centre of the road.

"One minute he tells me about an SR plot to kill Mirbach! In the next he sends in two SRs to prevent it! Incredible!"

Peters kept his eyes on the road.

"The idiot! He left it to me to save the treaty! And the chief conspirator, Weber, the agent-provocateur of British imperialism who was behind the Mirbach murder! Two interrogations, a piece of sausage and a ride home! Nothing!"

When the car missed the livery stable, screeched around to the left and headed back in the opposite direction Peters replied, "There was no evidence, comrade."

"You tell Derzhinsky to arrest the British imperialist, Weber. Conspiracy. Charge the bastard with treason, insurrection, murder, everything. Off with their heads!"

When the Rolls Royce jerked to a stop Peters jumped out, rushed inside and sprinted through the corridor to Derzhinsky's flat, where the lights were dim. A naked woman hurried into the bedroom and closed the door behind her. Peters breathed hard, tried to catch his wind and said weakly, "Lenin's furious. It's about Blyumkin."

Derzhinsky wore a silver kimono. He snuffed out a candle, switched on a light and looked through the window at the dark night. In the square outside Lenin stood next to his Rolls Royce and ranted to his secretary, arms flailing. Derzhinsky said to Peters, "Did you get the document?"

He nodded. "Sealed. With Alexandrovich's signature."

"I know what we need," Derzhinsky said. He threw off his kimono and donned his uniform. He took two champagne glasses into the bedroom and quickly returned.

"What?" Peters said.

"Something to capture his imagination. Tell him you've seen me with a pistol to my head. Go get him."

Peters rushed through the door, sped through the corridor and almost crashed into Lenin and his secretary, who were striding angrily toward Derzhinsky's flat.

"Comrades," said Peters. "Feliks has a gun to his head."

Lenin's face filled with horror. He hurried to Derzhinsky's flat, his secretary following closely behind, burst through the door. Derzhinsky faced the window, the pistol near his temple and his finger on the trigger.

"No!" Lenin shouted. "No, Feliks! Please!"

"I must," he replied. "I hate myself. It's all my fault."

"Feliks," Lenin beckoned, "lower that pistol."

"I can't face you, comrade."

"You've done your best. Any mistakes, any shortcomings, everyone forgives you."

"You may forgive me. You're kind. But kindness has no place in revolution. I cannot forgive myself. A professional would never have been so trusting with so much at stake. Yes, I sent Blyumkin, the Socialist Revolutionary, the Chekist, the turncoat. I sent him to save the German Ambassador. Instead he betrayed me. I sent him to save our treaty with Germany. Blyumkin, my little flower of the revolution. There is only one action for me."

When Derzhinsky's finger tightened around the trigger, Lenin's secretary raced across the floor, dove and slapped the pistol from his hand. It hit the floor and discharged.

Derzhinsky flinched.

Lenin and Peters raced across the room. Derzhinsky turned around. Peters picked up the pistol, looked at it in surprise and checked the safety catch.

Lenin embraced Derzhinsky. "There, comrade," he said with a gentle smile. "Try that again, I'll cut off your hands."

"Forgive me, Comrade," Derzhinsky said, faltering.

"We forgive you."

Derzhinsky took a deep breath, turned away as though some inspiration had suddenly taken hold and turned back to Lenin. "I resign," he said coolly. "Everyone must fear you. Tell them I'm gone, that Peters has the Cheka."

"What?" said Lenin. "Without you there is no Cheka."

"Be practical," said Derzhinsky. "People must know they can neither fail nor betray you with impunity. Even those close to you. I, for example. Or the SR betrayers."

"People must see that you've punished Feliks," Peters said. "There's no other way."

"Oh," said Lenin. "I understand. Feliks runs the Cheka in absentia. But have we proof enough to convict the SRs?"

Peters took a document from his pocket for Lenin. "This is the SR Central Committee's seal that got Blyumkin admitted to the German Embassy. The SR Alexandrovich signed it."

"Where did you get it?" said Lenin.

"It was on Mirbach's desk. I went to his office while you were with Colonel Bauer. Blyumkin used it to get in."

Lenin waved the document. "Proof that the SR Alexandrovich authorized this killing! You warned me about the SRs, Feliks! Now I understand! Kill the bastards!"

"What about political considerations?" Derzhinsky said.

"Forgive my stupidity. To hell with politics," Lenin said.

"I forgive you," Derzhinsky said.

Lenin and his secretary rushed from the flat.

Derzhinsky turned to the window and stared out at the Moscow night with Peters by his side.

"Purge the Cheka," Peters said with a smile of feline satisfaction. "The SRs are out. The Moscow Cheka is yours."

"There is still Petrograd. There's no time to rest."

Peters said, "I'll tell Artuzov to have Reilly shot."

"No, let Reilly be. I spoke with him this afternoon. I invited him to become our partner."

"What did he say?" Peters said.

"He said it would be more interesting to defeat me than to execute me. What do you make of that?"

"British arrogance," Peters said.

"I accept his challenge," Derzhinsky said as his pale face grew red and fury silently transformed his eyes. "But what is victory?"

"Victory," Peters said, "is getting what we want. Power."

"Oh, no," Derzhinsky said. "Our victory will consist not merely in getting what we want, but in making Reilly the means for doing so. Our victory will come not in Reilly's death, but in our turning his life into something useful to us."

Derzhinsky paused, looked outside and appeared to take inspiration from the deep Moscow night. An aura of Red energy enveloped him. He seemed to understand the answer to some mystical question.

Peters said, "What is it, Feliks?"

"I have learned much today," Derzhinsky said. "I have a worthy opponent in Reilly, perhaps even an equal. Now I see what will make my victory complete, and satisfy me."

"Your equal? Then what kind of victory will satisfy you?"

"I'll be satisfied when Reilly begs at my knee, not for his own life, but for my forgiveness. No, not for his own life, but for my approval of it."

Part VI: The Lenin Affair

July-August, 1918

47. What Went Wrong?

Rain swept clean the streets of Moscow on the morning of July seventh. Reilly arrived at the safe flat to find Sasha huddled up in a corner pool of water with his head back against the wall, soaked to the bone. He glanced at Reilly but did not get up. He wore an absent expression and empty eyes. Reilly sat next to him.

"I'm glad you made it through the day," Reilly said.

"You got smashed," Sasha said.

"We lost by a hair," Reilly said. "Popov told me the signal to start the SR uprising would come at the Congress at two o'clock. I built my timing around that. But they killed Mirbach an hour early and everything fell apart. If they'd carried it off at two as planned, we'd have done it."

"Don't you see?," said Sasha. "You were beaten by a mistake. Derzhinsky found out about the SR plot at the last minute and tried to use Blyumkin to prevent it. He thought he could stop the murder or at least wreck their timing, but failed. His failure ultimately stopped you."

"I didn't know," said Reilly.

"Yes," said Sasha. "They say he's out of the Cheka. That Lenin fired him. Others say he quit in a suicidal fit, tried to kill himself and that Lenin talked him out of it."

"Will Lenin keep the SRs in the Cheka?"

"He ordered their execution. Bad news for me."

Reilly looked at Sasha with apprehension. "Why?"

"I have execution duty this afternoon."

Reilly said, "You don't have to do it. You can get out."

Sasha sneered. "I'll go to America."

"I can get you out."

"And leave everyone else here."

"You're not a killer," Reilly said. "You don't have to go."

"Neither do you," Sasha said. "But you won't quit."

"All right," Reilly said.

"What will you do?"

"Re-group. Find out just what went wrong. Count my assets. What did they say about the Englishman, Weber?"

"Last night Artuzov and I arrested him."

"Where is he?" Reilly said.

"Derzhinsky has him hidden somewhere. I don't know."

"Where did you go to get him?" Reilly said.

"Nineteen Petrovka, apartment thirty-five. Books, boxes, bookshelves and bookcases everywhere."

Reilly was quiet. Then he said, "Lockhart has a contact."

"Who?" said Sasha.

"He won't say," said Reilly. "He got Latvian Colonel Bredis for me through Savinkov. When Mirbach was shot, he ran."

"Did the Allies land at Archangel?" Sasha said.

"No."

"Savinkov needed the landing," Sasha said.

"Dammit," Reilly said.

"What will you do?" said Sasha.

"Start over." Reilly climbed to his feet.

"You won't mind if I don't see you to the door."

Reilly saw the emptiness in Sasha's face. "You don't have to do it," he said. "We can bag the whole thing, get the family to New York. I can do it."

Sasha shook his head. "We started something a year and a half ago, Sidney. We made promises. All of us. I'm not backing out." He held out his hand. Reilly took it.

"I'll see you soon," Reilly said.

Reilly went to Petrovka number nineteen and asked to be taken to see British citizen Weber.

"Don't know the name," a worker said.

"Flat number thirty-five," Reilly said and dug into his pocket for some rubles.

"Won't produce someone who's not here," the man said.

Reilly put the money back in his pocket and took out his red Cheka card. "Flat number thirty-five," he said.

The man wiped his paintbrush on the edge of a bucket, rested it upright on a cloth and said, "We'll have to go up the back way." He led Reilly from the lobby to the rear of the building, took him up several flights of stairs and knocked on a door that bore the number thirty-five. The door opened.

"Good day, Doctor Andrianov," said an old woman.

"I beg your pardon, comrade," the man said. "This policeman wants to look at your apartment. Do you mind?"

A woman opened the door, glanced at the man but away from Reilly. "Go ahead."

Reilly went through a room that was sparsely furnished but freshly cleaned. "How long have you lived here?"

The woman glanced at Andrianov and said, "Thirty years."

Reilly went into the bedroom, which had only a bed and dresser with a white doily and a small, empty jewellery box. He looked in the kitchen, where a table and three stools sat near a window that overlooked a small back yard. The sink had several dirty dishes and cups filled with water.

On the stool closest to the window, partially covered by the table, was a book, Shelley's Verses. It had gold trim and looked expensive. An inscription on the inside of the front cover: "To FW. Patience is the greatest virtue." Signed with initials: Small M, Large C. He put it back on the stool and slid the stool under the table. In the living room, Andrianov whispered to the woman. Reilly cleared his throat and said, "You like Shelley?"

"What's that?" the old woman said.

"The poet," Reilly said.

"I've read Mayakovsky," she said.

Reilly said, "Oh, the contemporary Russians are quite good."

"Most of my acquaintances are pensioners," she said.

"Thank you for your cooperation," said Reilly.

"Good bye," she said and opened the door.

Dr. Andrianov nodded and said good bye. Reilly followed him through the hall, down the stairs and to the street.

"You see?" said Andrianov. "No one named Weber."

"I see," Reilly said and nodded. He went toward the Bolshoi Theatre and walked to the Arbat District.

At the German Embassy Rudolph Bauer took Reilly to the late ambassador's office, where dried blood covered areas of the carpet and remnants of shattered porcelain objects lay all around. Reilly saw a few bullet holes in the walls.

"It must have been a madhouse," Reilly said.

"Blyumkin's pistol didn't fire the bullets that hit the ambassador," Bauer said. He showed Reilly two pistols. Blyumkin had emptied one and its capacity was the same as the number of bullet holes in the walls and floors. Bauer's forensic specialist reported that the bullets in the walls and floors could only have come from Blyumkin's pistol. Blyumkin missed every shot. The two bullets taken from Mirbach's body matched the pistol of the second assassin, Andreyev. Blyumkin's minder.

"One a terrible shot and the other a professional."

"A professional?" Reilly said.

"An experienced killer," Bauer said. "The first emptied the chamber, panicked and jumped out the window. The second fired twice, killed the ambassador and left his pistol on the victim's chest. The mark of a Russian assassin."

"Who was he?"

"Name is Andreyev," Bauer said. "You say you couldn't find the Englishman Weber? He never lived on Petrovka?"

"I think he was moved out quickly after the murder. Or perhaps that's what Derzhinsky wants us to think."

Mueller said he saw Weber's Cheka interrogation.

"I know the Cheka went to number nineteen Petrovka and took someone described as Weber to Cheka headquarters," Reilly said. "Weber seems simply to have vanished. Or was he merely an actor? Did Weber really exist at all?"

Reilly contemplated whether or not the SRs could have been behind the entire picture.

It would have been too complicated.

Someone else must have been responsible. Who could it

have been? Weber? Lenin? Or *could* the SRs have fouled it up all by themselves?

Bauer said, "Look into it, won't you, Colonel Schaefer? You have agents at the British Consulate. It would be interesting to hear what they have to say."

Reilly went across the city to the British Consulate, where a cable from Savinkov waited for him. It said, "Have taken Jaroslavl. But the Red Army advances. We cannot hold out much longer. Where are your British troops?"

Reilly gave a note to the clerk and said, "London Centre."

"Your report?" Lockhart said.

"My complaint," Reilly said.

Lockhart nodded. "I need to speak with you." They went to Lockhart's office. "I just received a wire from London," Lockhart said and gave Reilly a decoded message. "Obtain fifty-thousand gold rubles from Reilly. Deliver post haste to Chicherin in Bolshevik Government.' What do you think?"

"I don't know," Reilly answered.

"Why would he want me to deliver money to the Reds?"

Reilly raised an eyebrow. "Lenin is selling a war secret or two. The director is the highest bidder. I don't know."

"Do you have the money?"

"In the consulate safe. Take what you need."

"You're keeping that much money here?"

"Running a counter-revolution isn't cheap," Reilly said.

"What are you planning to do with it?"

"I hope to find a reliable Latvian officer."

"Latvian?"

"I need to replace Colonel Bredis, the officer your Kremlin contact sent us. When Mirbach was killed, he ran."

"I'm sorry about that, Sidney. I feel responsible."

"But before I do anything, there's something you can do."

"Gladly," replied Lockhart. "Anything. Just name it."

"You can set up a meeting with your Kremlin contact. I want to meet him. I want to know what went wrong."

"Oh," said Lockhart. "I should have said *almost* anything.

That I can't do. He wouldn't go for it. Too dangerous."

Reilly looked displeased. Lockhart was taken aback.

"Let me spell it out, Lockhart. In my opinion, we could have defeated the Bolsheviks but for Colonel Bredis. You and Savinkov got Bredis through your Kremlin contact. You're right to feel responsible but your contact provided the introduction. He has the real responsibility. I want to meet him. I'll be very disappointed if you don't arrange it."

Without doubt the large flat had belonged to an aristocrat or a wealthy businessman before the Bolshevik takeover. Though it was lighted by only a few candles, Reilly could see doors that led to other rooms, paintings on the wall, expensive furniture, rich carpet and art objects in every corner. Near the window a plush high back chair faced away from two large sofas set across from one another. A cloud of smoke rose above it and spread through the room. A man in the chair crushed a cigarette in an ashtray. Lockhart gestured to a sofa. Reilly sat down.

"There's only one rule," the man who was out of Reilly's view said in Russian. "Don't ask my name. I agreed to come here because Lockhart told me you have some questions about the uprising. Go ahead and ask me what you want. I'll give you whatever information I can. But nothing personal."

"All right," Reilly said. "I want clarity about Mirbach and the SR uprising. In particular, two things bother me. The first is the assassination of the German Ambassador and the second is the Latvian Colonel to whom you referred us."

"What about the assassination?"

"It threw off our timing," said Reilly, "and wrecked our plan. They said a Brit named Weber was connected to the SRs and that they were plotting Mirbach's murder. Derzhinsky and Peters interrogated him and then released him. Who was Weber and why did they let him go? What was he doing? Where is he?"

"Weber was a nobody," the man said. "The Germans insisted that we bring him in for questioning. Derzhinsky released him to play on German fear that something would happen to the ambassador if he attended the Congress."

"They wanted the Germans anxious about the Congress?"

"That's right."

"So the Germans would keep Mirbach away. That's it?"

"That's it," the man said. "Mirbach was a reminder of our treaty with the Germans. Imagine the disorder his presence could have brought. A Roman holiday for the SRs."

"I see," said Reilly.

The man continued, "With Mirbach at the Congress the Bolsheviks could easily have lost control. So Derzhinsky sent Blyumkin to the German Embassy to persuade the ambassador that it was too dangerous to attend."

"He didn't know the dangers of sending Blyumkin?"

The invisible man laughed. "Do you think Derzhinsky wanted the assassination and the uprising? Are you crazy?"

"The result was the complete elimination of the SRs from the Moscow Cheka, and total control going to Derzhinsky."

"And the elimination of Derzhinsky too."

"Oh, come on."

"It cost him his job. A Cheka conspiracy? If there was a conspiracy it was by the SRs, probably the result of a grudge on the part of Spiridonova or Blyumkin. Petty. No more."

"It smacks of design," said Reilly.

"Reilly," said the man, "you're thinking like a Russian. You need a conspiracy to make sense of what happened. The truth is that the Bolsheviks were vulnerable, very unsure of themselves and grossly incompetent. They weren't capable of stopping the SRs, but the SRs were certainly capable of wrecking things for themselves. They just couldn't resist shooting Mirbach. So your timing was shot to hell. Your scheme wasn't wrecked by a Derzhinsky conspiracy or by a Cheka conspiracy, but by a bunch of SRs who were too stupid to come in out of the rain."

Reilly shifted his legs uncomfortably.

"And that's what you should have expected," the man said. "You thought you had planned for every contingency, every detail. But the truth is that you completely disregarded the most important element of Russian life. Which is fate. It thrives on your countrymen's penchant for self-destruction. It wasn't a conspiracy that undid your plans. It was Russian self-destructiveness, plain and simple. If you want to have another go at it, think about that or you're doomed to fail."

The man's words offended Reilly, not because he disbelieved them but because they rang true. He did not accept the cynicism in this explanation but had no better one.

"I want to replace Bredis," he said. "Can you help?"

"Maybe," the man replied. "But no promises. I'll let Lockhart know. That's all for now."

Lockhart nodded to Reilly, thanked his contact and led the way to the stairs.

On the afternoon of the eighth day of July, eight Chekists carried rifles from two black automobiles across a patch of grass, stopped and snapped to attention. One was Sasha. A long green branch shielded them from the afternoon sun. They turned toward the tall red stone wall around the Kremlin. Socialist Revolutionary Party members stood in a line, their backs to the wall. The Chekists raised their rifles and aimed them at the SRs, whose eyes showed defiance and not fear. Sasha's had only sadness. For the SRs, death by firing squad meant redemption for a violent life. For Sasha, the death of the SRs meant the death of his soul.

Someone said, "Fire!"

Eight shots rang out. Eight men fell against the red stone wall and thumped to the ground. Others removed the bodies. Eight more marched to the wall.

Someone said, "Fire!"

Eight rifles fired. Eight men fell to the ground. The bodies were removed, replaced with eight living men who would soon die. After them eight more died, then six men and two women, then eight men. At five o'clock they carried the last of the dead SRs to a flatbed truck and threw them over the side onto a bloody pile of bodies. The truck drove off. Seven of the Chekists marched toward their vehicles. Sasha walked to the tall tree whose long green branch had shielded him from the afternoon sun, bent over and vomited.

For several days, no one heard from the Chekist known as Timor Lipkin. For the most part, Sasha stayed in bed, the captive of physical pain that he knew originated with shame and horror. He had not regained himself by the following day, but for reasons that were beyond him managed to appear at the Lubyanka. The pale, ghastly face he wore, the hollow eyes that had witnessed the flight of his own soul, the quivering of lips that had nothing to say—these things were familiar sights to some in the Cheka. To men who had never killed until some circumstance that they had not imagined but had nonetheless chosen left them swimming in death and in the blood of their victims. That is why at first no one spoke to him until Artuzov approached him with a gentle pat on the shoulder. Not long after this, Derzhinsky appeared in the doorway of Artuzov's office. Everything stopped.

"Where is Comrade Timor Lipkin?" he said.

Artuzov looked at Sasha, who had glassy eyes.

Derzhinsky walked toward Sasha and looked down at him. "Comrade Timor Lipkin," he said in a soft voice.

Sasha rose silently, absently. Derzhinsky opened his arms, embraced and held him quietly as a father holding his son. He did not speak or move but kept him close.

Sasha was filled with horror, as though the devil had come to take him. He heard a distant, despairing voice that pleaded, "Run..." But he did not move.

Derzhinsky kept his arm around the neophyte Chekist who was now one of many baptized in blood. He led Sasha to the window that looked down on the Lubyanka Square, where men stood guard over empty streets.

"Our revolution will purify this corrupt land, Comrade Timor." Then his eyes captured Sasha, his voice unearthly, quiet, soft, yet filled with extraordinary power:

"That is the awesome responsibility of the Cheka. From each of us, that awesome responsibility demands superhuman sacrifice, a sacrifice that only a god is capable of. Oh, not merely a sacrifice of blood, but of something inside us. When we take human life, something inside us dies. Yet this is the demand placed upon us by our love of man, by our unique understanding of what is required to purify our world and make it into a paradise for all. This is our special knowledge, which can never be comprehended by ordinary men. With our sacrifice we take upon ourselves the pain and suffering of all. When we sacrifice the blood of the impure, we sacrifice our souls. But in doing this we make life possible for all. This is the legacy of the Cheka. And now this is your legacy."

Sasha, astounded, said nothing.

"You are Lazarus, risen from the dead. In this sacrifice, the spirit is reborn and life transformed, raised to a height not known by common men, but only by a faithful few."

He believes that he himself raised me from the dead.

Derzhinsky kissed the forehead of Comrade Timor Lipkin, held Sasha's cheeks and offered a final embrace.

As Sasha saw Derzhinsky walk from the office, he felt a tear crawling down his cheek and knew it was not his own.

A detachment of guards took Jacob Peters from the Moscow Station in Petrograd to the office of the Commissar of the Cheka Criminal Division, Comrade Volodia Orlov. "Derzhinsky sends his greetings," he said, "and the thanks of the Moscow Cheka."

"What for?" said Volodia.

"For keeping discipline among your agents and ensuring that the city did not experience what Moscow endured. An uprising that could have destroyed us."

"Peters," Volodia said, "are you blind? It was hunger and weakness that kept Petrograd quiet. Not me."

"Your superior might have behaved differently without you here. His Menshevik friends complain that food is scarce."

"Food is scarce. Only party members have enough to eat."

"There's not enough to go around, comrade. Let the city die. What matters is the survival of the Party. That's all. You have Derzhinsky's gratitude. You will be rewarded. Watch Uritsky carefully, to make sure he serves the Party."

In another office, Peters said to Uritsky, "Comrade Derzhinsky is counting on you to defend the revolution against a new and invidious threat. The British intend to overthrow us and install their own puppet bourgeois government. A dangerous British agent named Reilly is leading this conspiracy. His base is the British Embassy, which is in your jurisdiction."

"Yes, comrade," Uritsky replied. "Anything else?"

"You will lead a team of special agents that have been appointed by Comrade Derzhinsky. They will follow Reilly, infiltrate his organization and soon strike at the heart of the conspiracy. Here are the names of agents who will be involved," he added, giving Uritsky a document.

"Who are the Latvians? Orlov is the only name I recognize."

"They're Derzhinsky's men," said Peters. "Never mind. All you need to know is that this is Derzhinsky's top-priority secret operation. No one in the Moscow Cheka knows about it. Be quiet until someone contacts you."

Derzhinsky strode into Lenin's office, dropped a typed document on the desk and said, "This should amuse you."

Lenin took the paper. "Who sent it?"

Lenin read quietly, "Lockhart. 'Due to German encroachments we are adding reinforcements to the small number of British soldiers, already authorized by you, who are stationed at Murmansk to prevent a German seizure of the arms stores that they guard. The strengthening of this small force is based upon our agreed-upon mutual interest to counter threats both to our war efforts and to the territorial integrity of Russia.'" Lenin said, "Do you believe him?"

"The British are coming, comrade. What's more, the counter-revolutionary armies are almost at Ekatarinaburg and will soon try to liberate Tsar Nicholas and his family. If we don't stop them, the ex-Tsar will rally the Whites and the Allies. Either we act now or in several weeks we'll be fighting on two fronts. We'll move headquarters to the Urals and fight as guerrillas."

"What should we do?" said Lenin.

"Let the Allies know that if they invade, we will execute their diplomats and extend the treaty with Germany."

"Those are tough measures," Lenin said. "What else?"

"The policy of terror must be implemented."

"Not yet, comrade."

"And the revolt at Kronstadt?" said Derzhinsky.

"What revolt?"

"Don't you know? Forty traitors executed one of my men. Now Uritsky refuses to execute them without orders from you. This is the order," he said and gave Lenin a document.

Lenin quickly attached his signature. "What else?"

"Consider that Reilly is making plans to execute you. Think about the strength of the ex-Tsar if they liberate him."

Lenin threw his hands into the air. "More! More! More! I just signed an execution order for forty traitors and now you want premature terror! You want to hold Allied diplomats hostage *and* have Nicholas and his family executed!"

Derzhinsky clenched his jaw.

"If I do all this I won't be safe anywhere! The Allies, the Germans, even the Central Committee will be crying for my head. You can't use terror yet! Of the other crises, pick one!"

"The Romanovs," Derzhinsky said. "Kill the Romanovs."

48. A New Plan

The sky over Petrograd was a surreal and cloudless blue. Beneath the sky were factories, ugly in their emptiness. Worse were food lines with people whose factories had closed. Even worse were the numbers in documents hidden somewhere inside the Bolshevik Government that showed a decline in the city's population by almost half, almost one million over two years but most of it in the latest few months, since the Bolsheviks had moved the capitol to Moscow.

The weather was warm but the city of Petrograd cold. Years earlier, Peter the Great exiled his wife Eudoxia because she did not believe in the city that he had built. She retorted, "Saint Petersburg will stand empty!"

The city had not forgotten her words. Now the citizens believed that the curse of Eudoxia was real, that St. Petersburg, now Petrograd, was cursed. They recognized the city's vulnerability to the surrounding waters and to the swamps upon which it was built. They feared, just as the poet Pushkin had predicted, that one day the city would be swallowed in a tidal wave from the Gulf of Finland.

Now the citizens were moving away. Half had deserted. Half remained, the un-living, who no longer strolled on the Nevsky but stood in its queues. They heard that boxcars with food had arrived in the city. But at the end of their food lines they found rotten vegetables and mouldy bread. Would the un-living stay any longer? They were too weak to move so they stayed and stood lifeless in the food lines.

The British Embassy, on the Neva, was not impoverished. Food stores remained in the basement. Reilly arrived at mid-day. The Naval Attaché, Captain Cromie, opened the door and said, "You have a caller."

"Who?" Reilly said.

"Second floor," Cromie said

Reilly went upstairs to the conference room. As he turned the corner a knuckled fist flew out of nowhere and smashed his chin. His mind went blank. He crashed to the floor.

Sometime later a damp cloth drew slowly across Reilly's face and a bright ceiling light blinded him as he tried to open his eyes. His head ached and he tasted vomit. He raised his hand to his jaw, moved the jaw slightly left and right and looked up. Savinkov ran the cloth over his forehead and said, "I think you'll be all right."

"Did you do that?" Reilly said.

"I did."

"Why?"

"I thought you'd appreciate the symbolism."

"Oh," said Reilly. "It's good to see you too."

"It was for the thousands of troops your government promised but did not send. It was for six hundreds of my men who were butchered or executed, thrown in ditches and then buried by the Cheka." He ran the damp cloth across Reilly's cheeks and brought it under his chin. "There," he said. "You look better already."

"I had nothing to do with that," Reilly said, bracing himself with his elbows on the conference table where he lay. "It didn't exactly help me either, you know."

"Oh," Savinkov said, "I know. The pain in your head was not intended for you so much as for your Prime Minister. If you would be so kind as to deliver the message."

"You want me to hit Lloyd George?" Reilly said and lowered his legs over the side.

"Yes," said Savinkov. "That would be good."

"What are you doing here?" Reilly said.

"Hiding,' Savinkov said and took a cigar from the jacket of his uniform. He cut the end off with scissors and stuck the cigar between his teeth. "A good occupation for someone with a price on his head, as Lenin has placed on mine." He lit the cigar, blew a cloud of smoke into the air and coughed.

"Well," Reilly said, "you can't stay here very long. We're re-grouping. We're going to do it again on the twenty-eighth at a Central Committee conference in Moscow."

"What is it this time?"

"An Allied landing. Real support of the White Army."

"And the Latvians?"

"Your man, Colonel Bredis, jumped ship when Mirbach was shot. I need to replace him."

"Talk to Cromie," said Savinkov. "He has lots of friends."

"That's true," said Cromie, standing in the doorway. He walked to the table, put his fingertips on Reilly's chin and raised Reilly's head slightly. "Oh, bad luck," he said. "I daresay you'll be out of business if you do this to the Prime Minister. Black and blue. You should see yourself. But Savinkov is right. I may be able to help you with a Latvian."

"How soon," said Reilly.

"I'll make some calls," Cromie said. "What may I say?"

"It's just a feeler," Reilly said with caution. "Test their interest but don't give anything away." Then to Savinkov, Reilly said, "How long do you intend to stay here?"

"A few days, a week. I have to see my officers. I can field a few thousand. If they're still speaking to me."

"You're here alone?" said Reilly.

"More or less," Savinkov said. "I won't leave the city until I've spoken with Filonenko and Semyenov, my agents. They'll stay behind and represent me in Moscow and Petrograd. That way our communication will be better."

A woman appeared in the doorway and glanced at Reilly.

"Hello," Reilly said.

She was pretty, with a good figure and slinky dress that showed an ample bosom.

She smiled at Savinkov. "Introduce me, Boris."

"I don't know if I should," Savinkov said.

"I thought you said you were here alone," Reilly said.

"Sidney," Savinkov said as the woman came and stood next to him, "this is Mamie."

Reilly smiled. Mamie held out her hand as though she expected Reilly to kiss it. He glanced at it and then at Mamie's eyes. He put his hands on his hips. "We've met."

It was in St. Petersburg, before the war. Reilly had a new wife. Mamie had a Socialist husband. She still had him.

"He's my advisor," Savinkov said. "My sponsor."

Cromie came back in. "I'll have something for you tonight. Where are you staying?"

"Stay with us," Mamie said.

Reilly said, "No thanks" and gave the address to Cromie.

"Are you leaving so soon?" said Mamie.

"I'm sure we'll meet again," he said before turning to Savinkov and adding, "When do you expect your agents?"

"Any time," said Savinkov. "After that, I'll go to Kazan."

"You'll leave me a message, won't you?"

Savinkov glanced at Mamie. "You can talk to Cromie or to Mamie. They'll know how to get in touch with me."

Mamie frowned. "I thought I was going with you."

Reilly nodded to Savinkov and whispered to Cromie in the doorway, "She'll take on the three of us if you let her."

In the rail yards of Petrograd boxcars were filled with food requisitioned from peasant villages across Russia. The boxes were stamped, "Food delivery, Petrograd."

In Bryansk, a local Cheka boss said to the representative from the Moscow Cheka, "We're not getting much support from the local population. Food would ensure cooperation."

Lenin said, "Take a thousand out and shoot them."

A telegram came back, "One thousand executed per your instruction, but locals still defiant. Unless we bring some food to the city, there will be uprisings. Food will win their hearts and profit us." Profit was the operative word.

Soon the bills-of-lading marked "Petrograd" were exchanged for ones marked "Bryansk." Signed by Stalin.

Reilly's cousin and ex-lover, Elena Mikhailovna, worked with a man named Lev in the Department of Food Supply. They had fallen in love with one another and with their mission. When they met, Elena said, "We'll feed Petrograd."

Lev replied, "Yes, comrade, we'll feed it together."

Lev was unique because he smiled. He was attractive because he listened. He was brave because he swore he would never stop fighting for his ideals, which had become Elena's ideals. One afternoon they walked along the Nevsky and passed food lines that had recently grown longer.

"The food lines should be getting shorter," she said.

Lev said, "The most difficult part of food distribution is local. It takes time to get shipments to the shops."

"The lines should get shorter soon," Elena said.

"Yes," Lev said.

A day later another line of boxcars carried bills-of-lading that said "Petrograd." The steam engine pulled them slowly along the track and stopped while a workman fixed a switch to a different grading. Elena stepped up to the workman and said, "Why is that cargo going south and east?"

He said, "Comrade Stalin's orders."

"What is their destination?"

"Bryansk is south, Nizhny Sanarka is east, in the Urals."

Elena and Lev walked back to the Moscow Station. They wove through crowds in the station. Outside, Elena stopped and said, "It was almost a month ago. A month ago that Comrade Stalin approved our plan to feed the city. But every shipment of food gets re-routed to south or east. The people in our city are underfed, hungry and weak."

"I'm sure Petrograd will get its share," he replied. "But other cities need food too, you know. I'm certain Comrade Stalin will make sure the city gets its share."

The midnight sky was white. Beneath the white sky, where boards covered the windows of mansions, the shadows of mansions covered the street, which was dark and empty. At the end of the street was a small park surrounded by trees. Reilly stood there and watched a mansion that had windows instead of boards. In one of those windows a light flashed on and off. Reilly walked toward the building. The door was unlocked. Inside, another opened.

The man in the doorway was tall with steely, blue eyes. His grey uniform had red stars on shoulder epaulets. He was Latvian, and his brigade was Red. Cromie told Reilly that this officer wanted to turn White. His name was Berzin.

Colonel Berzin said, "I thought the Bolsheviks would respect the Fourteen Points of the American President, which support independence for all peoples. Lenin promised Latvia independence after the war. But Lenin is a liar and my men don't believe in him. We'd like to do business with you, Captain Reilly. I want to place myself under your command.

We'll help you overthrow the Bolsheviks if you swear to support an independent Latvia after the European war."

"What would be required?" Reilly said.

"Financial support, especially for some divisions who are being courted by the Germans. The Germans are also planning to overthrow the Bolsheviks."

Reilly smiled. "What's their offer?"

Berzin said, "Very high."

"The Germans will never give you independence."

"That is why I accepted Captain Cromie's invitation to meet with you. But we have no time to waste. The Germans are actively proselytising the Latvian soldiers in Moscow. And there are fifty thousand of us, Captain Reilly."

How much would the Latvians need?

"I'll take inventory and then give you a precise figure."

When Reilly saw Elena walking along the Catherine Canal embankment, he did not think she would acknowledge him. They had been intimate and had always loved one another. But she had become a socialist and now had responsibility in Lenin's government. He had become a spy and had got wealthy living a philosophy she found repugnant. She was an idealist who thought him a cynic. But she strode to the bench where he was sitting and said, "Hello, comrade."

"To what do I owe this honour?"

"To my failed belief in Bolshevism," she said.

She told him about trains with food that had been taken from Petrograd and sent south or east, about the food stores that had dwindled to nothing and about the food lines that were endless and growing every day with no end in sight.

"Petrograd is dying," Elena said. "People are going to die. Not in tens or dozens, but in thousands until no one is left. They steal peasants' grain and sell it to local Bolshevik bosses in the countryside and the villages. The locals barter it for anything profitable while Petrograd starves."

"Petrograd will not starve," he replied. "In a few weeks we

are going to replace Lenin. There will be ample food in the boxcars in the train yards at that time."

"How long will we have to wait?"

"One month. August twenty-eight. Can you hold on?"

"Yes."

"Can the city hold on?"

"I can get some of those boxcars unloaded and the food delivered, unless I get caught and shot. Why do they do this?"

"Because they need the troops elsewhere. The only way they can prevent an uprising here is to keep everyone weak."

"Everyone is weak. Their scheme is working."

"I could have told you."

"I didn't want to listen. What can I do to help you?"

"Can I use your flat tomorrow?"

"Why?" she said, looking at him with a half-smile.

"Can I use your flat?" he said impatiently.

She took out her keys. "Do you know the address?"

"I have the address," he replied.

"Can we communicate?" she asked.

"We can exchange messages in your apartment."

"I have an empty vase near the window. If your hand fits inside, you might find something from me."

Moura placed a tray with three teacups on the table and went into the kitchen that was just around the corner. She put on her eyeglasses and opened a book.

When Reilly arrived he noticed Moura reading a book by Hesse. She had been reading it for ages but was still on page eight. Lockhart took Reilly to the sitting room and said, "Per your request, I want you to meet a Latvian officer."

Lockhart brought in a familiar man. "Reilly," Lockhart said, "this is Berzin. Colonel, Captain Reilly." They shook hands but did not speak of meeting in Petrograd.

Berzin poured himself a cup of tea. "We can do more than help you overthrow Lenin," he said. "My men want action. I hear there may be an Allied landing up north. If so, we can join with them to form an unbeatable fighting force. We'll dump Lenin and help you defeat the Germans too."

"What can we do to help you, Colonel?" asked Lockhart.

"Get me a pass to your base at Archangel."

Lockhart went to type out the document.

Reilly followed. "Be careful, Lockhart. I'm not sure about Berzin. He's offering too much too soon. He acted as though we never met, but we did meet in Petrograd. He may be in it for the money, playing our offer against one made by the Germans. Or he could be one of Derzhinsky's agents."

"Too late now," Lockhart said. "I'll have to give him a pass. Otherwise he'll get suspicious."

"How far do you trust Cromie's judgment?"

"Completely," Lockhart said. "But there's no guarantee."

"Give the Lett a pass. Act like a friend. Test him later."

Reilly gave Berzin an envelope with money. Lockhart gave him a pass for admission to Allied facilities in the north. Maura went out. Lockhart said he had received word of a small added presence to the British contingent at Murmansk in the north.

"Are they're preparing to land?" Reilly said.

Lockhart said. "Not by this cipher. They actually want to protect allied stores from the Germans. But the Germans are sailing in the opposite direction, which will make us look like liars. I had to inform Derzhinsky even though it's just a few hundred and hasn't anything to do with the Bolsheviks. I wonder how he described it to Lenin."

49. An Allied Landing at Archangel

On August first, Derzhinsky reported that one hundred thousand Allied troops would land at Archangel. To Lenin, he said, "I told you the British would come."

"Are we prepared to evacuate?" Lenin said.

"We are prepared," Derzhinsky said. "But we have time. We should wait and let the conspirators make their plans. Information is coming."

"What do you know?" Lenin said.

"Reilly plans to arrest the Central Committee on August

twenty-eighth and have everyone executed. There is only one way to stop them, comrade, and that is complete terror."

"No. The political repercussions would finish us."

"Then postpone the meeting and destroy Reilly's timing."

"I can't do that," Lenin said.

But he did. In several days, when new reports revised the number of invading Allied troops down to six hundred, the Bolsheviks unpacked. Some measures set out against the Allied representatives in Russia were relaxed. Still, Derzhinsky continued to insist on his worst-case scenario.

Volodia, meanwhile, reported a visit by Peters, who insisted that Reilly was planning to execute the Central Committee. Uritsky rebutted with firm evidence, but Peters persisted: "Reilly wants to execute them."

"That's not what my sources tell me," Uritsky said.

"That's what I'm telling you, comrade."

Sasha had drawn tight the shades in his safe flat. One candle burned on a small corner table where the conspirators sat. "When will it end?" Sasha said, his eyes tired and empty.

"August twenty-eighth," Reilly replied. "At the Central Committee meeting in Moscow. Can you hold out?"

"I'll try," he said.

"I know how you feel," said Volodia. "I've been on the inside for more than a year. It's absolute hell. There are times when I feel that I am becoming like them."

"I've murdered people in cold blood," said Sasha. "I have nightmares about Derzhinsky every night. Worse, I have moments when I actually feel kinship with Artuzov. It's got to end or I'll lose my mind. Maybe I've already lost it."

"It will end," said Reilly.

"Artuzov may have Anna's flat under surveillance. I read an agent's report saying you had numerous women..."

"I have women agents."

"And that women are your weakness. Artuzov will try to plant a woman on you."

"Generous of him."

Volodia said, "We have an anti-Reilly team in Petrograd too, led by Uritsky. I'm on it, waiting for something to do. So far I've met with him a few times but have no assignments. They may have infiltrated your organization."

"I didn't know," Sasha said.

"He doesn't know about it," said Volodia. "It's secret."

"Two separate teams, unknown to one another?"

"Two teams that don't share information?" Reilly said. "Must be two different sets of objectives."

"One must be a shill," Sasha said.

"What do you think it means?" said Volodia.

Reilly said, "Derzhinsky has a story he wants to sell. Other than stopping us, what's his objective?"

"Power," Volodia said. "He has the Moscow Cheka and needs the Petrograd branch."

"How will he get that?" Reilly said.

"I'm not sure what to believe," Volodia said.

"Maybe the comrades don't know what to believe," Sasha said. "Maybe Comrade Lenin doesn't know what to believe."

Derzhinsky revised the number of Allied troops down to six-hundred and announced that the landing was just a test, a test that Lenin had failed. "Now," he said, "they will execute their real plan."

Namely, "Reilly's forces and a huge invasion. According to Uritsky, a putsch is planned for the twenty-eighth at our conference. It is an opportunity to defeat the imperialists once and for all. Postponing the conference will kill their timing. *Inconvenient* for us, but *salvation* for the revolution."

It was a forceful case. Lenin responded by ordering plans drawn up to move the government to the Urals.

Reilly crumpled Sasha's note.

"What's wrong, Sidney?" Anna said.

"A delay. Lenin's postponed the conference."

"What will you do?"

"I don't know." Reilly rang Lockhart.

"For how long?" asked Lockhart.

"Two weeks. We'll never be able to hold off for two weeks. I want you to talk to your contact inside the Kremlin. Tell him I want to stop. I'll talk to our people. Maybe it's best to wait until the White Army can take the cities."

"Wait, Sidney," Lockhart said. "Stop and think."

"About what?" said Reilly. "We've been broken. They're on to us. So we go to Plan B. We wait for the White Army."

"Let me see if I can set up a meeting," Lockhart said. "But I don't know."

On a dark and narrow street not far from the centre of Moscow, Lockhart led Reilly past a long row of houses abandoned by bourgeois owners who had fled from the revolution. Near the centre of the block, Reilly took Lockhart's arm, and stopped cold.

"Who is it, Lockhart?" he asked in an agitated tone. "Who is this mysterious inside contact? I don't like surprises. Tell me who he is now, before we go."

Lockhart took a deep breath. "If you insist on this, Sidney, we might as well go back. I promised anonymity. You want information. He has it. So be patient. I can tell you how I found him, if that will reassure you. The Director told me about him and indicated he thought he might be turned."

"What did he say when you met him?"

"That Lenin and Derzhinsky were much more dangerous than he had ever thought. He was looking for a way out but knew that once inside the Cheka, the only alternative was death. He said he knew it would take some time but eventually a counter-revolutionary attempt would be made against the Bolsheviks. He assumed I'd be involved in it and told me he'd do anything he could to help as long as he wouldn't be compromised. Today, when I told him there was a chance we might cancel our plans, he pleaded with me to reconsider. He really wants to overthrow Lenin. I think the Director was right. My man is half-turned right now."

"Lockhart, you're making my head spin. You're naïve as hell. Let's face it: Derzhinsky must have planted this fellow on you in the hope that he'd get information about me. But if C originated the contact- that's different. He's had years of experience identifying that kind of game and if he said the fellow is for real, well, I have to take him seriously. But he sent us to Bredis, too, who jumped ship, so he's suspect."

"I don't blame you for being sceptical," Lockhart continued. "All I ask is that you listen carefully to him and make your decision. I'll back you no matter what you do."

They walked to a house that was completely hidden in the darkness. Lockhart led the way around the side and to the rear. They climbed some wooden steps to a door. Lockhart knocked lightly, in three sets of two. The door creaked open.

"Lockhart here."

The door closed. Someone released a chain. The door opened halfway. Lockhart and Reilly slipped inside. Someone led the way up a flight of stairs, opened a door and then vanished. The British agents stepped into a room lighted by a candle with a high-back chair turned away from a sitting area.

"Hello, Lockhart," came the voice of the contact as a smoke cloud rose over the chair.

"I've brought Reilly," Lockhart said.

"Sit down and talk, Reilly. What's the problem?"

"My security was soft," Reilly replied. "Derzhinsky got hold of the plan. Probably my own fault. As a result the conference is off and once again our timing has been wrecked. We have no choice but to bag the whole thing and start over."

"Come on, Reilly," the man replied. "You never thought this would be easy, did you? If you bail out now, the whole thing will fall down and Lenin will be in power forever. You won't get another chance like this one."

"What does it matter to you?" said Reilly. "What does it matter, now or later? Why not wait until the Whites are ready to sack the city and take Lenin out then?"

"Sooner or later the balloon will go up and Derzhinsky will unleash a massive terror. Do you know how close it is to happening? It could be weeks, even days, before Lenin tells Derzhinsky to purify the country. What use will I be then? To anyone but Derzhinsky? And where will your supporters be then? I'll tell you where. They'll be running for Finland or Ukraine or Mongolia, the ones who are lucky, and they won't come back. And where will you be? In a comfortable hotel room in London, if you're fortunate. Everyone else will be lined up and shot. Who will stop Lenin then? Lloyd George? Hah. It's now or never, Reilly. It's you or no one."

Reilly raised an eyebrow. "There's too much I don't like."

"Oh, come on, Reilly!" the man shot back. "You're on the outside! You can leave whenever you want! You can go home to a normal life. But a lot of people have bet on you and your scheme to save Russia. Some have already died or are in prison. But others will be crushed if you give it up now. Win or lose, it's better to make an effort when Lenin finally holds his conference, even if you don't like the delay. If you don't, the opposition will fold and walk away. You can hold out for just a few weeks. But if you quit, Russia's finished."

The man put out the candle, stood and stomped to the door. "If you do quit, I'll see that you never make it back to London." He slammed the door behind him.

"Well," Reilly said. "There's a man with conviction."

"Perhaps he is Derzhinsky's man," Lockhart said. "But I agree with every point he made."

"You think we can survive the delay?"

"I don't know. We won't know unless we try."

"Is he right about the terror?"

"Your guess is as good as mine. But if we quit, we'll lose the ones who don't go over to the Bolsheviks in self-defence. It *does* seem like Russia's last chance."

Reilly stood up and said, "Let's get back to work."

Cromie had made a habit of hiding behind the curtains of his office, which looked out onto the embankment of the River Neva, the main thoroughfare along the river from Smolney Institute past the Winter Palace. He kept his spy glass with him at all times. Lately he had seen men watching the embassy. So had his adjutant, whose room was in the embassy rear and overlooked the street in the back, the long Field of Mars and the Military palace. Others at the embassy reported vagrants in the Summer Garden and speedboats idling in the nearby canal. Black automobiles cruised slowly past the embassy.

The Embassy was under close Cheka surveillance. On the night of August twenty-sixth Cromie received a message from Volodia that said, "Keep Reilly away from all safe flats in Petrograd. Believe Elena's flat is unknown to Cheka. In the best case, arrange for his escape. Net dropping. Cheka attack likely at Embassy. Evacuate."

Cromie got the message to Reilly, who responded, "Evacuate embassy. See you in Petrograd on thirty August, Balkov Café, twelve noon."

On the same day, Elena went to the rail yards to try to save another shipment of food for Petrograd, where food lines were longer than ever. The guard she had used on previous visits had been replaced by a man who eyed her suspiciously. She abandoned her mission and returned quickly to her flat. Along the way she saw that the number of armed guards on the streets had more than doubled.

50. Trouble in Petrograd

On August thirtieth Volodia arrived at Uritsky's office and found his Cheka superior with a bottle of vodka.

"Sit down, comrade," said Uritsky. "You'll have a drink with an old plunderer, won't you? Drink with me."

Uritsky poured a glass of vodka for Volodia. He raised his glass high and said, "Here's to the bloodiest bunch of sonofabitches in the world, comrade. The sonofabitches called

Bolsheviks." He gulped down the vodka. "But you didn't drink with me comrade. Why didn't you drink to my toast? To the bloody sonofabitches..."

Volodia looked at his watch. "Because it's ten-thirty in the morning. Do you want to put me on my back for the day?"

"You don't know what to say to a drunken Chekist."

"What should I say?" said Volodia.

"That I'm crazy. That the bloody sonofabitches are just lovers of peace and democracy. That rivers of blood are the only way to build a free republic where everything is normal, like in England." Uritsky lifted his glass.

"Better take it easy," said Volodia. "You don't need vodka. I'll make some coffee."

"Coffee?" said Uritsky. "I have coffee. Do you know why? Because I run the bloody Cheka and I can get anything. That's why I have coffee, comrade. Do you want some?"

"Yes," said Volodia. "Let's both drink some coffee."

Uritsky stood up, stumbled toward the window and stared outside. "Now there is the future of Russia."

Volodia went to the window and saw a youth on a bicycle.

"But what kind of future do you think Bolsheviks will give him? None. Look at him. See his eyeglasses. He probably reads. Do you know what he'll be reading soon? Nothing. Nothing but Red propaganda. Nothing but lies about our revolution. Do you know why? Because the Bolsheviks are terrified that someone might get an idea." Uritsky slipped. Volodia caught him and led him back to his seat.

"Why did you call me here, comrade?" Volodia asked.

"I don't want to die alone. I speak to no one. Who can I speak to? To comrade Derzhinsky? He'd have me shot."

"Why, comrade?"

"Because then he would know that I have contempt for him. For every bloody scheme he runs. For all the murders he has forced me to commit. But no more, comrade. No more murders. Why, you ask?" Because this comrade will die."

"What do you mean?"

"Power, comrade. No revolution. After all the struggles, all the years in exile, all of the schemes to overthrow the Tsar, what have we got? A government in power less than a year and already corrupt. Every Ministry. Head to toe. Only murder, bribes, extortion and theft. People in food lines. What else can they do? I have plenty of food and so do you. But they're starving. The citizens are starving and they're just bodies standing in line. The Terror has started."

Volodia wondered if his Cheka boss was testing him.

"But here's the worst, Your Honour," Uritsky said. "The very worst of all. A few months ago a Bolshevik eavesdropper reported that a few drunken sailors at Kronstadt had complained about not having food. Derzhinsky called it treason and had forty sailors shot. You know who had to execute that order. I did. Now I am 'The Butcher of Petrograd'. Well, to hell with Derzhinsky." Uritsky passed out on the floor, and quiet moans dripped from his mouth.

Volodia knelt down beside him and felt his pulse. "That's all you need to say for now," he whispered softly.

Volodia walked down the stairs, left the building and saw that the youngster on the bicycle was studying him with a frightened expression and seemed very anxious. He walked across the street and headed for his office.

When Volodia was out of sight, the youngster jumped off the bicycle, rested it against a building, looked behind him and walked through the door to Uritsky's office.

"Commissar," he called. "Commissar Uritsky?" He listened. From inside the office came a groan. The young man took a pistol from inside his shirt. "Uritsky!" he shouted. "I sentence you to death for executing forty young men at Kronstadt! I'm Kannengeiser and I sentence you to death!" The angry young man stepped into Uritsky's office and saw the Chekist sprawled out on the floor.

"Oh!" he said. "Uritsky is dead!"

He rushed out, jumped down the stairs and screamed, "They've killed Uritsky! They've executed the butcher of

Petrograd!" He jumped on his bicycle in a panic, tried to steady it as is wobbled, brought it under control and rode off.

Inside the building Uritsky opened his eyes, glanced over his shoulder and through a cloud of drunkenness saw a pair of boots near his head. Above him, someone said, "Why, that noise was the announcement of your execution, comrade."

Then a gunshot rang out, blew Uritsky's skull apart and echoed against the nearby buildings. A second shot coloured Uritsky's tunic crimson. The assassin lay his pistol on Uritsky's chest and walked casually down to the street.

A black Rolls Royce rolled to a door at the Kremlin. Derzhinsky leapt out and went inside. Peters parked the car and followed him into the building. Inside the office, members of the Central Committee talked in panic to one another. When Derzhinsky arrived everything stopped.

"I have news, comrade," he said to Lenin. "It's Petrograd."

"What happened? The landing?"

Every eye focused on Derzhinsky.

"They've killed Uritsky."

"No!" they shouted.

Lenin said, "You see, comrade, your resignation was premature. You're needed here. Take control of the Cheka."

The others nodded and shouted, "Yes! Yes!"

Derzhinsky said, "I serve the revolution and cannot think about taking power."

"Take back your power over the Cheka!" they shouted.

"Comrades," he said, "my debt to the revolution is not yet paid. I'm not fit for power."

"Derzhinsky, take back the Cheka! Save the Revolution!"

Lenin rose. "What about Petrograd, Feliks? Uritsky's dead, and you're in Moscow. Who protects us in Petrograd? Who speaks for The Party and the revolution?"

"Go to Petrograd!" they said.

Again, Derzhinsky looked aside, seemingly agonized.

"Feliks! The revolution needs you!"

Derzhinsky looked at Peters. "You'll remain in Moscow and guard Vladimir Illych?"

"I will, comrade," he replied, modestly.

"With your life?"

"I'll guard him with my life."

"Personal control, comrade!" Lenin shouted as Derzhinsky and Peters went toward the door. "I want you to take personal control of the Petrograd Cheka. If there is any resistance—executions! Kill them all!"

Outside, Derzhinsky said: "Is my train ready?"

Peters replied, "Yes. The Cheka troops are waiting."

Derzhinsky said, "Have Trotsky come to Moscow."

But in Moscow, all eyes were turned to Petrograd.

Reilly received a message from Latvian Colonel Berzin: "Abandon Moscow. The Cheka know everything. See me at British Embassy, Petrograd, Sunday, thirtieth, exactly noon. Go nowhere else. Petrograd Cheka searching for us."

Reilly contacted Anna, asked her to leave a note for Sasha at the safe flat and went to the station. But a huge crowd of people waited behind barricades set up by Cheka guards. A train sat idly on the tracks but no one could board. Reilly showed his Cheka identification.

"Sorry, Comrade," the guard replied. "But that train is reserved for top brass. No one else permitted. You'll have to wait three hours for the next train."

Suddenly the crowd lurched back as the Cheka started pushing with their rifle butts. Not far away several fired into the air and the crowd fell in upon itself. Then from the street came legions of armed troops, a Cheka detachment marching toward the station six abreast, boots stomping rhythmically in the muddy road. Derzhinsky was in their midst.

Reilly hid his face. A contingent of about one hundred boarded the train. The wheels of the train ground against the tracks, the train jerked forward and rolled away.

Volodia, who had cabled Derzhinsky about the Uritsky murder, waited with a full contingent of Chekists at the Moscow Station in Petrograd. They formed a cordon from the inbound track to two dozen motorcars waiting outside near Znamensky Square. The train arrived. Derzhinsky led the Moscow Cheka from the train.

"How many men do you need, comrade?" said Volodia.

"No more than I have, Your Honour. We'll will take charge. Send your men to the government buildings."

"Very well," Volodia said. "I have transportation waiting."

"Good. Drive me to the English Club."

One hundred Moscow Chekists went to headquarters, an equal number from the Petrograd Branch to the Smolney Institute and Derzhinsky, Volodia, and two armed assistants to the English Club.

"Shall I come in with you, comrade?" Volodia said, as his car stopped in front of one of Petrograd's older buildings.

"No, Your Honour," Derzhinsky replied.

They went inside. Volodia waited at the automobile. Moments later, Derzhinsky returned, followed by guards with the young man Volodia remembered from earlier in the day. Volodia took them to Cheka headquarters. Kannengeiser confessed to the crime, insisting that he had acted alone as retribution for Uritsky's execution of forty artillery officers at the Kronstadt Naval Base. But Derzhinsky asked leading questions, most related to Reilly.

Later, Volodia saw that the Moscow Cheka had seized all the files in the office of the Petrograd Branch. Derzhinsky had in fact taken personal control. When he was able to slip away, Volodia drove back to the Moscow Railroad Station and waited for Reilly. Then he took Reilly to Elena's flat.

51. Prelude to Terror

In Moscow, news of the assassin's capture redoubled the focus on Petrograd as distant, a land away, deeply troubled and in need of Party help.

In a meeting hall at a Moscow factory, hundreds of workers saw fury in Lenin's face. He glared, spit epithets at the "Allied butchers" and their imperialist lackeys and heaped on his audience every clichéd obscenity he could think of, a language that some imagined a precursor to terror.

"The lines are drawn between the parasitic banditry of the property-owning classes who masquerade under the slogans of freedom and equality. If the factories, plants and banks belong to the capitalists, to the smiling, blood-suckers who control people by putting pistols to the heads..."

The speech went on for nearly forty-five minutes.

Outside the factory numerous people waited for Lenin, hoping to speak with him or simply to see him. Several women stood near the door and a few men spoke nearby. A man in a black leather jacket leaned against a tree and looked at his watch. Ten feet in front of him stood a young woman.

The factory door opened. Lenin's secretary came through and walked directly to the car. Several others followed before Lenin emerged with a notepad in his hand. He stopped to write something on the pad and then turned to walk toward the car. An older woman emerged from the dark shadows and stepped quickly toward Lenin. When she spoke he turned around and recognized her face in the moonlight. They took two steps before the younger woman approached.

"Comrade Lenin," the young woman said nervously.

Lenin turned around and looked at the young woman.

"Comrade," she said, reaching into her purse. "Why must your Cheka steal food from railroad passengers?"

"What's that?" he said.

"Your food detachments are stealing food from the peasants and then selling it for a profit. That's not fair."

Lenin turned around and waved her away. She took a pistol from her purse, waved it at him, closed her eyes and squeezed the trigger. When the first shot came, everyone stopped. Lenin ducked as glass fragments shot by.

"Christ!" he said.

She fired another shot which hit a metal beam. Everyone fell to the ground. Then from behind the young woman came several shots. Lenin jerked backward but stayed on his feet. The young woman put the pistol back in her purse and stood there quietly until the man in the black leather jacket came from under the tree and threw her to the ground. Lenin faltered and struggled to walk. All around people were on the ground, some with bloodied clothes.

Lenin's chauffeur backed up the automobile as far as he could. The secretary and another man jumped out and tried to help Lenin into the car. He waved them away but fell into their arms. They dragged him into the car, which sped off.

Another black car pulled up onto the grass. The man in black leather opened the door, threw the young woman inside and got in. The car sped away.

Volodia waited while Derzhinsky interrogated young Kannengeiser at Petrograd Cheka headquarters. Shortly after ten o'clock, Volodia's telephone rang. He answered and then gave the receiver to Derzhinsky.

Without expression Derzhinsky said, "Yes? I see." Then he hung up and made a call. "Trotsky? Lenin was shot and wounded tonight in Moscow. I will return tomorrow. You are acting Chairman of the Central Committee, until a diagnosis can be made on Lenin. Allied plot? Yes."

Volodia broke away from Cheka headquarters, ran to Elena's flat and said, "Somebody shot Lenin tonight in Moscow. They don't know whether or not he'll live."

Elena said, "Serves him right."

"It's over," Reilly said.

"Forget counter-revolution," Volodia said, "and start thinking about survival."

"What do they know?" asked Reilly.

"I'm not certain," Volodia replied. "But they'll blame you for everything. You aren't safe anywhere. If you're smart, you'll move only at night, and then only away from this city. Don't bother with Moscow. I'll get a message to Anna."

"I'll have to go back to Moscow," Reilly replied. "I have agents all over, just young girls, Anna's age. I'll give it one last shot and go to the embassy tomorrow. Cromie may have heard about a landing. After that, get me to the station."

But Cromie had not heard about a landing. He learned about the Lenin shooting only when Reilly woke him at midnight with a telephone call. Before sunrise he got up and sat near the window, smoked cigarettes and let his mind race. A battleship drifted slowly in the river and dropped anchor a few meters from the embassy. The heavily armed cruiser pointed its big guns at the embassy. Shortly after dawn he called Reilly at Elena's flat and explained his situation. Reilly told him to evacuate. Cromie said he had ciphers to burn. He would go to the Balkov Café at noon.

On that same morning of August thirty-one Elena reported for work in a state of complete agitation and exhaustion. An official appeared at her door and said, "Come to Comrade Stalin's office immediately." In moments she stood across from Stalin, who sat in his seat.

"How are you today, comrade?" he asked.

"Tired, thank you, comrade. And you?"

"I'm concerned, comrade. Concerned about all these rumours I hear about a counter-revolutionary conspiracy led by the Allies. Concerned about the stories of foreign spies and agents who want to murder Lenin, destroy our revolution and seduce our women. Concerned that because of someone's treachery the people of Petrograd do not have enough food to eat and are forced to wait in cruel lines in the rain while food is diverted to areas where bourgeois prejudices destroy the people's loyalty."

"Yes, comrade," she said.

"Good," Stalin said. "But someone is not concerned about those things. Someone wants to destroy us. Please keep your eyes open and watch out for sabotage."

Disguised as a down-and-out Petrograder, Reilly ambled along Sadovaya Street to the Nevsky and made his way to the

Balkov Café. He was early. His meeting with Cromie was half an hour away. He wondered whether Berzin had made it to the Petrograd embassy as he had promised.

Outside black Cheka cars shot by. Reilly got away from the Balkov and went through the Mars Field. There he saw a dozen cars parked behind the embassy and many armed men. He walked across the field and approached a Cheka guard. He put a cigarette between his lips.

"Got a light, comrade?"

The guard lit a match. Reilly showed his Cheka identification. "What happened."

The Chekist led him to the front of the embassy and pointed to a body drenched in blood, lying near the front door. "That's Reilly, the British spy. He was executed."

It was Cromie, covered with blood and dozens of bullet wounds. Inside, Berzin appeared jovial until he glanced out to see Reilly. He turned serious.

Reilly hurried quickly away.

Somewhat later in the day, Elena waited in her office. Outside the streets filled up with black automobiles. Men in black and grey tunics scattered everywhere. She did not dare to leave but could not pretend to work. She stared out the window and waited. Derzhinsky appeared in her doorway. paled. She looked away, terrified.

"Greetings, comrade," he said.

Elena did not reply.

"What do you have to say, Comrade Elena Mikhailovna?" he said in a soft voice as he stepped slowly into the office.

"Nothing," she said.

"What would you say, Elena Mikhailovna, if a trusted comrade spent a night with a dangerous criminal who planned to subvert The Revolution by seizing control of the food supply? What would you say if that same comrade had countermanded Stalin's orders to move the food supply to areas that supported The Revolution? Would you not say that that person had betrayed The Revolution?"

Elena's mouth dried and her lips quivered. Her heart thumped inside her chest and seemed ready to explode. She forced herself to look at Derzhinsky. "I would say that Comrade Stalin and the revolution have betrayed the people."

Derzhinsky casually drew his pistol, put it near her temple and squeezed the trigger.

Reilly passed by the guards at number ten Torgovaya Street and raced to Elena's floor. Another guard stood outside. The door to her flat was open. He held up his Cheka papers.

"Where is the occupant?"

"Executed," said the guard.

Reilly swallowed his feelings, went to Volodia's and arrived just before dusk. "Lena's been executed," he said.

"I know," said Volodia. "I can get you on a train to Helsinki."

"Moscow," Reilly said. "Can you get me to the station?"

Volodia glanced through the window, saw that the sun was down and said, "You may have to be patient with Sasha. He's having difficulty in Moscow."

In Moscow, two long lines of Chekists faced away from one another on the platform with their rifles held low at the hip and pointed at the crowd of people hoping to buy tickets out of Moscow. Between the two lines a wide open space led from a cluster of black automobiles on one end to the very space where Derzhinsky would disembark from the train on the other. When crowds got too close, a Chekist opened fire. Some shots passed over the crowd. Some fell into it.

The train dragged into the station and ground noisily along the tracks until the steps were perfectly in line with the space opened up by the guards. Derzhinsky appeared in the doorway. The train stopped. He strode up to Peters.

"The Central Committee are waiting for you," Peters said.

They walked along the Cheka cordon and climbed into a black Rolls Royce which sped off to the Kremlin. When they arrived Peters went inside. Derzhinsky remained in the car.

In a large and ornate Kremlin chamber the members of the Bolshevik Central Committee made anxious comments to one another. "I heard the Japanese are going to join in the Allied attack on us. There are rumours about the Americans."

Peters came in and said, "Derzhinsky will be here soon."

The members talked among themselves. Peters said to Trotsky, "You are acting Chairman of the Central Committee, comrade," he said quietly. "Even the stubborn ones will listen to you. If you want to move Feliks to action, you'll have to persuade them, and Derzhinsky as well."

Someone said, "Not the French! Will the French also send their troops against us? Do they too want to surround us?"

Another replied, "All the West wants to surround us!"

Trotsky shouted and jumped onto a chair. "So let us be alone! Lenin will empower Derzhinsky to employ terror, our only remaining weapon against the western bandits! Give Derzhinsky the authority to use terror! Power to the Cheka! All power to comrade Derzhinsky!"

The members of the Central Committee shouted their agreement: "Let all the West betray us! We'll show them! Bring on the Terror!"

Derzhinsky stood in the doorway. The room fell silent.

"What's this?" he said. "What do I hear? Why, I hear my comrades' voices, my friends' voices, cry out for terror. And, of course, only terror can save us." He walked slowly to the centre of the large room and his eyes touched each person with gentle power. "But comrades, our wise comrade Lenin has political considerations that stretch beyond our petty vision. And comrade Lenin has insisted that the terror will come one day and that we will defeat our enemies, but now is not the time and we must wait."

"No! The revolution won't wait! It's time to act!"

Derzhinsky replied, "I say that we wait until our comrade regains his strength. Let the West attack us. Then we'll talk to Lenin about saving the revolution with terror."

"Comrades," said Trotsky, "We'll go to Lenin now and put our case to him. Comrade," he said to Derzhinsky, "if we can wake him up and explain the situation to him in a democratic way, will you agree to lead the Cheka?"

"Comrade!" they said. "Tell Trotsky to speak with Lenin!"

Derzhinsky filled his face with sadness. "Oh, poor Russia," he said, in a quivering voice. "What else will our revolution demand of us? How far can a man be stretched? What else will the British try to do to us?"

The small hospital room teemed with members of the Central Committee. Trotsky stepped quietly to Lenin's bedside. He leaned over. Lenin opened his eyes.

"Comrade," said Trotsky, "I have a message for you from the Central Committee."

Lenin looked up with glassy eyes.

"Comrade," Trotsky said, "the British enemy is at our door. There is no hope for us but the Cheka. Feliks has agreed to return. The Central Committee wants you to grant approval for the Cheka to employ terror against the enemy. You see how ruthless the British have been with you."

Lenin said, "Yes."

"All right," Trotsky said.

Outside they said, "All power to Derzhinsky!"

Anna sat at a small table with her friend Elizabeth and stared out at leaves that brushed against the window. In the distance the colourful onion domes of Saint Basil's Cathedral sat over the rooftops of the city near the golden ones at the Tower of the Resurrection. On thirty-one August, Moscow did not seem much different than on any other day.

"When will they come?" Elizabeth said.

"I don't know," Anna said.

"Maybe Sidney will come first."

"Maybe. But they'll come. Looking for Sidney, for me or for you, for Natasha or Sonya or Maria. They know he stays here. They know we're here. They'll come."

A black car turned the corner and drove up the lane. "Only the Cheka have cars," Elizabeth said. "They're here."

The car rolled to a stop nearby. Anna looked around the room for any incriminating evidence she might have left out. She found none. She walked through the bedrooms.

"Two men got out and are coming inside," Elizabeth said.

Anna stopped in Reilly's bedroom and listened to the thumping inside her chest. Reilly had left no sign of himself in the room. Anna walked back to the small table and sat down. Footsteps came up the stairs outside the front door. Both women closed their eyes and held their breath. Then came a loud pounding on the door.

"Open up! Open up or we'll break it down!"

Anna opened the door. "Greetings, comrades," she said.

Two men in black leather jackets walked in with their pistols drawn. One aimed his weapon at the women. The other threw everything around, searching.

"Where is Reilly?" one said.

"Reilly?" they answered, in unison.

He put his pistol to Elizabeth's temple. She trembled.

"Where is Reilly?" he said forcefully.

"You," he said to Anna. "Get undressed."

Anna slowly unbuttoned her dress, let it slip to her ankles, stepped out of it and stood in full-length undergarments The Chekist took it, examined and threw it back. The other returned from the bedrooms.

"We'll be watching both of you. You haven't got a chance. As soon as you make contact with Reilly a Cheka net will close around your necks. Then you're dead."

Anna held her dress in front of her. The men walked to the door. Suddenly, from the hallway came a scream.

"Oh, no..." Anna whispered. "Maria Friede."

In the hallway there was a scuffle. One Chekist stepped back and the other wrestled Maria into the flat.

"I know nothing!" Maria said. "I'm only a messenger! Don't hurt me!" She held her arms across her chest.

One Chekist tore away her sleeves. The other ripped the dress open and tore out pieces of paper with coded messages.

"You're under arrest!"

They threw Maria out the door and Elizabeth to the floor.

"Stop it!" Anna said. "You've no right to hurt these people! They've done nothing!"

The Chekists stood near the door and argued with one another. Then one said, "You two are under arrest."

"You," the other one said to Anna, "will be under Cheka surveillance. Soon you'll join your friends in jail."

The men pushed the two young women into the hallway, took them down the stairs into the street and threw both into their car. Anna watched the car speed away.

Horrified, a thousand thoughts filled Anna's head. She put on her dress, which contained important messages for Reilly written on cloth and sewn into the lining.

52. Executions

Sasha looked through the window of his office without counting the prisoners in the queue. They stood three or four abreast, and wound halfway around the Lubyanka courtyard. He raised a bottle of vodka to his lips. His body felt warm and light. Someone said: "Let's go, comrade."

Sasha gulped from the bottle again, tried to stick a cork into the top and clumsily put it on his desk.

In the courtyard below eight Chekists stood and watched as men and women with terrified, empty faces stood in line or walked nervously from a door near a small table that had a pile of documents on it. The documents were death warrants that the men and women had signed moments earlier.

Eight lined up at the far wall, which was filled with bullet holes. Sasha wondered how many of those holes he had made during previous executions, before his drunkenness set in.

The engines of half a dozen trucks revved loudly.

Someone yelled, "Ready!" And then, "Aim!"

Eight rifles pressed against eight shoulders, their barrels pointed at eight civilians.

"Fire!"

The bodies of eight former citizens spilled to the ground, their blood splattering all over. The wall behind them remained as before, with no new bullet holes. On the small table near the door that led to the courtyard, the pile of documents grew larger. Eight more men and women walked shakily to the wall.

"Ready...Aim...Fire!"

The rifle blasts thundered through Sasha's head. A chill shot through his warm body. He could not feel his legs. He tried not to look at the people standing in the line before him. But he recognized some faces anyway, including Anna's friend. What was her name? He did not want to remember.

"Ready, aim, fire!"

A flatbed truck backed up near the wall of bullet holes. Men in black leather threw bodies onto the wooden bed, which was stained deep crimson and brown. Soon the bodies piled high. When someone judged that the flat bed of the truck could hold no more cargo, the truck drove under the arch that led to the street. In the courtyard, even Chekists vomited. Someone gave the order to send them back when more flatbed trucks arrived, these with machine guns inside.

Reilly hid from the moment he arrived in Moscow. He changed flats regularly, each night staying with a different female agent who had not been compromised. One evening he rang Lockhart to ask about his plans to leave Russia.

"Not yet," Lockhart said. "But my contact in the Kremlin called a few minutes ago and suggested a meeting. You should come along. It may be your last opportunity to find out what happened. I'll have a militia escort. It'll be safe."

Later in the evening a black Ford stopped outside Reilly's flat. He jumped in and the car screeched away.

"Same as last time?" he said.

"Yes," Lockhart replied. "Same rules too. No names."

Reilly grumbled. The Ford came to a stop somewhere near the Kremlin. Reilly and Lockhart ran from the car to the rear entrance. The door opened. Soon they entered the large flat that was lit only by a single candle. The high-back chair was turned toward the window. On a table next to the chair sat a glass and a bottle of vodka. A voice said, "Alone, Lockhart?"

"No," said Lockhart. "With Reilly."

"Well, Reilly," said the man, "now what will you do?"

"I came because I have some questions."

"I'll give you what I can," the man said.

"What's the mood in the Kremlin? What does Derzhinsky have to say for himself?"

"He's depressed that they shot Lenin and killed Uritsky."

"Depressed?" said Reilly. "How? He's got control of both the Moscow and Petrograd Cheka organizations and now has no opposition, and with the Terror, absolute power. So he controls the government and the country. Why the hell is he depressed? He got everything he wanted."

"He's not blood-thirsty like Lenin, you know."

"Well, it looks like a set up to me," Reilly said.

"There you go again," said the man. "You Russians amaze me. You need a conspiracy to explain everything. If an owl opens one eye, it's a conspiracy. Reilly, you don't need a conspiracy to explain how the Terror started. Derzhinsky had almost nothing to do with it. After Lenin was shot, in one of his few lucid moments he called for Derzhinsky and ordered him to launch the Terror. Derzhinsky resisted. He didn't want the power they were forcing on him."

"Why not?"

"He knew that an official state policy of terror would kill any possibility for the government to sit at the peace table with the Allies when the war is over, for reparations against Germany. The Terror is not Derzhinsky's but is a logical extension of Lenin's paranoia. I told you this would happen."

"It happened because we went ahead, which *you* urged us to do. That *is* what put Derzhinsky in power."

"No doubt. But that doesn't mean he wanted power."

"It doesn't mean we're in a very good position either."

"You're dead wrong, Reilly. In spite of everything you're in a better position than ever to continue as the focal point of the counter-revolution. The focal point of an international anti-Bolshevist movement. Your government will sponsor you and the rest of the opposition. The Terror is your proof against the claim that will be made in your Parliament, that the civilized western world can do business with the Bolshevik Government. It's all the ammunition you need to persuade your superiors to support the Whites against the Red Army in the civil war."

Reilly looked at Lockhart and raised an eyebrow.

"What else would you like to know?" the man said.

"Who shot Lenin? Fanny Kaplan?"

"Of course. What did you expect? Did you think this was part of a 'Derzhinsky conspiracy?' Or that Lenin set it up himself? Listen, Reilly, if you want to stay in business you have to understand that some things in Russia are exactly as they appear. In Russia it's usually the Russians themselves who make a mess of things. Yes, it was Kaplan. Kaplan the SR, Kaplan the Russian. Like the killing of Ambassador Mirbach in July, it was a classic case of Russian stupidity."

"Why did she shoot him?"

"That's the stupidest question of all!" the man shot back. "She hated him! No hidden causes or conspiracies, no mysterious characters or secret motives. A simple situation, so simple the Bolsheviks weren't able to prevent it. They think in conspiratorial terms too. While they were out looking for your conspiracy, Kaplan slipped in unnoticed."

"They say she worked for me, that it's my fault."

"Of course! The Bolsheviks think the same way you do. You and Britain get the blame, but Kaplan was just another crazy Russian, acting alone. An angry woman who wanted it said that she killed Lenin. There's the conspiracy, Reilly."

"What about Kannengeiser, the boy who killed Uritsky, the director of the Petrograd Cheka? A single assassin?"

"Yes," the man said. "He wanted revenge for the execution of a friend who was among forty sailors from Kronstadt caught in some small anti-government scheme. The paranoid Lenin ordered Uritsky to execute them. Enter one young and angry Kannengeiser, who killed Uritsky all by himself. Another Russian just too stupid to come in out of the rain."

"I'm sure what you say is correct," said Reilly. "But the Mirbach murder gave Derzhinsky complete control of the Moscow Cheka. Then the Uritsky murder handed him the Petrograd branch. Finally, the Lenin shooting resulted in the Terror, which gave the Cheka absolute power over the Bolshevik Government. So now Derzhinsky runs the secret police in a police state and is the most powerful man in Russia. Somehow, it smacks of design."

"Think what you like. I can't force you to change your mind. That's all I can say." For a moment the man was silent. Then he said, "Lockhart, I need your cooperation this evening. The Kremlin Commandant, Malkov, will come to arrest you. You won't be harmed. You'll be released quickly. So don't resist. The alternative, if you flee, is Moura. They won't be easy on her. So let Malkov do his job."

Lockhart said with concern, "All right."

"Thank you," Reilly said.

"Not at all," the man replied.

From the third floor of the Lubyanka building Sasha glanced at the courtyard below, where regular rifle blasts echoed in the late afternoon fog. Or maybe, he thought, it was dust in the air that made it difficult to see the faces that he did not want to see, of the people whose lives would soon end. He tried not to think, having decided to act. The horror that filled him was buried somewhere, in some private place, but was ready to burst out at any minute.

I cannot forgive myself for this. I will not ask God to forgive me. It was my decision ...my intentions were good...but I tricked myself... or did I think I had to do what was necessary?...but it doesn't matter...all that matters is life...which I can have no longer...even if I live I am dead... as despicable as the men I hoped to defeat.

He put a single bullet in the chamber of his pistol and closed the barrel. He raised his arm and felt the cold steel press against his temple. His finger felt the trigger. But when the door opened, he took the pistol from his temple.

"No, Timor!" Artuzov said. "No!" He rushed toward Sasha, threw his arms around him and took the pistol from his hand. He dropped the pistol to the floor.

"We start over, comrade. The revolution starts life over."

Reilly wore a clean face, blond hair and a German officers' uniform. He stood outside Anna's door, knocked on it and stepped back when it opened.

"What is it?" Anna said. "What do you want?"

"I'm Sidney." He stepped inside and closed the door.

She threw her arms around him and her tears flowed. "They've killed everyone," she said. "All my friends."

Reilly closed his eyes and squeezed Anna next to him. "I didn't think I could feel more horror than I felt."

"I know," she said. "Forgive yourself, Sidney. Our friends hated the Bolsheviks for good reason and acted with their eyes open. They had no illusions."

Reilly held her tight and did not relax his grip.

"Understand the power you have over us Russian women. Such a romantic, handsome man. We can't resist. Be careful how you use us, be gentle and then ignore us, the way you ignored me. We're drawn to you like butterflies to fire. You're like fire in the night for Russian butterflies."

"Will you come with me?"

"I'm staying. You'll have use for me. I know your agents."

Reilly explained his scheme. He had made a small space in the woodworking at the floorboard. He opened it and removed a notebook. "Look," he said. "It can't be pried out. You have to lift it straight up. From straight on it looks seamless. Let's call it 'Ivan.' A message from me to you referring to 'Ivan' would mean to do something with my list of agents. More than a thousand." He slipped the notebook into the woodworking. Try it. Close the slat.

She easily followed his instructions.

"Good luck," she said, kissed him and added, "Someday."

Sasha came minutes later. He stumbled in with a bottle.

"Don't speak to me," he said, looking away. "I'm not the man I was. I'm a murderer. Don't speak to me."

"No, Sasha," she replied, pulled him inside the flat and guided him to a chair. "No, you are my Sasha. I know you've tried to save Russia. I knew what you'd have to do to convince them. You're not to blame, Sasha. They are."

Tears flowed down Sasha's cheeks. Anna embraced him, her nostrils filling with the stench of vodka. Then he started to laugh. "I'm starting over. I'm going away, tonight, going to America." He finished his bottle, dropped it clumsily on the table and watched it roll off and hit the floor. It did not break. "Do you want to go with me, Anna? To America?"

"I can't leave. I'm going to dance at the Bolshoi."

Sasha seemed confused. "Sidney?"

"He's getting out. By train with some German officers."

"Ahah!" he exclaimed, rising to his feet, his eyes crazed. "I'm going to the station too." He laughed a cynical and self-effacing laugh and walked straight to the door. "Do you want to come? If not, I don't know when I'll see you again."

"Where do you think you're going, Sasha?"

"I'm going to America. You can go with me."

"No, I can't," she said. "And neither will you. You'll get as far as the arch outside and sleep on the lawn. Stay here."

Sasha opened the door. "I need a fresh start," he said. "I think I can find it. Anywhere but here." The door closed.

Anna sat for a moment, surrounded by the empty space in her flat, closed in, alone, isolated, abandoned, empty. Abruptly she jumped up and rushed out.

Wanted posters with Reilly's picture were everywhere. At the Moscow Train Station they hung on every wall. Chekists moved through the crowds slowly, examining faces and comparing them to the smaller versions of the posters that they carried in their hand. But when Reilly arrived, he and the other men in German uniforms had a Cheka escort through the crowds outside the station. Inside, they waited for the train, standing defensively in an informal circle.

Sasha managed to find his way to the Station even though his drunkenness had not completely abated. His mind was slightly crazed; he got lost several times on his way. He looked like a tramp with his hair completely ruffled and his beard scraggly, his eyes bright red with big black patches below them and breath that wreaked of vodka. He stood for a while in the ticket queue, until it became clear that it was not moving. Then he marched to the front, to the mutters and growls of people who had been waiting forever in front of him. He showed his Cheka card to the agent and slipped some money beneath the glass window of the booth.

In moments a ticket to Petrograd appeared in front of him and he quickly headed for the platform. He stood casually, taking an occasional deep breath, making small attempts to clear his head. Luggage was all over and where there was no luggage were sheets, blankets or bags in which was stuffed everything that could fit. People who had left everything behind stood quietly or sat on a suitcase under the dense haze of cigarette smoke and dust that filled the vast station.

A young couple stood close to one another but looked away, defensively, protectively, obviously terrified that the Cheka could come up at any moment and separate, arrest or execute them. An old man stood with a ticket in his hand, a military jacket of some kind draped over his shoulders, its epaulets long since ripped away, more sadness than fear in his eyes. A few ladies stood with their backs to the wall and things they hoped to sell in order to raise money for a ticket.

Here was an old pair of trousers and there a golden clock, on the ground near one woman a silver set, a little tarnished but obviously expensive. If she were lucky it might fetch the required sum, and if not perhaps enough for a loaf of bread. Who would buy it? Everyone was dominated by a single thought: Escape. No one was shopping for bargains.

The crowd was hushed, silent, waiting with trepidation for the train to arrive, hoping that there was room enough inside for just one more person. Anna made her way through the crowds outside and pushed through the station entrance. Away from the platform there was some room to move. Closer to the area where the train to Petrograd was expected the crowd was thick. She slipped between people or barged through with one thought in her mind: Find Sasha!

She got to an open space near the boarding area. From outside the station came the ringing of train bells, and screeching of brakes as smoke shot above the train and disappeared into the haze against the high ceiling and hung there, thick and odorous. The crowd rolled like a wave.

Sasha ambled to the boarding area, trying only to deflect the densely packed bodies from him, awkwardly stepping over and around pieces of luggage and random possessions and even people who had not yet lifted themselves from the ground. Behind him the crowd fell in on itself as it tried to get close to the boarding area. No one could move. Soon everyone behind Sasha realized that the sudden change in the configuration of the crowd had reduced their chances to board the train. A woman stomped her feet in frustration, cursed and blamed her husband, who held several pieces of luggage. A man in thick glasses vainly waved his ticket in the air at the conductor. "We are loyal! Let us board!"

All around, faces were covered with anxiety. Moments before they had had some hope, but now only emptiness. A grinding screech of steel filled the station as the train slowed to a stop nearby, clouds of steam still billowing from beneath it. Reilly followed the German officers to the stairs, where they would be the first to board. They waited for a moment while the conductor adjusted something. Reilly turned around, glanced at the crowd and saw Sasha. The conductor opened the door and the group of German officers lurched forward. Reilly moved with them but remained in the doorway, held the iron railing tightly and pressed himself into the wall. He kept his eyes on Sasha, who swayed back and forth. Then he spied Anna.

He climbed down the steps, twisted through the crowd and the curses of those who thought he was German. He approached Sasha as Anna came into view followed by a militiaman, who said, "Stop! You are under arrest!" The militiaman took Anna's arm as several Chekists arrived.

"Why are you arresting her?" said one.

"She's with Reilly," said the other. "His girlfriend."

Sasha saw Reilly and staggered over to him. He glanced at Anna and the agents. "Think of something," he said.

Reilly put his arm around Sasha.

Then from nowhere came Artuzov. "Timor," he said, glancing at Reilly. "I've been looking for you." He came closer and said, "Who's the German officer, comrade?"

Reilly took a step back.

"Him?" said Sasha. "I fell on the poor bastard and he helped me up. Maybe not all Germans are sons-of-bitches."

Reilly held his breath.

"Thank you, comrade," Artuzov said to Reilly. But Artuzov was looking at Anna as Chekists hauled her away.

Reilly clicked his heels together and bowed. An announcement said his train would be delayed indefinitely.

Artuzov took Sasha's arm and hurried him through the crowd toward the exit. At Lubyanka he found Sasha a bed where he could sleep off his drunkenness.

53. Terror

The room was small, but large enough to hold more than the thirty women who sat on wooden benches or stood motionlessly. The ceiling was high and dark with peeling paint. The walls, tall, grey and filthy with slogans written in lipstick or pencil, had random blocks of cement torn away.

The room was silent, except that the sounds of revving truck engines came through the door at the far end. The door led to the courtyard inside the walls of the Lubyanka Prison. The Cheka brought trucks into the courtyard and gunned their engines in order to drown out the sounds of rifle and machine gun fire. When they heard the revving of the truck engines outside, the women knew that Cheka executions were being carried out. That is when the small room with slogans written on dirty walls by former prisoners who had been executed in the previous hours, was silent.

The women sat or stood and knew that their own time would come in the next few seconds or minutes, or if they were unfortunate in hours or days. These daughters, wives, mothers and sisters of their officially despised class had no names inside the Lubyanka Prison, only the epithet given them by the new masters of Russia, "Class Enemy."

A guard opened a door that led to an inside hallway. Suddenly everyone looked light-headed and breathless. Bodies stiffened. Lips quivered. Eyes opened wide or closed tightly. Outside, engines revved, spewing exhaust under the door to the courtyard. The guard called out three names. The woman sitting next to Anna jerked involuntarily. A pair of feet shuffled on the cement floor. Someone screamed.

"No! No! I've never hurt anyone! Please! No...!"

The woman next to Anna bit into her lip and stood. Another rose from her seat. The guard took the arm of the hysterical one and walked toward the door to the courtyard. He held out documents to the women: "Sign this."

"What is it?" Anna whispered to someone nearby.

"Death warrant," the woman replied.

One by one the women signed their death warrants. The guard opened the door. The smell of death, of the exhaust from truck engines, quickly filled the room. He stood aside as three women who had probably never seen one another before walked slowly through the doorway on shaky legs, holding each other's' hands, across the courtyard where others waited in a long line.

The guard closed the door. The engines in the courtyard revved to a high pitch. Exhaust poured under the door into the room and filled everyone's nostrils. Some whimpered. Some sniffled. Some sighed aloud.

In a brief moment of silence someone spoke out loudly through tears, "Why is such a man alive?! How can there be people like him, like Derzhinsky? How can Russia be taken over by murderers and liars? How can all the good people be put in prisons or executed?"

The answer came from the courtyard.

Within an hour, half of the faces in the small room had changed. Now forty women sat quietly or stood motionlessly as the gears of the revolution ground away, spending bullets in the courtyard of the Lubyanka, the revving engines of Cheka trucks blowing poisonous exhaust under the door of the small cell. The end was not far off.

How stupid we have been. In the old days Katya only stood in the food lines for just a few hours at a time. How luxurious that was. Ilya went out and never said where he was going, a typical teenage boy. How easy the old world was! Natasha and I walked along the Nevsky as everything changed around us... so many new experiences then, so many new senses stimulated, so much to hope for and to live for.

What do the British think of this? They think we're crazy, helpless and stupid. Maybe they will come and save us. I hear tanks outside. The British have come to save Russia!

The noise is not from British tanks, but from Cheka trucks in the courtyard. No one will come to save Russia. There are millions of us. Can they kill us all?

The people who lived in the mansions of Moscow are all gone. Did they take the train? Some were executed. But the smart ones ran when the Bolsheviks took power. They ran to the station and now they are sitting in cafes in Kiev. Maybe they are organizing something with Sidney. They'll ask the British to make Lenin give their houses back.

Mama will survive. She has no opinions but could be executed because of her class. The revolution killed Elena.

How many of Sidney's agents have survived? There are a thousand in Moscow. Some have been executed. But many have survived. In Petrograd, too. Volodia is in Petrograd. He's strong. How has Sasha survived? It only matters that he has survived. How he survived is unimportant. Sasha can do something to keep Sidney's network together in Moscow. If he can think straight. When Sidney returns.

Will Sidney return?

I believe in the possibility of a good Russian life. But our stories speak of so much sadness, foolishness and craziness, of unrequited love and betrayal. And now we aree completely betrayed by fate. Life is such a tease. You suffer, you think you have a reason to hope and then this. Just another time of trubles, like the others. Russia survived the others and will survive this one, the time of Bolshevik trubles.

Or is this the last one, the final time of trubles to which all the others were mere prelude? Are these the final days of Russia? Is this the latest terror or the last? Will God let that happen? Did God create Russia? Oh, God! Such a nightmare! When will I wake up?

The engines in the courtyard blasted away. Another cloud of exhaust shot under the door and filled the room. The other door opened and a guard entered from the hallway inside the Lubyanka. Everyone stiffened. He called several names. Someone sighed. Someone whimpered. Some feet shuffled. Several women stood on shaky legs and walked silently toward the door to the courtyard. The guard had them sign documents to make their executions legal.

Derzhinsky found Artuzov after searching for several hours. During a hurried discussion, Derzhinsky became angry, growled something and sent him through the doors toward the execution area. Then Derzhinsky raced through the entrance, jumped into his Rolls Royce and drove to the Petrograd Station.

The guard opened the courtyard door, called a few names and escorted some stunned, petrified women outside. Another followed him, glanced at a document in his hand, called three women and then looked at Anna, whose passport bore the name Eugenia Blum. "Blum," he said, "Come."

You should not cling to life when you are called to death, but go gracefully with forgiveness in your heart, and hope for the living. That's the only way. Now it's over, finished. The bread lines meant nothing, the sacrifices were all vanity, the hope and the agony wasted, the meaning you tried to give your life merely an illusion. You were loved, you loved someone and that's all there is. There is nothing more...

Anna floated through the room to the door and stepped outside behind the others. The guard followed and the truck engines revved.

Rev- rev- rev-olution.

Across the courtyard stood a line of people. They welcomed her with their eyes and beckoned her to their common destiny. Two trucks with machine guns aimed at the line of people. A guard strode along the line of prisoners and examined them. One of the women coughed. Another whimpered. The guard pointed to the end of the line.

The end of the line.

"Walk there, citizen," he said.

A woman took Anna's hand. Four stepped together toward death, until the guard took her arm.

"Not you, Blum. This way," the guard said and led Anna along the courtyard wall to a door. She followed as the engines revved louder and their exhaust fumes billowed through the courtyard. She coughed. He opened the door. Artuzov, standing inside, stepped up to her. The guard walked away.

Artuzov took Anna by the arm past cells filled with men and women soon to be executed. They went up a flight of stairs past offices with doors that said, "Comptroller, Reinsurance Division," or "Director, Life Policies."

It isn't real. I'm walking through a dream. I have already died. I have been executed. This is not real. Nothing is real. I am a ghost.

At the end of a long hallway thick black letters on a glass door said, "Disbursements, Personal Policy Claims Division." Artuzov opened the door, kept Anna by the arm and held high his red Cheka card. He took her through a crowd of Cheka agents and another door, then down a tall flight of stairs to the entrance. He said something to a guard, who got on the telephone. A car appeared.

"Ask her where she wants to go," Artuzov said to the driver and went back into the Lubyanka as the car drove off.

At the station Reilly stood with the German officers waiting to board their train to Helsinki. Whistles blew. The officers shuffled toward the rear steps of the train. Suddenly three guards pulled Reilly away. One of them, studying a wanted poster, said, "Reilly!" Two held Reilly by the arm and the third kept his pistol aimed at Reilly's chest. They began to move him away from the train and through the crowd, weaving, pushing others aside where they could.

Halfway to the exit Reilly saw Derzhinsky. At the same time Derzhinsky's eyes fell upon him. Reilly knew he was caught. He mentally prepared for a small exchange of words. Derzhinsky would approach, acknowledge him in some small way and order his Cheka custodians to take him.

But Derzhinsky subtly shook his head as though to say, "No," and looked away. Reilly felt his captor's grip loosen. Derzhinsky went to the exit. The Chekists followed him and Reilly quickly went back to the train. The whistle screeched as he boarded the steps of the last car, which soon moved slowly out of the station toward Helsinki.

Book Three:
Masterspy / Spy Masters

Characters Introduced in Book Three

Reilly's Wives

Nelly Burton – Reilly's third wife (Pepite Bobadilla)
Margaret - Reilly's first wife
(Nadine, wife #2, absent here)

British Agents, Spies

Herbert Fitch – Detective, Special Branch, London
White – Phantom agent, Moscow, later London
Weber – Phantom agent, Moscow, later London
Paul Dukes– British spy in Russia after November, 1918
Thomson – Director, Special Branch, London
Kell – Director, Military Intelligence, London

Bolsheviks in Line to Succeed Lenin

Kamenev
Zinoviev
Trotsky
Stalin

Groups

Phantom Group –Secret British spy centre in Moscow
London Centre –London Spy Service headquarters
The Trust – Moscow-based group purporting to be anti-Bolshevik

Part VII: Lenin in Power

54. Moscow, December, 1918

Anna jerked forward. She braced her legs against an army trunk and covered her face with folded arms. A screech came from under the floor of the train car, followed by a deep, long hiss and fountains of steam blowing through the cracks below. She opened her eyes, drew back the board that covered the small window next to her and looked outside. Groups of soldiers stood with rifles upright and as many civilians struggled with luggage. The train ground to a stop and the soldiers around her stirred. One jumped from the loose boards above her and pulled on filthy boots. Others stretched and climbed from their seats.

Anna pulled her legs from the trunk, slowly bent and lowered them to a filthy wooden floor. She reached under the rotting planks that had been her seat and bed for days and pulled up a white flowered bed sheet that was now grey. She undid the knot of the sheet's four corners and took an inventory of the inside contents: a change of clothes, photographs, books, an empty diary, two shoes, letters bound in twine, a gold chain with a metal likeness of the Bronze Horseman statue.

Everything I own.

She re-tied the knot, hoisted the bundle over her shoulders, stood and followed her traveling companions to the front of the car. She stopped at the door to look out at the station, over the heads of the troops waiting on the platform, where a red banner with white letters said:

"MOSCOW. WORKERS OF THE WORLD UNITE!"

She swung the bundle over her shoulder and climbed down the stairs to the filthy platform where countless men in Red Army uniforms waited to board the train to the south, where civil war raged. Standing in their midst, others in civilian clothes likely hoped the same train would take them to Kiev or to Odessa, where the Bolsheviks had not yet established control and, some said, life was still possible. The soldiers carried weapons and small duffel bags. The civilians had all kinds of luggage and even bed sheets like hers, tied into knots and stuffed with everything that would fit.

A chemical odour floated across the platform and filled Anna's nostrils, forced her to sneeze and cough and filled her eyes with water. She lowered her bundle to the platform, took a kerchief from her pocket, wiped her eyes and blew her nose. She sniffed, stuffed the kerchief away and again threw the makeshift luggage over her shoulder. She headed through the crowd with her arm bent and her elbow forward.

The crowd was thick and quiet. Suspicion filled the eyes of soldier and civilian. Anna imagined that when the train got past Kiev, passengers would separate into groups. One would try to escape from Russia. One would join the Whites and then engage the ones whose military caps had red stars- a third group -on opposite sides of bloodied battlefields.

The freezing wind cascading along the platform drew no attention. Anna shivered, pushed ahead and saw a hand painted sign above the door: "Citizens! Don't Spit! Fight typhus like you fight the bourgeoisie!"

She got inside the station and confronted the next crowd, a queue stretching around, ending at empty ticket windows. Like the crowds on the platform, those in the station were quiet. Faces that in February might have shown anxiety or anger were now sullen and weak. She remembered faces like those from revolutionary Petrograd, from Moscow during the Red Terror and from Kiev, where she had found sanctuary. She knew that the consequence of terror was emotional castration in the best case and in the worst, the death of the soul. She saw around her the former, deteriorating into the latter.

Hanging on the wall over the door, a poster with Sidney Reilly's face bore the words, "Wanted, Dead or Alive!" On the far wall near the main entrance another sign said:

"It is our duty to strangle the White Lackeys of Deniken!"

Under the sign was a handsome soldier, perhaps twenty but certainly not more than a year or two younger than she. Tall and muscular, his unbuttoned grey greatcoat and a red-star cap tilted back spoke of confidence bordering on arrogance. He followed her approach to the door with deep blue eyes peering through clumps of long blond hair.

She smiled. He looked at her with a contemptuous expression, as though he knew something about her that he did not like. Anna liked him anyway and did not look away for long until she reached the door. Even then, when she looked back and saw him staring, she smiled.

Low, grey clouds covered a dark December afternoon. Flurries danced in the air and thick, fresh blankets of snow covered the street. Anna climbed to the road and decided to wait there. Soon, she thought, a droshky would come for train passengers. A few rubles would buy her a short, even peaceful ride home. She was happy to be in Moscow.

Behind her, someone said, "We have no cabs, comrade."

Anna saw the soldier from the station. "No cabs?"

"No petrol."

"But droshkies..."

"No horses." He buttoned up his greatcoat.

"What?"

"They eat horses now."

She threw her hand across her mouth.

"They've eaten all the oats too, so it's just as well."

"I'll get a tram."

"No trams."

"No..."

"No electricity."

"Lord," she said quietly, "how will I get home?"

"I don't know, comrade."

Anna glanced down the empty street and said, "Long walk. Where can I buy food?"

She had eaten all the food she had brought with her from Kiev, well before the train got anywhere near Moscow. By now it seemed she had not eaten in days although she vaguely recalled that a Red Army officer had given her something.

Sausage? On the train?

"The shops are empty, comrade," the soldier said. "You might find a market if you don't mind paying extortion prices to the bourgeoisie or the kulaks. But most of what they've got to sell is filthy, old and rotten. Wash everything twice."

"Why?"

"Typhus," he said, shivering, holding his collar over his ears. "An epidemic since September. New graves every day."

Anna threw her bundle over her shoulder and let it slip down against her back.

"I've got an hour," he said quietly, "and a few rubles."

She could have felt insulted, but looked at him with the same patience she would have had for her younger brother. "Is that what you want?" she said gently.

"There's nothing else."

"There's feeling."

"You've been away too long."

Anna smiled. "A feeling shortage, is it?"

"You'll survive in Moscow only if you kill your feelings."

"You can't afford to do that. It'll eat your insides."

"Flesh is all the feeling you'll get here." He looked away, certain of his words and said, "Good luck getting home, wherever it is, if it's still there."

"Thank you," Anna said and watched him walk back to the station. She climbed over a mound of snow into the street and looked down a long stretch of white-crusted highway.

If it's still there?

The snow came up to the bottom of her overcoat. A furrow of boot steps turned into a walkway, where traveling was easier. Horseshoe impressions dotted the path.

No horses, indeed. But of course. The Cheka don't eat horses.

An hour later, with the cold cutting through her body, a dark, hunched figure moved toward her. Frightened, she stopped but then trudged along as the figure slowly approached, shapeless in an old overcoat, its head hung and gender indeterminable. Closer, Anna stopped and said:

"Excuse me, comrade, but do you know where...?"

The silent figure kept moving, its head low and shrouded in cloth, and disappeared behind her. Anna continued on, hungry, her legs aching and her body weakened.

If it's still there?

A glowing fire at a nearby corner cast an unearthly shadow on the remnants of a house. Ragged children huddled around a flame and watched her approach as though ready to counter-attack. Two boys came from the shadow with wood.

Anna stepped away and struggled to another intersection, where more dark figures stood around fires in the cold, dark afternoon that was close to night. Suddenly aware that her toes had no feeling, she stopped again, wiggled them and tried to bring them back to life. She wondered how long it would be before her feet froze, she would stop and then fall.

Is it still there?

On the next block two fires blazed in metal barrels. Between them stood several women in heavy overcoats, scarves wrapped around their necks and over their fur hats. They had cleared away the snow and in its place put products to sell: religious icons, a Bokhara rug, two walking sticks in the snow wearing a blue silk smoking jacket. A fur coat and a few books. Food on a piece of cloth: three eggs, a slab of bacon, a pat of butter and a jar of something that looked like preserved fruits or vegetables.

The bourgeoisie, selling their things for train tickets out.

"How much?" she said, nodding at the food.

"Four hundred," said one of the women.

Anna took off her gloves, reached inside her overcoat and stuck her hand under her sweater and through her blouse. She clutched some bills and gave them to the woman.

But the woman jumped back. "The devil, girl! You crazy?"

Anna looked at the woman in confusion.

"British currency? You'll get us all arrested or shot."

"Bloody hell," Anna said, taking back the money that Reilly had given her before he escaped in September. She was exhausted and dull-witted. She cursed herself for the lapse. She reached again into her coat and found rubles.

"Four hundred, you said."

The woman took it, tucked it inside her overcoat and wrapped the food in cloth.

Anna took the small bundle. "Four hundred rubles," she said, untying the knot in her bed sheet. "That's twice what I earned at work in the last two years."

"You may be crazy, girl. But you're not poor."

"I'm poor now," Anna replied and stuffed the small bundle into her bed-sheet, tied the corners back into a knot and threw it over her shoulder. On the next block children stood in a snow bank, chopping the carcass of a horse.

Or is it a dog?

Farther along, the remnants of other house frames stood like chopped skeletons, or less, kindling taken from their bones like meat cut from the bones of horses, sustenance for freezing citizens of the New Moscow. Sheremetyevsky Street, where Anna had lived until three months earlier, brought her heart alive. The lot on the corner was vacant now, the older house that had occupied it torn down for firewood. But there stood Number Five Sheremetyevsky.

It's still there!

She crossed the street and smiled at the peeling paint, the rusty iron fence, the archway and snow-covered courtyard.

We survived the Terror! My home! My neighbourhood! Lord, when have I felt such joy?

Joy overtook her, lifted and comforted and relieved her, repaid her for her sorrows. But a glance at the top floor of the house revealed light in the window of her apartment and shattered the joy in a flurry of heavy, sinking, heartbeats that seemed, somewhere beneath the surface, perfectly normal.

Inside, Anna saw that the light in the window was really the full moon reflected in a mirror. She was relieved, but sad. She was, she thought, the only survivor. But in a few days Anna found a young woman called Olga, in a local market. She had worked for Reilly. Now she was selling potatoes.

55. Petrograd, January – February, 1919

On an icy afternoon in early January, a railroad train departed from Moscow, the daily northern run to Petrograd carrying hundreds of people. Scheduled to depart at seven the previous evening, for some reason left the station seventeen hours later. It rolled through dangerous territory and stopped occasionally so that Red Guards could secure the rails and ensure safe passage. It travelled through country and villages already secured by the Bolsheviks. It stopped many times so the Cheka could check the documents of passengers, take some of the people off the train and shoot them in the beautiful white countryside. It arrived in Petrograd six days after it departed from Moscow with roughly half of its original passengers.

Anna made it all the way, through Cheka searches and treacherous snow drifts, through greedy hands that seemed to stick out from everywhere to beg for food. She got through the constant stream of suspicious and threatening eyes that stayed open, defensive and changed by the terror, until exhaustion made consciousness impossible. When the train stopped in Petrograd the weary passengers rose slowly, checked the knots in their sheets or blankets and walked to the platform like lost foreigners. Anna put herself in the middle of the lifeless crowd and moved as they moved, slowly and without expression, horrified by their gaunt and empty faces. Inside the station, people drifted even more slowly and lifelessly. There life seemed covered by an even-greyer layer that hid other colours. But she was outside when the true spirit of New Petrograd exploded in front of her and countless shades of grey saturated everything. Outside, Petrograd had lost its colours and was a city of grey.

Anna barely glanced at the cab stand off the Nevsky Prospect because she knew even before she got there that she would find no taxis. At Znamensky Square just across the street she saw three cannibalized horse carcasses and one in process, its flesh hacked away by hungry men and women and cooked over a barrel of burning wood.

Anna was no stranger to the boards that covered so many

windows in Moscow and had begun to cover windows in Kiev in the recent months. She remembered boards on windows in Petrograd along the Moika and on her own Fontanka Canal. How long had it been since the boards started to come down for firewood? She half-remembered: it was when the exodus was in full swing. Even so, every so often she had been able to find an open shop or café.

Today the boards were almost gone. Whole houses had come down. The skeleton of the city's great thoroughfare, the Nevsky Prospect, recapitulated the frames of houses that still stood or the bones of horses that remained after the flesh had been taken. Petrograd was a city of skeletons.

Two men stood on the carriage path under the red brick arch at Anna's red stone house on the Fontanka Embankment. "Who are you?" one said.

She approached and said, "Excuse me. I live here. I'm Anna."

"The hell you do," the man said. "I'm house commissar."

"My mother lives here," Anna said. "I did too but I moved."

The man said, "What's her name?"

"Katya," said Anna.

"She's the quiet bourgeois woman," he said to the other.

"May I go in?" said Anna.

The house commissar eyed Anna with suspicion and something that looked like anger. But the other one said, "You better take her, comrade. You don't want her alone in people's rooms. If she stole something you'd get the blame."

The house commissar gestured with a twist of his head that said, "Follow me." Anna hurried along, went up the steps and followed him into the foyer. It was not the foyer that she remembered, where on all but the coldest of evenings she would stretch her legs and exercise on a metal bar that Sasha had put up for her. Instead of a wide room with stone walls where the family always left their shoes and put on slippers stood a partition and a makeshift door.

"What happened to the foyer?" Anna said.

"It's my bedroom," the house commissar said.

Anna glanced into the kitchen, where the old oak table had been replaced by wooden boards. One broken piece of the old kitchen door rested against the others and Anna read something that Ilya had inscribed on it years earlier:

"Anna is studying English so she can marry the King."

A rope hung through the kitchen, a clothesline for woman's undergarments. A woman stood near the sink and took out wet clothing. "Who's that?" the woman said. "You throwin' someone out? Somebody executed?"

"Nunna yer business, comrade," he said and pointed to the back stairway. The stairway was dark. He walked first and Anna followed, her hands searching blindly for the wooden rails on both sides. But the rails were gone.

Firewood.

At the top of the stairs she glanced down the hallway into her old room, where two children fought, a woman bent over and a strange odour floated in the air. Someone slammed the door shut. The bathroom door was closed and bolted. A young man with wire-rim glasses came out of Reilly's old room, walked toward the back stairs, ignored Anna but said to the house commissar, "Good morning, comrade."

"Hullo," the house commissar said and pointed to Katya's bedroom. Then he knocked on the door, which opened. The house commissar said, "This lady claims you're her mother. There's no over-nights without official permission, but if the lady needs a place to stay I'll close my eyes for a few days."

"Thank you," Katya said.

The house commissar wandered down the hall, opened a door and examined a room. Then he stepped out, closed the door and went down the front stairs.

"Come in," Katya whispered.

Anna stepped cautiously toward Katya, as though treading through a paper-thin dream, unable to believe that her home had been turned into a cheap boarding house. She stopped and opened her arms.

"Not here," said Katya. "Inside."

Anna went in. Katya closed the door and put her arms around her. "I'm so happy to see you, darling," she said.

"When did this happen?" said Anna.

"September. One day I came home and a family had moved into the front room. Then others came. The house commissar threw me out but the Housing Authority they gave me permission to stay." She swept her palm toward the end of the room. "This is my part, except the bathroom, which I share with three other people and two children."

"What happened to the bath in the hallway?"

"They said it would use too much water so they locked it. But I think the student who lives in Sidney's room uses it sometimes in the middle of the night."

"Wait a minute, Mama," Anna said. "Did you say you have to share your bathroom with five other people?"

"Yes."

"I can't believe it." Anna examined the room. Katya's four-post bed was gone and a small mattress lay in its place. Her mahogany dresser rested under the window at the far end of the room, near the bathroom. But in place of her eighteenth century writing table was a smaller round one, cheaply made, next to a small stove. A few pieces of wood sat on the floor nearby. At the other end a rope hung. The room was small and that was good. It was only big enough for one and for the present, at least, Katya had it all to herself.

"It's not so great when one of them comes in and uses the toilet in the middle of the night. I haven't slept in ages."

"Who are they? Who put them here?"

"Just people," said Katya. "A worker's family, a student, upstairs a single worker and a young couple. Two men in Ilya's room died from typhus last month. We'll probably all die of typhus. They'll put someone there too. Twelve in all."

Anna shook her head in disbelief. "How are you?"

"I don't know," said Katya. "I took some of our things out to the carriage house and the commissar didn't seem to mind. I hid some more in the attic and in the basement but soon I'll need to start selling it off so I can pay the rent."

"Rent?" said Anna.

"The basic rent is fifty rubles," said Katya. "But I'm a bourgeois class-enemy so there's a surcharge of nine-hundred fifty rubles. Then there's the Red Army Fund, which is fifty for everyone else but two hundred for me."

Katya continued. Anna imagined her mother turning grey.

"The government has a proletarian literature drive, so we have a House Proletarian Literature club. They have meetings that are free for the workers but I pay an extra hundred a month for them. There's talk of a new Red Flying Fund and a Revolutionary Culture Fund, and each will cost something extra. I pay thirteen hundred a month. I'll run out of money soon if I buy food. So I have to sell my things."

"Can't you get a job somewhere?" said Anna.

"I could wash someone's clothes for a few kopecks but that's about all. I haven't given up. I know others who managed to get working papers and food rations."

Anna felt ill. She went to the bed and lay down. Then she sat up. "Mama, I have to get away. Let's go for a walk.'

"Let's go," said Katya.

They went quietly down the stairs, trying not to inconvenience the other residents, not so much out of politeness but because neither had any desire to speak with them or to face their insults. They left through the back door, walked around to the front and went under the archway to the road. Instinctively they started toward the Nevsky, but it was too much a reminder of the current state of things so they turned around and walked in the other direction.

Anna noticed someone leaning against the wall under the arch, smoking a cigarette. He seemed to glance back at her and Katya, smiling. She took Katya's arm and walked a little faster. They walked up Gorohovaya, where a grey cloud hung over a certain house, the stench of automobile exhaust filled the air and a low, distant mechanical noise rumbled through the street.

"Oh, no," said Anna.

Katya said, "Number Two Gorohovaya. I didn't think."

Katya led Anna down a different street, turned onto another and walked a few more blocks past Saint Isaacs Cathedral. They reached the Admiralty, passed a few sentries and into a wide lawn that led to the Neva Embankment and beyond it to the River Neva and the Gulf of Finland. They walked across the snow-covered lawn, where several children were throwing snowballs near a statue. Anna stopped.

They walked around the statue, ducked a few snowballs and went to the Neva Embankment where they stood at a stone wall as the wind swept in from the Gulf waters.

"What are you going to do, Mama?"

"I don't know," Katya said.

"Come to Moscow. I've an extra bedroom. Otherwise they'll put someone else in it. It'd be good to have you there."

"I keep thinking things will change," said Katya. "Sidney came back on his way to London. He said the British might try to save us. I can't leave the house, Anna."

"Can you buy food?"

"Some," said Katya. "Enough to survive."

"Where do you buy it?"

"On the street. But the only legal places are run by the state and they have huge lines, armed guards, bad apples and stale crackers. A few cafeterias have food just as bad."

"That's it?" said Anna.

"I've heard of some other places where the bagmen go, but if you're there when the Cheka come you can go to jail. Then it's over to number two Gorohovaya. Executions there every evening at seven and sometimes in the daytime too."

Anna suppressed a laugh. "Inquisitions at six. Executions at seven. Matinees on Saturday."

"Oh, Anna!"

"I'm hungry and have money," Anna said. "Let's eat."

"There's a market at Vladimirovsky. It's a walk."

"I've been sitting in one position for days, Mama. My legs can use the exercise."

Katya pulled her black scarf up over her nose so the collar of her overcoat reached over the bottom of her fur hat. Anna made a small adjustment to it.

They walked back past the Bronze Horseman to the Admiralty and over to Gorohovaya. They put their heads down and fought against the wind that blew against them to Zagorodny and then walked toward the Nevsky, but crossed a few blocks before it and came out at a church near a small park. Some kiosks were set up, sellers had food and wretched looking people stood still in long queues.

One queue twisted around a corner, filled with people who had brought their own possessions to sell: old clothing, crockery, toys, nick-knacks, books, pots or pans and stamps, everything they could not eat or set on fire. In another, people waited to buy food, everyone expressionless, avoiding contact. The sellers and buyers who ran the place, the speculators, tended to their transactions quickly with one eye to merchandise, one on the customer and both glancing regularly at several other men who stood statue-like on the edge of the market. These in turn watched the streets like hawks prepared to dive at any moment.

Katya and Anna stood near the closest of these protectors and surveyed the market. "It's complicated," Katya said. "I have a friend, a protector called Anatoly."

The protector called Anatoly glanced over. Katya turned away. He walked closer, examined Katya, looked at Anna and offered a slight bow. "Zabloky, Anatoly Vladimirovich. Ladies," he said, "a thousand pardons that you must see me in such a sorry state, but alas, the circumstances do not permit more formal attire." His overcoat was filthy and ragged and his red scarf seemed about half its original size.

"In fact, if I may be permitted a modest boast, in my earlier years as a country squire my social status might almost have equalled your own. Indeed, madam, one could say we are quite nearly birds of a feather." He shrugged, twiddled his fingers under his chin and said, "You know how it is."

"We do," Katya said.

"How may I serve you today, ladies."

"We came to find some food," Katya said.

"I can help," he said. He bowed, ran off to one of the kiosks and was back in a moment with a bag of sausage, bread and cheese. "With my compliments," he said. "When you come again look for me. I'm at your disposal."

Anna went up to him and spoke into his ear. "Anatoly, my Mama needs to sell some of her things. The house commissar is draining her savings with all sorts of charges."

"Ah," he said. "I know such charges. I pay them too."

"Help her to sell some things without those terrible lines?"

"Indeed," he said. "But what about work?"

"I'm willing," Katya said.

"Let me see. I might be able to do something."

"What?" Katya said.

"You could work as a seamstress with others in your situation, you'd get money and you wouldn't need to put on a working-class accent like most of the bourgeoisie do."

"That would be wonderful," Katya said.

"Where is the factory?' Anna said.

"A small place off Suvorovsky," he said. "We have a government deal. Red Army uniforms. Where do you live?"

"Fontanka, near Nevsky," said Katya. "I can walk."

"Come in the evening," he said. "Day after tomorrow."

Suddenly a shrill whistle blew from the far corner of the market. In an instant the kiosks disappeared and the people manning them fled everywhere. The people in the queues drifted slowly toward the streets as two Cheka cars slid to a stop on Kuznechny and another one jumped up off the street from Vladimirovsky. The Chekists leaped out and blew their whistles, took a few people who weren't fast enough to get out of the way and threw them into the cars. Katya tucked her bag under her overcoat.

"This way," Anatoly said, guiding them past one of the Cheka cars. "Good afternoon, comrade," he said.

"Go away, Anatoly," the man said, "or we'll arrest you too."

"One hopes the state will protect its loyal servants," he said, walking more quickly.

At the next block he said, "Will these tidbits suffice?"

"They're fine," said Katya. "Thank you."

"I'll see you day after tomorrow, then." He bowed, nodded at Anna with a smile that said he might really have been a country squire in some distant life, and walked slowly away. Evening was setting in. It was about six.

The women walked quietly back to Sherbakov Street. The streetlamps, which worked intermittently, were out. A few men were quarrelling near the corner at Fontanka. Katya took Anna's arm. They walked along the embankment and turned under the arch. Abruptly someone stepped back quickly from the carriage path, surprised by their sudden presence. He dropped a cigarette, stepped on it and smiled as though about to speak. Katya grabbed Anna's arm. They hurried past him to the back of the house and went inside.

"What's wrong?" the house commissar said. "Cheka?"

"No problem," Katya said.

"Well we don't want no trouble here. Remember that."

They tiptoed upstairs, cooked a small dinner and soon went to bed, Anna on Katya's small mattress and Katya curled up on a small divan.

"He was a foreigner," Anna said as she lay on her back and stared at the ceiling.

"Who?" Katya said.

"The man outside, under the archway."

"How do you know?"

"He smiled," Anna said.

"Did he?" Katya said.

"And he looked me in the eye."

"I didn't see that."

"He couldn't have been Russian," said Anna. "Not now."

"Maybe he's crazy."

"He could be a crazy Russian. No, he's foreign. British."

"Are you worried?" said Katya.

"No, Mama. Just curious."

Katya drifted away. Anna lay there with open eyes. The moon illuminated part of the back yard and the carriage house. Anna looked out. Nothing moved. Petrograd was quiet. She threw her legs over the side of the mattress and slipped her dress over her night shirt. She took her boots and overcoat, tiptoed to the door and went quietly down the stairs. At the kitchen, the house commissar growled, "What's your problem? Everyone wants to sleep and you're up walking. Don't you bourgeoisie have any consideration?"

"Sorry," she whispered. "I'm going outside for a cigarette. I didn't want to disturb anyone with my smoke."

The commissar grumbled, turned back inside his room and closed the door. Anna put up her collar, stuck a cigarette between her teeth and opened the door to the back yard. She went down the steps, lit the cigarette and walked toward the carriage drive. She kept the cigarette between her teeth, smoke billowing into the air, hoping she could pass for a man in the night. When she turned onto the carriage path she looked at the archway and saw the man still standing there. She stepped up quietly, her hands in her pockets, blew some smoke into the air and said, "I say, old man. You aren't lost, are you?"

He laughed quietly.

Anna said, "If you're lost, perhaps I can set you straight."

The man laughed until his laughter was no longer quiet.

"Be quiet,' she said. "Besides, what's so funny?"

"You are," he said.

"Isn't my English good enough?" Anna said.

"You're English is quite good."

"You're a foreigner and an Englishman," she said. "What are you doing here?"

"That depends entirely on you," he said.

Anna took a step back. "I don't know what kind of girls you have in England, but I'm not like that."

"No," he said. "What's your name? I'm Paul Dukes."

"Dukes?" she said.

"Dukes, but call me Paul. Are you Anna?"

"How did you know?"

"I work with Reilly."

"Oh!" she said in a screaming whisper, her hands over her mouth and knees bent as though about to spring into the air.

"Reilly sent an introduction letter with his messenger to your Moscow address. About Ivan. But when he returned he said you weren't there. I'm going to Moscow myself in a few days. Is there a place we can talk?"

"Not now," she said. "In Moscow. I'm going in a few days. Have a messenger leave your contact information and suggest a meeting place. Did the messenger leave the letter?"

"Reilly said you would know where to look."

"When I've read Sidney's letter I'll contact you."

"All right," Dukes said with a chuckle. "By the way, what made you come out?"

"You smiled at me so I thought you were a foreigner. No one here smiles, especially the kind of people who might be watching from under an archway. I came out on a hunch." She sucked in a cloud of smoke, blew it into the freezing air and tossed the cigarette into the snow. "By the way, do you know where he is?"

"South Russia," he said in a whisper. "Working with General Deniken and the White Army."

"Oh," she said slowly, imagining Reilly might stop to see her. "See you in Moscow."

"Good night," Dukes said and walked toward the Nevsky.

Anna turned around, walked back along the carriage path and went inside. She took off her boots, walked quietly up the stairs and into Katya's room. She undressed and lay down on the mattress. The light of the moon had passed from the room. The outside was dark and noiseless. She thought of how dangerous going out to meet Dukes could have been and silently approved of herself for not letting caution rule her. Or fear, the way it seemed to rule everyone else. In a few minutes she closed her eyes, turned over on her side and drifted off.

In the morning Katya made some tea and they ate the remaining sausage and cheese. Anna told Katya about her escape to Kiev, about men who lit cigarettes with thousand rouble banknotes and about the soldiers she'd met on the train back to Moscow. Katya told Anna how Volodia had come in a hurry one night and said he'd heard from Reilly.

"He can't come without raising suspicion."

"Neither can Sasha," Anna said.

"Ilya's in another world. You're all I have left."

"They executed Natasha and our friends," said Anna.

Katya almost did not react. "They didn't execute you."

"I have a friend. Olga. She's nice. A dancer."

"She's alone?" said Katya.

"Her father was a General. Shot."

"They're taking the old white generals into the Red Army," Katya said. "Sometimes they arrest their families and hold them as hostages until the officer does what they want him to do. Then they kill most of them anyway."

From there Katya walked up Suvorovsky to a factory that made uniforms for the Red Army. In Moscow, Anna found the letter from Reilly, which instructed her to introduce Dukes to 'Ivan.' She smiled with delight: Reilly's network was about to come alive. Anna was back in play.

Part VIII: The Assassinations Revisited

56. November, 1918, London

Reilly arrived back in London in chilly, wet weather and spent a few days burrowed in his flat writing and typing his report. In a week he would deliver it to C, his superior officer, and arrange a debriefing. He finished writing late in the evening, went to bed and awoke to a particularly warm, sunny day. Good weather for a London November.

Without much deliberation he put a towel in his bag and

drove to a lake outside London that vacationers had abandoned months earlier. He tore off his shirt, dropped his trousers, dove into the water, swam out and stopped in water over his head. He held himself afloat with slow-moving arms and legs and let a lukewarm sun bathe his face. He stayed like this for several minutes and then swam back to land.

His pants and shirt hung from a tree and his shoes rested on an adjacent rock. He dried and dressed and went for his shoes but stopped when he saw an envelope protruding from one. It had a single line and number six pencilled on the front. The single line meant it had a cipher inside written in invisible ink and had originated with White, the British agent he had seen in New York, speaking with Trotsky. Viewing a message with these markings required a vegetable substance that he could likely procure at a food market. The number six meant the message inside was urgent.

Reilly stopped at a market and bought what he needed. At his flat he set the cipher and a book called "Ovod" on his desk. Ovod, Russian for "Gadfly." Once the cipher was made visible Reilly would have to extract a series of numbers and look in the book for the associated letters. Only then could he put together words and sentences—or additional code. It was a cumbersome system that he and White had devised in a flurry of rookie excitement more than twenty years earlier. However serious the message might be, he knew that at some point White had smiled at the thought of Reilly taking the time and effort to decipher the meaning:

"I am Lt Fr. Weber," the cipher said. "I received this schema from my Superior Officer Cpt White. In July of 1918, I can attest, Derzhinsky ordered the murder of the German Ambassador. Trust no other explanation." Here, to Reilly's surprise, was testimony according to the infamous phantom Weber: Derzhinsky had sent Blyumkin to kill Mirbach. Treasure, of a sort, for Reilly. *I thought so too.*

If White had ordered Weber to make this communication, Reilly could deduce that both had been in Moscow in July, 1918.

Reilly had witnessed White's meeting with Trotsky in January, 1917. That implied a connection between these two very secret British agents and the Bolsheviks. But did that mean that C, too, had connections to the Bolsheviks?

British Intelligence Director C sat at his desk, behind which a glass-front cabinet resting against the wall displayed two dozen weapons. A window overlooked the street and to the right two smaller windows looked out onto the rooftops of Whitehall Court. Farther to the right, on the wall near his desk was a world map with pins in various areas. Attached to the pins were small red and white flags. C pulled a white flag and smiled as he dropped it in a desk drawer.

When the metallic clicking sound of the secret lift rolled through the hallway, C pulled a flag marked 'WC2' from the Moscow area and dropped it into his desk drawer. Reilly marched through the hallway, where a long table displayed various small inventions, inanimate, pending modification or simply the attention of the inventor or one of his visitors. He saw a tiny photo camera, an extended-distance listening device with a wire that terminated in a polished cylindrical wooden earplug, a metal gadget of indeterminate function that seemed to require electricity, several other mechanisms made of wood or metal whose use was unclear. There was a mechanical fishing lure, a writing pen that could fire a single bullet, and a bucket. Near the window in the front sat a mahogany Grandfather clock that C himself had built.

"Hello, " C said as he rose, offered Reilly one hand and closed the desk drawer with the other. "Welcome home."

Reilly brushed snow from his black overcoat and draped it over a chair. He glanced through the window as gloomy grey clouds filled the skies. "What a miserable place Moscow is," he said and shook C's hand. "There's water in the air, and it turns to ice. I've never missed England so much. The rain here is paradise after that." He sat down, took out his kerchief and patted beads of sweat from his brow.

"You look no worse for the wear, Captain," C said and sat down. "So, your love affair with Russia has cooled."

"No, but at the moment there's no bloody food and everything's filthy. They tear down houses for heating fuel and kill people who speak the language correctly."

On C's desk sat a newspaper and Reilly's report, which was a thick typed document. C turned the newspaper around and slid it across his desk. The headline said:

"British Agent Pays 100,000 For Failed anti-Lenin Coup."

"I'm flattered," Reilly said

"The Herald will have a field day. Could discredit the Service." He hesitated for a moment and continued, "I'm trying to keep you out of the papers. But Thomson from Scotland Yard took the American Ambassador to the Foreign Office. They say you sold out your own plot to oust Lenin."

"What?"

"An American agent who worked with Basil Thomson on an Iowa farm years ago. Worked for you in Moscow. Got a letter out of a Bolshevik prison, said you were a Bolshevik double agent. Now the Foreign Office is asking the same question. Of course I told them it was insane and untrue."

"Who was the agent?"

"Named Kalamatiano. Butyrki Prison. He wrote it."

"The Bolsheviks wrote it. Get him out. He'll go crazy there. They take you out to the execution courtyard, make you sweat for quarter of an hour and then send you back to your cell. I don't know what he really thinks, but that's unimportant. Get the Foreign Office to speak to the Americans and the Bolshies and get him out."

"I will. Nonetheless it would be prudent for you to go to south Russia on assignment to General Deniken, away from London until you disappear from the public mind. There's a civil war there and the Foreign Office needs information. I have another man on assignment with the Foreign Office. You'll both go. Analyse and propose. Do you agree?"

"I do."

"Now, as to your report. C opened his desk drawer, absently took out a pen knife, opened it and tapped the blade lightly on his wooden leg. "I've studied the blasted thing and still don't understand why your mission failed. First in July and then again in August. What on Earth happened?"

Reilly leaned forward in his seat. "We made two attempts to stage a coup against Lenin. Both times assassinations threw off our timing and cost us control."

The penknife blade rapped loudly against C's wooden leg.

"In July we came close. But a Socialist Revolutionary..."

"An SR?"

"Yes, an SR called Blyumkin shot the German Ambassador. Wrecked our timing and split up our coalition. Gave Derzhinsky the excuse he needed to execute the opposition SRs inside the Cheka. Gave him complete control of the Moscow branch of the secret police. On a platter."

The knife blade tapped faster. "What about Blyumkin? Who sent him to kill the ambassador?"

Reilly said, "The German Embassy thought it was an SR scheme, set up by the British. The Bolsheviks blamed me. Some said Derzhinsky was behind it, since it removed his opponents from the Cheka. But one of my agents inside the Moscow Cheka said Derzhinsky did it after finding out my uprising scheme was about to succeed and the purpose was to disrupt our timing. It's also possible that Blyumkin was acting on his own behalf. After all, everyone hated the Ambassador. He was an arrogant prick."

"What do you think?"

"Don't know," Reilly said, "perhaps a few things." Not a word about Weber.

C looked flummoxed and said, "You know that the PM promised a landing in the north. It was sure to guarantee your success. But then in July he cancelled it."

"I do," Reilly said.

"We had to do something to support the White generals, to support Savinkov in Jaroslavl, to divert everyone's attention to

Moscow. When I heard the landing was cancelled, I knew you'd fail, so I ordered an agent working with the SRs to activate a contingency he had developed for just such an emergency. I ordered him to get Blyumkin to the German Embassy to shoot Mirbach."

"You were behind the murder of Ambassador Mirbach?"

"Sorry."

"Who was it? Hill?"

"No."

"Who?" Reilly said with abundant coyness.

"Top secret."

"Bloody hell."

"Sorry."

Now Reilly had two conflicting explanations for the Mirbach murder. Who was really behind it?

The blade hit C's wooden leg with an unnerving ping.

C said, "Tell me about August. What happened then?"

"We planned to arrest Lenin and the Central Committee at a big meeting in Moscow. They postponed the meeting, but we thought we could wait it out. Then SRs shot the Petrograd Cheka Commissar and the same night they shot Lenin. That allowed Derzhinsky to take control of the Petrograd Cheka from his opponents and gave him the ammunition he needed to convince the wounded Lenin to approve the Red Terror. The Cheka murdered thousands and put us out of business."

Reilly did not say that Derzhinsky had let him escape.

"And what is your view? Was it all an SR conspiracy?"

"Might have been," Reilly said. "Might not have been."

"What?"

Reilly shrugged.

"There is something else, Reilly. Unpleasant surprise. In late August I heard Derzhinsky had put Latvians inside your organization. I couldn't cable the embassy because Derzhinsky had it bugged and any effort to tell you would have got you killed. I stood fast and took other actions."

"Such as?"

"Well, eliminating Lenin would have been good if it had worked. I don't know whose idea it was to use Fanny Kaplan, but none of her shots hit him. The real shooter was Savinkov's man. Unbeknownst to Savinkov. Semyenov."

"Lord!" Reilly said, burying his face in his hands. "You did it again. We had a chance, if you'd left things alone."

"Well," C said, "what actually happened was that Trotsky took interim power. If the bullet had hit its mark, we'd be dealing with Trotsky now, not Lenin. Trotsky is reasonable."

"You gave Derzhinsky complete control of the Moscow and Petrograd Cheka. You put him in charge of the secret police in a police state. You turned Russia over to a very bad man." But Reilly was thinking of his time in New York, when he had seen British agent White in Trotsky's office on St. Marks Place, and of the cipher he had received from Weber.

If the point was to put Trotsky in power in any event, I was just a diversion. All of my loyal agents who died....

"Oh, Lord," he said again and shook his head.

C saw Reilly's anger. To minimize it he presented an idea he knew Reilly would love. He would fund a Russia desk, bring in outside resources and put Reilly in charge of it. Their own setup, including a secure "safe house."

"You'll be the centrepiece of the international anti-Bolshevik movement. All the resources you need, in secret place with secure communication."

Reilly nodded. "Yes, exactly what we need."

"It will be in place when you return. Of course, technically you'll separate from the service." Then he turned to another item. "I've got a new man with experience for Russia. Name is Dukes. Someone should get over there and pick up the pieces of your agent network in Moscow and he's the best man. Do you have a list of your Moscow agents?"

"I have an agent I trust. He can speak to your man."

"How many remain?"

"I don't have a count. Give Dukes my number."

On November eleventh the King announced the end of the

war and victory over Germany. A few days later, Reilly left for south Russia, where he thought he would find Savinkov. Paul Dukes left for Moscow with a letter to Anna from Reilly, written in a code that only she and Reilly knew.

Reilly had two explanations for the murder of the German Ambassador that had caused his failure.

Who really sent Blyumkin to the embassy that day? C, as he himself stated? Or Derzhinsky, as White and Weber insist? What is the importance of believing one or the other?

By April, the snow in London had given way to moderate warmth and birds were nesting on the rooftops of Whitehall Court. The mist had vanished from the outside air. But a blue-grey haze of pipe tobacco floated under the ceiling of C's office. He stood at the end of a long table and fiddled with one of his little gadgets, an invention he did not remember ever having explained, the purpose of which he had himself long since forgotten. He remembered that he had hidden a trigger mechanism of some kind beneath the smooth metal surface that his laboratory had developed specially for him during the war. He recalled that a certain general had tested the device in the field during live action in France, reported that it was a success and tried to order a large quantity for his men. But C could remember neither what the device was supposed to do nor the name of the officer who had used it.

He put it carefully on the table and took up a walking stick from among numerous other devices. This one he knew. He slid the handle away from the shaft and revealed a thin, sharp sword. He took an awkward step on his wooden leg and thrust the sword forward into an imaginary opponent.

"Ah!" he whispered.

A metallic clicking sound came from the end of the hall as the secret lift reached his floor. C sheathed the sword, limped to the centre of his office and stared down the hallway as the door to the lift opened and Major Fothergil got out. As he walked around behind his desk and sat down, Fothergil came in with a thick file under his arm. C rested the sword against the glass front and folded his hands on his desk.

"You look upset," said Fothergil. "What's wrong?"

C drew his hands apart, palms up, and shrugged.

"What happened? Why did you want Reilly's file?"

"You know how much I've backed Reilly's anti-Bolshevism. But his blind zeal could catapult him and the Service into view. Might put him out of business. Might encourage the British Reds to take up arms in the factories.

"To complicate matters, there's a growing service envy in Military Intelligence, Naval, Special Branch. Each wants control over secret information regarding Russia. There is a power struggle brewing here that could become dangerous."

"What's it got to do with Reilly?"

"Controversy, Major. Reilly's going in that direction."

"How?" Fothergil said.

"A lunatic banking scheme for south Russia, for one thing. And he won't stay in Russia to report on General Deniken."

"He's coming back?"

"He cabled me to say he wants to attend the Paris Peace Conference in a few weeks. He says the Americans must be prevented from sponsoring Soviet participation. Can you imagine such hubris? An agent who tries to dictate policy to a foreign power, to our American cousins, no less. I'm afraid when he gets here he'll discredit the service, then go to the Paris peace talks and discredit the crown."

"Tell him to stand down," said Fothergil.

"Reilly sometimes fails to follow orders, especially when he's playing his own game. He's losing focus, Major, just as I feared. There seems no way to get him under control, other than to keep him in isolation in the new safe house. There is criticism enough, rumours that he was or is a Bolshevik infiltrator. Probably, of course, because our establishment, blast it to hell, hates Jews. In that sense Reilly can never fit here, that is, in the class of the British elite. That is something that arouses my own sympathies," C continued, "because of my own experience.

Nonetheless, now I feel I must distance myself and the Service from him. Do you see my conundrum, Major?"

Fothergil nodded.

C picked up the thick file that Fothergil had dropped on the desk. He flipped through a few pages and looked sadly at Fothergil. "This business about Reilly's bigamous life, two past wives and no divorces. We may have to use it."

"You want to discredit him, C?"

"No. Just limit certain schemes. What else can I do?"

"I hate to be involved in this sort of thing."

"That's why I trust you, Major."

"Just what am I supposed to do?"

"Plant this information in certain places; and if Reilly gets too close to the edge, I'll send another agent to dig it up. He'll have no choice but to re-focus."

"What will the subject be," Fothergil said.

"The first wife, Margaret. A conniver, to be sure. But find what you can. I'll find a way to put her in play if the need arises. It will be harmless enough, but the message will be clear: stay focused and don't shoot yourself in the foot."

"I've never envied you your job, C. It's an ugly business."

C nodded grimly. Fothergil got up and took the thick file.

C rose, took the walking stick and the two went to the lift.

"Look!" C said.

Fothergil turned around. C thrust the walking stick towards the Major's abdomen. When Fothergil instinctively took hold of it C slid out the sword and raised it into the air.

"Surprise, Major! The element of surprise! Crucial!"

Fothergil's eyes bulged. The lift made a metallic noise as it reached the floor. C slid the sword back into its scabbard and leaned on it as Fothergil opened the lift door.

57. Margaret and the Jaroszynski Plan

In April of 1919, Reilly returned from southern Russia after several months with the White Army General Staff in the Civil War. For the first few days he had avoided British Intelligence, stayed at his flat, made appointments to see bankers and worked his way through many of letters that the desk clerk had accumulated, from friends, political allies and business associates. Many more had contributions for his anti-Bolshevik crusade; not a small number came from admiring women. Word had spread rapidly after the newspapers ran stories of adventure and derring-do that romanticized his attempts to stop Lenin. He was undisputed world champion of the anti-Bolshevik cause.

Reilly lay on the couch in the sitting room of his London hotel suite with his eyes closed, his hands folded back behind his head against the arm of the sofa and his legs crossed. His bags sat on the far side of a mahogany table and a glass with a trace of brandy sat on the table. In a saucer between the glass and a pistol, the ashes of a not-quite-smoked cigarette lay like a dried-out worm. On the far end of the room, near the window that overlooked neighbouring rooftops, a Victrola played and replayed the first ninety seconds of a tune from Nick LaRocca's Original Dixieland Jazz Band. The song was lively but not loud enough for Reilly's senses. He chortled in his sleep, uncrossed his legs and his shoe fell to the floor. He drank coffee and went to C's office.

C stood with a smile and said, "Welcome home, my boy."

"Hello, C," said Reilly, accepting C's handshake.

"What the devil is that?" C glanced at Reilly's binder.

"My reports from south Russia," said Reilly. "Some you've seen in my ciphers. Some I prepared on my journey back. It's a civil war that Deniken can win. I came back because some things we can do now."

"Well, good," C said. "How can I be of service?"

"First, I have a plan to secure the areas won by the Whites, so that they don't fall back into Bolshevik hands. Those areas need immediate economic benefits if Russians are to believe capitalism is superior to Bolshevik Communism. To do that we need investment bankers to step in. But no one will touch Russian investments without guarantees, so I've persuaded the Polish banker Jaroszynski to underwrite it."

"What?" C said, sitting straight up in his chair. "Karol

Jaroszynski? The Polish banker? He'll underwrite it?"

"Every farthing. All we need is the commitment of the British and American banks. Once they understand Jaroszynski will indemnify them, they'll fight to get in."

C wrung his hands together and stared away, his lips and jaw twitching. Unconsciously he opened his desk drawer and reached for the pen knife. He brought it out, opened it up and began cleaning under his fingernails. "I don't know," he said. "I don't know. It could be controversial."

"Not at all, C," said Reilly. "The fact is that I've already made a dozen appointments It's just a question of..."

"No, no," said C. "It's out of the question. You're going to the Paris Peace Conference and we've booked your passage for tomorrow. They'll be no time for meetings. We can't let the Bolsheviks upstage the democracies in Paris."

"You don't mind if I go?"

"Not at all," C said and coughed from deep in his throat.

"As I was saying, I've made a dozen or so appointments for when I return, starting next week. It won't take more than two visits to get a contract signed. When I've wrapped up the British bankers I'll go to New York and bring on the Americans. I'll have the project up and running in a month."

"A month," C mumbled, somewhat in surprise.

"We'll start a corporation now and borrow against the proceeds. The White Army can start to operate effectively now. Word will spread throughout Russia. The Bolsheviks will be out of business by September. Guaranteed"

C tapped the pen knife on his wooden leg in an irregular rhythm, as though keeping time to several tunes at once.

"September, is it?" he mumbled. "Guaranteed. Hmm." C tapped the knife louder and faster, put his pipe to his lips and though the flame was out, sucked on it. He handed Reilly an envelope. "Passage and expenses."

"Thank you," said Reilly.

"I may ask you to stay a day or so extra."

"In Paris?"

"Yes."

"I want to return as soon as possible for the bankers."

"Never mind about that. In fact, I'll do it myself while you're away. Give me your appointment book."

Reilly looked oddly at C, but took a typed sheet from his pocket and gave it to him. "Those are the bankers, the dates and places. Are you sure you can handle this?"

"Of course," said C. "I didn't realize it at first, but that American scheme to put Lenin's representatives at the peace table is downright subversive."

"You agree with me?"

"Yes. And you're the only one in the world with the savvy to scotch it. Otherwise the bankers might think we've changed allegiances from the Whites to Lenin and pull out."

Reilly got up. "I understand George Hill's going with me."

C mumbled something instead of a reply but then said, "Yes, Hill's going but I may bring him back a little sooner."

"All right," Reilly said, "See you next week."

"When you return I'll take you to your new venue, the safe house from which you can run our anti-Bolshevik campaign."

One week later a taxi stopped outside the Albany Hotel. The driver took two suitcases from the boot. Reilly paid him and walked into the hotel as the concierge came for his bags. They took the lift upstairs, where Reilly got on the phone.

"Whitehall Court, please," he said.

"Yes?" C said.

"Reilly."

"How did it go?" C said.

"Perfectly. Took me forty-eight hours and a couple of phone calls. The Bullet Plan to seat the Bolsheviks is dead and buried. Have you spoken to the bankers?"

C hesitated and then stammered, "You know, I want...that is, banking is blasted confounding, if you ask me...I made some...that is, I spoke to several...but you know, Reilly, you're so much more persuasive than I. Why don't you call them? By the way, I've taken care of the safe house for you. We'll take a drive and inspect the place together, give you the keys. Good luck with the banks."

"All right," said Reilly.

"Let me know the result."

Reilly hung up, called the concierge and requested a bottle of Napoleon, pheasant and whatever messages awaited him at the front desk. He took off his overcoat and slid into his slippers, and in the bedroom exchanged his sport coat for a sweater. He sat to eat and read a stack of messages. Twelve were cancellations from the bankers. Twelve out of twelve.

What's happened? What did he do? I had them chomping at the bit, ready to go. What can I do now?

He called Lockhart. But before he could finish a sentence Lockhart said, "Sidney, Melbourne, the banker called yesterday. He wanted me to vouch for you, and I did. He said you wanted to speak about Russia."

"Yes," Reilly said. "About the banker Karol Jaroszynski, who will underwrite the reconstruction of south Russia."

"Well it seems he was all in until C called him. He said he'd had to postpone your meeting until he could look at your bona fides. I told him not to worry."

"I think C hates the plan, Bruce. I don't know why."

"I spoke to Churchill. He thinks C is concerned about the rivalries among the services. C doesn't want anything remotely controversial and thinks that no matter how solid the plan, if you're involved there could be a scandal."

"I see," said Reilly.

"Well," said Lockhart, "don't worry. Winston wants to meet with us tonight. He'll back the plan and see the bankers himself. Meanwhile, go to New York and see what you can do there. Don't bother with C. Other things on his mind."

"Where should we meet?" said Reilly.

"I'll pick you up at eight o'clock."

"All right," said Reilly. "I'll see you then." He glanced at his watch and saw that it was almost three o'clock in the afternoon.

He went back to the dining table, picked on the pheasant for a while and got up to turn on his Victrola. After the first ninety seconds of the tune from Nick LaRocca's Original Dixieland Jazz Band he put a coin on the arm of the phonograph and let the recording play all the way through. He played it again just to hear it again without interruption.

Churchill liked the Jaroszynski Banking Plan and said he would speak to each of the potential British investors while Reilly was meeting with the American bankers in New York. Reilly was relieved. As he strode through the lobby a pretty young woman caught his eye. He smiled and walked to the lift. She put down a book, got up and walked after him.

"Good evening, Mister Reilly," she said, an art portfolio under her arm. "I'm Caryll. I'd like to speak to you about my drawings. I'd like to solicit your help in selling them."

Reilly grinned, held out his hand and said, "Hello, Caryll."

The lift came. She followed him as he got on. "I've wanted to meet you for so long. Since last summer."

The operator glanced at Reilly, who nodded slightly as the operator closed the door. "Do you always call at this hour?" Reilly said, examining his watch but glancing sideways at her. She had a round face and soft skin. From some angles her long hair appeared light brown but in the light of the lift Reilly saw a predominance of red. She was confident but neither bold nor arrogant: visiting a strange man at midnight seemed perfectly normal. Her eyes were blue, determined and, although unlined, seemed wise. Reilly imagined he would not have noticed her in passing on the street. She was homely but attractive.

"No," she replied. "If I had called for a meeting and you had agreed I would have tried to arrange something more convenient. But I've come a few times and each time you were going away somewhere. I was afraid you'd go away again, not come back for months and forget about me."

The lift shook as it stopped and the door opened. Reilly let her out first and then pointed the way to his suite. He took her coat, put it in the closet and gave her vegetable juice.

"What's the urgency?" he said.

"I think I know you," she said matter-of-factly.

She opened her portfolio and looked up at Reilly. "Perhaps this isn't the time."

"Go ahead."

"I'm sorry if it's inconvenient, Mister Reilly."

"You can call me Sidney."

"You can call me Caryll."

They spoke for an hour. Reilly was struck by her worldliness and intelligence, but tried not to notice her wisdom. He agreed to show her drawings to his friends.

What is this? Who sent her? What is she doing here? She looks at me with trust and confidence, as though I'm special, and seems to know me. There's something about her that leaves me wary, whether it's her vulnerability or my own natural mistrust, there's something. She has Anna's innocence. I can't look her in the eye. Who is she?

Caryll got up, put her portfolio under her arm and gave him a card with her name and telephone number. "I know you'll be away but I want you to call me when you return. Our talk is unfinished. I think we have much to say to one another. If I don't hear from you, you'll hear from me."

She smiled and walked to the door. Reilly hurried after her and got her coat. "I'm glad you came," he said, holding the jacket while she put her arms through the sleeves. "But I'm not as special as you think. You think about what I did in Russia and imagine a romantic and even noble adventure. Well, it wasn't. I tried to do something good but as a result many people died and I don't feel very good about it. So when you think about me, if you do, remember that I'm a fellow with good intentions who's done some terrible things. Maybe no worse than some, but no better than anyone else."

"So you think," she said. "Next time I'll tell you what I think. Good evening, Mister Reilly." She smiled slightly, opened the door and walked toward the lift.

Reilly watched her ring the buzzer for the lift. Then he closed the door, went back to the sitting room and glanced at the drawing. He turned it on its face, switched off the lamp and went to bed. The next day he went to New York.

When Reilly returned to London several weeks later he had the look of a victorious man. A Rolls Royce limousine brought him from the pier to the hotel. His new suit carried a label that said, "For Sidney George Reilly by Chesterton Tailors, Seventh Avenue, New York City, May, 1919." The driver carried his luggage into the Albany without waiting for the doorman, and Reilly followed slowly behind, as though to allow his admirers a prolonged glance. As he passed the concierge came up to him, offered his hand and said, "Welcome home, Mister Reilly."

"Hello, Dobson," Reilly said.

Dobson kept pace as Reilly entered. "Mister Reilly, I'm terribly sorry. The new man, Jenkins, well he didn't know any better ...but you see there's a woman and he thought..."

But Reilly's attention was taken by the women near the concierge's desk who stood up, smiled and approached him. It was Caryll, more attractive now than he remembered.

"So the problem is, Mister Reilly..."

Reilly brushed Dobson's arm. "Thank you, Dobson. But never mind. It's all right."

Dobson looked curiously and said, "Very well, sir."

"Hello, Caryll," Reilly said.

She came up and touched her cheek to his. "Welcome back, Sidney," she said. "I couldn't wait for you to call so I came here. I have some things for you."

"Well, good," he said, taking her arm and walking toward the front desk. "Messages?" he said to the clerk.

The clerk gave Reilly a handful of envelopes. Reilly kept them in one hand, took Caryll's arm with the other and walked to the lift. The driver passed by, looked at Caryll and then glanced at him. "I put the bags inside your door, sir."

Reilly nodded. The lift arrived. The operator glanced at Caryll, looked as though he had something to say to Reilly but said nothing. In a moment they walked down the corridor toward his suite. Reilly put his key in the lock, opened the door and stood aside so Caryll could enter first. He stepped inside, stopped and sniffed the air.

"Whiskey, cigarettes and perfume," he mumbled. "Let me get the window." He took a few steps toward the sitting room and suddenly the overhead light went on and a woman appeared in front of him in his bathrobe.

"Margaret!" he said to his first wife. "Why are you here?"

"I've come to sleep with my husband," she said, glancing victoriously at Caryll. She was in her early forties with dark curls and reddened eyes.

Reilly looked at Caryll and back at Margaret. "You are *not* my wife," he said.

"Don't be silly," she said. "Of course I'm your wife. You've never divorced me and we've been married for more than twenty years. Why should I stop being your wife now?" She carried a cigarette, looked around and tapped the ashes into the pocket of the robe. "Who does she think she is?" Margaret said, "The little tart in the door."

"What are you doing here?"

"I didn't mean to interrupt you, love," she said. "After all, I know how important your peccadilloes are to you. Does your little whore have a name?"

Reilly turned to Caryll and said, "Excuse me," and took Margaret away by the arm. He threw her into a room, shut the door and locked it. He hurried back to Caryll, who stood in the doorway. "We were married for a short time years ago."

A crash came from the room where Margaret waited.

"She's unbalanced and comes when she needs money. I may have her committed."

"You have my number," Caryll said.

"I'll call you later," he said.

Caryll went out and closed the door behind her.

Reilly went back into the flat and let Margaret out of the room. "What are you doing here?" he said forcefully.

"I thought you wanted to see me."

"I do not want to see you."

"Your friend delivered a letter from the old man. He said I should come if I needed anything."

"And of course you need money."

"That shouldn't concern you. I'm applying for loans."

"Loans? Who's going to loan you money?"

"Oh, all the bankers want to see me, Sidney. I've a dozen appointments in the next few days. And I have an attorney."

"What bankers?"

"Your favourites. The ones you want to bankroll your Russia plan, as I understand it."

"What do you want, Margaret?"

Margaret lit another cigarette, shook the match until the flame disappeared and dropped it on the carpet. "If I'd known you were in London I'd already have half," she said in a cocky voice as she blew a cloud of smoke in his face.

"Half of what?"

"Half of you." A dress and a pair of black shoes lay on the floor near the hallway.

"Sit down," he said.

"Fix me a drink."

He walked away. She sat on the sofa. He went to the bar, tore the top from a whiskey bottle and filled a glass. He brought it back and put it down hard on the coffee table. "Why are you here? How did you find me?"

"The old man wrote me. Chap named Hill brought me."

"When?"

"The letter came three weeks ago. George came a week later. I arrived yesterday."

"How did you get in?"

"Key at the front desk. I showed our marriage certificate."

"You have to go," he said, voice low and eyes intense.

"But I don't want to go," she said with an affected pout. "I only just got here."

"What do you want?"

"Half of whatever you've got. What have you got?"

"Not enough to satisfy you."

"A million would be a good start."

"Where did you get that figure?"

"The old man said you were doing well."

"If you think you're going to get your hands on my money, forget it." Reilly's insides churned. He knew he looked agitated and cursed himself for getting caught by surprise. He felt naked and that made him angrier.

"Think again, Sidney. If I go to the bankers, say I'm your wife and plead poverty, what will be your chances of keeping them in your Russia banking scheme. Less, I think."

Reilly looked at her icily. "You wouldn't dare," he said.

"No? Desperation leads a lady to desperate measures."

"You're no lady," Reilly said.

"I *am* desperate," Margaret said.

"Are you willing to go away?"

"It would break my heart, but I suppose I have my price."

"Your price is absurd." Reilly got up and went to his library. He opened a desk drawer and brought out a stack of banknotes tied with a thick string. He slammed it down next to Margaret's whiskey glass and said, "One hundred thousand. A one-time offer." He drew a pistol from his jacket and unlocked the safety catch. "Take it or leave it," he said. "Now or never. Take it and go." He held the revolver at her neck and leaned in close. "If I ever see you again, believe me..."

It's all she understands.

Margaret shook. Her eyes shifted. She licked her lips.

"Take it or leave it. I'm playing your game, Margaret, but if you hesitate another second I'll change the rules.

She scooped up the stack, held it tightly to her breast and looked at him with a hurt expression. "It's only fair."

"Take it and get out." He pushed the barrel of the pistol into her temple and glared hatefully at her. "Now," he said.

Suddenly Margaret stood up, raced across the room and stashed the money in a sewing bag, which appeared to be her only luggage. She dropped the robe on the floor, put on her dress and slipped into the shoes.

"Don't spend the night in the city," he said, "just get out."

She looked almost longingly at him, but any regret she may have felt was buried under fear. She walked to the door like a queen at a court ball, opened it and turned back to him. He strode forcefully toward the door. She opened it, jumped into the hotel corridor and slammed the door behind her. He pulled the chain into its latch, turned around and leaned back against the door with his body shaking and his teeth grating. He held up his pistol and moved the safety into lock position.

58. The Counterfeit Massacre

Reilly stormed through the hallway on the top floor of Whitehall Court, threw open the door to C's office and went in. C looked up, jerked back in his seat when he saw Reilly and took up his walking stick, terror written in his face.

"What's wrong?" C said as casually as he could.

Reilly stomped across the room, threw away the low-back chair and stood over C's desk. He leaned forward on his hands. C slid back into the glass-front case that held his show-weapons. He put one hand on the trunk of his cane and the other on the handle.

"Tell me what's wrong," he said nervously.

"You brought Margaret in to wreck the Jaroszynski Plan. You knew you weren't big enough to beat Jaroszynski, me and Churchill, so you reached under the belt and sent her to ruin me with the banks."

"I did nothing of the sort."

"Well, back off or I'll go to the press and tell them that you're trying to wreck Russia's only chance to survive. Back off, Commander. Back off now or I'll go to the press."

C swallowed hard and said, "Now, Captain, bring that chair back here and sit down. You're mistaken."

Reilly swung the chair back into position in front of the desk, sat on the arm, leaned in and said, "Let's hear it."

C rested the walking stick against his desk, opened a drawer and took out his pen knife. He pulled out the blade, glanced at it absently and tapped it gently against his wooden leg. "You see, Captain, according to Administrative Rule number four-oh-five of the Code, all services directors are required to compile certain information about their agents. When we are audited by the Compliance Office we must answer all questions concerning the background of agents."

"You see, I went ahead and set up the safe house and put you in charge of it. I got the Prime Minister to fund it and had to order the usual investigation."

"You brought Margaret to London to see me."

"No, Captain," said C. "No, not on purpose. It seemed innocent enough when she said she was going to send you a card and wanted to know your address. In my gentlemanly zeal it did not occur to me that she would come herself."

"Rubbish. You sent her to talk to the bankers."

"Oh, dear me. What have I started? I did. I did, indeed. She said she needed help and I felt responsible. I sent her to apply for a temporary loan with certain guarantees that I was sure you'd appreciate. I volunteered to underwrite it myself since it sounded urgent. But when the banks started calling, well, I knew then ... I do apologize. She took advantage of my good nature. Apparently she'd gone to almost all of the banks. I realize I made a terrible mess of things."

"What is it about the Jaroszynski Plan that bothers you?"

C replied, "Well, it could be considered controversial."

"You started the controversy by bringing in Margaret."

"But of course I wouldn't do anything to get in the way, even if I disapproved a great deal, which I do not."

"Bloody hell," Reilly said and stood up.

"Wait a minute, Captain. I have more to tell you."

"What?"

"Sit down."

Reilly again sat on the arm of the chair.

"I showed your report on south Russia to the Foreign Office and they agree with it. Your Jaroszynski scheme's going to be a big success. The Foreign Office even authorized a disbursement for Paul Dukes, who took your place in Moscow. So you see,

Captain, although at times it may not be obvious to you, I am your biggest supporter."

"How much did you get?"

"I sent Dukes one million by courier. While you were away. By now it's all in the hands of your agents, thanks to Dukes... and your friend Anna."

"One million," said Reilly, sitting up. "That's better than my whole budget for the Lenin operation. That's very good. He can run my network on a million."

Anna? I've never mentioned her to him.

"Yes," said C. "I acted on the recommendations you made in your report. All of them. Because we understand one another, Russia now stands a good chance to become whole again. One day, because of us, your young friend Anna will be able to go to bed without fear that the Cheka are going to burst through the door. I'd say that's the result we both want. Now get out of here and let me finish my reports. You're not the only spy I have to account for, you know."

Weeks later Reilly was at his library desk, opening envelopes. One was from Lockhart, who had heard from someone in south Russia. The banking scheme was working. Areas won by the Whites were staying White. General Yudenich was poised to take Petrograd. There had already been small uprisings. Moscow was awaiting Deniken's army, which was not far away and rumoured to be planning a huge offensive designed to take the city and smash the Bolsheviks.

There were other messages from bankers who wanted in on the banking scheme. British bankers, French and some Americans, even a Japanese trust wanted a piece of it. At the bottom of the pile was a larger envelope delivered by a courier who had just come from Moscow. There were two letters inside. One was from Sasha. The other was addressed to him in Anna's handwriting. Sasha's was written before Anna's so he opened and deciphered it.

"Sidney, we are well. Anna is dancing again and very happy,

working with Dukes quite successfully. I am close to Derzhinsky, Peters, Artuzov, am amused by their confidence when I know the forces that are building around them and circling in for the kill. General Deniken is outside Moscow, General Yudenich has his eye on Petrograd and Dukes is just waiting, chomping at the bit for the final attack on Moscow, ready to take control and bring Savinkov to power. This may be my last letter from the inside, my last letter to you before you come back. I will see you then, in a public place with none of the fear I have endured for the last two years. It's so close and I know we will be successful. Still, I cannot wait, and I cannot wait to see you and Volodia.—Sasha."

A lightness filled Reilly's body. He hadn't realized that the moment of victory was so near. He put Sasha's letter down, opened Anna's and noticed that some of the ink had been smeared and diluted with water. But it was legible.

"My dear Sidney—A few weeks ago a courier arrived with a tremendous amount of money for Paul Dukes, which we quickly got out to all of your agents here, a massive undertaking. We received the news that the Whites are coming and maybe the British, got everyone ready and waited for further word about our liberation day. Every day seemed to bring the moment closer and I think no one here could sleep with such anticipation.

"But this week something changed. At first some of our people disappeared, and then more. But now it seems they are all gone. Arrested, maybe executed. Sasha says Lubyanka and Butyrki jails are filling up, executions every day.

"Today Dukes came here in a hurry and said the money was counterfeit. He got out by rail. Instead, we got it out to our agents and Derzhinsky's men followed it to them. Sidney, what have I done? I want to die."

C sent counterfeit money.

Heat began to rise up through his chest. He crumpled the letter in his fist and walked toward the bathroom.

It led Derzhinsky to my network and killed my agents.

Instead he turned to an adjacent closet and opened the heavy wooden door, slipped in behind his overcoats and closed it, sealing himself away.

He held Anna's letter to his heart as an unfamiliar surge of horror pushed itself up from somewhere inside him. His whole body strained as he fought its approach to his throat, and resisted with all his strength as it burned slowly up inside his neck like fire. He clenched his teeth, groaned and tried for endless moments to push it back down. But his strength caved in; it exploded through his jaws and mouth.

"Nooo...!" he screamed. His fists cracked against the sides of his crimson temple as it roared more and more loudly, spending his breath, sucking the air out of him.

"Nooo!" he bellowed as a constant stream of unimagined pain gushed from his body and filled him, an ocean of blood from a nightmare turned real.

His body writhed uncontrollably. He fell limp to the floor and cried into his palms. Tears flowed from his eyes but did not extinguish the fire in his face.

Reilly spent the following week trying to get more information about events in Moscow. Unable to find anything in London after two days he went to Paris, where a large Russian exile community had grown since the revolution and where he had numerous reliable agents and other contacts. After a few days one of his Moscow agents arrived with a small piece of the story: he had evaded a Cheka search on his flat by hiding on a rooftop, fled to White Russia, got out and found safe passage to Paris. He agreed to speak with other survivors to compare notes and deliver a full report as soon as possible. Reilly returned to London and received the agent's cipher:

"All received expense funds from centre [Dukes] but the notes were all counterfeit. Cheka searches began immediately with about 95% arrests. Entire Moscow network believed destroyed with some survivors able to get to Paris or Berlin. No known civilian agents remaining. Three inside Cheka [Sasha,

Volodia and Arkady Semyonovich] believed safe. All others executed. If more, will inform you, etc. – Maxim."

Reilly seethed. The "money" that C sent to support Dukes had created a trail that led the Cheka to every one of Reilly's agents. As on other occasions C's attempts to help Reilly and the anti-Bolsheviks had resulted in disaster. He waited a day for his anger to subside to a manageable level and then, with his heart thumping mercilessly inside his chest, went to Whitehall Court. He stormed out of the secret lift and down the hallway to C's office and found C standing at his desk. But when he heard C shouting into the telephone receiver he stopped cold in the doorway and listened:

"I don't give a damn what you say, Thomson. He was your man. He's ruined more than a few of mine. So don't tell me about his poor immigrant family and how hard he's worked to get himself out of the slums! All I want to know is how he turned out to be a crook!" C put his hand on his hips, garnered all his energy in his brow and growled, "Your courier may have got one of my best men killed. If Dukes doesn't make it out, there'll be hell to pay."

C slammed down the phone, crumpled a paper into a ball and threw it wildly at the wall. He glared at Reilly and said, "I don't want to hear your complaints either."

Reilly's anger dissipated somewhat as he saw C's crimson face and the strained jaw that stretched his skin in rage.

C slid into his chair. "I used a courier called Strasky to send the money to Dukes in Moscow. I got him from Thomson, who said Strasky had been an effective agent at Special Branch. But he never told me about Strasky's financial condition. If I'd known he was bankrupt I'd never have given him that money."

"What are you talking about?" Reilly sat down.

"Strasky, the courier. Turned out to be a crook."

C continued, "He bought counterfeit money with the million I gave him for Dukes, delivered the bogus notes and kept a fortune for himself. The counterfeit money led Derzhinsky to everyone who worked for Dukes."

"My network was wrecked by a petty crook? A nobody?"

"Apparently so," C said in a trembling voice.

"I doubt it. I think Derzhinsky planted counterfeit money on you, so Dukes would get it. A classic set-up."

But who did Derzhinsky use to do this?

"Oh," said C. "No. I don't think so. We'd have discovered any counterfeit money here before it got out. Strasky was a crook." C shook his head.

"Maybe Strasky worked for Derzhinsky."

"It wasn't political. He simply needed money."

"Strasky carried messages in and out of Russia without difficulty for almost a year," Reilly said. "That would have been nearly impossible without Derzhinsky's help.

"He had our help all the way up to the border," said C.

"He was working for Derzhinsky, old man." Reilly sat in the chair, crossed his legs and accidentally kicked C's desk. He rested his chin on his fist. "It's all a set-up."

"Perhaps Strasky's easy transit across the Russian border should have given us pause. But to say that Derzhinsky originated a counterfeit scheme in order to destroy our Moscow network— well, that's giving him too much credit."

"He's a criminal genius," said Reilly.

"An opportunist. He was watching Strasky, discovered that Strasky'd brought counterfeit money to Moscow and knew it could only be going to the opposition. So he dropped a net. He's smart. But don't overestimate him."

"Tell me about Strasky." Reilly's anger was quieted. C seemed nearly as agonized over the disaster as Reilly himself. It appeared that one way or another, C had played into Derzhinsky's hands and could not have prevented the catastrophe. It seemed that C's own anger over the matter could create difficulties in his already-strained relationship with Basil Thomson, director of the Special Branch, from whom C had obtained the courier Strasky. In such circumstances Reilly always slipped into the role of reasoned advisor in order to keep C from boiling over. Although this usually worked, at the moment C's face was crimson and his brow thick with beads of sweat. Reilly waited for calm.

C looked sadly at Reilly. "Strasky was a Russian immigrant who worked for Kell at Military Intelligence. After the Russian Revolution I told Thomson how dangerous I thought the Bolsheviks were here in England and suggested he look to the immigrant community for some help in his investigations. But Thomson's budget was cut, so Kell gave him Strasky. I got Strasky from Thomson when Dukes went to Russia. He looked like the perfect courier."

"Kell to Thomson to you. So he worked for Military Intelligence, Scotland Yard and the Secret Intelligence Service. What a goldmine for Derzhinsky."

"If Derzhinsky had known, he'd never have used him on such a trivial operation."

"Trivial? Not for us and certainly not for Derzhinsky. It's just how he would've used someone with Strasky's understanding of our services before bringing him back."

C shook his head. "Think what you like, Reilly. And while you're at it, think about who should run foreign intelligence. Kell thinks it should be Military Intelligence. Thomson wants his Intelligence Directorate to do it."

"What do you think?" said Reilly.

"It shouldn't be a military question. And Thomson – well, you can see he's demonstrated remarkable incompetence where foreign intelligence is concerned."

"Kell can make a case for Military Intelligence."

C leaned forward on his desk. "Too many cabinet members are impressed with uniforms. Parliamentarians melt at the sight of ribbons on a general's chest."

Reilly's brow was non-committal.

"Military men think only in military terms. We need someone with a broader view."

"That would be you."

"That would be us."

"Not at the expense of the Special Branch or Military

Intelligence. If you lose them you might as well give the Bolsheviks the key to London."

Again C's attention roamed out to the rooftops of Whitehall Court. As he glanced back at Reilly his pen-knife appeared out of nowhere, blade open, and started to tap on his wooden leg. Just as abruptly his peppered moustache crawled down over his upper lip, his jaw stiffened and he said, "Then, Reilly, there's the question of whom to trust on the most sensitive matters."

"Whom to trust?"

"It's not always clear."

"What?"

"Information gets out. Lord knows how."

"You don't trust Thomson?"

"A leak becomes a rupture from which a steady stream of information flows."

"In the Special Branch of the Directorate of Intelligence?"

"You are needed temporarily in South Russia. Military information is leaking. Go plug the leak. Look at Deniken's intelligence methods, fix the problem and come back. We've got our own trouble brewing here too. Will you do it?"

"When?"

"Tomorrow or the next day."

"I'll need three days to clean things up."

"Very well, then, it's three days and no longer." The telephone rang and C lifted the receiver. He smiled, nodded a few times and said, "Thank you, Major." He dropped the receiver on the switch hook. "Good news from Helsinki," he said. "Dukes made it out of Russia. Our people have him."

59. A Party For Blyumkin, May, 1919

The concierge brought Savinkov's cable very early in the morning. "Come immediately to Paris," it said and gave an address unfamiliar to Reilly. The signature, "B. Viktorovich," told Reilly that the message was both authentic and urgent. Reilly left his coffee in the kitchen sink and had a driver take him directly to an airfield near the coast. He might have flown solo but recognized his own exhaustion. Instead, he paid for a pilot's service, went to sleep before the airplane was out over the Channel and by late afternoon had found his way to a cheap hotel in a poorer section of Paris.

Reilly greeted Savinkov with more emotion than the latter had ever seen him express. His voice quivered when he said, "I'd have killed myself but for the friends we have to help. Sasha, Volodia, Anna, Katya. We can't let them be taken."

"What the hell are you talking about?" Savinkov said. He took Reilly by both arms and sat him down at a dining table covered with documents and maps. "What did you say?"

"You don't know?" Reilly said.

"I don't think so," Savinkov said. "What is it?"

"C sent money to Dukes. A million. Anna and Dukes got it out to everyone. But it was counterfeit, a roadmap for Derzhinsky. Executions are probably still going on."

Savinkov said quietly, "No. I didn't know."

Neither spoke. Savinkov made coffee and they smoked.

Reilly said, "If you didn't know, why did you want me to come? What's so urgent?"

Savinkov watched a cloud of smoke and said, "Blyumkin."

"You mean the little piss-ant who shot the German Ambassador and blew our timing?"

"You haven't heard. He went back to Moscow."

"No doubt they've put him in front of a firing squad. Serves the bastard right."

"You don't know," said Savinkov.

"Oh, but I do," Reilly replied. "You know who put him up to it?" Reilly chuckled and said, "You want to know?"

"It was Derzhinsky," Savinkov said.

Reilly laughed. "That's what I thought. After all, it bought Derzhinsky control over the Moscow Cheka. But C told me he sent the assassin. He thought we'd fail, so he activated a contingency to kill Mirbach."

Savinkov slowly shook his head. "Derzhinsky."

Reilly continued, "C said he ordered it. When the British scotched the landing in the north, he thought we didn't have a chance. So he ordered a contingency, a sleeper named Weber, who got the SR Spiridonova to find a patsy for an assassin. Weber told me Derzhinsky was behind it. You agree? Why?"

"Blyumkin went back to Moscow," Savinkov said, "but they didn't execute him. Derzhinsky and the whole Cheka threw a party. Hats and balloons and all that. Gave him a good Cheka job. Welcomed him like a brother. Now, do you still think C was behind the shooting?"

Reilly said, "Bloody hell. What do you make of that? Why would C take responsibility for wrecking our plans? I might have wrung his neck. He couldn't predict how I'd react."

Savinkov said, "He was protecting Derzhinsky."

"Why?" Reilly said, almost rhetorically.

"What have we got here?" Savinkov said.

Reilly said, "C sent counterfeit cash, which led Derzhinsky to our network. But they may have been working together on something that wrecked our counter-revolution earlier-Mirbach. What else? What's the story?"

"What should we do?" Savinkov said.

"I have other business with C," Reilly said. "It may take some time, but I'll try to get him to talk to me. I want to hear what Sasha and Volodia think about it." Reilly looked at his watch. "I'm going back to London."

But Savinkov had something else. "Lenin is unloading his war-chest of diamonds. Wants to buy a British newspaper." He gave Reilly an envelope for the London Metropolitan Police. Reilly said he would take it to Inspector Herbert Fitch.

Savinkov took Reilly to the airfield. As he said goodbye to Savinkov he extracted a promise that Blyumkin would never be discussed outside his role as an assassin. No one would know that Reilly and Savinkov knew Blyumkin had returned to Moscow. Reilly's pilot flew him home. By midnight he was asleep in his own bed.

60. Inspector Fitch

On a dismal, foggy evening a Special Branch Inspector called Fitch stood between two houses on a small street in a cheap section of London. He wore a walrus moustache and a Deerstalker hat that protected both his neck and face from the drizzle. A mahogany Calabash pipe drooped from between his teeth, and once in a while he would blow out his cheeks and a circle of smoke would drift over his head. His hands rested in the pockets of his tartan overcoat, one with a pencil, the other with a pistol. He shifted his feet from time to time but his eyes never left the house across the street, where every so often a man would come or go. He looked at his pocket watch, took a small pad from under his coat and wrote on it with the pencil. He put the pad in his coat, took out a box of matches and re-lit his pipe.

Someone approached the house across the street, climbed the stone steps and knocked quietly on the door. The door opened and the visitor went inside. Fitch again checked his pocket watch, wrote something in his notebook and took an umbrella from the side of the house next to him. When a light appeared in a certain room across the street he stuck the umbrella under his arm, left his secluded spot between the two houses and crossed to the other side. He climbed the stone steps, adjusted the pipe between his teeth and tapped on the door with the handle of his umbrella. In a moment the door opened a crack and someone said, "Who is it?"

"Fitch," he said calmly. "Special Branch."

When the man behind the door went to close it, Fitch thrust his umbrella into the crack with lightning speed. "Open up," he said. "I want a word with Pritkin."

"There's no Pritkin here."

"Open up." Fitch looked at his pocket watch and said, "You have 'til the count of ten." He counted, "One, two..."

The door opened and the man moved back. Fitch went in and took off his hat. "Good evening, gentlemen," he said to two who stood in opposite corners of the room. One wore a sweater and seemed at home. The other was tall and thick with a heavy, wet overcoat, bare feet and a nervous look.

"What do you want, Fitch?" the comfortable man said.

Fitch glanced at a pair of boots behind the door and guessed that they belonged to the man in the wet overcoat. "Diamonds," he said. "I'm here for diamonds."

"No diamonds here. Now, be a good chap and go."

"I smell diamonds," said Fitch.

"You've caught a chill, Fitch. Your nostrils are clogged."

"Nevertheless, I have certain impressions based on fact. Number one, you work for the Daily Herald. Number two, this gentleman just got off the boat from Petrograd."

"He's my guest. He just arrived. So what?"

Fitch smiled. "I smell diamonds." He looked at the shoeless man. "Just got off the boat, did you? Pritkin?"

The Herald man turned to the other. "Yes, he's Pritkin."

Fitch glanced at Pritkin's bare feet and said, "You'll catch your death of cold if you don't put something on your feet." He poked his umbrella between Pritkin's toes. "You should put something on those feet..." Fitch turned and lifted one of the man's boots with his umbrella. "...like this!"

"He just took them off, Fitch. They're wet."

"They don't seem too wet to me...comrade. But they do seem heavy. What do you suppose are the odds that he took them off because they weigh too much and are cumbersome to walk in? What would you say to that?"

"You idiot, Fitch," said the man, "What do you want?"

"Diamonds, as I said." Fitch took out a pocket knife, opened the blade and held it at the top seam of the boot. "I can make your boots lighter so you can walk in them. You'll have less risk of catching a cold."

"Go away, Fitch!"

With a single motion Fitch slit open the top of the boot. When he turned the boot upside down diamonds poured onto the floor. He took the other boot and did the same as Pritkin cringed. "Do you have a small sack of some kind?"

"You bastard, Fitch."

"You wouldn't want him arrested for smuggling."

The man opened a drawer in a dark table near the door. He took out a small burlap bag and tossed it to Fitch.

"Thank you, gov'nor," said Fitch. "Now stand away." The man moved back and stood next to Pritkin, hands on his hips. Fitch tossed the boots to Pritkin, who caught one after another on the fly. "See how light they are now? They'll be much more comfortable." He bent over, collected the diamonds and put them in the sack. He stood without taking his eyes off the two men, tossed the sack a few inches into the air and caught it as it came down. He put it into his pocket, took his umbrella and looked at Pritkin. "You Soviets will have to find another way to pay for propaganda in England. And you," he said to the other one, "Find an honest way to meet your paper's expenses."

Fitch put on his hat, swung around and poked the door open with the umbrella; but as the door closed behind him caught it with his elbow. The man peeked through the crack.

"What now, Fitch?"

"I expect that my friends from Military Intelligence or the city police will visit. Give them my best regards, will you?"

The door closed. Fitch heard cursing. He climbed down the steps, put his umbrella under his arm and walked away.

Reilly sat alone in the rear of the tavern with his back to the wall and watched Fitch amble slowly past the bar in his Deerstalker hat in hand. Fitch dropped the hat on Reilly's table, clenched his pipe between his yellowed teeth, took a pinch of tobacco and lit the pipe.

Reilly grinned, gestured toward an empty chair with an open palm and said, "Hello, Fitch."

Fitch blew a cloud of smoke into the already-hazy tavern and sat down. Reilly nodded at the waiter.

"Give my friend his choice. In fact, a double of his choice."

At a table on the far side of the room three young women laughed with two older men. One of the women looked at Reilly and smiled. One of the men looked at him and glared.

"What would you like, inspector?" said the waiter.

Fitch sucked on his pipe. “Ale, same as Reilly’s.”

“Two?”

“Now and later.” Fitch grinned. “I have a good story.”

“I love a good story, especially if it’s funny.”

The waiter walked away. Fitch took the pipe from his teeth, leaned forward and said, “It doesn’t have to be a funny story, does it? I’m not good at funny stories.”

“Make it as sad as you like,” Reilly said, leaning forward again. “And you can tell it any way you want. You can go from start to finish, or give me your conclusion first and we’ll drink to the details afterwards. Now go ahead, Herbert.”

“You wouldn’t mind?”

“I don’t mind.”

Fitch reached around, pulled out a bag from his overcoat and called to the waiter, “Bring a bowl!”

From several tables away the waiter replied, “Of what?”

“Empty.”

The waiter brought a mug of ale and a bowl, put them both on the table in front of Fitch and walked off. Fitch opened the burlap bag, loosened the twine and spread it with his fingers. He poured the diamonds into the bowl.

Expressionless, Reilly said, “Tell me about the intercept.”

“Tonight. At the home of the editor of the Herald. The Bolsheviks want a beachhead here. The Herald is available.”

Reilly said, “Does Director Thomson know?”

“In principal. I showed him what you gave me.”

“But C doesn’t know?”

“No,” said Fitch.

“Why not?”

“He’d want his Secret Intelligence Service put in control.”

“What about Kell?”

“He’d want Military Intelligence put in control.”

“Who knows?”

“Thomson, Churchill, you and I, the PM and Lord Curzon.”

“I don’t want to be the one who tells C. Let Thomson.”

“Here’s what I think,” Fitch said. “The Secret Intelligence

Service begins at the sea and takes in the world. We begin at the shore and take in the Kingdom. But where the Bolsheviks are concerned we should be partners, not competitors. If Thomson and C won't cooperate, we should."

"What do you want from me?" Reilly said.

"At the moment, just your ear. We and the Soviets may negotiate a trade agreement."

Reilly said, "How do you know that?"

"Thomson got it from the cabinet."

"And the Prime Minister?" said Reilly.

"He wants to see how far The Herald is connected to the Bolsheviks. He doesn't want to look stupid. How can we fight the Bolsheviks and trade with them at the same time?"

"We can't," said Reilly. "You've got the goods on The Herald. Go public. No one would invite the Soviets then."

"That would wreck the code breaking operation."

"Is that why Lloyd George is holding off?"

Fitch glanced quickly between Reilly and his ale, took a drink and said, "Can you find out what C knows about it?"

"I can try," Reilly said. But he was going back to South Russia in a day or two. He referred Fitch to Hill or Fothergil but said he would look into it before he left. "One more thing," he said. "Can you come with me in the morning? Can you do line work?"

Fitch looked dumbstruck. "What?"

"Can you do line work, telephone listening setups? I need someone I can trust. I'll go out of channels for this one."

"Thompson just canned a specialist for moonlighting."

"You trust him?"

"Completely."

"Bring him. I'll get him some cash."

"I'll stop by in the morning."

The next morning's sun broke over a nearby chimney and a comfortable June breeze blew in through the window. Reilly put his arm over his eyes and covered Caryll's eyes with his hand. She squirmed, rolled part way onto his body and snuggled into his neck. He pulled the sheet over her shoulder and she whispered, "Thank you." He lay on his back, stared absently at the ceiling and the clock on the table. He nestled his fingers into the hair at the top of her neck.

"Class in an hour." She opened her eyes. "I'm glad you're back. Wish I could stay. I'm having dinner with my mother tonight. Doctor Stone invited us to a tea at Pusey House. They've started an Anglo-Catholic Congress. They think the Catholics and the Church can talk to each other. I'll learn about the Catholics."

When Caryll dressed, Reilly took her hand and led the way from the kitchen. She smiled, kissed him again and opened the door. Fitch stood outside.

"Excuse me," Fitch said, surprised.

"Hello," Caryll said, and "Good bye." She went to the lift.

"I'm sorry," Fitch said as he came inside, took off his overcoat and went to the sitting room. "I thought we'd get a good start. I told Casper, my sweeper, we'd get him early on."

"Just in time for coffee," said Reilly. "Sit down. Black?"

"Sugar," Fitch said. He sat on the sofa.

Reilly put a tray on the table. Fitch dropped two lumps of sugar into his cup. "You're excited," Reilly said.

"I have reason to be," said Fitch. "The Bolsheviks have sent a delegation to hold trade talks with the government. And they've sent more money to the Daily Herald. We can trace it. We've got enough to keep the trade talks from getting off the ground."

Reilly shook his head. "It's more complicated than you think, Herbert. The Red Army is about to attack Warsaw. Some cabinet members and Parliament want to help the Poles. The Left will pressure the government to stay out of it."

"We could have demonstrations," Fitch said.

"Yes. You may have to use that decrypted information for a pre-emptive strike, and release it before they start talking about British intervention in Poland."

"They want to keep it quiet to protect the code."

"What does Thomson say about revolution here?"

"He thinks it's possible. What does C think?"

"I'll ask him," said Reilly.

"Don't say anything about the decrypts," Fitch said. "You've never heard of them."

61. Decrypts, 1920-21

Reilly stood in the doorway and watched C at the front window of his office, looking out at the nearby buildings.

"Take a seat, Reilly." Reilly shook C's hand and sat. "How was south Russia?"

"I'm not optimistic," Reilly said.

"What did you find out about intelligence leaks?"

"The leaks are from somewhere else, not Deniken's camp. Derzhinsky has an informer somewhere along the line. Here or there. Anything is possible."

"Then what's wrong?"

"The White Army. Troops change sides overnight. White generals can't control their officers. They stage atrocities and pogroms. The civilians are fickle and I don't blame them."

"How is the banking plan working?"

"The troops undermine it with their recklessness."

"Not surprisingly," C said.

"I saw the Whites chase the Reds from a village. The Whites disappeared without securing the territory or bringing in any food or economic assistance. Half came back the next day, raped a few dozen Jewish women and hanged as many men. The survivors begged the Red Army to return."

"Is there any hope of a White victory?"

"Little that I can see."

"Is this an overall pattern?"

"The Reds are gaining ground and the Whites are moving south. They can't retreat forever. The next round of the struggle will take place somewhere else. Europe or Britain."

Reilly had returned from Russia through Warsaw to meet with Savinkov and his 'Green Army,' The Red Army wasn't far away. The Poles said they thought their only hope was British intervention. Reilly saw a story unfolding.

"We'll hear a patriotic call from the Cabinet and Parliament to send British troops."

"They're trying now," C said.

"Then a Left, 'No British Troops in Poland' movement."

"Correct," C said.

"The Soviets sent a delegation to negotiate a trade agreement with the government."

C shifted in his chair. "The Prime Minister says trade will mean jobs for British workers and very bonnie Bolsheviks."

"Nonsense," said Reilly. "Lenin is subsidizing the Left and at least one of the papers, the Daily Herald. Building a propaganda machine, just as in Petrograd in 1917. What's holding the Prime Minister back?"

"One never knows."

"One bloody-well does know when one can read the other side's mail," Reilly said. "Here's what will happen: Left protests against British intervention in Poland and the subversive activities of the Soviet Trade Delegation."

"Yes. Revolution here is a frightening possibility."

"We have real evidence," Reilly said.

"Which we cannot release."

"Why not?" Reilly said.

The pen-knife appeared as if by magic. As the blade began to tap quietly against his wooden leg, C said, "There will likely be more decrypts and more damning evidence against the Soviet Trade Delegation."

"Wouldn't be surprised," Reilly said.

"Kamenev is the only highly-ranked member of the trade delegation who is connected to the Moscow Soviet and the Communist Internationale. Imagine that one day soon we intercept a direct communication between Lenin and Kamenev, leaving no doubt whatsoever that Kamenev's real objective is to organize factory workers' militia groups across England. Just as Lenin did in Petrograd in 1917."

Reilly leaned forward. "Yes?"

"Imagine we could then prove that what Lenin and Kamenev really want is to use the trade talks to disrupt the British political process, inciting workers to revolution. Not the whole delegation. Just Kamenev. In Moscow, Lenin."

Reilly squeezed his chin. "The delegation would remain and our code breakers would still be in business."

"Right," said C. "And with the discrediting of Kamenev, both the Internationale and Lenin would be taken down a peg around the world. Lenin would no longer be able to duck responsibility for his schemes by blaming the Internationale. In Moscow, Kamenev would become a pariah."

A smile worked its way across Reilly's lips.

"I hear Lenin's in and out of seclusion," C said. "The pistol wounds and more. I hear he has syphilis. He won't last long."

"So, who takes Lenin's place when he dies?" Reilly said.

"We can't sink the whole ship at once. Now there are five. A corpse and four men waiting in line to take its place."

"Lenin the corpse. And Kamenev, Trotsky, Zinoviev, Stalin."

"If we eliminate Kamenev, it's one down, three to go. When one remains, the house of playing cards collapses."

Reilly smiled. *Beautifully simple and far-sighted. It's brilliant. Only a true anti-Bolshevist could have imagined it. If only...*

If only Lord Curzon, Foreign Minister and Chairman of the Intelligence Committee, could be kept at bay. If only Churchill could take a longer view. If only no one jumped ship and released the documents prematurely.

Reilly had asked Fitch to cover Casper as the latter examined the telephone line connections at C's safe house. They stopped by to tell Reilly that C had installed cumbersome listening devices that did not represent a real challenge at present, but that the house could be accessed from a secret entrance. A listener with even a primitive device could overhear conversations from anywhere in the house.

Telephone conversations might also be monitored from the telephone company exchange. Otherwise Casper did not know whether surveillance could be done remotely. He had also located radio transmission facilities that C might or might not have intended for Reilly's use.

Reilly took Fitch aside. "It's a good house but with all that equipment I can't use it. C may want to put someone in there to listen to me. Leave it alone and I'll use it appropriately. Now, Fitch, you know London. Could you find something for us to use outside of channels? Something unobtrusive for private meetings, but not too far away. Access by car. Cash payment."

In just a few days Fitch brought the address of Reilly's new safe house. Casper was there at that same moment, doing his first daily examination. But almost at the outset, Casper was called to Brighton to care for his aging father.

Fortunately the next day brought the Frenchman Laurent to Reilly's flat. He had taken a Russian lady back to France. She had disappeared with a painter from Montmartre and his heart was broken. He had come to London to seek solace. It did not help that French Intelligence had turned him over to the Foreign Legion after discovering that he had worked with Reilly in Russia. Though he escaped, rumours had surfaced in Paris that Reilly and Laurent were double agents working to sabotage allied anti-Soviet intelligence efforts.

"Svetochka?" Reilly said.

"I know," Laurent said. "You told me so."

"Want a job? I could use a housekeeper and a watcher."

"I was hoping you'd say that, Mister Reilly."

Caryll held a Bible and walked through the hotel lobby. A driver passed her, smiled but looked somewhat confused at the sight of the Bible. It struck the Concierge, too.

Reilly's girl, after all.

"They managed to get several hundred Catholics and Anglicans in the same room to hear the lecture," Caryll said. "No shots fired. Not a bad start."

"Good lecture?" said Reilly.

"I liked his view of Jesus as a man who succeeded not simply because he was the Son of God but also because he saw the necessity of faith and sacrifice in saving humanity."

The telephone rang, and Fitch was calling. "Sorry if I'm late. Did you speak to C?"

"Yes."

"What's he think about the possibility of revolution?"

"He agrees with Thomson but is against releasing decrypted information now."

"Why?"

"I can't comment," Reilly said. "But follow a Bolshevik named Kamenev."

"Yes," said Fitch. "Of the Soviet Trade Delegation."

"Tell the code breakers. It's where you build your case."

"That's what C says?"

"That's what I say. Do you have anything new?"

"Yes," said Fitch. "The unions met and agreed to hold strikes against intervention in Poland. We're afraid of a general strike, with streets filling up all over the country."

"What would the army do?"

"We don't know. Thomson and Wilson would like to talk with you, off hours."

"Wilson?"

Fitch cleared his throat. "Field Martial Sir Henry Wilson, Chief of the Imperial General Staff."

"He wants to see me?"

"Thomson told him about our conversations. Wilson claims to know about you. Can we arrange something for tomorrow night? Out of the way?"

"Yes," said Reilly. "Come here. I'll have the staff make arrangements for you to use the back way."

"I'll call you after I speak with Thomson," Fitch said.

Reilly hung up.

"Is something wrong?" Caryll said. "Should I go?"

Reilly crushed his cigarette in an ashtray. "No. Stay." He went back to the sofa. "You were talking about the importance of faith and sacrifice." He sat next to Caryll and put his hand on her shoulder.

She touched his fingers. "You've sacrificed so much."

"Such as?" he said, scratching his neck.

"You've risked and sacrificed everything for Russia."

"I've risked a little," he replied, "and sacrificed nothing."

"You're modest," she said, leaning forward to kiss him.

"Modest I am not. And I haven't sacrificed anything. I'm no saint. I believe in what I'm doing but I don't think I need to die for it. Alive, I can influence people. Dead, I'm no good to anyone. I will not become a martyr for my cause."

"But you would."

"Not if I had a choice. It would achieve nothing. Without me the whole anti-Bolshevik movement would splinter into factions. Millions of Russians would lose hope. My importance depends on staying alive, not in sacrificing myself. Would I die for a friend? Yes. But I want to live as long possible."

"You give yourself no rest," she replied.

"I don't want you to have illusions about me."

Caryll said, "All right, no illusions. You are imperfect." She moved closer and slipped her hand inside his shirt. "Make love to me now and we can talk philosophy later."

In the morning, Caryll walked through the hallway. "I'll call you tomorrow," she said as she brushed Reilly's cheek.

When she opened the door they saw George Hill standing outside with a briefcase under his arm. He smiled at Reilly, glanced at Caryll and said, "Oh."

"Excuse me," Caryll said and left the flat.

Hill turned to Reilly with an amused expression and said as he stepped by, "Your wind must be quite good, old man."

"She's older than she looks," Reilly said.

"She'd better be."

"What have you got?"

Hill took a few documents from his briefcase. "I hope her father doesn't have a service revolver left over from the war."

"What's this?" Reilly said.

"Enough information from the government code people to send Kamenev and Krassin packing. Or to prison. They're putting money all over the place. The cabinet's in an uproar. Lord Curzon gave me these in the hope that they would convince C to back the release of the information."

"What did C say?" Reilly said.

"He didn't have time to look. He said I should see you."

"C has a good reason not to release the information, George, and he made me promise to keep quiet about it. That's final," Reilly said. "For the moment."

"There's talk of a general strike, you know," Hill said. "The information in the decrypts may be all that quells it. Some of our people are starting to twist the PM's arm to send troops to Warsaw. C's cutting it a bit close, don't you think?"

"Have you talked to anyone from Military Intelligence?"

"They're tearing their hair out," said Hill. "The Soviet Army is bearing down on Warsaw. Kell is desperate to release the information to discredit Lenin."

"Call me late tonight," Reilly said. "I'll have a clearer picture then. But now I suggest you go back to C and tell him you need to understand his thinking. Tell him I clammed up. Maybe he'll talk. Then when I know more we can go in together."

Hill nodded, put the decrypts back into his briefcase and left the flat. Reilly took another cup of coffee and went back to his newspaper. Inspector Fitch called to say the meeting with Thomson and General Wilson would be at nine that evening. When the conversation finished, Reilly put a few garments into his bedroom closet and called the maid.

Thomson and Wilson, two of the highest ranking officials in the government, were in awe at the depth of Reilly's insights. Both men and many around them believed Lenin would soon launch attacks on Britain, using disaffected factory labourers and underpaid troops. Both wanted C to cease his resistance to publicizing the contents of the decrypted documents. Wilson was so filled with fear of a Bolshevik insurgency that he was preparing to move troops to the city as a contingency. Neither Thomson nor Wilson trusted C. All evening they pressed Reilly to get C's support to release the decrypted documents.

Churchill called. "Got a whale for you, Sidney. Hold on."

Arkady Semyonovich, one of Reilly's best agents, now assigned by Derzhinsky to the trade talks, took the line. He offered pleasantries and good news that Anna, Sasha and Volodia were well. Then he said, "Lord Winston tells me you're reading Lenin's mail."

Reilly went silent.

Arkady said, "Here's something for you, Sidney. Derzhinsky's reading *your* mail."

Churchill came back. "Hear that? He's got our codes."

"Does he know we're reading his mail?"

Churchill asked Arkady and came back to Reilly. "Thinks so. We have to assume so. White Army codes too."

"Christ. How did he get the codes?"

"Arkady thinks it's an inside job." Churchill said that he too suspected a leak somewhere in the intelligence services. Reilly cautioned not to jump to conclusions. In the background he heard Lockhart ask why Derzhinsky had not changed the code.

"Someone wants us on the other end, perhaps to kill the trade talks or to discredit Kamenev," Churchill said. "Derzhinsky's work, of course. But a trade agreement means a lot. Money, commerce and the possibility of a British loan. It would mean he could put as many spies as he wanted in London. Why would Derzhinsky sabotage all that?"

They *had* to persuade C to speak with the Prime Minister. But C said the timing was wrong. Not far off, but not yet. Couldn't give up control. It would be days or weeks.

Fitch said, "Yesterday I intercepted another Bolshevik smuggler taking jewels to The Herald. Today Kell at Military Intelligence asked Wilson if troops were near enough to London, just in case. Tonight Wilson called Churchill and brow beat him to take it to the papers. Churchill sent a courier to you moments ago with decrypts. Wants you to deliver them to the papers for Curzon first thing tomorrow. In other words, Curzon sent you, bypass C, and shut up."

Reilly was back by seven the next morning.

C called and said, "Kamenev is out. The PM pulled his visa. The press are running a letter from Lenin to Kamenev with orders to infiltrate the army and labour unions."

"Who tipped the press?" Reilly said.

"Curzon, the weasel. Got the information from Thomson."

Reilly's phone rang once again. Arkady would return to Moscow the following day. He warned Reilly that starvation was coming to Russia, that the grain harvest had failed and they could not feed the population. Reilly should be aware, because the Soviets already knew it was impossible. They would beg for help and the Foreign Office would ask Reilly.

"Give the Soviets nothing- no money, no food- unless they satisfy very hard terms-- like disbanding the Cheka. Aid will hurt Russians who resist the Soviet Government. Don't be tempted by compassion. It works the opposite way."

"Who's left to resist?"

"Sidney, we've had disturbances in the provinces, factory strikes in Petrograd, a Red Army disgruntled with Bolshevik power. We may see an uprising at Kronstadt Naval Base. There's much resistance to the Bolsheviks. Starvation will add more. Don't let your Prime Minister fall for it.

"What else?" Reilly said.

"The Red Army has lost at Warsaw and they're retreating. Warsaw won't need British troops."

"Nor will London," Reilly said.

"So you need not worry about anti-war demonstrations."

"I know what C will say," Reilly said. "He'll say he knew it all along."

62. Source BP11, 1921-1923

"I knew a great deal more, too," C said, an arrogant wrinkle on his brow melting into a general expression that Reilly thought a cross between modesty and helplessness. He pushed an open file across his desk.

Reilly looked at the top paper and said, "What's this?"

C glanced at the ceiling with starry eyes. "A sort of parallel reality. Not quite of this world, yet not of the next."

Reilly shuffled through a dozen or so documents in the file, stopped on a few and then closed the cover. "A new source of information on the Soviet Trade Delegation?"

"I'll call him Source BP11. He gave me advance summaries of the same cables that the Code and Cipher Department decrypted. That's how I knew we'd get Kamenev."

Reilly sat back in his chair. "That's why you fought against releasing the decrypts."

"Right. I had to keep the decrypts flowing to gauge the authenticity of BP11's documents."

"Now it makes sense," Reilly said and sat back in his chair. "But you haven't proved BP11 absolutely reliable."

"Not yet. I should have an answer soon. Yet God knows I may never be ready for it."

"Why?"

"Because if these documents are authentic, someone I've trusted for years has let us down, perhaps even..." His voice trailed away like the echo of a fading thunderclap.

"Who?"

C folded the pen knife. "I shouldn't have mentioned it." Then he lapsed into trivialities, though lines in his forehead did not fade. Reilly thought he was preparing himself for a blow, and bowed out hoping not to contribute.

"I'll tell you what I think and then ask your help."

C stood up straight and leaned on his cane. "BP11's documents purported to show that one of our men has turned. We may now have a Soviet mole in the Services."

"What can I do?" Reilly said.

C turned stern. "Prove Source BP11 a fraud," he said, "and his reports false. Rescue our man from infamy. Do that and you'll have earned my undying gratitude. Start with a man called Opperput. He sends Source BP11's material to me. See Savinkov. I'll give you everything you need."

After a moment in silence, Reilly said, "Who is it?"

C winced visibly inside, turned to Reilly, faced him squarely and said, "Thomson."

A chill shot through Reilly's veins.

"Forgive me," C said. "I'll have Fothergil deliver everything this evening. Let him know what you think. I don't want to be involved in this. I'm ill, I tell you. I've got to get away."

Reilly fought an impulse to call C an idiot.

Source BP11 may be authentic, but Thomson is no traitor.

C turned, gave him a barely perceptible nod and limped to the window. He glanced back from the corner of his eye but then peered outside with his head held high and his face stoic. Reilly went back to the Albany.

C's strategy was working. Kamenev was now out of the picture in London and they were shorting his stock in Moscow. Most no longer counted him among Lenin's possible heirs. Now the dying Lenin had three possible successors: Zinoviev, Trotsky and Stalin.

On the following day Reilly went to Paris to see Savinkov and to test Opperput's bona fides.

"Yes," Savinkov said, "I know the name. And the man. He may be the key to a successful counter-revolution."

"He's sending C decrypts from a source he calls BP11."

"They must be the real thing."

"Because you think Opperput's the real thing?"

Savinkov's hope in Opperput came from the man's suggestion that a new organization was growing in Moscow, an anti-Bolshevik group exploiting criticism of Lenin's government. Opperput had identified himself as a member and trusted messenger who had top secret access to high level information on the Soviet-British trade talks. To Savinkov, he had credibility. The organization, Opperput said, wanted to persuade Savinkov to return to Moscow, lead the opposition and take Lenin's place.

"Think of it, Sidney."

"I'm thinking of it," Reilly said.

"The Reds are in trouble. Food, money, dwindling support,

an uprising at Kronstadt base, protests favouring open markets, revolt against Communism. An organization ready to step in and take control. All they need is us."

"You, perhaps. Did they issue a formal invitation?"

"The time isn't quite right. But soon."

A message from Volodia cast doubt on Opperput: "Remember that with these people, nothing is real. Opperput, or whoever he is, is certainly Derzhinsky's man."

Reilly knew it would be like Savinkov to convince himself that Opperput and his organization were on the level. He knew also that Derzhinsky was going after Russian ex-pats in London and Paris, and probably New York and Amsterdam. Good strategy: bring the opposition home to attest to the success of the revolution and then make them disappear. There were stories. Savinkov's was the latest and most fantastic. But source BP11 was linked to Opperput, who might open a window into Derzhinsky's strategy.

Volodia said, "If Opperput says Source BP11 is real, then source BP11's material is made in Derzhinsky's laboratory. Thomson's credit is good. C's been had."

That stayed with Reilly as he tried to get Savinkov's visa approved in spite of C's efforts to keep him out. In London Savinkov impressed some and not others. By the time he returned to Paris many thought him a spent force, a great man whose time had passed. Reilly thought he saw C's hand in Savinkov's demise.

After speaking with Savinkov, Thomson called Source BP11 a fraud and questioned C's intentions. Reilly suspected pettiness: Thomson's power was on the wane and C's sway over the spy services expanding. Powerful forces were buying into Source BP11's credibility, and Thomson felt his ground slipping away. Reilly wondered if that coloured his judgment, even though he too doubted the authenticity of Source BP11.

63. White's Story, 1923

Reilly's safe house came with a lake, swimming privileges and a rowboat. His part of the lake was just a cul de sac, little more than a pond, but private. This was an attraction, though he was more at home at the Albany. But by 1922 privacy- no fire engines, police whistles, people on the street, loud language or barking dogs- was priceless.

So it was the issue of privacy that was first brought into question when a lovely blond face broke the calm waters in front of him. Almost as quickly came the instinct to survive, which wrapped his hands around the naked woman's wrists and forced her hands through the water's surface.

"I left my knives in the pantry," she said and smiled, keeping her hands on his chest as she embraced him with her legs and a long, wet kiss. She pulled away. "I'm your birthday present," she said. "Happy birthday, Mister Reilly."

"You're four months late," Reilly said and smiled.

"I'm eight months early," she said and laughed.

Reilly was quite prepared for love-making, which began immediately and without interference from laughter. Sometime later she broke away and though she felt warm inside said, "The water is cold. Did you bring a towel?"

They swam to land, towelled and dressed. She said her name was Nelly, that she had been sent as a gift with a message and produced an envelope with a pencil line.

"Weber, or White?" he said though she shrugged. "Well, you might as well make us dinner- if you have time- while I try to make sense of this message. Do you cook?"

"All things in moderation," she said. "Do you have food?"

"When I have a cook. There's a market on the road. We can stop. You have some time to plan your menu."

"Where are you taking me?"

"Home, the Albany Hotel." As they reached his car he said, "How'd you get here?"

"He drove me."

"Who?"

"Weber or White, I suppose."

"How were you planning to get back to the city?"

"He said you would take me."

"Did he?" Reilly said. "Where do you live?"

"He said you'd take care of that too."

They stopped at a market, bought food and then went to the Albany. Nelly cooked and Reilly deciphered the message, which was a familiar name and the telephone number of an obscure London hotel. After dinner he called. White was in hiding. They met in the morning at the safe house.

"They spot me, I'm dead, see?" White said in an odd version of Hungarian-accented English and foreign cadence.

"Who?"

"Bolsheviks, Brits."

"Are you armed?"

"No. Anyone else in the house?"

"A watcher. Laurent. Invisible. I trust him."

"All right, you trust him. But I *would* prefer privacy."

Reilly gave White a pistol and sent Laurent to the dock.

"How's that, White?"

Three fingers to a puckered lip demonstrated his approval. "Very good of you, Reilly. Very good of you."

"So, what do you want? What have you got for me?"

"That's just what I like about Sidney Reilly. You try to get comfortable with small talk and he sets you straight to the point. Professionalistic, you know? Of the highest order."

"You saw Trotsky in New York in January of 1917. Did C send you? What did you discuss?"

White had his own idea how to deliver his story. To do that he went back not to 1918 when Reilly tried to overthrow Lenin, not to his own 1917 meeting with Trotsky but to 1910, to a jewellery store heist called "The Siege of Sidney Street."

"First we have some catching up to do. First, I give you background, all right?"

"So what are the facts?" White began. "Ten years ago- all right, maybe twelve - some Bolsheviks from the Russian immigrant community robbed a London jewellery store. The press used the name 'Peter the Painter' for one, real name Jacob Peters. C got him off the street ahead of the police, kept him safe and maybe turned him. Another man came with him, perhaps Derzhinsky, all right? They're inseparable, after all. Or maybe they met later. Who knows? What I'm getting at, Reilly, is that these fellows share a common history. My theory might be off by a degree, but nonetheless, there's a link between C on one end and Derzhinsky and Peters on the other. I think it began with Sidney Street.

"So, in 1918 in Moscow my instructions from C came through Peters. Who was Peters really working for? And Derzhinsky? In other words, who was working for whom?"

"All right," Reilly said. "Let's not worry about the bottom line yet." Moscow, Summer, 1918. Who was Weber? What did he have to do with killing Mirbach?

White began a re-introduction of sorts, saying that the whole thing had so many tiers that he had to lay it all out one piece at a time so he wouldn't get too confused.

"Ah, to the point, that's where we should begin, isn't it? I built a good little network over the years, not everywhere, but where I thought I might be useful. Budapest, Moscow, New York. When C needed something done, a little gambit, a burn, something substantial, he'd contact me. My locals would set it up, do what was needed and then disappear. C paid a stipend that kept them happy.

"Now Freddy Weber, you know, he's an able agent. He trained at London Centre, went to Moscow and became an English teacher. Under my wing but on C's payroll, see?

"In 1916, I saw insurrection and revolution looming on the Russian horizon. With C's help I put Weber on to some opposition groups. No, not the Leninists, they were too dangerous even then. But the Socialist Revolutionists, the SRs, were open to discussion like real democrats. Weber actually built his own tribe, maybe a dozen or so, all ready to go but who knew where? You know what I mean, Reilly?"

"Mmm," Reilly said. "And the Mirbach assassination?"

"Right," White said, "essential background. Listen carefully, Reilly, because this may change your life. You need to understand the details and how they add up."

"To Weber and Mirbach, please," Reilly said impatiently.

"So Weber had some interesting horses in his stable. A few he got from London Centre, in particular two fellows called Semyenov and Filonenko, both lefties and either could thread a needle at fifty paces, just in case we needed to discourage someone or drop them dead. You thought C sent them to Savinkov. No, C got them from Derzhinsky and sent them to me. Per C's orders I got them to Savinkov. They watched, took notes, sent ciphers and waited for orders.

"Another was a real revolutionary, crazed but beautiful, with muscle for a brain, a woman called Spiridonova. A born SR, a total bore. Now I mention her only because she had an SR cell, and ran a brat named Blyumkin, one of the SRs Derzhinsky took into the Cheka to appease Lenin.

"Now, who's Blyumkin? Well, to start off he's a young man who thinks highly of his own prospects. He boasts that Derzhinsky has given him a big assignment and guess what? Derzhinsky has put him in charge of security at the German Embassy. A German-hater, right? At the German Embassy.

"Imagine, Reilly, just days before the Mirbach murder, Blyumkin the Brat boasts that he's going to kill Mirbach, even says the orders come from a Brit called Weber and that behind Weber stands the SR Spiridonova and behind her, Derzhinsky. He goes into a café and puts this into a poet's ear, Mandelstam. Imagine, our boy on a bender, announcing it like a special performance of Macbeth. Chaliapin is back in town to do an encore of Boris Godunov, you know what I mean? Really thought he was top boy. Crazy."

"Why would Derzhinsky rely on someone like that?"

"Blyumkin was out of the mainstream and had no track record. Only a few SRs knew him. It was a big assignment that Blyumkin wouldn't want to miss. He was easily controlled, too. His shots completely missed Mirbach. In the end his Cheka minder, Andreyev, did the actual killing."

Reilly said, "So Derzhinsky wanted no one on the inside to

know. Hence Blyumkin and your man Weber. Who else?"

"The chain of command was Weber to Spiridonova to Blyumkin, so Derzhinsky could blame the SRs and the British for the murder. You'll see a pattern here. So if you ask me who was behind the Mirbach murder, I say it was Derzhinsky. C admits to sending him too, but in light of what you now know, that's really an admission that C was an accomplice in Derzhinsky's scheme. Or vice-versa.

"Now, you ask about Weber. His job was to control Spiridonova, by which I mean to control Blyumkin. He kept the two running in place until they were needed."

"By you?"

"By Derzhinsky."

"Right," Reilly said sceptically, "What is C's actual role?"

"Well," White said, "that's the rub, isn't it? Because we don't really know what kind of partnership he had with Peters and Derzhinsky. Was C just trying to put Britain in a position to deal with a reasonable Russian Government led by Trotsky? Was he inadvertently serving Derzhinsky's rise to power, used by the master? Or was he serving a master?

"A question without an answer for now, Reilly, but pending, maybe. Was Derzhinsky C's agent, building his own base at the same time? Endless variations."

White then moved to the Lenin shooting. "Instructions from C come to me through Peters: Semyenov will shoot Lenin at the Mikhelson Factory. Many still think the shooter was Fanny Kaplan, but she was a foil, delivered and taken away by Peters' men. Semyenov shot Lenin. Then with Lenin in the hospital, Derzhinsky put Trotsky in power."

White continued, "Whereupon Trotsky sent Derzhinsky to Petrograd to rid the city's Cheka of Menshevik Party opposition. Then what do you know, enter another nut-case. This one was a young right-winger named Kannengeiser, shot Petrograd Cheka Commissar Uritsky and then ran off to The English Club. So blame the English. Blame Reilly. But do you want to know who really killed Uritsky? None other than Filonenko,

Kannengeiser's Cheka control and Semyenov's pal. One of C's twin gifts to Savinkov. Courtesy of Derzhinsky."

"Did Boris know?"

"Of course not. He was in hiding."

"God," Reilly said. He breathed deeply and thought, "C was running Blyumkin, Semyenov, Filonenko, Weber and White and maybe Kannengeiser. All the assassins who led to my defeat. But who was top man? C or Derzhinsky?"

Reilly said, "Tell me about your meeting with Trotsky in New York City in 1917."

"Oh, that," White said. "There, you might find a motive. I delivered a letter from C. Trotsky was friendly but said nothing. We made small talk. No substance."

"Nothing?" Reilly said.

"Nothing," White said and gave his full theory. "But I can imagine a scenario that would go something like this with C and Trotsky together somewhere, out in a rowboat like yours or along the lake, somewhere private. C might say, 'Britain is concerned that a revolution in Russia could get very messy. From our point of view we prefer not to have Russia leave the war. We believe you feel that way too because you think like a good military man, you have political skills and you know Russia would benefit later at the peace table. We do not claim to understand Russia and our own revolutions are in the distant past. But you do understand Russia and have a profound sense of what revolution means. Do you agree that a revolution, out-of-control, could stick Russia with a leader who knows nothing about economics or business? Lenin, that is?

"Trotsky might have said, 'Yes' to that. But privately.

"C would continue, 'Do you agree that this would spell doom for historic friendships between Russia and the West?'

"Trotsky might agree and even point to common interests, such as winning the war, keeping trade alive, checking German military ambitions, saving the food supply in the south; the need to maintain Russia's honour in war in order to keep public support. My theory, of course, all right?

"C would add his patented seductive flattery: 'You see, we cannot do all this by ourselves, we're simply not smart enough, not capable and what's more we can't comprehend what the Tsar is doing to Russia, but we know it's disastrous so we are sympathetic in principal to the revolution. Russians need a father figure, but not a Tsar. A Father Frost image, perhaps, but neither Tsar Nicholas Romanov nor Vladimir Lenin. It might be you, Trotsky. Otherwise we are at our wit's end. We know of no one else. You are our last hope.'

"Trotsky might wonder what C is asking him to do. C would reply that history would take its own course. 'Everyone's best guess is that even if Lenin were to get the revolution started, he would not likely survive it. By one turn or another. That's simply the way political architecture works. The one who takes down a kingdom is not necessarily the one to lead the government that replaces it. At least, not for long. Should that suggestion prove prescient, we would prefer that you be the new architect, the re-builder. With full support from the Western powers, of course.'

"Later Semyenov would come along, assassinate Lenin, put Trotsky in command and Derzhinsky in full control of the Cheka. A true partnership. They'd blame the West of course but eventually things would settle down and relations would normalize. Without the fanatic called Lenin."

"Not quite how it worked out. And I'm not a good foil."

"Now don't vote yet, Reilly. You may have been a perfect foil. But don't assess how you may or may not have been used, not yet. Face it, we're spies. Pawns in someone else's game. Some things we just have to take on faith."

White had said almost everything he thought needed to be said, at least for the moment. Perhaps more would come when Reilly had had time to digest everything. Reilly did not think the conversation finished. He wanted to hear Savinkov's opinion, to speak to Volodia Orlov in Berlin and to hear what C had to say.

Reilly let White stay in the house for safety and said he

would be away no longer than two weeks. Laurent would be there too and Fitch would visit. Plenty of food, a case of brandy and some vodka. A crystal set too, but not so much on the air. Reilly went back to his flat at the Albany and had a heart-to-heart with Nelly. That evening he did not return a call from Caryll. He wired Savinkov that he would visit, typed up a summary of White's statements and went to bed. In the morning Nelly drove him to an airfield where a private plane and pilot were waiting.

Reilly recounted White's story to Savinkov. He started with the theory that C had met Peters and Derzhinsky in 1910, possibly at the Siege of Sidney Street. He described how Derzhinsky had sent the agents Semyenov and Filonenko to C, and how they might have come with instructions from Derzhinsky to turn them over to Savinkov but have White eventually use them to assassinate key people. He talked about Blyumkin the Brat, whose murder of the German Ambassador Mirbach had been appropriated by C but in fact was initiated in its finished form by Derzhinsky. Purpose: throw off Reilly's timing and kill the coup.

Savinkov tried to keep his cool but became bug-eyed as Reilly described their betrayal. "Used from the beginning."

Reilly was unsure whether C was a traitor or an inept Machiavellian patriot. He had reservations about White, not on the factual level, but on his reasons for telling Reilly his story. What did White want Reilly to believe? Were C and Derzhinsky simply serving their own overlapping interests? Was C a traitor or a bungler? Derzhinsky had controlled Reilly and Savinkov and C had made it possible.

Then, after a long silence, Reilly remembered that after the Lenin shooting, when the Red Terror began, he escaped by train among some German officers. Before he boarded, Derzhinsky saw him in the crowd but let him escape.

"Why do you suppose? Because I had let him go in July?"

"You're crazy," Savinkov said.

It took Reilly no time at all to visualize the chain of events. Derzhinsky had purpose: to make Reilly the centrepiece of the international anti-Bolshevik movement. Method: get Reilly safely back to London Centre and tell C to start stroking him. Let him believe he's top man. Purpose: Derzhinsky obtains control over all international opposition to the revolution, all enemies and even his own funding. C as Reilly's controller. Reilly as Derzhinsky's fund raiser. *That's* why Derzhinsky let him go.

Savinkov said, "Did you know that Semyenov went to Moscow and they celebrated his return? The man who shot Lenin ate with Derzhinsky. Like Blyumkin. Prodigal sons."

White had not spoken about that. Perhaps he did not need to mention it. He had already painted enough of a picture for Reilly to ask certain basic questions about C.

"Perhaps White wanted to leave one fact for you to discover on your own," Savinkov said, "to cement the doubts he had planted about C. Perhaps White wanted to create a scenario with which you would confront C. A scenario C could rebut by admitting to all but his last line of defence."

Reilly closed his eyes. "That he is a Bolshevik mole. That he has been working for Derzhinsky all along. That we have been nothing more than Derzhinsky's tools."

What is real?

Savinkov took two pads and gave one to Reilly. "Damage that C did. Write it out. We'll compare notes."

The exercise went through a call to room service and dinner, through bottles of wine and champagne and in the morning a pot of coffee. They agreed their joint list might be incomplete, and that they could have misinterpreted some of C's behaviour. That the worst case was merely a theoretical scenario that had to receive the greatest scrutiny. What did they actually know? What was really knowable? Answer:

That C had White start a dialogue with Trotsky in 1916;

That C and Derzhinsky set up the Mirbach murder which ruined the July plot to overthrow Lenin, which let Derzhinsky purge the enemy SRs from the Moscow Cheka;

That C and Derzhinsky were behind the Lenin shooting, which ruined the August plot;

That C and Derzhinsky were behind the Uritsky shooting, which gave Derzhinsky the chance to take over the Petrograd Cheka and launch the Terror;

That C sent Margaret, Reilly's ex, to the bankers in an effort to discredit Reilly's banking plan for Russia;

That C sent counterfeit bills to Reilly's Moscow network that let Derzhinsky identify and destroy it;

That C tried to discredit Thomson of the Special Branch?

That C tried to keep Savinkov out of London and likely acted to discredit him while he was there?

Of the list, only the last two were questions.

Next they tried to set out certain scenarios that might come into plan when they confronted C with any of the matters they postulated. What would be true in any case? What would be his last line of defence? What would be the best case and the worst, given what they thought?

The best case would be a conclusion that C had had the foresight to imagine how Lenin would ruin Russia's economic prospects, which would make Russia nervous and probably hostile toward capitalist countries such as Britain. How would C articulate this?

Savinkov as C: "Yes, I did all those things, I used people and some died. But I was doing it for Britain. That's why I communicated with Trotsky. And yes, I know I was used by Peters and Derzhinsky. But I acted to protect both you, Reilly, and England. And even if I made some mistakes I'd do it pretty much the same all over again. After all, we almost put Trotsky in power. We couldn't have done much better than that. And as for your sacrifice, the failings I made you suffer, well you've heard it before. I hated it. But you know very well I was right."

"Right," Reilly said. "Best case. He did it all for Britain."

"How will C explain himself if he's Derzhinsky's mole?"

"Same way," Reilly answered. "He might bemoan being used

by Derzhinsky but the pitch would work out the same way, just more indignant. He would give it all away, right up to his last line of defence. 'I should have seen the Red Terror coming but you can't predict these things. Now, with Semyenov back in Moscow, well, that's proof that I was duped. Forgive my mistakes, I tried... but I'd do the same things again in the same circumstances."

"Either way," Savinkov said, "it will come out just as White gave it to you. That's why he gave it to you as he did, one line short of C's last line of defence. Confront him head-on. If we don't buy, we'll take him away for interrogation."

Reilly said, "And face a firing squad in the morning? No thank you. We'll be deliberate, one step at a time without alarm or resort to force. Get everything out, on the table. Let him assemble the pieces himself

Gradually C would either feel the noose tightening or lose patience, try to hit Reilly with his walking stick and throw him out. That would indicate innocence. But if C were guilty, he would want Reilly buy into each point.

64. C's Story, 1923

Reilly went to C's office and started his 'questioning' by raising the return of the assassin Semyenov to Moscow.

C coughed, rubbed his eye and said, "I knew it. I knew Semyenov was the shooter. I sent him. Didn't I tell you? Yes, he went back to Moscow in June."

"No," Reilly said. "You said you were behind the Lenin shooting. You didn't say Semyenov was the actual assassin."

"Oh," C said. "Don't suppose I wanted to open that particular can of worms with Savinkov around. Don't suppose I told you who killed Uritsky, either, did I?"

"Who was the shooter?"

"University boy, Kannengeiser. No, Filonenko, Semyenov's pal. You understand why I was reluctant to use names."

"Why did you send them to Savinkov?"

"Control. I knew Savinkov would keep them busy. Then, if I needed to put them in play I could do so quickly."

"Why did you need a foil?" Reilly said.

"Except for Shakespeare's Caesar, every successful political assassination in history has used a lone, local fanatic to affix the blame, and a straight shooter not far away."

"How did they know to go to the English Club?"

"They thought we were behind it."

"The English Club's got nothing to do with the English."

"It's all in the name, Reilly," C said. "The ethos of the name, a quiet suggestion to let people draw their own conclusions."

"I see," Reilly replied. "Is there anything else to know, anything interesting? An American journalist wants an interview," Reilly lied. "I should go see him rather than let him wing it." This was Reilly's supposed rationale for aggressively questioning C and he knew it was thin.

"Careful, Official Secrets Act, a fifty year moratorium."

"I didn't start the fire," Reilly said. "Someone's got to guide him away from the story. Or should I send him to you?"

"Lord, no," C said. "Keep him away from me!"

"What should I say if he raises the question of a Soviet mole in British Intelligence?"

"What?" C said in a loud voice. "A mole? Why would he say that? Who says there's a mole in the service?"

Reilly waited as C fumbled and grasped his neck.

"The American agent, Kalamatiano said so," Reilly answered. "Don't you remember? Thomson from Special Branch took the American Ambassador to the Foreign Office and then came to see you. Accused me of being a Bolshie spy who intended to undermine Britain's efforts in Russia."

But C had turned pale and was breathing deeply. He lay his head on the back of his chair. Reilly got up, hurried around the desk, dabbed his handkerchief in a glass of water, patted C's head and loosened his necktie.

"I confess," C began.

"What?" Reilly said. "Confess to what?"

"I'm not well. I have spells. Sometimes my breathing..."

"Shall we get you home then, C?" Reilly said.

"I'll get strength. Next time. Mind how you go, Reilly."

At the safe house, White said, "How far did you get with C?"

"Just his story. He sent Blyumkin and Semyenov to eliminate the German Ambassador and Lenin. I said nothing about a link to or agreement with Derzhinsky and Peters. He got upset when I mentioned the possibility of a mole. Just a reference to accusations against me. But no giveaway. I'll let go for a week, then raise the question of a link to Peters and Derzhinsky."

"Derzhinsky," White said after a silence, "I think he wants you back. Alive. It's a psychological game, to prove his manhood, his revolutionary virtue. A challenge you laid out in Moscow. I got it from Peters. Remember why Derzhinsky ordered Blyumkin to kill the German Ambassador that afternoon? It was because Peters had come to him with news that you had done the impossible, that you had got the Monarchists, SRs and Latvians to agree to an insurrection, and that you were on the verge of succeeding.

"During the uprising you had Derzhinsky as a prisoner and could have killed him. You told him it would be more fun to defeat him than to execute him. You wanted him to know that you would be master. Right?"

Reilly said, "Yes. Who told you about it?"

"Peters," White said. "That same evening. Peters volunteered to have you killed, but Derzhinsky said no. He wanted to control you, to put you in a subordinate position and have you admit to his superiority, even approve of it. He said you were his equal but thought he could dangle you from a leash. He won't kill you. He wants to lure you back."

"He's trying to lure Savinkov back even now."

"See now, Reilly, he has made you his own agent through C, and he has used you to control all of the Bolshevik Government's enemies, and even to raise financing for the Cheka. Just as Peters said he would. To buy time to build mastery over all the intelligence and secret police organs. To allow the Soviet Union to become strong enough to stand on its own. Peters said he wasn't surprised that Derzhinsky let you go at the station."

"He wants my approval. How very strange," Reilly said.

"He *needs* your approval and will do anything to get it."

"Peters was unusually open with you, White."

"At that point," White replied, "I had no reason to doubt that Peters was C's man. I thought he just needed someone to talk to, and it couldn't be Moura Budberg, his girl. It would have been all over Moscow. Starting with Lockhart."

Reilly laughed. "All over Moscow, indeed," he said.

That evening Nelly cooked dinner, served a good claret and took Reilly to bed. It was mostly conversation. Nelly seemed to share a mutual interest in a partnership, not so much of sex, though that was all right too, but something intellectual and strategic. Not based on romance, though there was nothing wrong with romance either. She was intrigued, intensely curious about her new lover and asked question after question.

Reilly admitted to having two women, Anna in Moscow and Caryll in London, both early twenties, wonderful and purely innocent, both supremely worthy of his respect, both eliciting the need to protect and neither apparently destined to hook Reilly with a commitment.

"What is it about innocence?" Nelly said. "Why do some men feel the need to preserve it in women, to protect it from everyday danger? It becomes a mission. Like seduction. Yet men are also drawn to depraved women, prostitutes and the like. What man ever gave sympathy to a Prostitute?"

"Christ did. I do."

"Yes," Nelly interrupted with a loud laugh, "you and He."

"But some girls should remain innocent," Reilly said, trying to remember his own time of innocence. "Innocent girls don't know how to protect themselves."

"I'm certainly no innocent," Nelly said. "But I'm not a bad sort of girl. Some might say I have a certain virtue."

Reilly acknowledged that he could love innocence, which allowed him to give without demanding trust. But virtue came from choosing well. It turned on loyalty to a standard or to an ideal and not to a person. Thus it could not betray. Reilly believed Nelly virtuous. This let him feel an altogether different and far more reliable trust than any relationship he had experienced: its intimacy did not bind, limit or threaten. It required no protection, but brought forth in Reilly a rare respect, natural and pure, and real devotion. Within limits.

"Feeling better?" Reilly said. He glanced at a copy of *The Gadfly*, on C's desk, a book with a history.

"Better but not chipper," C said. "What is it now? The Foreign Office sent one of their top boys to test me on our meeting. It's hard to deflect their questions. They act like inquisitors who haven't earned their brass knuckles. They're sure you're odd man out, a renegade Jew and a Bolshie agent. I can only defend you so far."

Reilly did not reply.

"So, you have come to hound me again. Remember the Official Secrets Act. If the Foreign Office hears of our discussions, they'll fry us both."

"My first question is, how did you found Blyumkin. Did you have agents hidden in Moscow? Did one of them identify Blyumkin and take him under wing?"

"Reilly, I managed the whole affair precisely as you would have done. Of course I had sleepers in Moscow."

"Names would help."

"Damn you, Reilly," C said. "Don't you interrogate me."

"C, it's between us and goes no further." Reilly pushed deliberately to test C's breaking point. A quick snap might suggest C was innocent but angry at Reilly's impertinence. But patience might mean the opposite, a guilty suspect's uncertainty as to where he should draw the line in order to appear cooperative when his real motive was to persuade that a full picture could be built of little give-aways.

But C was a masterful inquisitor himself and knew its psychology well. "Careful, Reilly," he said. "Weber. Worked for White, the Hungarian. Managed my contingency operation just in case your mission became impossible."

"Weber controlled Blyumkin," Reilly said.

"No. Weber controlled Spiridonova who controlled Blyumkin. She was not mine. And she may have been a double. In the end it was Derzhinsky, not Weber, who gave Blyumkin the order. C said nothing about Andreyev, Blyumkin's minder.

Andreyev was Peters' hit man, a common thug in need of greater autonomy than working inside Derzhinsky's Cheka would allow. Peters told White he was a professional killer. Two shots, as the German Bauer had said, one to the brain, one to the chest and then leave the weapon on the body, a calling card and a warning.

"Now, C, you told me that you arranged the Mirbach and Uritsky killings and the Lenin shooting. Where did you find the assassins, Semyenov and Filonenko?"

"It may have been Weber. No, a Latvian. No, an SR who went to the embassy a year earlier with bona fides that someone vouched for. Cromie, perhaps, but maybe Field-Robinson. Yes, I think that was it, an SR friend of Field-Robinson or Cromie."

"You told Savinkov to take them but sent them to White."

"How...? No, not exactly. Someone else directed them to White." C's penknife began to tap on his wooden leg.

"Peters?"

"What, how...?"

"Process of deduction, old man. I suspected you picked up an asset or two at Sidney Street. Years of cogitation led me to think it was Peters. I'd have taken him too. Must have been quite valuable."

The pen knife dropped to the floor and C bent down to fetch it. For a moment Reilly imagined C emerging with a pistol. End of interview. End of Reilly. But C sat up and rapped the blade ever more quickly and asked if he could be of further assistance.

"Out of curiosity," Reilly said, "did we get anyone else?"

"It was a very valuable acquisition," C said. "You can't imagine what came of it."

"What?" Reilly said with an admiring smile.

"Tip-offs. Information about socialist crimes in London. Advance warning of other robberies, attacks, bombings. Treasure, Reilly. Information I passed to the Tsar's intelligence that prevented killings and disasters. A gold mine. On that alone I could have written a book about Russian revolutionaries. Savinkov, Spiridonova, Azev, the Irish mob and all the rest."

"What about Trotsky?"

"Yes, yes," C said with a triumphant smile.

"The Pole, Derzhinsky? Did he send you treasure?"

C coughed and dropped the pen knife again. He kicked it under the desk. "Mind getting that, my boy?"

Reilly got it, folded the blade and put it on C's desk.

"Did you say Derzhinsky?"

Reilly smiled like a Cheshire cat. "The Pole."

"Well, Reilly, heh, you have done your homework. We'll keep this one from the American journalist if you don't mind."

"I don't mind."

"All right, Reilly," C began. "I suppose you are the one person who deserves a full accounting. Your theory about Sidney Street was spot on. Ditto Derzhinsky. Brought me good information all the way, really made quite a hero out of me with Scotland Yard and the Foreign Office. When the revolution became inevitable I thought Trotsky might be useful. Sent White to deliver a proposition. We'd remove Lenin, though of course not in so many words, and Trotsky would get control and keep Russia in the war. With Derzhinsky's approval. Failed, but Trotsky *was* a bug on the German Army's arse."

"Who were you dealing with in Moscow as I was trying to put together a putsch?"

"Peters. He spoke for Derzhinsky."

"What was the deal?"

"Overlapping interests. Get rid of Lenin and install Trotsky. Ensure your safe passage home. And everyone else's. A seat for Trotsky or Derzhinsky at the peace table with victory won and Russia on our side."

"What happened afterwards? Did you continue to speak?"

"The truth, Reilly, is that I realized when Derzhinsky started the Terror that he had used me and that if I continued the communication I would be risking too much. I sent a letter thanking him for seeing to the safety of our men and informing him that I would make no further communication. That was the end of it. Are you satisfied?"

Nothing about Margaret? Nothing about the counterfeit money that destroyed my network? Nothing about what he did well after 1918.

C breathed deeply and mumbled something unintelligible. Then he became quiet and stared out the window at the rooftops of Whitehall Court.

Reilly got up and turned to the hallway. He heard C wheezing and said, "Sure you're well, Commander?"

But C stayed silent and continued to stare glassy-eyed at the rooftops outside. Reilly took the lift down and drove to the outskirts of London to see an old friend.

"Major Fothergil," Reilly said and stretched out his hand.

"How goes Captain Reilly?" Fothergil replied. "Brandy?"

"Yes," Reilly said and followed the major into his library.

Fothergil was a friendly man, a devoted servant of C's who years earlier had brought Reilly and White into the Service.

"What inspires this visit, old friend? How can I help you?"

"A mutual friend is behaving oddly, Major. It's C."

"How so?"

"What's he doing with a copy of Voynich's book, *The Gadfly*, on his desk? It's nearly thirty years old and I can't imagine he went out and bought it himself."

"Well, I think actually I gave it to him," Fothergil said.

Twenty five years earlier Reilly had laid claim to an affair with the author, Ethel Voynich. He said that he had told her the story of his unfortunate childhood and that she had used Reilly's tale as the story of Arthur, the hero in her novel, *The Gadfly*. It was just one of Reilly's wild, exaggerated stories, and a lie at that. Nonetheless Fothergil had always believed that the fact of Reilly's telling it was demonstrative of his psychology and answered questions that C and Fothergil had posed many times. Why, for example, was Reilly so obsessed with going back to Russia as its heroic leader?

Reilly's father had disowned him. Perhaps, if Reilly became leader of Russia, his father would notice him and feel remorse. C thought it was a fascinating theory and read the book in the hope of understanding more about his mysterious agent, perhaps to predict his behaviour.

"When?" Reilly said. "Why is it sitting on his desk?"

"Are we speaking man to man, Sidney, in confidence?"

"Of course."

Fothergil poured more brandy. "Several things come to mind. First, for some time he was concerned you might do something to discredit the Service. You are after all a free agent and not exactly someone he can control. You approach your mission with zeal. He ordered me to deliver your file; I brought the book too. He wanted me to look for ways to discredit you and to make a case that you could be a mole. He wanted to create a new legend in case he needed to discredit you. He had me find Margaret's address and get it to Hill."

"Bloody hell."

"A set up to discredit you *just in case*. But only if you became a threat to the Crown, though I knew you never would. Rumours about you have surfaced in any event, and not just in the Service, but in social circles. Look at Sinclair, C's replacement, who accused C of harbouring red-brick sympathies for you."

"Replacement?"

"That's the second point. C is not well. He may have a year, a couple of years but it could be months or weeks. Sinclair has his own men studying all the Intelligence Service files. He started with yours and studied all agents who had served in Russia. He's even interviewing cabinet members."

"How do you know?" Reilly said with some alarm.

"One of Sinclair's top boys came here to see me with all sorts of questions. Your professional successes and failures, marriages, suspicions. Is Reilly a double, a triple? Of course I told him to go to the devil. But that won't be enough to stop them if they really want to ruin you in high circles, as I think Sinclair is determined to do. He seems to think you're helping Lenin arrange revolutions everywhere, Germany, France, America and Britain. Churchill, by the way, answered much as I did. He's a loyal friend. Lockhart, Hill and Dukes too. Kick Sinclair's arse. But everyone is afraid of revolution in Britain. Some think the Bolos could actually pull it off if they had you on their side."

"They don't," he said. "What is it, Major?"

Fothergil nodded. "I'm afraid it's the obvious. You lack Oxford and Cambridge credentials, old man. Background. So you are forever red-brick, new school. Your blood is common. And, you're a Jew.

"I'm told a number of professors at both schools are hostile to this attitude, by the way. It's an embarrassment. Britain can go nowhere so long as the propertied classes remain stuck in the Eighteenth Century. C made a list of them. Sinclair hates you, Sidney. The professors, however, hold you in high regard."

"Does C have a role in this?"

"Lord, no," Fothergil said. "C took his degree at the Royal Naval College, hardly Oxford or Cambridge. But C has the sympathy of the gentlemen, especially the Conservatives. The death of his son, remember?"

Reilly and Fothergil sipped their brandies.

"Doesn't paint too bright a picture of my prospects, does it?"

"I'm afraid not, Sidney."

"Fothergil, if you trust me enough to speak to me as you have done, perhaps I can persuade you to do something else."

Fothergil just sat and sipped. Then he leaned back. "Sidney, if C discovers that your file went missing there'll be hell to pay."

Reilly shrugged. "Give me just one day. I want more than the file. I want C's list of university professors."

Fothergil rolled his eyes.

"C has had dealings with Moscow," Reilly explained. "I know he has used me to identify Derzhinsky's enemies, including my own agents here and in Russia. I don't know whether Derzhinsky simply used him, or if C went over sometime back. I need to see what he's put in that file."

Hearing these words, Fothergil felt that he had no choice but to deliver. Reilly returned the following evening and went through the heavy file, taking notes on some documents and laying out others to be photocopied. He finished just in time for Fothergil to return the file before reporting to work in the morning.

Reilly enjoyed a wide reputation as a decisive man. If most thought him headstrong, few found him indecisive. But when he took a soft chair in Savinkov's sitting room he dropped his head and said, "I just don't know."

The evidence seemed irrefutable. The assassinations that had wrecked his plans, the counterfeit money C had sent to Moscow with which Derzhinsky decimated Reilly's network. There was C's attempt to poison the thinking of the bankers in order to discredit both Reilly and the banking plan for south Russia. More recently was C's solicitous demeanour and patience with Reilly's questions. Enough, he thought, to convict anyone. Anyone but C.

And arguing against conviction: Reilly's own sympathies.

"A grouch with a temper like a mountain lion. But not a mean bone in his body."

"Piece by piece one could explain it all," Savinkov said. "But Fothergil came on board quickly enough and White seems to be pushing you toward a guilty verdict. Their instincts are based on the same suspicions that you have."

"There's no reliable test," Reilly said. "He explains everything in terms I understand but the totality gets to me."

In the end it wouldn't matter whether C had been turned or simply found himself in an impossible position. He had worked for Derzhinsky. He had given Derzhinsky information. He had given information to the enemy. Technically and legally that was treason.

"Now you've got to find out what other damage he's done,"

Savinkov argued. "Has he put other moles into the government or the Service? It's a huge operation you've got on your hands. Unless you want to take him away and interrogate him. Or leave it to Churchill and his friends."

Savinkov came to London to stay in Reilly's safe house in the hope that he, Reilly and White could put their heads together and make sense of things. Churchill thought C was beyond reach. But C was dying and Sinclair, who hated Reilly, was the likely replacement. Why shouldn't Churchill take the case to Sinclair, who would start a quiet investigation to assess the damage? Reilly, meanwhile, would create the impression that he was headed away from politics in favour of business ventures and the quiet of civilian life. At the same time with White, Savinkov and perhaps Fitch of the Special Branch, he would investigate discretely, based at the safe house. Churchill could get all relevant information to Sinclair who would, presumably, do something.

Then there was Nelly.

"Will you marry me?" Reilly said. "I need respectability."

His pitch was so dull that Nelly said, "Oh, Lord. What next? You think I can help you look respectable? Get rid of those French vases and most of that Napoleonic gaud."

"Dear," Reilly said.

"Chuck all of this old furniture..."

"It cost a fortune."

"It's new money. Give it to the poor and let me do some interior designing. Write me into your will. Love me?"

"Yes. But it's a practical affair. I need to redo my image. Respectable but common. Working class and clinging. Not on the ascent, just holding off the fall. Get the picture?"

"Then 'Nelly' may be too respectable. We'll use my stage name, 'Pepita.' Foreign sounding enough. Déclassé at Oxford."

"Good," Reilly said.

"Deal. I'll start planning a wedding."

Nelly went shopping with a purse full of cash and a victorious smile. While she was out Fitch stopped by with an acquaintance, a near-double of Reilly.

"Who's this?" Reilly said.

"Say something else," Fitch said.

Reilly quoted a few lines from Kipling. Fitch held up his hand. The double repeated the lines just as Reilly had spoken them. Reilly went silent and serious. He eyed Fitch and said, "What is this?"

"Something you might find useful. Or just amusing."

"Most people would say that one Reilly is enough." But Reilly imagined the benefits of a double, the illusions he might create and what value they might bring. "I'm Sidney Reilly," he said and shook the man's hand. "Come in and have a brandy."

"I'm Sidney Reilly," the double said. "I'd like a Brandy."

"Brahndy," Fitch said.

"There's time for prahk-tice."

The three sat for a while with Fitch very amused at his accomplishment and Reilly's mind ablaze with schemes. The guest was an American actor called Cedric. He was looking for work in London, something to put on his curriculum vita.

"I'll put you on retainer, Cedric. That means you can do as you like but be available for a call. Interested?"

Cedric agreed. The door opened and Nelly brought several shopping packages into the room. She spied Cedric, smiled and said, "Good Lord, Sidney. Now what are you doing? Is this a test? What if I kiss the wrong Sidney?" It was a joke. Close up she could tell the difference. But only close up.

Savinkov was the first victim. Cedric answered the door. Savinkov gave him a bottle of Champagne and a close, studied look. Savinkov spoke. Cedric answered as Reilly. Nelly came in and kissed Cedric's cheek. Savinkov wrinkled his nose. Reilly came in, put on a hat, shook Cedric's hand and said, "Good to see you, Captain Reilly."

Savinkov said, "Well, what...?"

Smiles all around. "This is Cedric," Reilly said. "We may be working together. We'll spend some time here and take our show on the road."

Reilly and Cedric talked for a week. Cedric read from Byron and Kipling until Savinkov and Fitch could close their eyes and not know who was speaking. The next act ran for White, who noticed nothing unusual in Cedric's demeanour until Reilly entered. White laughed loud and long.

Nelly meanwhile wrote out wedding invitations and per Reilly's instructions sent one to C and one to Sinclair, two each to Churchill, the Cabinet Ministers, Reilly's former Service colleagues and friends, and Nelly's Theatre friends. The invitation announced that Pepita Bobadilla, actress, and Sidney George Reilly, Businessman and Engineer, would marry. It listed her credits and mentioned her late playwright husband. They would honeymoon in New York.

As expected, C attended the wedding and wished Reilly and "Pepita" well as they departed for the boat.

"Good bye, my boy," C said. "Go well." He grasped Reilly's hand with both of his and squeezed.

"Rest yourself," Reilly said, smiling gently at C. "Happy you came. Wouldn't have been the same without you."

From that point it was Reilly all the way to the safe house. After that it was Cedric with his arm around Pepita, waving to people on the dock, carrying out Reilly's deception.

65. Kill The Witnesses, June, 1923

The strategy table alternated between arguments and card games. More than once Savinkov deliberately wrecked a straight or a full house to pronounce upon C's disloyalty or Reilly's tentative sympathy for the old man.

A message came for Reilly. Coded and worth half a day of deciphering, it was from Volodia Orlov, now one of Derzhinsky's men in Berlin. His message:

"Derzhinsky intends to kill every foreign partner he had during the revolution, everyone who could bear witness to his cooperation with the British. Probably not Reilly or Savinkov, but certainly the phantom agents and C. Ibrahim the assassin has been sent abroad."

"That means Britain," Reilly said.

"Russian xenophobia," White said.

"Derzhinsky is Polish. This is very careless. Sending a hit man to kill two British agents and the Director just when Russia is pressing Britain for economic support. Why now? Why not wait? This could cost them an important loan *and* Derzhinsky's reputation. What's going on? What is he doing?"

White said, "I'd wager no one knows that Derzhinsky worked with C in 1918. He wants no one left to tell the story. Get me out of here."

White called Weber in London and told him to pack. Savinkov drove White to Weber's flat and then took both to an airfield. Reilly called his pilot and got transportation for them to the port at Calais and then passage to New York. He gave White the keys to the safe house on St. Marks Place.

Laurent, now acting as Reilly's bodyguard and driver, sped to Kensington. Though a short drive, Reilly feared in his gut that he was too late. Ominously, as they arrived another car crept away. The door to C's apartment was not quite closed. Laurent covered Reilly's back, his pistol drawn. C sat slumped back in a chair with a light turned on and a book on the floor near his feet. He opened and closed his eyes.

"Sorry, Commander," Reilly said, hoping C had dozed and he had merely wakened him.

C pointed to a spec on his white shirt. Blood. Reilly opened the sleeve, rolled it up and found a spot of blood on the inside of his elbow joint. Just a pin prick. An injection.

"So sorry, my boy," C mumbled and shut his eyes. He held his heart and said, "Forgive me."

Those were his final words. The housekeeper stirred. Reilly got Laurent through the door and slipped out.

Reilly called Churchill with the news. Churchill sent his own agents to sweep C's flat. Not until the next day did Churchill contact Sinclair, who swept it again. The next morning Savinkov, Reilly and Laurent went to Paris. Savinkov went to his hotel to meet Opperput. Reilly and Laurent went by by train to Berlin to see Volodia Orlov.

They took a good hotel suite. Laurent contacted Volodia to request a meeting at a remote location. There, he took Volodia through the building to a car parked in the rear, from which they drove to a flat elsewhere in Berlin.

Volodia first delivered personal information. Sasha had remained inside the Cheka, now called the OGPU, and had earned Derzhinsky's confidence. Katya was still working in a clothing factory in Petrograd where Anatoly was now director. They would open a kiosk to sell some of the clothing produced in the factory. It was the New Economic Plan, NEP, capitalism to quiet criticism. Run by Derzhinsky. Implemented by NEP-men. Initiated after an uprising at Kronstadt Naval Base, probably to prevent worse. Put down by a reluctant Red Army with Cheka bayonets at their backs.

Sasha had told Anna of Reilly's marriage to Nelly. "I wish Sidney a lifetime of happiness. He is my one true love and our love is not bound in time or space, but exists always and forever; one day we will be together."

Volodia, too, had kept Derzhinsky's trust, and had a good assignment in Berlin. He was Derzhinsky's watcher sent to observe one Munzenberg, a young German Communist working with Soviet specialists toward a German revolution.

66. Opperput and The Trust, 1923

In London, Savinkov's new associate, Opperput, came to Reilly's flat with an issue that required Reilly's attention: Savinkov's general disposition. Opperput had seen Savinkov and Lockhart in a Prague night club. Lockhart, then British Ambassador to Czechoslovakia, seemed happy and made the rounds with diplomatic greetings and jokes. But Savinkov sat in a corner with a dour expression, brooding, pathetic, drinking heavily, his sleeves rolled up exposing needle tracks.

"You would be wise to help him," Opperput said, "if you want to make further use of him."

"Why can't you help him?" Reilly said.

"I know you have doubts about the viability of The Trust and our hope to replace Lenin with Savinkov. Under the present circumstances I also have doubts. Which puts you in the middle, Reilly. I must convince you that The Trust is real and that our plan is well-conceived and perfectly workable."

"I have no opinion," Reilly said. "But I do know that our friend is desperate to believe in something that will put him back in Russia, preferably in a position of power. As far as The Trust is concerned, I have no way of knowing whether it is viable or not. But as a general rule, I trust no one without proof. You have shown me nothing. What should I think?"

Opperput opened a notebook. "What do you see?"

"A map of Berlin. Brandenburg. Landwehr Canal, where they left Luxemburg's body. Tiergarten. So what?"

"Notice the circled streets and numbers."

"How would it be used?" Reilly said coyly.

"The circled areas are Communist arms supply depots." On a second page he pointed to the addresses of the key German revolutionaries. Then, he showed Reilly a timeline culminating in attacks on police stations at year's end.

"Where did you get it?"

"We have someone in Zinoviev's office. You see the initials in the corner? Approved by Derzhinsky."

"Authentic?"

"You wanted proof," Opperput said. "Here it is. It represents more than mere trouble-making in Germany. It's a blueprint for taking over Europe. After Germany, England, then France. The start of world revolution. Zinoviev's plan. With Derzhinsky's blessing."

It looked too detailed to be real. But the logic was so tight it might be true.

"If you want proof, send the police to any of the arms depots. If they hesitate, tell them to start here." He pointed to an address. "A German Communist called Munzenberg. A ringleader. But act quickly. Zinoviev and Trotsky are pressing for action. If they succeed, they have much more detailed plans for revolution in Britain. And the British Labour Party is restless. If you hope to stop insurrection in Britain, first go to Germany. Fail, and The Trust is finished. Zinoviev will be first in line for power, probably with Derzhinsky's support. But if you stop the German Communists, the world will accuse them of betraying the revolution, starting with Trotsky, Zinoviev and Derzhinsky. The time will be right for Savinkov. If he's sober."

Reilly said, "What about me? Can't I go back too?"

Opperput was prepared for the question. "We'd like nothing better. But no one else outside Russia could fill your roll as the proven champion of anti-Bolshevism in the west. Who has your ethos, your contacts, your depth of vision? Who else could raise funds for us? The way we see it, the current movement here must continue to operate as it has, with perhaps more of an eye to fund-raising and stopping Derzhinsky's agents in the west. Otherwise The Trust will have little foundation and will lose the confidence necessary to move ahead."

In Berlin, Reilly showed the documents to Volodia.

"Where did you get them?" Volodia said.

"Russian man called Opperput. Associated with a Russian group based in Moscow, 'The Trust.' They say they're anti-Bolo and want Savinkov to go back to replace Lenin. Boris says they're the real deal. I thought they were fake, but the information looks authentic to me. What do you think?"

Volodia looked at the pages, asked for a photograph and said, "You mean that *if* the file is real, The *Trust* must be real?"

"No," Reilly said. "But if I really *can* use it to stop revolution in Germany, well, that's different. I'd have to think about it. We know Lenin and Derzhinsky want world revolution. What better place to start than Germany?"

"Don't assume anything," Volodia said, "any connection, any therefore, any fact. You can't know. You're likely to be wrong."

Reilly explained more. "Your young German revolutionary, Munzenberg, is working closely with Zinoviev and Trotsky. Kamenev is out of the picture."

"And Derzhinsky?"

"Trying to get back into Lenin's good graces along with

Stalin. Opperput said just what C said: take them out one at a time and you'll have no one left. Opperput says we can kill several birds with one stone. Eliminate the most dangerous German Communists and that'll take Lenin's zealots down a notch and slow revolution in Britain."

Volodia shook his head slowly. "Two issues bother me. First, it's too easy. Second I won't be able to see anything clearly until I know why Derzhinsky sent his hit man Ibrahim after his foreign partners from 1918. Strasky, White, Weber and C. The only conceivable reason is a desperate need to hide all the 1918 links back to him. But who would care?"

"He doesn't want any loose ends."

"You and Savinkov are loose ends. He let you go at the train station in Moscow and is not going after you now. He spent the others but not you. Why not? What purpose do you serve? What use are you to Derzhinsky? He must be certain you don't know any of this."

"All right," Reilly said. "My eyes are open. Now talk to me about The Trust. Could it be real? Is there a chance they could put Savinkov in power?"

"Maybe. If Savinkov has agents in Moscow."

"He does, and they're begging him to go in."

"Ten to one they've been turned. Think extortion. But as far as the German Revolution is concerned, it might not be a bad idea to consider Opperput's evidence. Get it to the authorities, but don't go to the police yourself. Send an agent, give him a legend and get him out right after delivery."

One of Reilly's established agents in Berlin was a jeweller with contacts all over Europe. He brought in a Scandinavian man to take the information to the Berlin police and get a receipt that he took back to the jeweller. Another agent delivered the receipt to Laurent, who took it to Reilly. The signal for the German Revolution was given New Year's Eve, 1923. It was put down easily by the Weimar police in Berlin.

Across a room filled with cigar smoke, balloons and women in expensive black dresses celebrating New Year's Eve, Hugh Sinclair, C's successor, glared open-eyed at Winston Churchill and Basil Thomson. He stomped across the floor to Reilly and growled quietly, "Your relationship with The Service was terminated some time ago. Yet you involve yourself not only in the affairs of this state but in the affairs of foreign states as well. Stay away, Reilly. We've nothing to do with the likes of you. You're nothing but a ... "

But as Sinclair continued, Nelly, or "Pepita" as she was now known, stepped between Reilly and Sinclair, smiled softly and put her lips to Sinclair's ear.

"Happy New Year, Huie," she said. "Now piss off."

It was after midnight. Sinclair got his overcoat and left. Churchill and Thomson looked at Reilly and beckoned him to bring "Pepita" across the room.

"Happy New Year, Pepita," they said nearly in unison. Then, looking at Reilly, Churchill raised his glass and said, "Congratulations, what?"

"What?" Reilly said.

"They say you tipped the Berlin Constabulary, who have taken in a fortune in small arms and explosives, as well as innumerable German Revolutionaries just setting out to despoil Weimar's Republic. So," Churchill raised his glass again and said, "Congratulations."

"Thank you," Reilly said.

Thomson leaned in and said, "This very evening, in fact."

"Don't worry about Sinclair," Churchill said. "He's upset that he had nothing to do with it and that my agents brought home the news."

"He won't like that a Jew set up the bust, either," Reilly said.

Later, Inspector Fitch stopped at Reilly's flat. Instead of attending a New Year's party he had gone to the docks to interdict a clique of Russians with jewels and secret documents.

"The Russian Communists have made progress here. They want a loan from Prime Minister Ramsey MacDonald, a trade agreement and diplomatic representation. Yet Trotsky and Zinoviev press British Communists to build cells in the army so they can stage revolution in London. Are they crazy?"

Reilly said, "Is MacDonald a Communist?"

"MacDonald's actions count, not his thoughts. He could be pure as snow but a loan to the Soviets, a trade deal or diplomatic recognition makes him dangerous. It's not his soul, but his best-intentioned actions that might threaten us."

"If Thomson agrees, how does he propose to stop him?"

"He agrees but says it's up to the politicians."

67. The New Legend, 1923-25

"I've got it!" Savinkov said as snow covered the streets outside his Paris hotel.

"What?" Reilly said.

"We'll invest in my old Green Army, White Russians and Poles who hate the Reds. Greens. The last anti-Bolshevik fighting army in Europe. All we need is cash. Eh, Sidney? Eh?"

"The Greens. Sounds like a Christmas tree. Or a salad."

Savinkov looked as Opperput had described: glassy-eyed and drugged. He sat down, rolled his sleeves and exposed the needle tracks in his arm.

"We can't do it without you, ace," Savinkov said. "Maybe you have something stashed away? Something you could take to auction? Something to buy a little help?"

Something to buy drugs.

"My law suit in Philadelphia is a possibility," Reilly said. "Maybe half a million. A split. Otherwise, I'm not much good. I leave in a week. I'll write you when it's finished."

There: little Eddystone-by-the-Delaware, where a tiny drop of a lawsuit might fall unnoticed into Reilly's huge financial bucket. There: Philadelphia and New York, where banks kept fortunes for Sidney Reilly, unknown to anyone else. Certainly unknown to Savinkov. And a good time and place to invent a new Reilly.

Savinkov steadied himself, his hands on Reilly's shoulders.

"Quarter of a million! That's perfect! I knew you'd do it! That'll get us off the ground."

"We'll see," Reilly said. "It's no cinch. My lawyer has to persuade the court that Baldwin owes me for shells I brokered for the Russian Army. You never know."

"Then buy a Philadelphia lawyer and pay him right. Sidney Reilly, who damned near threw Lenin out of Russia, that's who your lawyer is representing!"

"Don't assume anything," Reilly said, by which he meant, "I'll sit this one out, Boris Viktorovich. Because we're old friends I'll do something small for you, but now even *you* are part of a deception I am creating for Derzhinsky. Even *you* must believe I am nearly indigent, useless, no longer a player. You, my friend, are also only an illusion. Sorry, old man, but that's the only way we can win it."

That night, near Moscow, Vladimir Lenin died of syphilis.

Reilly felt badly after his talk with Savinkov. True, Savinkov's "Greens" might be brought back to life if they had serious western backing. They could fight successfully against the Red Army for a period of time. But the Russian Civil War was over, the Reds had driven the Whites into the Black Sea and Savinkov's original Greens had disbanded.

Moreover, in recent years Savinkov had largely discredited himself with drugs, hangers-on and a lavish life-style that now had him on the edge of bankruptcy. His support had dried up and his friends were almost all on the way out. Whether or not he really believed in his Greens, the anti-Bolshevik military forces needed a miracle. Even Reilly, whose hubris knew few bounds, did not delude himself into believing he could save a Savinkov who in the end would not be saved. Without Savinkov, nothing would bind the Greens.

No, Savinkov believed his only hope lay with Opperput, who continued to tell him he could still lead Russia and that he should let The Trust take him back to Moscow. But Savinkov, a terrorist and not a general, craved a military victory before accepting a civilian sceptre. He wanted to ride into Moscow like Napoleon, victorious, and not slink in some night at the behest of White Russians who were just storytellers or hero-worshippers. He pouted that Russian fate had teased him with grandeur that he deserved but then turned to deprive him of his moment of greatness.

Upon returning to London, Reilly had much of his collection of Napoleana packed and shipped to an auction house in New York. Giving what small profit it raised to Savinkov would help Reilly convince Derzhinsky, that both men were desperate has-beens: men on their last legs, their fortunes gone, down on their luck, down, if not out. Word would quickly find its way to Moscow. Derzhinsky would think that, having picked off Savinkov and stuffed him into Lubyanka Prison via Opperput, he could lure Reilly back too and reel in his greatest catch of all. Or so Reilly wanted Derzhinsky to believe. Step one.

In New York Reilly prepared his lawyer on how to present his case. He signed an agreement with an auction house to publish a hard-cover catalogue of Napoleonic items he wanted to sell along with a commitment to stage an auction. He sent Laurent to the British Consulate to find out who might be there upon his return trip. He bought an expensive pool cue. Then he and his attorney, Robinson, boarded the Broadway Limited to North Philadelphia, from which a hired car took them to Delaware County, first to an inn in the small town of Swarthmore for a night's sleep and then to Eddystone where his case against Baldwin Locomotive and Samuel M. Vauclain would be heard.

The judge had the presence of a Thomas Nast cartoon sketch of Boss Tweed, sitting in his chamber on a high chair that looked like a throne. He alternatively chewed on and smoked a cigar. He held a billiard stick like a sceptre.

Reilly waited while Robinson spoke to the judge.

"Who the hell are you?" the judge said in a cloud of smoke.

"My name is Robinson. I've come to open an account."

"You want to bribe me to get a favourable verdict?"

"No, sir," Robinson said and gave him the new pool cue.

The judge opened the case, took out the cue and rolled it between his palms to test for curvature.

"Good stick," the judge said and put it behind his throne. He reached down to shake Robinson's hand. "MacCraken," he said. "Frank MacCraken. This'll go nice in my new pool hall down' Chester. But honest, you can't bribe me when you're up against Sammy Vauclain. You can't compete with Sammy Vauclain. They're naming streets after him down' Chester."

"No, sir," Robinson said. "My client expects to lose. So he wants to invest ten grand in your Chester pool hall."

"He wants to lose?" Judge MacCraken said.

"For appearances. It's worth something to him to create a certain impression with the press. I'll make a short argument on his behalf, Your Honour will deny the petition and then my client will respond with some unpleasantness. The press will report it. Your Honour need pay no heed. Okay, sir?"

MacCraken climbed down from his throne, nodded Robinson into the courtroom and put on his robe.

Delaware County justice.

Reilly and a few others stood up and the bailiff cried out:

Oyez-Oyez-Oyez-Honourable-Justice-of-the-Supreme-Court-of-the-Commonwealth-of-Pennsylvania-Frank-MacCraken-this court is in session." Bang went the gavel.

"Counsellor?" the judge said.

Robinson rose from his seat and lectured the court in sum:

"The greatest enemy of the United States of America is the Soviet State of Russian Communism. Sidney Reilly is our greatest champion in this fight. Twice he almost stopped Lenin from taking power and almost threw Lenin out of power once he had taken it. He is still fighting Communism today, Your Honour. But he needs funding because he has already invested all his assets in America's freedom. Please consider his case to receive commissions he earned years ago before this crusade began, so he can lead us to victory."

Reilly put a small piece of soap in his mouth.

"That it?" Judge MacCraken said.

"I have a lot more stuff you can read, Your Honour."

"The Court rules in favour of the defence."

Reilly jumped up and screamed at the judge and then growled in an apparent fit. Reporters wrote furiously. Cameras flashed. Reilly continued, but louder. Soap bubbles foamed on his lips as his eyes bulged. His face went crimson.

"Gentlemen, come into my chamber." Judge MacCraken closed the door behind him. Inside, the judge asked Reilly if he was a politician or an actor and whether he thought there was any difference. Was that really soap he had slipped into his mouth? "The soap bubbles had a good effect. Overall, Counsellor, it was a good performance, but I still don't get it."

Reilly smiled and wiped his lip.

Robinson gave the judge an envelope containing ten thousand. The judge put the envelope in his pocket, took up the pool stick and said, "You fella's any good at this sport?"

"Sure," Reilly said, wiping away a cluster of soap bubbles.

"Then come for dinner at Sammy Vauclain's mansion in Rosemont. The girls will be there but afterward we can shoot some billiards on his new table. You know Rosemont?"

Reilly and Robinson looked emptily at one another.

"Right. Where are you staying?"

"Strathhaven Inn, Swarthmore," Robinson said.

"Nah. Nothing but mosquitoes in the crick this time of year. Sammy will put you up, get you to the train in the morning. I'll have my man pick you up at five."

Robinson drove Reilly back to the Strathhaven Inn.

"Must be unpleasant to have to sell yourself short like that," Robinson said.

"I have an agenda," Reilly said. "Losing this case was a necessary part of it."

In New York City Reilly dismissed the attorney with appreciation for a good performance. He neither shaved nor changed his clothes. He collected from the auction and took some of the money to Savinkov's investment account at Kuhn Loeb. He went to the British Consulate and waited until his friend Field-Robinson came out, as Laurent said he would. He looked at Reilly and shook his head.

"What happened, old man?" Field-Robinson said gently.

"A bit down on my luck, Robbie. Bad lawsuit."

"So I read," Field-Robinson said. He came closer and spoke low to Reilly: "Anything I can do, old man?"

"No. Maybe, yes. Can you spot me fare back to London? Maybe twenty? I've come up a bit short. I swear I'll pay you back. Buy you dinner. You'll see."

Reilly's old friend put several hundred in his open palm. He shook Reilly's hand as though for the last time.

"G'bye," Reilly said.

"Mind how you go, Sidney," Field-Robinson said, almost as though he thought Reilly might not get to the ship.

Field-Robinson went back into the Consulate. Reilly and Laurent went to the ship. On the first night of his voyage he spent hours wondering how long it would be before Derzhinsky heard of his misfortune. How long would it be before he sent someone like Opperput to London to persuade him to join The Trust, and Savinkov, in Moscow?

Nelly met Reilly at the pier and drove back to the Albany.

"How was it?" she said and poured a brandy.

"As I expected. Won twenty bucks from the judge after dinner with the defendant, Sam Vauclain. Vauclain thinks he would have won anyway. Might have done."

Nelly said, "some friends stopped by in the last few days. Hill, Dukes, Lockhart. They wanted to know if you're all right, could they help in any way. Maybe you laid it on a bit thick. Your friend in New York certainly got the word out."

"Might have done," Reilly said. "The important thing is that Derzhinsky hears the message from several sources. 'Reilly's out of business.' I want him to think he can approach me with one of his little Cretans like Opperput and suck me back to Moscow, where he can con me. Well, Nell, I'll go back when it's clear that he can be had. All I wanted to do in America was start the burn, get people saying things he can follow to his own conclusions. Then he'll lay a trap for me and, who knows, I might just step into it."

"You'll have him right where he wants you. Where is that?"

"In Moscow, with a chance to turn the table."

"Meanwhile," Nelly said, "I hear talk about labour unrest and revolution here. Maybe we should go to the suburbs."

Reilly thought for a minute. "Might be smart to sell this apartment and refurbish the country place I've been using as a safe house. So you'll have a good place when I go. Right, Nell?"

"It's a good deal for me, but change makes me queasy."

Opperput's envelope was the same kind in which he had delivered the downfall of the German Revolution.

"It's not the same revolution," Opperput said, "but it is the same idea, just more urgent. It's Zinoviev again and Derzhinsky trying to buy into the British Labour Party."

"The MacDonald Labour Government won't last. We'll have a new election."

Opperput continued, "Derzhinsky and Zinoviev can do a lot of damage before that. Britain just granted the Soviets diplomatic recognition. More recognition is bound to follow in the west. They're negotiating a big loan. The British people would never approve of what they're doing if they knew. But as of now all you have is a few shipments of diamonds to a half-assed newspaper owner who has no idea how to run a business. That won't convince anyone.

"But what will you do," Opperput said, "if the Soviets get their hands on real money and start buying pieces of the British Army? And what will you say if that money comes in the form of a loan from the British Government? Will you sit on your butt while the British Government lends Derzhinsky and the Soviets forty or so millions so they can buy the British Army and stage a real revolution here?"

Reilly sat back in his chair. "What did you bring for me?"

"All the proof you need to get support against the Labour Government. You won't have a revolution in London and The Trust will have hope in Moscow."

"What is it?" Reilly said as Opperput opened the envelope. "This is a small photographic copy of a letter written by Zinoviev, intended for the Chairman of the British Communist Party. It contains instructions for opening Communist cells in the services, the army first, and for taking over the Labour Party and eventually the government. I don't know if he delivered it yet. Yet. But everyone I know says it's an accurate description of Derzhinsky's plan for world revolution. Starting in Britain.

"You'll know how to read it, to magnify it, to copy it onto real Soviet stationary. I don't know how to instruct you in applying it. But at some point I believe- we believe- it could come in very handily. Especially if Zinoviev replaces this government-by-committee that Stalin is leading at the moment. You could get it to the press, to Churchill and his people, even to the Liberals. But you can't allow the MacDonald Government to succeed. It would be death for Europe. In five years you'd have the Red Army all over Europe. They've already ordered new uniforms. Prime Minister Ramsay MacDonald will pay the tailor."

Opperput rose to his feet. "I wish there were something else I could say to persuade you of the dangers at hand. It's much more than Russia at stake. By the way, best regards from Savinkov. Good day, Reilly."

Reilly immediately called Laurent with instructions to change the venue in Berlin and to inform Volodia Orlov.

The jeweller in Berlin had the proper facilities for producing enlarged photographic copies of the miniature letter. Reilly waited alongside the jeweller as Laurent peeked out through the blinds covering the glass front door, which the jeweller had bolted shut. The process took several hours; both Reilly and the jeweller smoked many cigarettes. When two copies were dried, Reilly put them in an envelope, making sure no one else saw them. The jeweller had absented himself so that Reilly could finish the process privately.

Reilly and Laurent then drove to a new hotel, a slight improvement over the one they had previously used. Laurent took a trolley to Volodia Orlov's flat and left a letter requesting a meeting. He met Volodia in a new facility and took him to a flat he had just obtained for this purpose.

"Is there a translation?" Volodia said.

"This is the only document I was given. But it's clear. Can you authenticate the handwriting as Zinoviev's?"

"I think so. I have a party document on file."

"Does the content ring true?"

"Perfectly. It reads like speeches I heard Zinoviev give to the Central Committee."

"How quickly can you deliver?

"I'll be called back to Moscow soon. I'll get started now."

"I suggest we find you a quiet hotel room where you can write. Such as our suite. You can always say you were away for a day or two because you found a woman."

"Right," Volodia said.

"Laurent," Reilly said. "Take Volodia back to his flat and wait while he gets something."

"Mr Reilly? Waiting could spoil everything. How long?"

"A minute," Volodia said. "Just around the block."

Mobility was everything to a good watcher. Laurent took his duties seriously.

"Just drive the car around the block, Laurent," Reilly said. "It's all right. I can't risk keeping Volodia there for long."

"Wouldn't it be better, Mister Reilly, if I were his bodyguard? If Cheka goons come for him..."

"Once round the block," Reilly said with a slight smile.

"I'll just stop up the street a bit and keep 'er warm."

"That's fine," Volodia said.

Reilly shrugged, palms up. "Then right back to the hotel."

The jeweller suggested a name from Reilly's past to set up multiple distribution channels for the forged letter in London. He had run messages between Reilly and Boyce, his Station

Chief in Russia during the Summer of 1918. Most importantly he had coordinated movements among Reilly's allies- SRs, the White Generals, the Latvian Brigade, and Reilly's own agent network. Had Reilly disposed of Lenin then, he would have owed a large debt to British agent Donald Im Thurn, who was now in Berlin.

Volodia's counterfeit came out perfectly. The stationary was the kind known to be used in Derzhinsky's office. Even the typewriter used for the translation into English was of the kind the Bolsheviks used, the Remington, impounded from a Tsarist Ministry when the monarchy fell.

Long and complicated did Reilly and Donald Im Thurn make the trail of the Zinoviev Letter, from Volodia Orlov's Berlin studio to the British press and Parliament, with mysterious twists that fooled everyone who ever tried to follow it. The copies that went out days before the election left no doubt that Prime Minister Ramsey MacDonald's political career had hit a bump and that his Labour Party and the socialists were, for the moment, a bad bet.

The British electorate turned MacDonald out in favour of the Conservatives, scotching the British loan to the Soviets and the British Revolution. Reilly wondered who would fall next.

As the election results were announced an expected letter came from Savinkov: "My doubts about The Trust have been resolved by Opperput and the Dehrenthals, whom you must remember from the embassy in Petrograd. They have taken personal responsibility for my safety on the journey that Opperput has organized for me. My next letter will reach you from the Kremlin, from which I am told I will dispense justice on behalf of all the Russian people. I am in Amsterdam and leave presently for Moscow. Godspeed on your own return to dear Mother Russia, which I await."

It was no time at all until news came that Savinkov had been arrested by the new Cheka, the OGPU, and was awaiting trial in Lubyanka Prison.

Opperput arrived again to explain that the arrest was part of a complicated deal that would see a trial and a suspended eight-year sentence. What had gone wrong? Opperput's Trust associates explained that Savinkov had insisted on the arrest of key Bolsheviks, who would be put on trial upon Savinkov's release. If Reilly or the new British Government led by Conservatives could guarantee a loan to the new Russian Government led by Boris Savinkov, such a government would be established in fact, without Bolsheviks.

Opperput congratulated Reilly on a superbly forged Zinoviev letter, though he did not know the identity of the forger. What he did know was that the letter had helped to defeat the MacDonald Government and sink the Soviet loan. He spoke also of the damage the letter had done to Zinoviev in Moscow. Stalin had gained by accusing Zinoviev of interfering with the revolution and running his own foreign policy. Some said he had undermined the British Revolution.

The clique of four that became a troika when Kamenev fell, had lost another forceful member, Zinoviev. Now just two men sat in Lenin's seat: Stalin, who was trying to appear a moderate, and Trotsky, who had lost support in the Central Committee and was quietly biding his time.

But Reilly did not trust the results. Shutting down the German and British revolutions seemed too easy. Who had sent Opperput to Reilly with all that treasure? An anti-Bolshevik group called The Trust? Derzhinsky? Or both?

Reilly felt listless, a loss of energy he guessed came from a long period of intense work followed by a dead stop. Zoom, screech, crash. An ill-defined state of depression. He thought the best remedy would be aspirin and work. Nelly wanted a Christmas tree, so out they went and cut down a small pine near the lake at Reilly's country house; then presents, visits to an orphanage and a hospital. Finally, just after Christmas, a letter from Volodia arrived from Berlin:

"Last man standing says build socialist society in one country before exporting to the rest of the world."

Stalin was the last man standing. In a recent Moscow speech he had made a statement that had got socialists talking. *Socialism in one country*. What did it mean? Was Stalin bucking Party history, that is, the history of Man, which carried international revolution at its core? And how had *Derzhinsky* reacted to such a radical, even counter-revolutionary notion?

Reilly and Laurent went to Berlin on New Year's Eve. Laurent got Volodia to the hotel. Reilly did not want to stay in the cheap place they had been using. And he wanted room service available to bring brandy all night. Laurent spent the evening in a corner of the hotel lobby with a newspaper in his hands and two pistols under his sport coat.

"What happened to the World Revolution we've all heard so much about?" Volodia said. "Lenin's legacy, and Stalin's."

"I don't like the smell of it," Reilly said. "Opperput brought enough material for us to kill two bloody revolutions. In order to prevent world revolution. In order to stop the spread of Communism. To get Savinkov back to Moscow. Now Savinkov's been arrested and Stalin is speaking out against world revolution. What's going on?"

"I don't know," Volodia said. "I won't know until I'm posted back to Moscow. Then I'll see Sasha and Arkady Semyon'ich. Perhaps they're close enough to Derzhinsky and Stalin to make sense of it."

"Volodia, I'm in a real haze," Reilly said. "Can you get me back there? Can you let them know I'm coming?"

Volodia set it up through his own agents, the few who had survived the Counterfeit Massacre. They were, after all, Reilly's most loyal men. In weeks they would get Reilly through White Russia to a house near Moscow, the location to be determined by Sasha and Arkady Semyon'ich.

During those weeks Reilly visited Cambridge and Oxford Universities to meet with the professors on the list prepared by C and provided by Major Fothergil along with Reilly's file. He introduced himself as Karlov, a friend of the late Director. No one had followed up on C's final contact though a few had identified students who might be candidates to speak with representatives of the Soviet Government Department of Foreign Affairs. That is, with Derzhinsky's men.

"I'm Yakushev," said the man standing in Reilly's doorway. "From The Trust." He had good posture, a military moustache and fine teeth.

Yakushev's pitch must have been the same as Opperput's to Savinkov. But Opperput was gone now, found out and executed by the Soviet State for crimes unknown. This, Yakushev said, had forced a change in Trust strategy. After Savinkov's arrest the Trust had undergone some internal turmoil. Their survival depended on funding that came from western anti-Bolshevik groups that no longer trusted them. Most were holding back, waiting to see what would happen, what Reilly would do. Yakushev understood that of all people, Reilly had the greatest influence on them and their pocketbooks and must now be the most suspicious. So it was Reilly on whom the Trust would focus.

"Odd situation, no?" Yakushev said.

"Not really," Reilly said. Of course, no matter what Yakushev had to say, Reilly would not believe him. "If you can change the opinion of your greatest critic, you have a chance of staying in business. And," he said, "you might just convince me. Opperput, after all, delivered good information that led to the destruction of two major European revolutions. International Communism is dead. Courtesy of Opperput's Trust."

Opperput, the liar who seduced Savinkov.

"So I have an interest in The Trust and might even accept an invitation to visit Moscow. And perhaps you can get Savinkov released from prison. For God's sake, Derzhinsky must know he's impotent and useless. And The Trust must also know they could never have counted on him as a leader. Get the poor bastard out of jail, and I'll give The Trust some consideration. But now I'm off to New York. Fellow owes me some money. Call me in six weeks."

But Reilly was not going to New York. He was going to Moscow. He called Boyce, his old Station Chief from 1918, and Field-Robinson, who had just returned to London. He had given Yakushev their telephone numbers.

Part IX: The Grand Inquisitor

1925-1926

68. The Tiers of Deception, Spring 1925

"I didn't think," Arkady said. "I just dove in. If I had known it was Stalin crying for help I'd have let him drown."

It seemed the whole, small dacha was filled with cigarette smoke. Sasha, Volodia and Arkady smoked one papirosi after another and Reilly smoked his American Camels.

The dacha was miles away from Moscow and access required a car. At the same time, though it was seemingly buried in the forest, there was a long view from the room at the top, over the trees and to the access road more than two miles way. The dim lights in the distance were surely less dim close up, but they provided a four mile marker and line of sight to the entire length of the access road. The main road was unpaved, covered with dirt. Laurent could warn Reilly if a Cheka car approached.

The dacha was a gift from Stalin in return for Arkady's demonstrated loyalty in saving Stalin's life. Arkady knew, however, that the water was shallow. Had Stalin thought to stand up he would have found himself a full head above the water level.

With the dacha came a car and driver who doubled as a guard, posted at the opening to the main road. Actually, like Arkady, the guard was one of Reilly's own agents who survived the Counterfeit Massacre of 1919. The dacha had belonged to a duke before the revolution. "No trespassing" warnings suggested that someone very high up, perhaps even Derzhinsky himself, lived there. Even higher up, Laurent thought he saw the entire universe and all of Russia at night.

The dacha contained everything, including food that Arkady had bought at the "company store," where Bolshevik Party members went to shop for foreign goods, silk stockings and food. But perhaps the chief asset of the place was that Arkady had himself selected it as Stalin's gift. No one knew of it but Arkady and his driver. Since Arkady's specialty was cartography, the dacha had been removed from the Intelligence Section's few maps of the area. He and his guard *really were* the only people who knew of it.

Reilly stood near a window. Arkady, Volodia and Sasha sat nearby. Reilly said, "Let's review what we know, shall we? I'll tell you what I've discovered and what questions I have. I'll give it to you chronologically. A ten act play, a drama. Listen to me, point by point. I'm looking for a story to emerge. Let's see if these events are related in any kind of pattern or are simply random acts that have nothing to do with one another except that collectively they are my excuse for failing to stop Lenin. Tell me if I go too fast:"

"Act One. During the Summer of 1918 we tried to overthrow Lenin. Our July attack was undone when the murder of German Ambassador Mirbach upset out timing. Our August scheme to arrest Lenin and the Central Committee was lost when Lenin was shot. Then the murder of Cheka Commissar Uritsky gave Derzhinsky full control of the Petrograd Cheka. The Red Terror began. Then Derzhinsky let me escape.

"These shootings were run by Derzhinsky himself. His partner was the Director of London Centre, C, the very man who sent me to overthrow Lenin. C said he thought I was failing, so he activated a contingency plan. He found it safe and expeditious to partner with Derzhinsky, who shared some of his goals, for example keeping Russia in the war.

"My question: how were they partners? Was C Red?"

They discussed C's role and partnership with Derzhinsky. C may or may not have been Derzhinsky's mole but there was no doubt that he worked with the enemy. That was treasonous.

"But," Reilly said, "after the Red Terror of 1918, Derzhinsky may not have needed C to control me. I was predictable. Perhaps C's cooperation with Derzhinsky in 1918 was practical and technically not treason on C's part. Maybe it ended after the Terror of 1918. But maybe he was Derzhinsky's mole for life. Red? Maybe. Maybe not. Maybe C had his own reasons."

"Act Two. In 1919 I developed a banking plan to pump money into the economies of the south Russian areas won over by the White Army. C tried to stop me by bringing my first wife, Margaret, to London and taking her around to visit the prospective bankers. Stopped me cold, until Churchill stepped in. Was C working for Derzhinsky? Or did he just think I was a loose cannon, dangerous to his career?"

"Act Three. When I escaped from Russia after the events of 1918, I left intact in Moscow a network of more than a thousand agents. At first only Anna had access to this list, which we called 'Ivan.' I instructed her to share the list only if she received a letter from me suggesting that she introduce a named individual- Paul Dukes, for example- to Ivan. 'Introduce Mr X' would mean 'give Mr X the list'. In other words, give the list to Dukes. No one else saw that list, nonetheless it was compromised in a very clever way.

"In 1919, C took on agent Strasky from Thomson at Special Branch, who had got him from Kell in Army Intelligence. With the support of the Foreign Office C sent one million rubles to Dukes, who now ran my Moscow network. Dukes, Anna and some others got the money out to my agents to keep them in business. But the money turned out to be counterfeit, and created a trail to most of my agents. Derzhinsky's Cheka picked them off one by one. We called this the 'Counterfeit Massacre.' Strasky disappeared after delivering the cash to Dukes. We think Derzhinsky intervened at some point, took the real rubles and substituted the counterfeit bills, which must have been very easy to mark and spot. C sent the money and said it was a mistake, that he was betrayed. I don't know."

"It seems clear to me that items one, two and three were C's doing, whether as Derzhinsky's mole or as a well-intentioned bungler. But as we go on past this point, both before and after C's death, I think I see Derzhinsky's footprints. So, let me continue first to the question of world revolution, which was Lenin's stated goal and Britain's greatest fear for years, and second, to the power struggle in the Kremlin. Who would replace the ailing Lenin upon his death? The favoured candidates were Kamenev, Zinoviev, Trotsky and Stalin.

"These two questions are deeply intertwined: support for world revolution and Lenin's possible successors."

"Act Four. In the early twenties London prepared for trade talks with the Soviets. We were able to decode Soviet ciphers and intercepted communication from Lenin to Kamenev, a trade delegation member, with orders to plant communist cells in the British army and labour unions. We discovered that Derzhinsky was reading our mail too. We made some of the information public in order to eliminate Kamenev. The reluctant PM cancelled Kamenev's visa and sent him packing. That finished him in London and largely discredited him in Moscow. Of the four candidates to replace Lenin, three then remained: Zinoviev, Trotsky and Stalin.

"Here is the interesting thing: Derzhinsky knew, because he was reading our mail, that we were on to Kamenev. But he never changed the Soviet code. He never told Lenin or Kamenev. He never tried to hide the incriminating communications between the two. He never tried to stop us from destroying Kamenev and hurting Lenin. Why not? Was he inept? Did he dislike Kamenev? Didn't he realize he was playing into our hands?

"Let me add that ever since 1918, we believed that Lenin and his cronies were completely committed to International Bolshevism, that is, to fomenting foreign revolutions. No one ever questioned that assumption. That is background for everything we did from 1918 on."

"Act Five. C told me that he fought against releasing the incriminating cables between Lenin and Kamenev, because he was receiving the same communication from Moscow, decrypted and summarized by someone he called 'Source BP11.' He wanted the current code kept secret because it was necessary for authenticating Source BP11. I agreed: had we released the compromising documents, our decryption project would have been blown. Little did we know then that Derzhinsky was already on to it. So C convinced many that Source BP11 was very important.

"But where did it come from?

"Source BP11 had a very interesting point of origin. And you will see that this point of origin becomes the centre of a number of very clever links. C originally obtained Source BP11 from Opperput, a mysterious Russian who identified himself as an associate of the most important anti-Bolshevik group in Russia. His first known appearance in our evolving drama was as delivery boy to C of Source BP11 decoded materials. How did he get it? He said he had access to officials at the highest levels of Kremlin policy-making. Genuine strategists. The Thinkers of the Revolution."

"Act Six. Opperput, Scene Two. Opperput sends Source BP11 communication to C. He speaks to Savinkov in Paris, and pitches a line that warms Boris' heart: his organization, The Trust, is poised to take over the Soviet Government. Its members include the very powerful. They need just one more thing to overthrow the Bolos. They need Savinkov.

"Savinkov is charmed by this story. He is desperate to return to Russia and ready to believe anything that will feed the fantasy that this is possible. If Opperput can pull it off, would Savinkov agree to return to Russia to lead the government? Savinkov flirts with Opperput, asks for supporting evidence to dispel his doubts. But he's hooked."

"Act Seven. Opperput Scene Three. 1923, Opperput knocks on my door and asks for help. Savinkov is not taking very good care of himself, he says, suffering from drink, women, bankruptcy and a host of other ills. If he keeps it up he'll be no damned good to anyone, to me or to The Trust. 'We know that you, Reilly, are a sceptic, and we would be too. So I've brought you a proof that I hope will convince you to speak to Savinkov on our behalf.' Long story short, he gives me photographed documentation of a pending Bolo revolution in Germany, full details, maps, names, munitions sites, everything. He encourages me to get the information to the Weimar police in Berlin. So done. The German Revolution fizzles, and with it eventually, Derzhinsky's top boy in Berlin, Munzenberg. It looks like Derzhinsky has taken a big fall indeed.

"My doubts, I must say, are very nearly resolved. Everything I read tells me about Lenin's commitment to world-wide revolution, and those candidates to replace him are enthusiastic. Opperput cannot be Derzhinsky's man, for Derzhinsky is as much an internationalist as Lenin. That is, if he has any credibility left at all after the fall of Kamenev and the destruction of the German Revolution. In early 1924, Lenin dies."

"Act Eight. Opperput Scene Four. The next year Opperput comes with information about the coming British Communist Revolution, whose architect, Zinoviev, has written down his instructions to the British Communist Party and signed the document for posterity. The so-called Zinoviev Letter. This is a bomb with unusual explosive reach, designed to destroy the liberal MacDonald Government, a British loan to the Soviet Government, the British Revolution, Zinoviev and Derzhinsky, all in one blow. Very heady stuff.

Strategy: take the letter to the papers just before the British elections in October to destroy all prospects for a liberal government. Elect the Conservatives and the rest will follow suit. I take the information to the press, the MacDonald Government loses, the Soviet loan is denied and the British Revolution is kaput. England can sleep at night.

"Have no doubt, British conservatives think they are big winners here, though the letter itself is probably not the only cause of this turn of events. Still, Derzhinsky must be very close to folding. And in Moscow, Zinoviev is discredited.

"I'm a big hero too: I've pushed Derzhinsky right to the edge.

To Savinkov, Opperput now looks like St. Vladimir. Even I think I see the glow of his halo. Our boy Boris is on the way back home, all right. But when he gets there he is arrested and imprisoned. Opperput makes a curtain call in London, delivers a very fishy sermon and exits stage left, never to surface again.

"Still, he has taken out Kamenev and Zinoviev. Of the original four, just two candidates remain to replace Lenin."

"Act Nine. Earlier, C confirmed that he and Derzhinsky worked together in 1918 via C's Phantom agents, White and Weber. Last year an inside source told me that Derzhinsky sent a hit man to England to get rid of all three. I got White and Weber out of the country and went to C's place, where someone had just injected poison into C's arm. In a minute he was dead. I discovered that courier Strasky of Counterfeit Massacre fame, had also been executed. All of these people had some close connection to Derzhinsky and to C.

"Now what do you make of this? Neither my name nor Savinkov's was on Derzhinsky's hit list. Why did he let me escape from Moscow in 1918 when he had me in his hand? Both times Derzhinsky kept me alive. Why?"

"Act Ten. For all we can see, International Revolution is still holding centre stage in Moscow. But from backrooms we hear new lines spoken. Stalin takes the stage. 'Stay home,' Polonius tells Laertes. 'There's nothing for us in Paris. Just dangerous revolutions, and spies all over. No foreign adventures for us. We have everything we need right here in our country. Socialism in one country: to the West we say, stay out! To western Socialists, we say, stay away!

"Trotsky still touted international revolution until Stalin made that speech. But Stalin's support in the Central Committee kept Trotsky quiet about internationalism. Stalin, who was on the rise and needed to be seen as a moderate, never mentioned it again. Now Lenin's four possible successors are whittled down to one, Stalin. Lenin's credo of sponsoring foreign revolution has been transformed into no foreign revolution at all."

"So," Reilly ended his peroration, "what's this all about? Where are international communism and world revolution? Where have they gone and why? It makes little sense to me."

The first question was answerable: Derzhinsky kept Reilly alive so he could use him, and had been using him since 1918. They agreed that the execution of Strasky and the hit list containing White, Weber and C meant that Derzhinsky was desperately trying to cover up his involvement with C, eliminating witnesses to all connections with London Centre and the shooting of Lenin. Why?

The most contentious issues concerned Derzhinsky's position on international revolution. Did he favour it or not? Of equal importance was the corollary question of who would succeed Lenin. Answering those questions required a closer look at Opperput. Was he Derzhinsky's provocateur or someone genuinely in favour of overthrowing the Bolsheviks? These questions were deeply intertwined, since Opperput delivered genuine gold that struck a big hit against international revolution, and by implication against Derzhinsky. Moreover, "Opperput destroyed two possible successors to Lenin. So far, Opperput is our man."

"But that was not so for Savinkov, whom Opperput delivered not only to The Trust but by implication, to the Cheka. To Derzhinsky. Does that mean Opperput was Derzhinsky's man, or a zealot who made a fatal mistake?"

Sasha said, "Compared to what he did for us, Savinkov's arrest should be seen as beyond Opperput's grasp. He couldn't have prevented it. He wasn't Derzhinsky's man."

"The question is," Volodia said, "how can we reconcile these two seemingly incompatible facts? What's the common ground between Opperput's serving our interests and his working for Derzhinsky?"

"Logically," Reilly said. "There's common ground only if everyone has been wrong about international revolution as a staple of Bolshevism. Only if Derzhinsky didn't really want revolution in Germany or Britain. So there's common ground only if Derzhinsky's interest, on some level, is the same as what we perceive our interest to be. The other Bolsheviks want or wanted international revolution. Why would Derzhinsky not want it?"

Volodia said, "He's backing Stalin, which represents a radical change in strategy."

"No," Reilly said. "A change in objectives. After that, a change in strategy. What is the new Bolshevik objective?

Arkady said, "A new policy: Socialism in one country. No more foreign adventures. Avoid the quicksand of the West."

Volodia said, "You mean no more investing in foreign revolutions that they can't control."

Reilly said, "That they can't afford. They wanted a loan from Britain because they were nearly broke. Look at Britain and Germany: even after a destructive and expensive war, their economies are relatively resilient. But Russia's economy is a disaster, worse every day. Their redefined objective was to prevent bankruptcy." Reilly dropped his drink. "Yes! Soviet Russia was running out of money! If revolution had succeeded in Britain or Germany, they'd have lost their leadership and gone broke.

"Derzhinsky alone must have seen this coming. Zinoviev *had* to be stopped! Up to this moment, no one in Europe has understood this, not the intelligence services, not the brightest minds at Cambridge and Oxford."

After a few shots, wherein Reilly and his friends sat amazed at their new hypothesis, Reilly said, "What is Derzhinsky doing with Germany?"

Arkady said, "They made secret deals. Maybe he sold out the German Revolution to the Weimar police or intelligence service. All he had to do was to get the details to you, Sidney. He would have known just what you would do with them."

Arkady poured more vodka and for a while no one spoke.

Reilly repeated his thought. "What's the deal with Germany? What does Derzhinsky want? What value can he deliver to the Germans other than the German revolutions? The answer to that is the key to this puzzle."

After a break, Reilly said to Sasha, "Do you have my German identification and passport at your safe flat? If you can get me to the Polish border, I can get to Berlin and be back in five days."

Sasha said he would bring the documents the next day. Arkady would get him a disguise, take him to Byeloruss Station and ride with him as a Cheka escort to Minsk, where other agents would take him into Poland, from which he could easily get to Berlin.

Anna's embrace might have lasted forever. "My God," she whispered, "It seems like no time at all has passed since you walked out of my flat seven years ago."

Sasha had brought her, and after Reilly had left with Arkady, Sasha would drive her home.

Time had passed and life had taken its toll. Her skin was dry and older and her hair greying. At thirty. For the former-bourgeoisie, Moscow was a city of stress. Amazingly her flat was on the Bolshevik protected list and no one else had been allowed to take the small bedroom in which Anna's roommate Olga slept. Most of the other flats in the building were occupied by Party people.

Olga's father was a White General who had helped Reilly in 1918 and had been arrested that autumn. Shortly thereafter Olga began her affair with Derzhinsky. That had kept her father and the apartment safe and the women in good food. Party Food. From the company store.

"Mama Katya is coming to Moscow to stay with me. They shut down the kiosk she and Anatoly were running under the New Economic Policy. They took Anatoly away. She had enough money to buy a ticket south. I expect her tomorrow. But she's in pain. A tooth. They can only kill the pain with vodka, and she doesn't drink alcohol. What a mess."

"I can take both of you to London and you'll never have to think about Russia or money or vodka again." Reilly's heart told him to abandon his plan and get them out right away. "Please

Anna," he said. "I want you in London."

She knew that he meant it and saw love in his eyes.

"I'm going away for a few days and when I come back I have to speak with my friends. I can get all of you back if you want to come. I want you with me, Anna."

"That's silly, Sidney. You're married."

"It's a marriage of convenience. It doesn't matter."

"Convenience?"

He smiled. In a flash this older and gloriously beautiful Anna transformed him completely. He thought of all the opportunities he had surrendered to vanity and greed. But in this moment he understood that he did not need Russia any longer. He did not need any of the glory it might bring him. He needed this woman who could still look at him with confidence, whose innocence had not faltered despite a decade in hell.

"Stay off the street, Anna. Keep Katya away from the dentist, no matter how bad the pain. Don't go to work or anywhere else. Stay in your apartment. Promise me?"

"Yes," she said. She did not say that she had no job or that the headmaster at Moscow Conservatory had revoked her honours and diploma for refusing to sleep with him.

Reilly saw Arkady's automobile arrive. He embraced Anna and said, "For the next few days until I return you have only one job, and that is to survive. Do you understand?"

Her embrace tightened; she did not reply. The dream could evaporate at any moment. She dared not even blink. Reilly might disappear without the door even opening. Such things happened in Moscow.

Reilly kissed her once again and went to the door. In a moment he vanished and Anna thought for a second that he had never come at all. But she felt his moisture on her lip, and her heart, which had been still, began to beat rapidly.

Reilly would go to Berlin and come back. He and his friends would spend the time needed to make sense of everything. Then he would take Anna and Katya back to Europe. He worked out a plan with Arkady that would take the four by train to Poland, where agents would meet Reilly, Anna and Katya and take them across the country into Germany and across to France, where Laurent would meet them. They would spend a night in Paris and move the next day to the port at Calais, take a ferry across the Channel and drive down to London. Volodia and Sasha would come later, depending on Reilly's report from Berlin.

In 1918, after Lenin took Russia out of the Great War, the German Government opened an embassy on Arbat Street in Moscow. It was there that SR Blyumkin was reported to have shot German Ambassador Mirbach. It was also at this location that Reilly, playing the role of a German spy, met with German spy chief Rudolf Bauer, who now received him warmly in Berlin. He answered Reilly's questions in the belief that higher-up German policy-makers had requested his advice.

Bauer said Derzhinsky had cooperated with German Military Intelligence for years, starting in November of 1918, when he delivered information that destroyed the planned "November Revolution" of the German Communist Party.

Bauer explained that this had been a pre-condition for a secret deal between Germany and Soviet Russia to rebuild their armies with German War technology and conscripted Russian labour. A new Red Army was now under construction. For Germany, a new German Army would be fuelled by revenge and hate for the Allied war victors. A new, secret military treaty would follow, linking Germany and Russia against their European enemies. Then a final war.

What did this imply for Soviet support of international revolutions and International Communism? That, Bauer answered, was an issue that died with Lenin. Derzhinsky himself had promised to quash Soviet efforts to build up Communist movements in Europe, as long as the joint military rebuilding project continued.

"Then what was the real Soviet objective?"

"Very simple, Colonel Schaefer. Can you imagine a more formidible military force than one combining the Russian masses and German technology? At some future time we will initiate a war and completely occupy Europe. Finally, there will be a real European peace."

Reilly said, "The Soviet Union is still pushing revolution in India. Look at what they tried to do in Britain and Germany. Do you really trust Derzhinsky's word?"

Bauer said, "He destroyed Lenin's scheme for International Communism. Starting with Germany and Britain."

Reilly shook his head. "You don't mean to say that the future of Europe will be shared with Russia?"

Bauer said, "Let us leave the question of strategy there, Colonel Schaefer. Our plans do not call for a Russian partner in the domination of Europe. Derzhinsky claims the Bolsheviks don't want revolution in Europe, that revolution in their own country is enough. But we're not fooled. They want world domination, not world revolution. Their tool will not be the writings of Marx and Lenin, but the new German weaponry of the Red Army. Not ideology but raw brute force. Of course, we will not let that happen."

Reilly's head spun. He had not imagined a Russian strategy without ideology. But Bauer had made complete sense. Marx, Lenin and ideology were a collective sham.

Reilly preferred a circuitous route back to Moscow, this time to meet Arkady in Grodno and to take the night ride from there. Reilly re-thought the meeting with Bauer. Arkady was quiet, as though very tired and in a particularly bad mood. Reilly thought that was a result of too much concentrated stress that would likely continue until Anna and Katya were across several borders and heading to Paris. That would improve Reilly's mood too. He let Arkady sleep while he thought about what he would do. As the train sped on, Bauer's words played in his mind: *Not ideology, just raw, brute force. Not world revolution, but world domination. Not Communism, but a massive Red Army.*

At the dacha, Sasha and Volodia also seemed anxious and unhappy, as though they felt the three would not meet again. A poignant sadness seemed to hang over the dacha. Reilly repeated Bauer's description of the agreement his government had made with Derzhinsky, and by extension, with Stalin.

"Stalin doesn't believe in anything. Derzhinsky can persuade him to buy his scheme and believe he thought of it himself, that it was his idea. Never mind how Kamenev, Trotsky and Zinoviev had been undercut, going back at least as far as 1922. Stalin might imagine that anyone so consistent and patient in his planning bore watching. But as long as Derzhinsky could deliver, he would sit at Stalin's right hand.

"The undoing of the British Revolution was not accidental. Derzhinsky intended it in order to keep British power out of the socialist picture until the Red Army became dominant. The elimination of Kamenev, Trotsky and Zinoviev likewise pushed the philosophers out of the military's way. Stalin knew his competitors were being knocked off one by one. Surely he imagined it was because of Derzhinsky's confidence in him."

But Derzhinsky's plan to deal with and then betray Germany was surely what Stalin liked most. Derzhinsky was Stalin's treasure, his own personal Cardinal in the Kremlin.

Reilly said, "At any cost, Derzhinsky must be stopped, seduced, killed, replaced. Bolshevism contains the seeds of its own destruction. But a Russia run by Derzhinsky would be far worse until it finally destroyed itself."

"What is his weakness?" Sasha said.

"He tried to destroy the witnesses to his collaboration with C in 1918. He fears what might happen if the information got out. The operative word is 'fear.'"

"Fear?" Volodia said.

"Perhaps Stalin," Reilly said. "But yes, 'fear.' He's gone to extraordinary lengths to keep his methods secret."

Sasha said, "Stalin would take a big step back, especially with the news that Derzhinsky worked with the British."

"Sasha," Reilly said, "he ordered the Lenin shooting. What incredible hubris. Stalin would shoot him on the spot."

Sasha continued, "Right. And he kept everything to himself:

working with C, the Counterfeit Massacre, the assassins, Strasky's murder. Stalin would feel betrayed. Derzhinsky the treasure would become Derzhinsky the suspect, Derzhinsky the threat, Derzhinsky the enemy, the late Derzhinsky, Derzhinsky the statue."

"And there," Reilly said, "you have Derzhinsky's weakness. His Achilles' heel. Fear of Stalin matched by moral vanity."

Then Reilly stood. "Derzhinsky is sending feelers, hoping I'll bite on the Trust's invitation."

"No doubt he needs you to take back a good report on the Trust," Sasha said. "Its funding supports the spy service. He'll take you in, show you paradise and send you back."

"Reilly turned to Arkady, "Now let's get Anna and Katya to the train. We're going back to London."

Whereupon silence fell all around.

"Sidney," Volodia said through a constricted throat, "Anna's been arrested and possibly executed."

Reilly's expression was unchanged.

Sasha said, "Her roommate Olga is Derzhinsky's lover. She went in, Arkady thinks, to join the Cheka to save her father, the general who worked for you in 1918. Derzhinsky's blackmail."

Reilly's eyes closed.

"That's not all, Sidney," Arkady said. "Katya arrived from Petrograd just after we left for Berlin. Her tooth was causing terrible pain. She went to a hospital, where they drugged her, took her to the wrong room by mistake and instead of pulling her tooth amputated her leg."

Reilly slowly sat down.

Sasha said, "Anna's friend Olga left a letter for Anna. When Katya came back from the hospital she found it. It was a short apology for joining Derzhinsky's OGPU. Through the drugs they had administered, Katya thought the letter was from Anna, that Anna had abandoned her. She jumped from the window. She's dead, Sidney. Then the Cheka came for Anna."

"Dead?" Reilly said in disbelief. "Katya and Anna dead?"

"Katya is dead," Sasha said.

Arkady said, "At Lubyanka they say Reilly's girlfriend was executed. I don't know for sure."

No one thought Reilly could stand the final piece, so they stopped speaking there for a time. But silence was impossible for long: the Bolshevik press had just reported that Derzhinsky had rejected Savinkov's offer of service. In despair, the report stated, Savinkov jumped to his death in Lubyanka prison.

That night the group stayed together for Reilly's sake. After lights were out Laurent came downstairs to secure Reilly's pistol and kept guard all night.

It would be fruitless to recount Reilly's agony in words. He had never been given to self-recrimination. At most he judged himself at fault to correct or learn from a mistake.

The self-hatred he felt when his friends left him alone was the greatest pain he had ever suffered, worse even than his misery upon learning about C's Counterfeit Massacre.

For most of the night he thought of Anna. She was gone. Katya was gone. Could either really be gone? Reilly knew he had hurt others, though he had never really tried to hurt anyone. Neither had he helped when helping might have jeopardized his position. He had tried to help Russia, but where did his greed and vanity fit into that, especially in view of the young people who had believed in him and died in his service? Had he been brave? Sometimes. Did he take risk himself? Sometimes.

What of all the people he had sent on risky missions while he slept in comfortable, luxurious hotel rooms? What had he sacrificed? Other than those who loved him? He had thought himself a messiah. But Christ had chosen to suffer and die for mankind. Reilly had let mankind suffer for Russia while he himself lived in comfort.

"It's not the end of the world. There's still hope. There's still love. We can win."

Anna's words from the Red Terror. Reilly was leaving Russia during, and Anna would remain in Moscow. "I still have hope, Sidney." Could Reilly soothe himself with these words?

All night Reilly slept in shadows of evil and impossibility. His father's voice, filled with contempt, came back to him: "You were an evil child, and lived your life as the worst of men. It's your fault those women are dead. You are a fool. Do you really think a bad man can do good?"

And all night Laurent stayed unseen in the doorway, his back against the wall, just in case Reilly gave way.

69. The Burn

But Reilly did not give way. Nelly was touched by his story, cried with him at the loss of Anna and Katya and promised to do everything in her power to help.

Boyce and Field-Robinson had spoken with Yakushev. Both knew Reilly's opinion of the Trust. Both lied bare-faced to Yakushev, encouraging him to persist in his efforts to get Reilly into Russia to face the Trust. After all, the Trust was probably the best thing for the now-dispirited, seemingly poor Reilly. Russia, they said, would lift his spirits after a few failed business ventures and steep losses. Going back to Russia after such a long absence would be good for him.

Yakushev, of course, was only an agent of the Trust. He could make no promises. The most he could do would be to contact Moscow and ask The Trust to send Savinkov's friends, the Dehrenthals, to London.

"What exactly *is* 'The Trust?'" Churchill said.

"Derzhinsky's most brilliant scheme," Reilly answered. "A Moscow-based organization that claims to be anti-Bolshevist. It uses a core of Cheka agents to manage people they have extorted, bribed or threatened to perform certain things.

"One example is their campaign to take Savinkov out of play by persuading him to return to Russia. Now they are bringing exiles back from Paris, New York and London with great promises. Derzhinsky's men seize all assets when they arrive.

"They have tentacles across the world, people who influence or control anti-Bolshevik groups and can raise fortunes.

Derzhinsky uses this money to finance his entire Cheka. But suspicion has grown and profits are down. Derzhinsky thinks he can use me to repair its tarnished image. He must be stopped."

"Savinkov," Churchill said and bit his cigar. "Was he pushed or did he jump?"

"Everyone says he was pushed. I think he jumped. He tried to get Derzhinsky to take him into the government and Derzhinsky said no. Savinkov was depressed to begin with and simply gave up. He believed that when he could no longer contribute, the bill for his Terrorist murders- Plehve, the Grand Duke, the rest- would come due. He believed that a terrorist killing could only be justified with an act against the enemy that would result in the terrorist's own death."

"The Russian Orthodox Church and the Russian Terrorist," Churchill said. "God. What an alliance."

"It was a message to me that my take on The Trust is correct. That's what his suicide was intended to say."

Churchill lit the cigar butt. "What else?"

"I believe C may have been a mole. He may have been trapped and his intentions may have been patriotic. But we have no way of knowing how much he gave to Derzhinsky."

Churchill nodded slowly.

"And he may have brought someone in as a replacement. That's what I think. But I have no proof. Everything has to go, Winston. The codes, networks, assignments, everything. We have to rebuild everything, top down. And we have to eliminate Derzhinsky. He's the greatest criminal genius we've ever come up against."

"Do you have a strategy?" Churchill said.

"I've cultivated the impression that I'm a spent force that Derzhinsky can use for his own purposes. It's taken more than a year, but I believe I have put *that* illusion in play. Derzhinsky and his Trust now think I can be had almost as easily as Savinkov. Soon I'll go back to Russia."

"What?"

"I'm going back. You should assume that whatever C did not give them, I will tell them. Assume they know everything. You'll start from scratch. You, Sinclair, Lockhart, Hill, Boyce, Dukes, Fothergil, Herbert Fitch from Special Branch. Rebuild. I'd be no good here. Nobody trusts a Jew."

"What do you think you can accomplish?"

"If I can convince them that they and their ideas have sway over me, I may be able to influence Derzhinsky."

"Answer my question. To what end? Derzhinsky is not going to invite you for dinner and give you an opportunity to cut his throat. Are you serious?"

Reilly said, "Once I'm there I'll find a way."

"You're delusional."

"You never know."

Churchill shook his head. "Sidney," he said, "what about your friends, your career, your reputation, your fortune, even your life? You can't give all that away. Just to expose The Trust. People will think you were a traitor all along."

"That's right. You'll have to shout it the loudest, because if they think this is *my* scheme, I'll be dead before I get anywhere. Derzhinsky must believe this was his idea. So create a legend, a story, how you discovered I was Derzhinsky's man, the first Soviet mole in the British Government and make sure it gets back to Derzhinsky. Call Fothergil and Lockhart. Tell them to re-write my file."

Churchill said good luck and took his hand. "You're right to assume we have no secrets at the moment. Still, you're paying a high price for your patriotism."

"It's not that. I'm just re-paying a few debts. If I didn't try, if I stayed here, I'd be haunted. I'd never have a good night's sleep. It's selfishness, Winston, not patriotism."

Reilly would write back as a signal that he had got far enough with the Dehrenthals. He would also send incriminating letters so the Intelligence Service would be certain to sweep his flat, clean their own houses and change their codes. Over the next few days he wrote letters to

Churchill and Lockhart. He gave them to Nelly with instructions to go to Helsinki to mail them after he departed.

Mame Dehrenthal arrived with her husband, Savinkov's close advisor. Soon Reilly disappeared from London. Churchill received the promised short note and incriminating letter. Lockhart too, though his was so overdone that he laughed out loud when he showed it to Churchill. It was a simplistic lecture in praise of Internationalism, the same Internationalism that Derzhinsky had destroyed. The Bolsheviks had lots of it, Reilly said, and they'd conquer everything with it. Internationalism is the future. You can dance to it. Just wait and see. Reilly must have been enjoying himself when he wrote it and added a final salutation: "Believe me, Lockhart."

"Believe you! Believe you, indeed, Sidney Reilly. Hah!"

"Bravo," Churchill said. "Put that letter into Reilly's file. Better still, frame it."

Churchill's housekeepers swept Reilly's flat before Sinclair could send in his men. On September twenty-fifth Reilly arrived in Moscow and met the members of the Trust.

The first day and night of meetings with the Trust members were uneventful. On the second afternoon Artuzov came and announced that the meeting was over. Immediately, obedient Trust members got up and filed out. Artuzov gestured to the door and Reilly walked ahead of him to an automobile. Two guards awaited in the rear seat. Artuzov started the car.

"I was concerned you'd send me back to London."

"It would be best for you not to speak," Artuzov said. He drove through the arch into the courtyard of Lubyanka. Artuzov went in first and started up a flight of stairs.

The two guards took Reilly to a lower room. They were, in Reilly's language, low-level inquisitors, thugs who worked a prisoner over until he broke and spilled information they wanted. Then they would beat him some more. Reilly said nothing. He thought their questions amateurish: "What is your real name? How long have you spied for the British? Who helped you to plan the assassination of Ambassador Mirbach? The shooting of Lenin...?" Of course, Derzhinsky would never have prepared them with any mysteries he really wanted solved. The point of the questions was to provide a rationale for beating him. All the while they punched Reilly, threw him and kicked him in the ribs when he fell. Softened him up, they might have said, with pain just short of unbearable.

"Idiots," he thought.

"Speak!" they said.

But after time Reilly was so silent that they judged he could not speak. The session went long, into or perhaps through the next day. Time ceased to exist. The inquisitors hit harder whenever his eyes closed. After two days Reilly knew he had at least another day to endure. He was right. Three days without sleep in all. Finally, after the third day the inquisitors broke and one brought Reilly water.

Reilly tried to say something but failed.

They imagined he had endured all he could.

Reilly clumsily spilled the water on his chest, closed his eyes and lay his head and shoulders against the wall. An inquisitor got a second cup of water. Then they left him alone. It was a few hours, Reilly guessed, before Derzhinsky came in followed by the inquisitors. With a gesture he told them to lift Reilly to his feet and follow to another room. They dropped him on a cot and disappeared.

"Why did you come back?" Derzhinsky said serenely.

"I'm finished. I've nothing left."

"Do you think I have something for you?"

"No."

"I told you once that you could make a choice," Derzhinsky said. "Once. We have nothing more to say." He left the room. A guard closed the door. The filthy window under the ceiling showed no light. Reilly passed out.

Sometime later Artuzov brought him a potato, coffee and a photograph of Nelly. Artuzov said nothing but slipped out the door and later reported that Reilly had wept all night and kissed the photograph as though it were alive.

The following morning a guard brought a pot with warm water, a rag and a change of clothes. Reilly, still in extreme pain, slowly cleaned himself and awkwardly dressed. Derzhinsky came in and offered a cigarette.

"American," Reilly said, surprised, as Derzhinsky struck a match and lit it.

"What do you think of Savinkov?" Derzhinsky said.

"Savinkov alive or Savinkov dead?"

"How did he die?"

"Suicide," Reilly answered.

"You don't think he was pushed?"

"No. I imagine Russian Orthodox theology in the mind of a Russian terrorist," Reilly said through his agony. "He incurs a debt when he commits murder and must atone for his crime. He must sacrifice his own life for the revolution. Savinkov longed for atonement in your approval. He failed to get it and therefore failed to atone. His only choice was suicide."

Derzhinsky, looking surprised, walked away.

A guard brought coffee the following morning. Another came in to bandage his wounds. Reilly felt somewhat better. Derzhinsky came in and sat on a stool.

"How would you judge the Cheka, in its earlier years?"

"I could not judge it. But I can see it in a way similar to my view of Savinkov's thinking. Men with higher vision lead faithful disciples. The tasks are ugly and require discipline. The leader must take full responsibility and impose a rigid structure, create fear, dispense penalties, forgiveness and atonement. I think that's why Savinkov came back."

"It's why you came back."

"Savinkov was desperate. He knew he could do nothing, and preferred to die."

"Then why are you here?"

"I have come to hate the British elite. I possess a world of information. I'm a goldmine. It is, if you will, my atonement."

"But it will not save you."

"I have no wish to be saved."

"You will write your protocol, a confession going back to the beginning. Then interrogation, painless if you cooperate."

Reilly nodded weakly.

Derzhinsky walked to the door. "You're right about Savinkov's suicide. I did not imagine you would understand."

"I was raised in Grodno," Reilly said. "Sometimes it's part of Poland and sometimes part of Russia. So I am both. My Polish side can observe the Russian with some detachment."

Derzhinsky looked quizzically at Reilly, smiled and closed the door behind him.

That was Reilly's first victory. Until that moment, no one had ever seen Derzhinsky smile.

They came days later with a worn suit of clothes, Soviet grey, a stretcher and a sheet.

"I have to dispose of a little matter," Derzhinsky said. "Can you remain absolutely still for three or four minutes?"

"I can hold my breath for three minutes," Reilly said.

"Good. We'll do it in three. We're going to stage a viewing for the press. Let them photograph you as though dressed by an undertaker. We will announce your execution. Then we'll continue our business. Get dressed. Ibrahim and Artuzov will carry you into the courtyard and in two or three minutes take you back to your quarters. Sidney Reilly will be officially dead. Your new identity is Comrade Karlov, a Russian from Berlin. A defector from Germany, a top Intelligence officer who knows the mind of the German High Command. I will prepare Stalin to meet Karlov."

After the make-up artist finished, they took Reilly on a stretcher into a private room in Lubyanka Prison. Members of the press photographed his 'body' and were dismissed.

They took Reilly to a private Lubyanka apartment that was clean and well-supplied. Reilly sat at a desk near a wall filled with books and wrote his protocols, a description of his activities from 1917 to the Red Terror of 1918, first person point of view. Artuzov and Ibrahim studied the protocols and gave them to Derzhinsky, who returned them with questions. The sessions went smoothly and the new, professional Inquisitors reported to Derzhinsky that Reilly was cooperating fully.

This was true, except for certain details that would have confused the interrogators. He gave them everything they could comprehend and nothing more: he had come to Russia with orders from the British Prime Minister to overthrow Lenin and put Russia back in the war for Britain's sake. He had tried twice and failed both times. The first failure came when an SR shot and killed German Ambassador Mirbach, forcing Reilly to abandon his plan. The second failed when Lenin was shot and the Cheka launched the Red Terror.

"Good," Derzhinsky said when Ibrahim brought a transcript of the early sessions. "Facts, not opinions."

"Yes," Reilly said to Artuzov and gave a second layer of details to please the Inquisitors.

Derzhinsky showed satisfaction with Reilly's cooperation and rewarded him with small things such as a clean military-like uniform, leather boots, a better apartment in Lubyanka and occasionally vodka, whisky or wine.

But petty rewards were less important than occasional opportunities to personally engage Derzhinsky. Reilly had developed a keen interest in his captor's expressed belief in himself as a visionary. There Reilly observed what he had long suspected was Derzhinsky's Achilles' Heel: a conflict between his moral vanity and fear of disclosure before the brutish Stalin.

Now began the most critical phase of the interrogation, in which Reilly aimed to control the Inquisitors' perceptions of how much knew and what he really believed. Success here could lead the Inquisitors to think that they themselves, not Reilly, were masters of their own discoveries.

The first and second phases of interrogation had consisted of plain narrative and known characters, and led to the conclusion that the British Director launched contingency plans that undermined Reilly's scheme. Reilly believed he had set the stage for the third phase, in which he would reveal the the Director's "Phantom Group" of invisible agents.

"To start with, I was well-positioned with the German Embassy in Moscow. They mentioned a double named Ginch. I can't be certain, but I think he was an SR whom the Germans turned."

"So?" Artuzov said.

Ibrahim wrote furiously.

"Before the July uprising I met there with Intelligence Chief Colonel Bauer. He asked me to investigate something Ginch had reported, a British plot to kill Ambassador Mirbach run by an unknown British agent he called Weber."

"Weber?"

"Yes. I thought I knew every British agent in Moscow. But I had never heard of agent Weber or about any plot to kill Mirbach. The British Colsulate organized a search for him. Station Chief Boyce even cabled London with the question, but they replied that they didn't know Weber either. I concluded that the so-called Weber did not really exist except perhaps as a brilliant fiction created by Derzhinsky to confuse the Germans.

"Later I discovered that Weber *did* exist," Reilly said. "He was one of the British Director's Phantom Group. He ran the SR Spiridonova, who ran Blyumkin, who is blamed for the assassination. But in fact Blyumkin was a foil, someone who could be blamed while the real assassin got away. The shooter was Andreyev, probably another of the Director's phantom agents. In any event the man behind the Mirbach murder was my superior officer at London Centre."

"What? How did your Director explain that?"

"He said it was a contingency plan to sabotage Lenin's treaty with Germany. He said he activated it because he thought I was about to fail."

"Hah!" Artuzov said. "You were a hair away from success!"

"I thought so too," Reilly said.

Artuzov remembered that at the moment in question he

personally delivered critical information to Peters that proved Reilly's forces were about to overthrow the Bolshevik Government. Based on that information, Derzhinsky ordered Blyumkin to kill the German Ambassador in order to throw off Reilly's timing. Because Reilly was about to succeed.

"But the Director was in London," Reilly said, "and I was in Moscow. He had no idea how close I was to success."

Artuzov judged that Reilly seemed to buy his Director's rationale, which meant that he knew only half the story. Reilly did not see that the murder of the ambassador had dual but interdependent causes: Derzhinsky and the British Director had collaborated on the Mirbach murder. Their common link was Weber. Technically, both were traitors. But, Artuzov surmised, Reilly could not know this.

Reilly knew that the Weber link was proof enough for Artuzov that Derzhinsky had secretly collaborated with C, the enemy. He knew this would be of great interest to Artuzov the Inquisitor, but insufficient to alarm Artuzov the policeman. For that, a second proof would be necessary.

Artuzov moved on to Kaplan and the Lenin shooting. "Did the Kaplan woman, who shot Lenin, work for London Centre?"

"Oh, no," Reilly said. "She was a nothing, a minor SR agent, run by the SR Spiridonova."

"Who ran Spiridonova?"

"The phantom agent, Weber. But by the time Kaplan came into the picture, Mirbach was dead, Spiridonova was in prison and Weber was out, recalled, released, escaped, but gone. This is when Weber's superior officer arrived in Moscow, a London Centre phantom named White. He order Kaplan and Semyenov to kill Lenin. But Kaplan was as blind as Blyumkin. Semyenov, her handler, stood right behind her and fired the shots that nearly killed Lenin, and then escaped."

"What?" Artuzov said, "Semyenov was one of the British Director's phantom agents?"

"Yes," Reilly said. "The Lenin shooting came out of London

Centre. Blyumkin and Kaplan were foils and the real assassins were phantom agents. Off the books, so to speak."

Off the books of British Intelligence. Off the books of the Cheka. But well-known to two spy masters.

At first, Artuzov was absolutely certain that Semyenov could not have taken orders from White and the British Director. But then an electric feeling of panic rolled through his stomach. He realized that the Lenin shooting could have come out of London Centre, but only with Derzhinsky's approval, that is, only on Derzhinsky's specific orders.

Semyenov was Derzhinsky's man. Artuzov had read his reports from General Kornilov's headquarters in Mogilev in 1917. Semyenov and Derzhinsky were closely connected.

Artuzov knew something more: Semyenov escaped after shooting Lenin and returned to the Cheka four years later. Derzhinsky welcomed him and put him to work in a responsible Cheka position. The man who shot Lenin! Just like Blyumkin.

Reilly could see that this troubled Artuzov much more than the Mirbach killing. It was his second proof of Derzhinsky's collaboration with the enemy. Worse, this was not collaboration against a common war enemy such as Germany, but a direct attack on Lenin and the Revolution.

The Inquisitor twitched. His body tingled and his hair stood on end. He calculated the implications and then abruptly, in horror, asked himself whether *Reilly* knew that Derzhinsky had ordered the murder of Lenin. He became desperate to know absolutely that Reilly did not understand the value of what he had just revealed.

Artuzov said, "So, I suppose both White and Weber got out of Britain. Did either contact you?"

In other words, "Reilly, how much do you *really* know?"

"In time, as the director tried to win back my confidence, he told me a little about them, as I mentioned. Later, they came to me in a panic. They had been targeted by assassins but escaped. I was sure the British Director issued the assassination order. I went to confront him, but the Director himself had just been murdered. They said it was a heart attack. But I found him myself with fresh needle marks in his arm. Someone had injected him with a poison that mimicked a heart attack. White, Weber and the Director. Without doubt an assassination plot. But who ran it? Army Intelligence? Special Branch? Churchill? I just *can't* be sure."

But Reilly knew that Artuzov *was* sure.

Artuzov thought of Yagoda, one of Derzhinsky's backroom boys, a specialist in poisons and the delivery of poisons into the body. A man who enjoyed his work. A man whose genius had stretched the bounds of tradecraft.

Ibrahim cleared his throat.

Artuzov's hair stood on end for a second time, at the sudden realization that things were so badly out of control as to lead to executions. "All three of us," he thought, meaning himself, Reilly and Ibrahim. How could he get control of *this*?

Artuzov swallowed hard. Beads of sweat formed on his brow. What could he do? Informing a desperate Derzhinsky might get him executed. But going to Stalin presented almost as much danger. Here was proof of Derzhinsky's disloyalty. Stalin would rightfully feel threatened and betrayed on all counts: re-enter Yagoda. A quiet death by poison, a state funeral, a viewing, a parade and a statue. And he might shoot the messenger.

Artuzov turned to Reilly. He seemed to have something to say but kept quiet. The two Inquisitors walked to the door.

Reilly said, "Comrades, if you and Comrade Derzhinsky feel I'm cooperating, would you get me another pack of American cigarettes? Your Russian papirosis are giving me a sore throat."

Artuzov and Ibrahim stood in the doorway as Reilly casually lay back on his cot with his hands behind his head.

Then came, "Karlov." It was Derzhinsky's voice. "I have some questions for you. Artuzov and Ibrahim will return."

"Excuse me, Comrade," Ibrahim said to Derzhinsky. "We need a private moment together at this time."

Derzhinsky nodded. Ibrahim followed him out.

Artuzov, filled with information, uncertainty and fear, stood helplessly in the cell doorway, glanced at "Karlov" and moments later rushed off.

In a few minutes Ibrahim returned and said, "Come with me, please, to Comrade Derzhinsky's office."

Ibrahim announced Reilly and went away. Derzhinsky poured a glass of brandy. Reilly was certain he saw his captor's hand shake, almost imperceptibly, as he put the snifter down. He gave the glass to Reilly and turned to the courtyard below, the courtyard of executions, where blood had saturated the ground. He was dressed in his most formal military uniform for a speech to the Central Committee that he was expected to make later in the day. He beckoned Reilly to stand with him.

"Reilly, do you see what we have done, how much we have accomplished? Would we have succeeded had we used your western methods, elections, worrying how the peasants would vote? Asking citizens to take Christ, Church and state on faith, praying for miracles and longing for bread? Impossible. But Bolshevism, the very opposite of faith and miracles, can speak of success. We know your expertise, even excellence. But it is old world excellence and can never succeed where we succeed. Surely you know this. So why do you come to bother us with the ways of your old world?

"Do you remember when we met during the insurrection in July, 1918? Do you know where Lenin sent me just after that? During the uprising, SRs severed telegraph lines all over Russia. Lenin sent me to the Siberian Urals to a village called Nizhny Sanarka to assess reports that the local peasants were threatening an uprising because of the food shortage, which was everywhere. I hoped to help the local Cheka boss, Comrade Pikhanov, to calm his people. They were literally *his* people, since he was Comrade *Father* Pikhanov, both an Orthodox priest and Chekist.

"When I arrived, the villagers were wandering around, waving their arms in the air in desperation, despair and hunger, pulling out their hair. Men were beating one another and women were setting each other on fire. Children were throwing stones like balls and hitting other children with sticks. It was complete chaos and very close to disaster. I introduced myself and Pikhanov took me aside and asked what I thought he should do to make the people orderly. Would I attend his church and pray with him for the peasants? What, he asked, would Lenin do? Pikhanov looked at me with great expectation.

"I replied, 'If you think a church service, communion and prayer will bring order to your people, by all means take them to church. But if this method fails to bring them in line with Party discipline, I will have no choice but to shoot you dead. There is only one way, and that is Party discipline. Here is what you shall do. Find ten good men and give each a rifle and ten bullets. You can find ten, can't you?'"

"'Yes, yes,' he said.

"Then bring them here, have them select one hundred villagers and put those villagers against the wall of that barn. Then give the signal for them to fire and keep firing until all hundred are dead. In the presence of all villagers, men, ladies and children. You and your loyal Chekists will not be shooting people, Comrade, you will be disposing of the old ways and giving your living villagers something to believe in. As must eventually be done all over Russia and finally the world. I promise you that, *ad majorem gloriam Dei*, sacrifice will bring your village back in line with sacred Party discipline. By giving them something to believe in. Do you know why, comrade?

"Comrade Father Pikhanov said, 'No.'

"You believe that the gentleness of Christ will feed the people and give them faith. But where there is no bread there is no faith, and where there is no faith the people crave discipline and yearn to see power. When your loyal soldiers kill one hundred, you will immediately see discipline, and that will serve your village until bread comes. Where Christ asked for faith, the Bolsheviks demand fear. The delivery of bread will be the work of The Party, and everyone will know it. But it will be treated as a miracle.

"I said, 'Go now, Comrade Father, and do your duty. Or I will kill you and appoint someone else. Do not worry about God forgiving you. I will forgive you, the Cheka will forgive you. You and your comrades may make their confession to me. I will listen. Later I will tell Lenin, and he will explain all to the Central Committee. They will understand your plight and permit no further difficulty in your loyal village. And then your citizens will be happy. Go now, comrade.' Of course I showed him my pistol, fully loaded.

"In no time ten good comrades stood with rifles aimed at one hundred randomly selected citizens of the old world. Comrade Pikhanov gave the order to fire, and all one hundred fell to the ground. Instantly, as I had promised, the village citizens became quiet and went about their business. I admit I felt a tear come to my eye. I have not lost my humanity.

"You see, Reilly, here is the great contradiction that your world has failed to confront: what is the inevitable result when the world relies for sustenance on Christ's failed doctrine of faith and free will? Those people, waving their arms and beating each other with sticks, were faithful and full of free will. But faith and free will brought them nothing but chaos, uncertainty and harm. Pikhanov the priest was nothing compared to Pikhanov the Chekist. With Chekisty, the eyes and ears of Bol'shevism, he produced no miracles yet gave them something to believe in, to rely on, to fear. Now they lack free will, but they believe. If they lack faith, fear makes them virtuous. Now Nizhny Sanarka is a model of Chekist virtue, a paradigm of Party discipline.

"So you have come back to Russia, and you see that we are successful. You can say nothing to me because you are a product of the old world that has already failed. You and your world of faith and love have failed. You have left us with no choice but to instil fear in the absence of faith. You have left us no choice but to replace the Church with the Cheka. And you have given me no personal alternative than to take up the task that Christ left unfinished and to root out the delusions he left for mankind.

"Reilly, don't you see that our methods are necessary because the methods that Christ used, that you and the West used have all failed so ignominiously? Don't you see the mess that Christ, the churches, governments and democracies have left for us to clean up? Yet you come to me, even with the best of intentions, with ideas born of failure. For god's sake, will you never stop trying to hinder us? Will you never leave well enough alone?

"The answer to that question is self-evident. You are not a visionary of our Bolshevism, but of the old world. Regardless of your good intentions you can never serve us. That is why you must be executed as a symbol of the old ways that are already in the process of decay. Now go back and give the Inquisitors what they ask for, and let that be your catechism, your absolution and your contribution to our new world. It's all you can do.

"As the Sword of the Revolution, my responsibilities are great and terrible. As the Conscience of Bolshevism, I forgive your transgressions but order your execution."

Derzhinsky put a death warrant on the table and ordered Reilly to sign it so as to ensure the legality of the execution. The guard opened the door to take Reilly back to his cell.

Half an hour later Artuzov opened the door to Reilly's cell. He was out of breath and for the first time armed with a chest-belt, holster and pistol.

"Get up, Reilly," he said.

Reilly rose as Ibrahim arrived breathless and armed.

Artuzov nodded to Reilly. "Follow me, please," he said.

They went to Lubyanka courtyard, got into a black Ford and drove under the arch and through Moscow to the Sparrow Hills. They stopped at a clearing. Artuzov opened the boot and gave shovels to Reilly and Ibrahim. "Follow me," he said.

It took nearly an hour to prepare the grave, during which time not a word was spoken.

At the same time a black Rolls Royce stopped at a guard's station outside the Kremlin. Derzhinsky got out and saluted the guard, who stood at attention and returned the salute. Derzhinsky went inside and walked to a large chamber where the Party Central Committee were gathered. As he entered the comrades rose together as one. When he reached the podium they seated themselves quietly and out of respect, as though anticipating some great or dreadful announcement. Peters went to the front, handed him a scribbled note and a tray with a glass of water. Derzhinsky put the tray on a table at the side of the podium and read the contents of the note. He cleared his throat.

"I am not surprised," he began, "that certain factions of the Central Committee have taken it upon themselves to limit the power of the spy service. They say that the methods we employ are harsh and give us a bad name even among comrades across the sea. But what is the spy service? This is an elementary question that deserves a straightforward answer. The spy service is first of all The Revolution, which is always under attack by the West. Remember, our enemies did not come to us with the Revolution and hand it to us for free. We took it. Well, we paid for it in blood. Their blood. So shall it be when we are attacked. We are always under attack."

At this moment Stalin, sitting in the first row, jumped to his feet and applauded. The comrades followed suit and seated themselves as one.

"Some say the spy service is like a police force. No, we exist not to react to crimes against the state but to anticipate our enemies, to catch them before they act in order to protect The Revolution. The Revolution is its own judge and jury and cannot wait for justice in the western sense. The West is the very enemy we must attack and destroy, so how could we judge ourselves according to so-called western judicial standards? For here in Soviet Russia, even long after we have achieved true paradise, the West will always be at our throats, conspiring to surround, attack and destroy us."

Again Stalin and the Central Committee jumped up,

applauded and seated themselves.

"We will always have comrades who say that our methods are too harsh, that our proper function is to gather information or to arrange assassinations. But no. The greatest power of the spy service, its very highest purpose, is not the gathering of information or the elimination of enemies, but the power to control the minds of the masses in our everlasting war against the West. That is why only fools want to limit our power."

Derzhinsky took a sip of water. Peters came to get Stalin and led him out as Derzhinsky continued with his remarks.

Reilly stood at the edge of his grave, his shovel thrust upright into the ground and the cold barrel of a pistol at his neck. He had done everything possible to bring his scheme to fruition. He had sacrificed his fortune, friendships and reputation. In moments he would surrender his life.

He had set his master plan in motion knowing that he would probably not live to see the outcome. The plan would succeed or fail without him.

Reilly put a cigarette between his yellowing teeth. He had been captive in a Soviet prison for months, during which time he had received American cigarettes as a reward for his cooperation. The Inquisitor had promised him tooth powder too, but later confessed that there was not a gram of tooth-powder left in Moscow. It was the only information Reilly got from his Soviet captors that he believed.

The Senior Inquisitor took a match from the front pocket of his black tunic and lit Reilly's cigarette. As Reilly took the smoke into his lungs, he mused on one remaining question. The Senior Inquisitor read his mind. "Well, was it worth it?"

Reilly offered a slight smile.

Ibrahim, the second Inquisitor, raised his pistol to Reilly's skull. Artuzov, the less excitable Senior Inquisitor said, "What's funny about that? Did you think we would *not* execute you?"

"I couldn't ignore what Lenin and Derzhinsky were doing to Russia," Reilly said. "People were starving in Petrograd. They killed millions with the Red Terror. I had to act. Call it atonement for a corrupt life, if you wish."

"It's over now. Perhaps you want some archaic ritual, like incense or Last Rites?" the ex-Catholic Artuzov said.

"Get on with it." Reilly took a final drag on his papirosi and flipped it into the freshly-dug grave as the Inquisitor backed up behind him and said, "Goodbye, comrade."

Two pistol shots followed. A lifeless body collapsed into the grave. The gunfire echoed for a moment. Then the hills overlooking the city of Moscow fell silent.

"Christ!" Reilly said and looked at Ibrahim's body, motionless in the grave, as a mist of blood sprayed over him.

They buried Ibrahim and walked toward the car. Reilly was speechless for a while but eventually said, "Your Comrade Superior won't be very happy with you."

"If you mean comrade Derzhinsky," Artuzov replied, "I'm told he met an unfortunate end late this afternoon. Ibrahim, Derzhinsky's loyal servant, therefore had to follow. Consider it a moment of homage, an expression of his devotion to his master."

Reilly wiped his hands on his trousers. Artuzov continued:

"My new Comrade Superior, Stalin, has rewarded me for revealing what I deduced from certain information related to our interrogation."

"What was that?" Reilly said.

"I calculated that Derzhinsky collaborated with the British Director and our British enemy in 1918. I also concluded that he attempted to assassinate Comrade Lenin. He was tried on the spot, judged guilty of treason and executed this very day."

"Treason?" Reilly said. "You say he collaborated with my Director? He ordered the Lenin shooting? Comrade, that's incredible! It explains everything!"

"So it does," Artuzov said with a certain, humble pride.

"But comrade," Reilly said, "execution?"

"As I left Stalin's office, he rang Yagoda. I imagine execution by poisoning. Something tasteless mixed with water."

Reilly breathed deeply. "Where are you taking me?"

"You'll stay in your own remote dacha. Henceforth, no one will ever hear the name Reilly. You will be Karlov as long as you live. You'll have little contact with the outside world." He drove up a long dirt road to a dacha, clutched the hand brake and gave Reilly a key. "I'll return in an hour with some supplies. Please, Reilly."

"Karlov, comrade. I'm not going anywhere."

Artuzov returned half an hour later with a few boxes of food from the company store, and blankets, soap, tooth powder, a bottle of Georgian wine, wine glasses, a few books and numerous packs of American cigarettes. He said he would return in the morning and that Karlov should concern himself only with a good night's sleep.

With Artuzov away, Reilly poured a glass of wine and sat down. The door opened. The voice was unexpected.

"I told you it wasn't the end of the world, Sidney. I told you there would always be hope and love. Now you know I was right. Derzhinsky's gone and we are together."

Reilly did not know if Derzhinsky, Artuzov or Arkady had kept Anna alive. But she was alive.

"I was right, wasn't I?" Anna said.

"Yes," he said weakly, his throat swelling, "you were right. You were always perfectly right."

Anna poured a glass of wine, put it on the table and hugged him from behind. Cheek to cheek she felt tears on his face. She kissed the moisture.

"Artuzov will let me stay," she said. "He thinks that's the only way to keep you here."

"I hoped they would think that way. They kept you alive for seven years. They needed you almost as much as I did. Almost as much as I do."

"But in a different way," Anna said.

Reilly took Anna and for the first time kissed her passionately. Then he said, "Yes. A very different way."

A Back Word
By the Author and Editor

Nearly a century ago, Vladimir Lenin's Bolshevik party took power over Russia. The party, later known as the Communists, won by wholesale deceit and ruthless murder. Above all, it won by imposing a level of state terror that far surpassed both its predecessor, the Tsarist Monarchy, and its own historical model, the French Revolution.

While the Bolshevik leaders were ruthless men, willing to do anything to gain power, the primary architect of the murder and terror was Feliks Derzhinsky, founder and first director of the Bolshevik Secret Police, the Cheka (later, OGPU, KGB). This same Secret Police, under various names, has held Russia and its satellites captive ever since. First it was a tool of Derzhinsky, then a tool of Stalin. Since Stalin's death in 1953, it has made itself more and more obviously the real ruler of Russia.

Among his Chekists, Derzhinsky was revered almost as a god, and that reverence has persisted to the present day. This is no accident: Derzhinsky himself cultivated the appearance of selfless, almost saint-like devotion to the Bolshevik cause. He acted the part of a man of feeling who was depressed by what he was doing, but was forced to shoulder the burden for the sake of the Revolution. Many Western scholars consider Derzhinsky an evil genius, though some say his brilliance is overrated.

The author feels that, on the contrary, Derzhinsky has been *underrated.* Some of his plots have never been uncovered, although they set the course of the Soviet state and made critical contributions to the horrors of the century. This too is no accident: he covered his tracks well. One person may have uncovered enough of those tracks to see how dangerous Derzhinsky really was: his major antagonist, the British spy Sidney Reilly.

But the Reilly of Robin Lockhart's *Ace of Spies*, the reputed prototype for Ian Fleming's James Bond and the subject of modern fictional legend, Reilly the superspy, is *not* the subject of this book.

Nor does the author believe in the Reilly of modern intelligence legend, the traitor and Soviet mole of Robin Lockhart's subsequent recantation, *Reilly: the First Man.* Both the superspy legend and the first-mole legend were fabrications, originally devised by Reilly himself. Then they were seconded at different times and for different purposes by British and Soviet spy services. Having something to hide, each organization arranged for strategic leaks to prop up one legend or the other.

By now there is probably no one left on either side who feels that Reilly's story will endanger their power and reputation, or that of their organization. There may be no one left who even knows about it. In 1991, the author met with Lev Bezymensky of *Novaya Vremya*, then one of the leading KGB experts on Reilly, the "Lockhart Plot" and the Revolution. Bezymensky commented, "Every new director of the KGB has sorted our files on Reilly. There remain very few original documents." KGB chief Vladimir Kryuchkov was reported to have personally reviewed Reilly's file in the 1980s.

Yet the almost surreal story told in *The Private War of Sidney Reilly* shares with much other truth the quality of being stranger than the corresponding fictions. It will probably not find much support from historians, although three of the acknowledged experts have conceded that it is possible. One, Soviet journalist Bezymensky, thought it the likeliest interpretation.

Historians prefer to find that historical forces beyond any one or two individuals are stronger than the individuals who happen to be in a position to direct those forces. They do not happily acknowledge the total responsibility of even the Hitlers and Stalins of the world, much less the Reillys and Derzhinskys.

The Historians' account seeks a sense of inevitability, partly because like the rest of us, they do not want to believe that our world is the result of catastrophes that did not have to happen. As scientists, they are also justifiably concerned about the career-blighting effect of being labeled "conspiracy theorists."

Nevertheless, those of us who are not professional historians have a legitimate citizenly interest in well-argued conspiracy theories. We want to know the *kind* of thing that *may* be happening behind the facade. And if we are sane and responsible, we will not use that knowledge to argue that all, or even most, mysteries are really conspiracies. What we will do is to fight for transparency and accountability in the construction and use of power, because our fears of being manipulated for the gain of a few are legitimate and realistic.

Reilly's legacy has grown primarily from the superspy legend. The results of that legend are still with us. Who knows how many Western spies found in Reilly and the fictional James Bond their first fascination with the exercise of backstairs power? More significantly, the superspy has surely provided a subliminal background influence on those who debate particular secret operations.

Derzhinsky's legacy has been an organization that ran one of the most oppressive police states in the history of the world, and certainly one of the least transparent. The conjunction of these traits is, of course, no accident. But we tend to forget that however the twig was bent, the tree of tyranny was nourished in the soil of idealism and trust. Apart from Derzhinsky's own henchmen, literally everyone's trust in him was misplaced, even Lenin's.

The author believes that, despite the allure of stealth and force, the proprietors of Derzhinsky's legacy still retain the power to build a new, constructive narrative. This story, then, poses a question for them and for idealists of all kinds: are there not levels of power with which *no* one can be trusted, however well their professed ideals may match our own?

Allan Torrey, Author
Bill Barus, Editor
New York, September, 2014

ACKNOWLEDGMENTS

The Private War of Sidney Reilly is dedicated to Carolyn Marks-Blackwood and Bill Barus, and is offered in memory of two friends and mentors whose encouragement was a pre-condition to the birth of this book, Robin Lockhart and F. Reese Brown.

Carolyn Marks-Blackwood is a photographer and movie producer who contributed to earlier versions of the book. See her work at www.cmblackwood.com.

The author wishes to express his deepest gratitude to Bill and Barbara Barus, who contributed substantially to this book and its sequel, in research, editing and story development. Bill's current undertakings are non-fiction books in philosophy and history of religion. Barbara is an author of epic fantasy novels.

F. Reese Brown was Publisher and Editor-in-Chief of The International Journal of Intelligence and Counter Intelligence. He gave this author his first opportunity to publish and provided valuable subject matter, advice, criticism and encouragement for the writing of this book.

Robin Bruce Lockhart, author of *Reilly: Ace of Spies*, was an early, enthusiastic supporter, reader and critic of the book. He had a deep respect for ideas and enjoyed engaging others such as the author, whose theories and interpretations were sometimes at odds with his own.

There remain dozens of contributors, without whose assistance and support this book would still be hiding at the bottom of a desk drawer. A partial rendering includes:

Publisher-editor Carolyn Penzler Hartman and literary agents Henry Morrison and Clyde Taylor; Professor Wilson Carey McWilliams, Nina Berberova, Dr. Lev Bezymensky, Artiom Borovik, Professor Richard Spence, Allen Douglas, Eduard Gudava, Barney Melsky, Steven Lawrence, Vladimir Zhelezniakov, Nikita Mikhalkov, and the staff at the Museum of the Revolution in St Petersburg, Russia.

Special thanks to Professors Linsey Abrams (Director, CCNY

MFA Creative Writing Program), Samantha Gillison and Lisa Reardon of Gotham Writers; to Anne Wilburn, Larry Tool, J. Wilfred Gagen, Carol Botwin, Irwin 'Sonny' Fox; to Elena Kuzmicheva, Alexandra Goncharenko, Lyuba Abramova and Olga Torrey.

Thanks to Roberta Sorensen and Kathleen Weakland for design, and to Roberta Sorensen, Rhona Danzeisen and Gerry Waterfield for careful readings, commentary and criticism.

The author wishes to acknowledge and thank Executive Coach **Virginia Russell**, who helped him to put the completion of this book at the top of his priorities. For more about her work, see her website: russellconsultingintl.com

The author thanks Russian Historian and novelist Marina Osipova, whose review and critique have contributed to this Second Edition.

EXTRACTS FROM:

Richard Pipes, *The Russian Revolution*, Vintage, 1991. Portions appearing as quotes were extracted, shortened and re-crafted by the author for language and context. Included: Kerensky's July, 1917 Congress speech, cables between Savinkov and Kornilov, the Hughes conversation between Kerensky and Kornilov, and other cipher communication.

N. N. Sukhanov, *The Russian Revolution, 1917*, Princeton, 1983. Speeches by Lenin and Kerensky at a July, 1917 conference, quoted by Sukhanov and extracted, shortened and re-written by the author.

In all cases the author has endeavoured to retain the original context and meaning of the materials used.

Made in the USA
Charleston, SC
22 April 2016